AN UNOFFICIAL GRAPHIC NOVEL FOR MINECRAFTERS

REDSTONE JUNIOR HIGH

DRAGONS NEVER DIE

BOOK 3

CARA J. STEVENS

ART BY WALKER MELBY

SKY PONY PRESS
New York

Copyright © 2018 by Hollan Publishing, Inc.

Minecraft® is a registered trademark of Notch Development AB.

The Minecraft game is copyright © Mojang AB.

Sky Pony Press books may be purchased in bulk at special discounts for sales promotion, corporate gifts, fund-raising, or educational purposes. Special editions can also be created to specifications. For details, contact the Special Sales Department, Sky Pony Press, 307 West 36th Street, 11th Floor, New York, NY 10018 or info@ skyhorsepublishing.com.

Sky Pony® is a registered trademark of Skyhorse Publishing, Inc.®, a Delaware corporation.

Minecraft® is a registered trademark of Notch Development AB.
The Minecraft game is copyright © Mojang AB.

Visit our website at www.skyponypress.com.

10 9 8 7 6 5 4 3 2 1

Library of Congress Cataloging-in-Publication Data is available on file.

Cover design by Brian Peterson
Cover and interior art by Walker Melby

Print ISBN: 978-1-5107-3797-6
Ebook ISBN: 978-1-5107-3800-3

Printed in China

Designer and Production Manager: Joshua Barnaby

REDSTONE JUNIOR HIGH

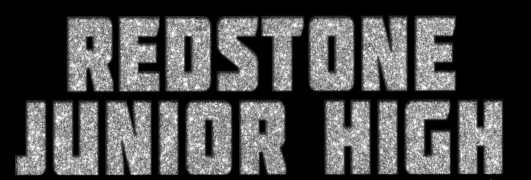

MEET THE

PIXEL: A girl with an unusual way with animals and other creatures.

SKY: A redstone expert who is also one of Pixel's best friends at school.

UMA: A fellow student at Redstone Junior High who can sense how people and mobs are feeling.

CHARACTERS

MR. Z: A teacher with a dark past.

PRINCIPAL REDSTONE:
The head of Redstone Junior High.

SMITE: An evil villian with a ninja army who does everything he can to disrupt the realm.

GALI & OMOL GHOSH:
Uma's worldly and adventurous parents.

INTRODUCTION

When Uma shows up at Pixel's house over summer break, it's not just for a friendly visit. It's to bring chilling news of the Ender Dragon's death. Never before has their world suffered such a great loss. Uma now holds the one item that the Ender Dragon left behind and both girls must protect it with their lives.

The girls return to Redstone Junior High with a sense of purpose and a secret much bigger than the both of them. But what used to be a safe haven for students has been ravaged by the Ender Dragon's destroyer, Smite, and his evil cohorts. Not only has the school been turned upside down, but it's also overrun with mobs seeking protection from a wave of attacks on their homes. Pixel, Sky, Uma, Principal Redstone, and the other students must teach these mobs to fight back for their homes before Redstone Junior High becomes a battlefield and the Ender Dragon's legacy is lost forever.

Will the Ender Dragon finally be avenged or will Smite and his crew wipe out every last ounce of hope for a return to peace and normalcy?

CHAPTER 1

THE SECRET

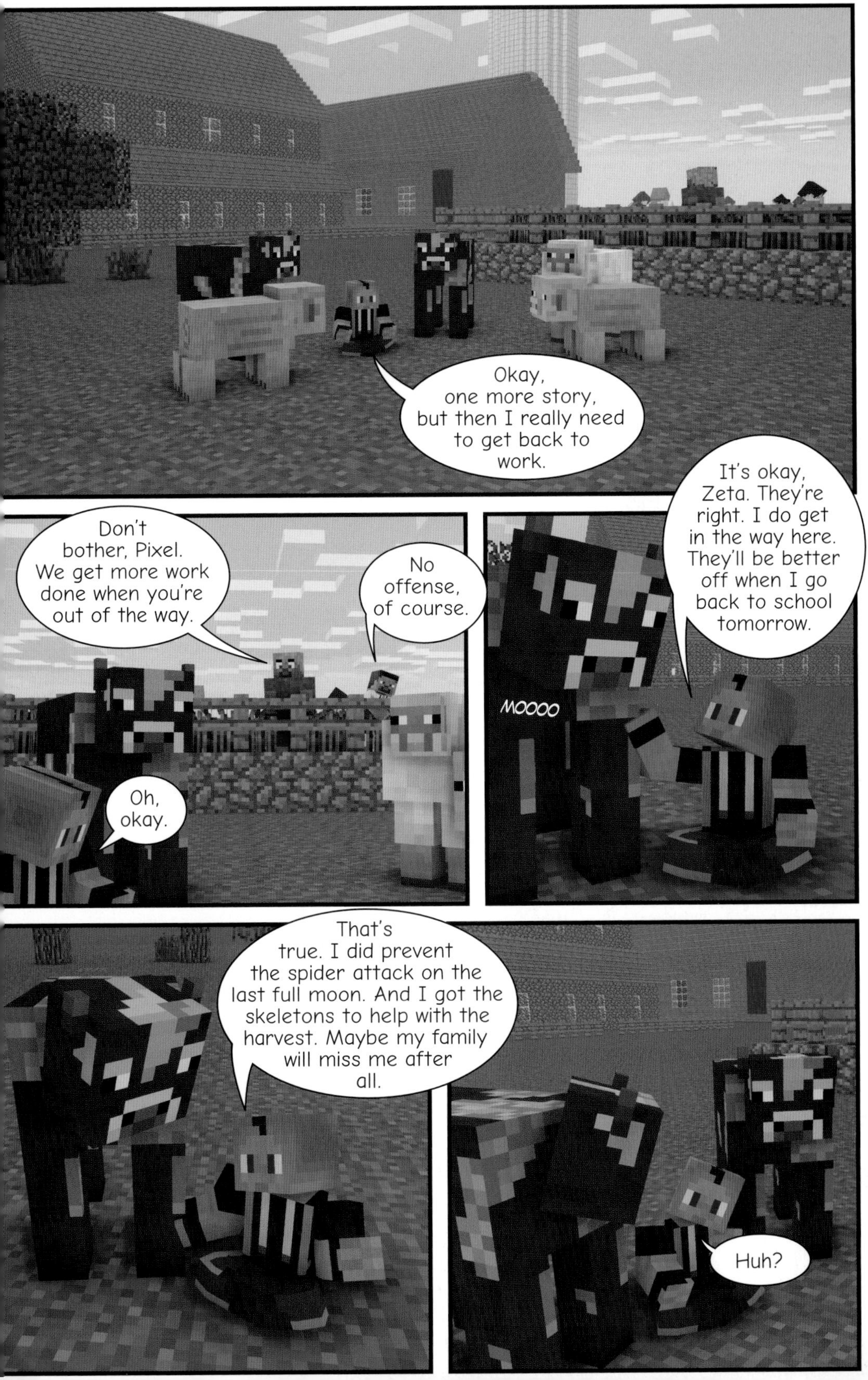
Okay, one more story, but then I really need to get back to work.
Don't bother, Pixel. We get more work done when you're out of the way.
No offense, of course.
Oh, okay.
It's okay, Zeta. They're right. I do get in the way here. They'll be better off when I go back to school tomorrow.
MOOOO
That's true. I did prevent the spider attack on the last full moon. And I got the skeletons to help with the harvest. Maybe my family will miss me after all.
Huh?

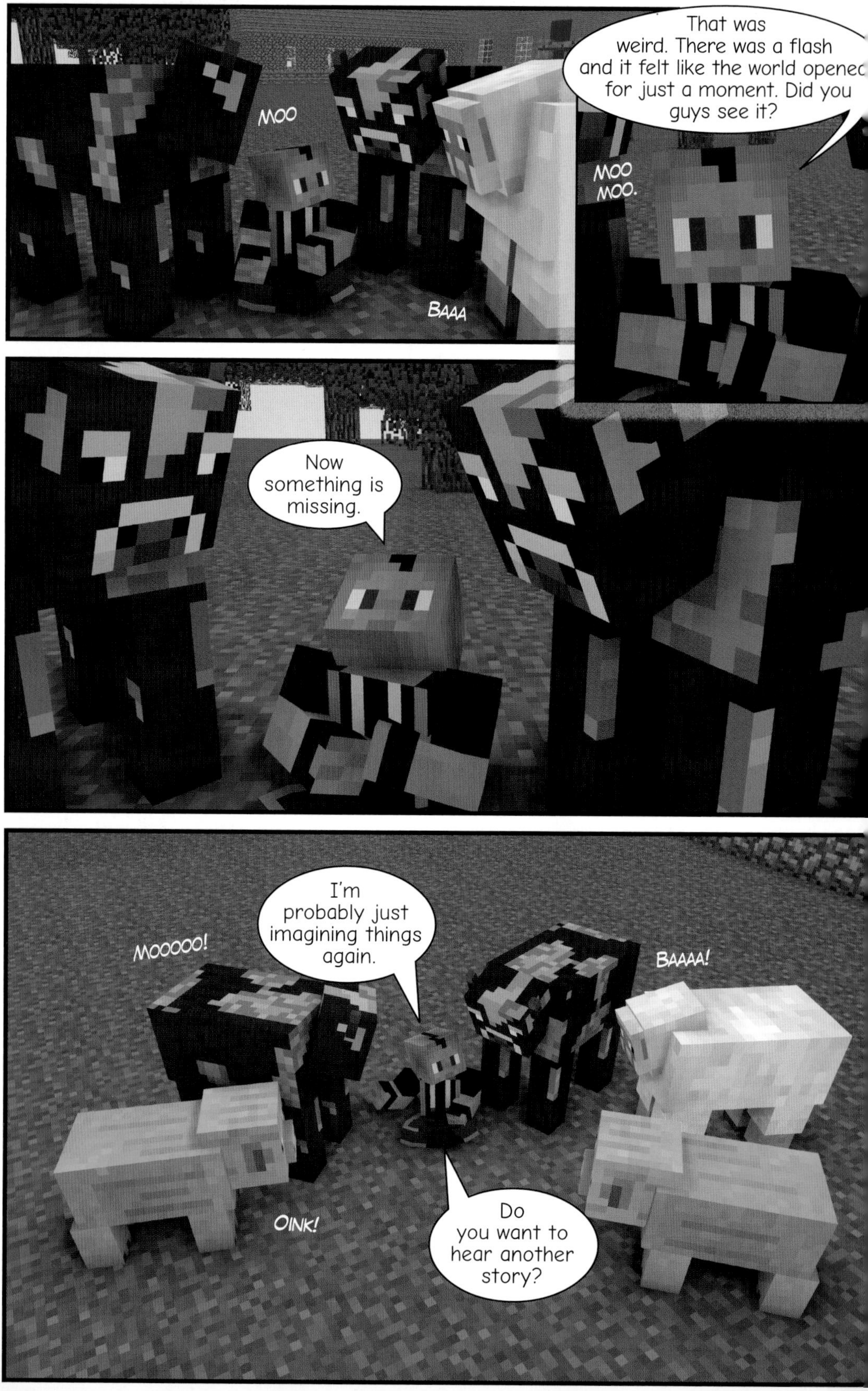
MOO
BAAA
That was weird. There was a flash and it felt like the world openec for just a moment. Did you guys see it?
MOO MOO.
Now something is missing.
MOOOOO!
I'm probably just imagining things again.
BAAAA!
OINK!
Do you want to hear another story?

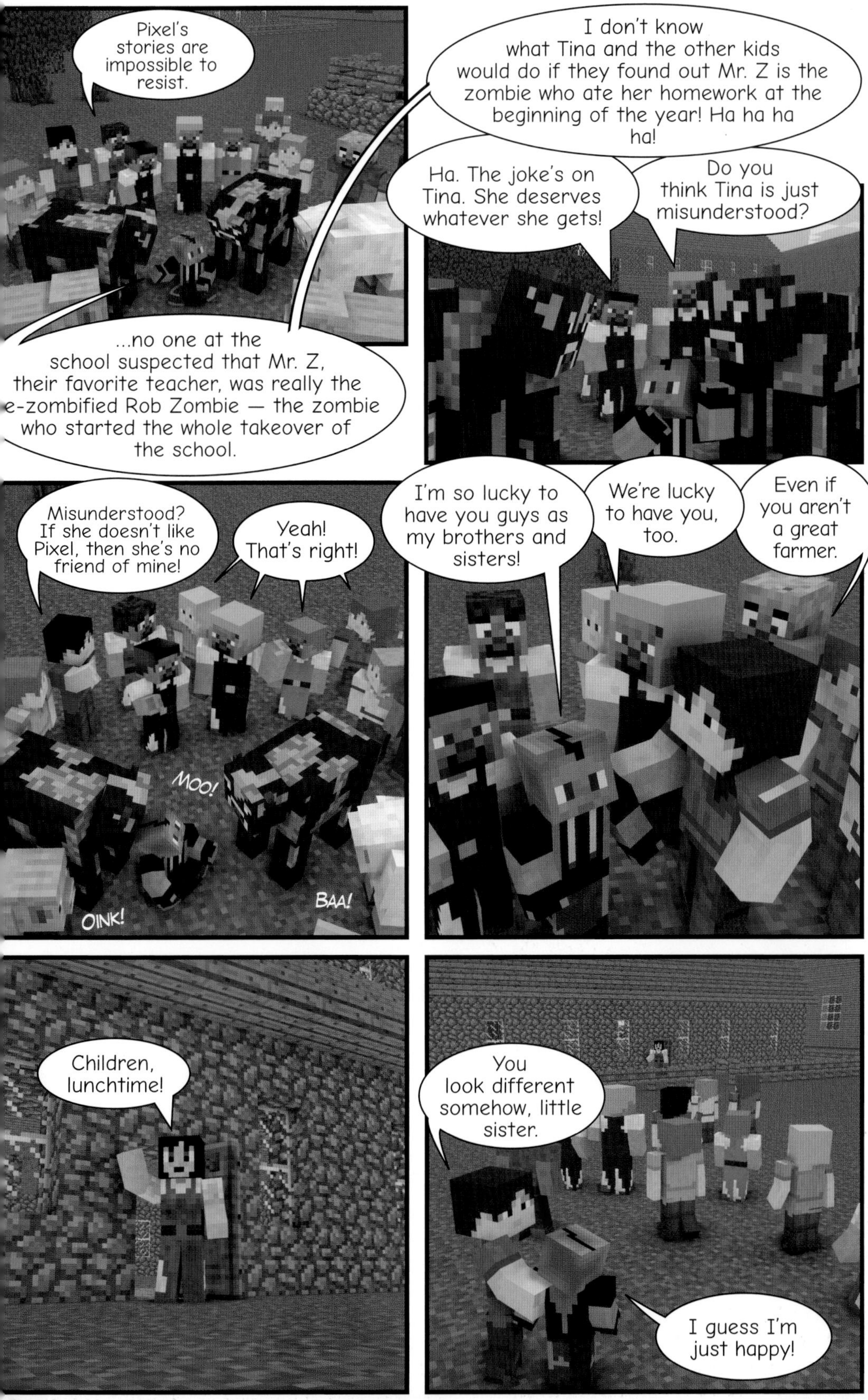

Pixel's stories are impossible to resist.
...no one at the school suspected that Mr. Z, their favorite teacher, was really the e-zombified Rob Zombie — the zombie who started the whole takeover of the school.
I don't know what Tina and the other kids would do if they found out Mr. Z is the zombie who ate her homework at the beginning of the year! Ha ha ha ha!
Ha. The joke's on Tina. She deserves whatever she gets!
Do you think Tina is just misunderstood?
Misunderstood? If she doesn't like Pixel, then she's no friend of mine!
Yeah! That's right!
MOO!
OINK!
BAA!
I'm so lucky to have you guys as my brothers and sisters!
We're lucky to have you, too.
Even if you aren't a great farmer.
Children, lunchtime!
You look different somehow, little sister.
I guess I'm just happy!

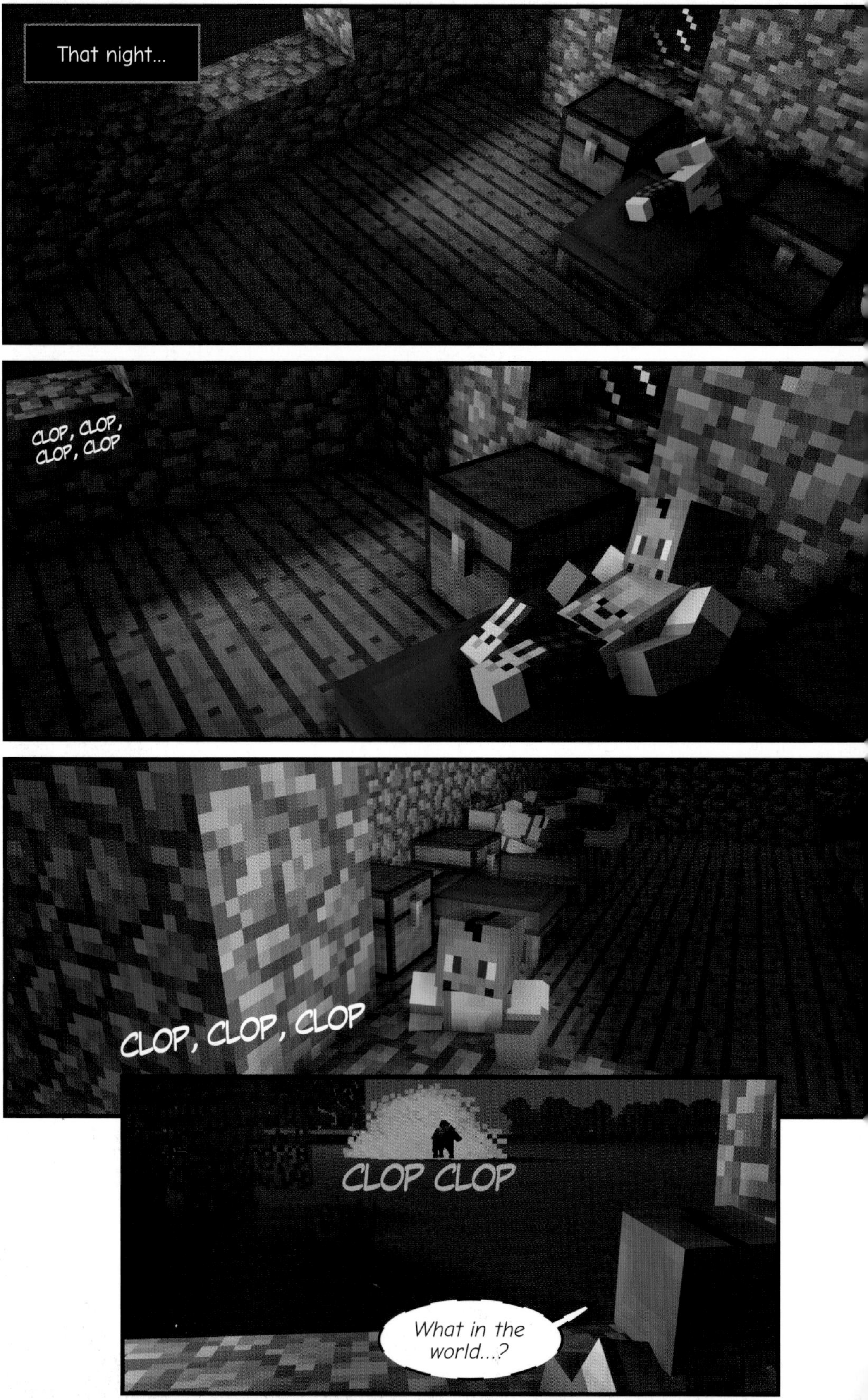
That night...
CLOP, CLOP,
CLOP, CLOP
CLOP, CLOP, CLOP
CLOP CLOP
What in the world...?

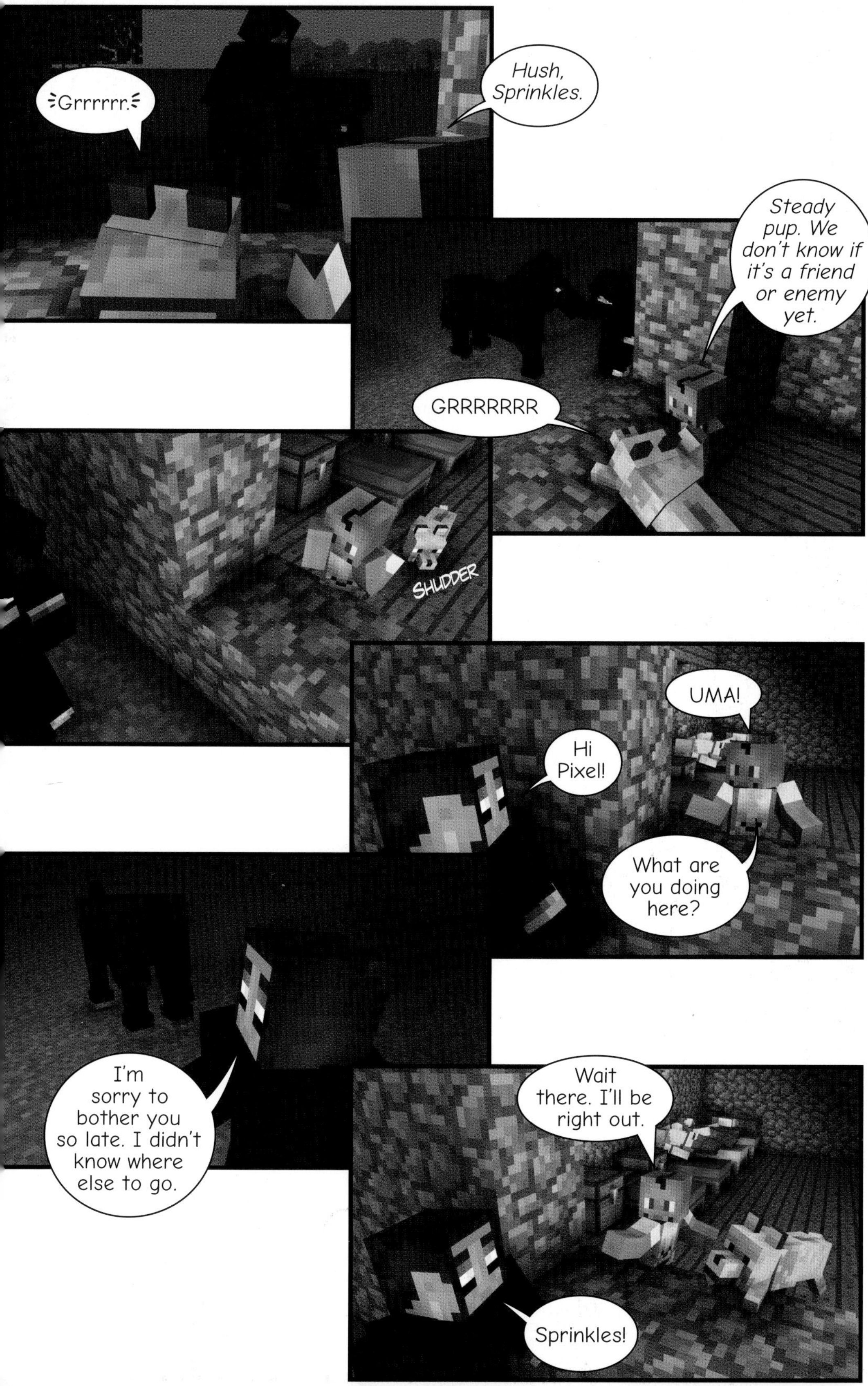
Grrrrrr.
Hush, Sprinkles.
Steady pup. We don't know if it's a friend or enemy yet.
GRRRRRRR
SHUDDER
UMA!
Hi Pixel!
What are you doing here?
I'm sorry to bother you so late. I didn't know where else to go.
Wait there. I'll be right out.
Sprinkles!

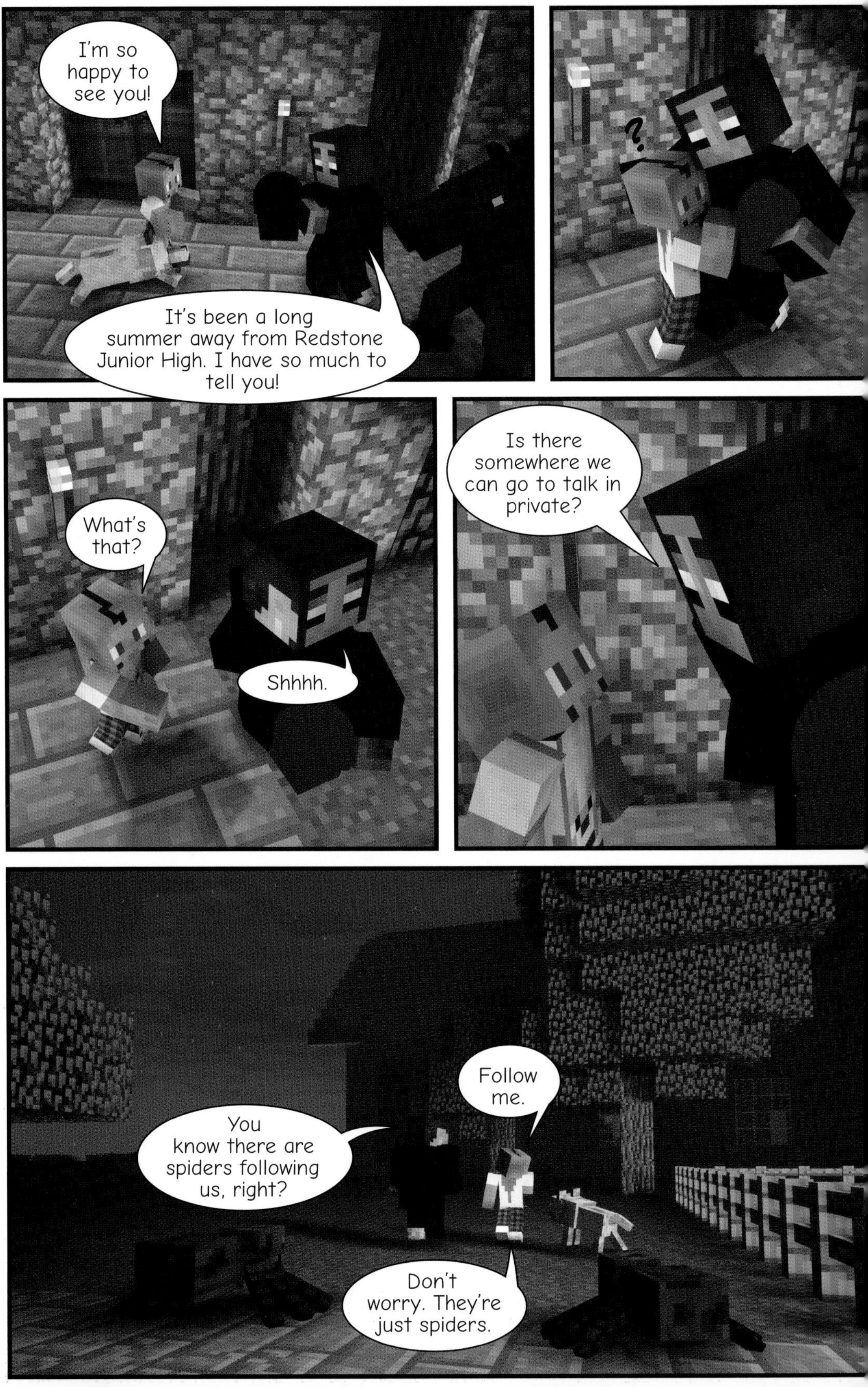
I'm so happy to see you!
It's been a long summer away from Redstone Junior High. I have so much to tell you!
?
What's that?
Shhhh.
Is there somewhere we can go to talk in private?
Follow me.
You know there are spiders following us, right?
Don't worry. They're just spiders.

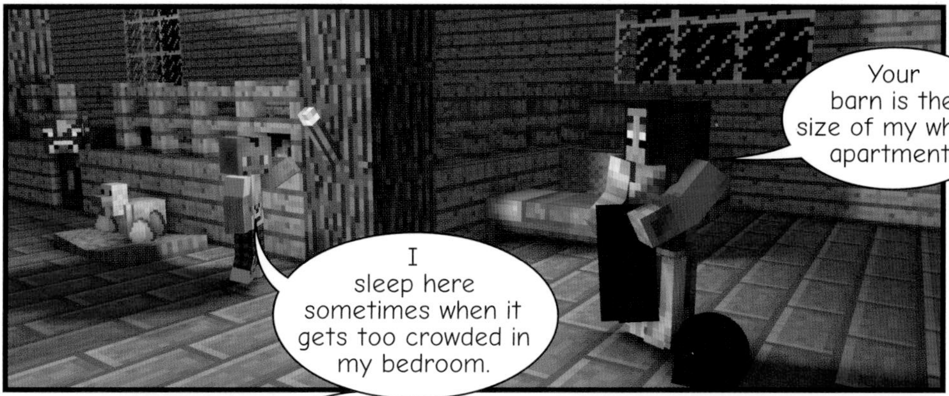
Your barn is the size of my whole apartment!
I sleep here sometimes when it gets too crowded in my bedroom.

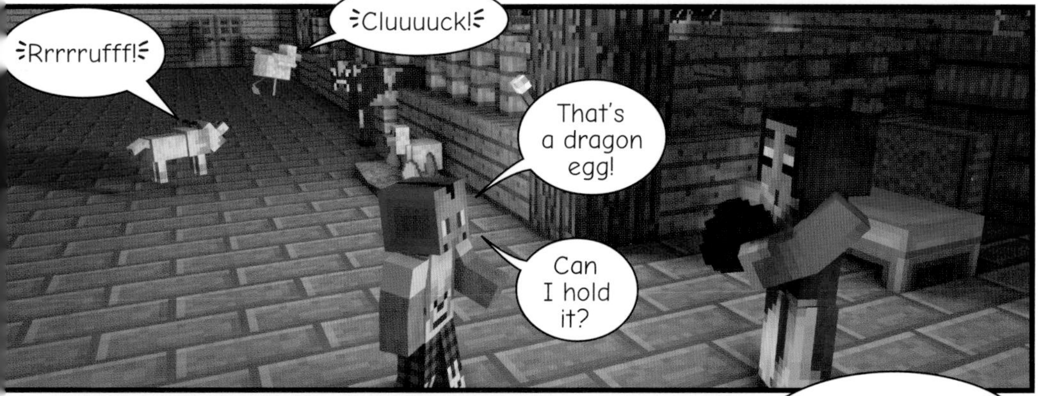
Rrrrrufff!
Cluuuuck!
That's a dragon egg!
Can I hold it?

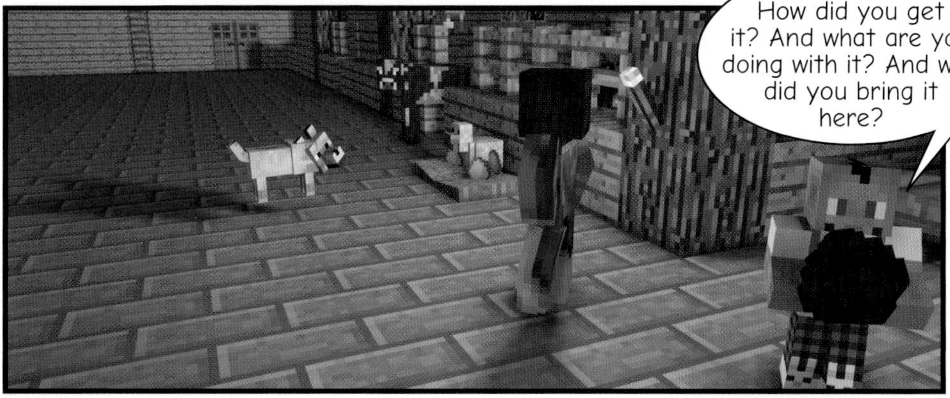
How did you get it? And what are you doing with it? And why did you bring it here?

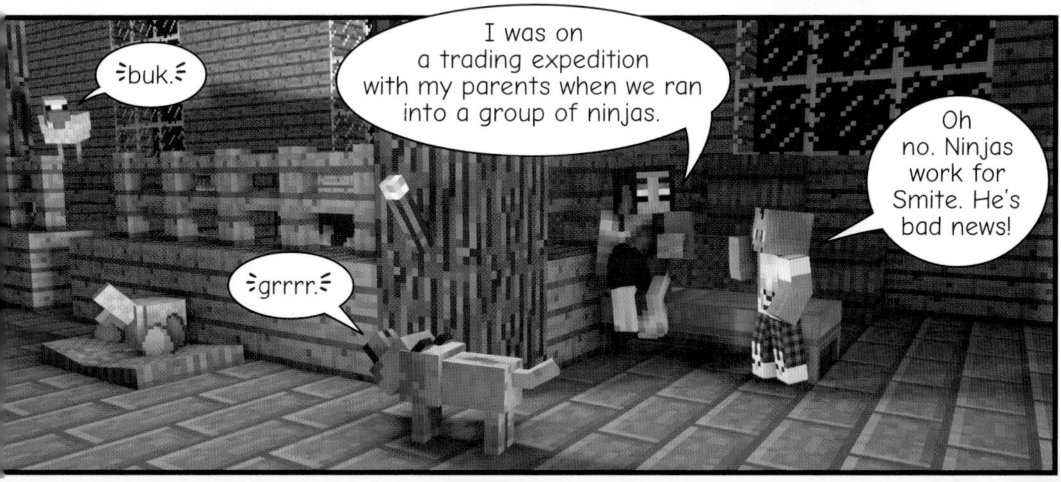
buk.
I was on a trading expedition with my parents when we ran into a group of ninjas.
Oh no. Ninjas work for Smite. He's bad news!
grrrr.

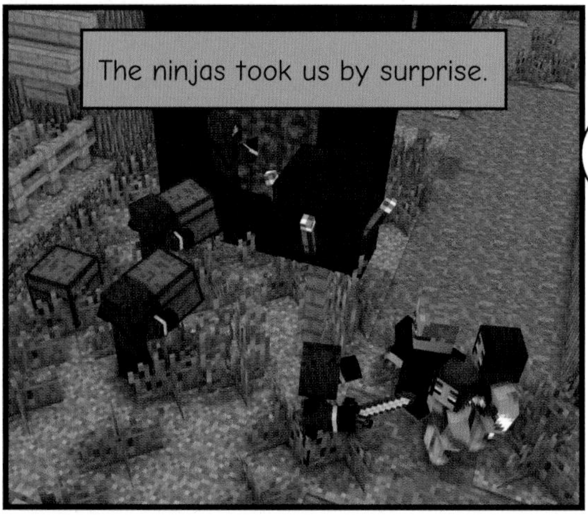

The ninjas took us by surprise.

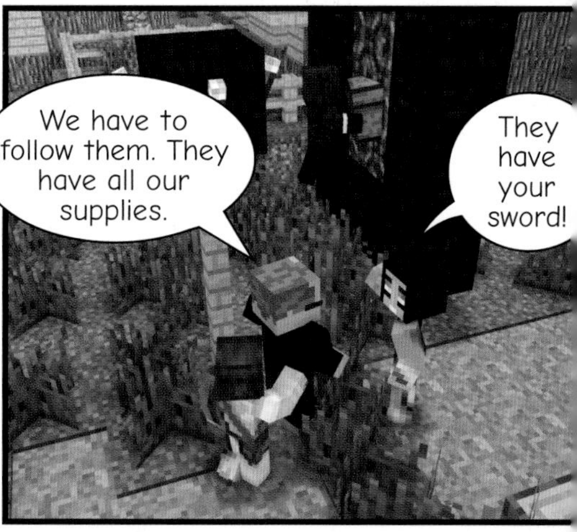

We have to follow them. They have all our supplies.
They have your sword!

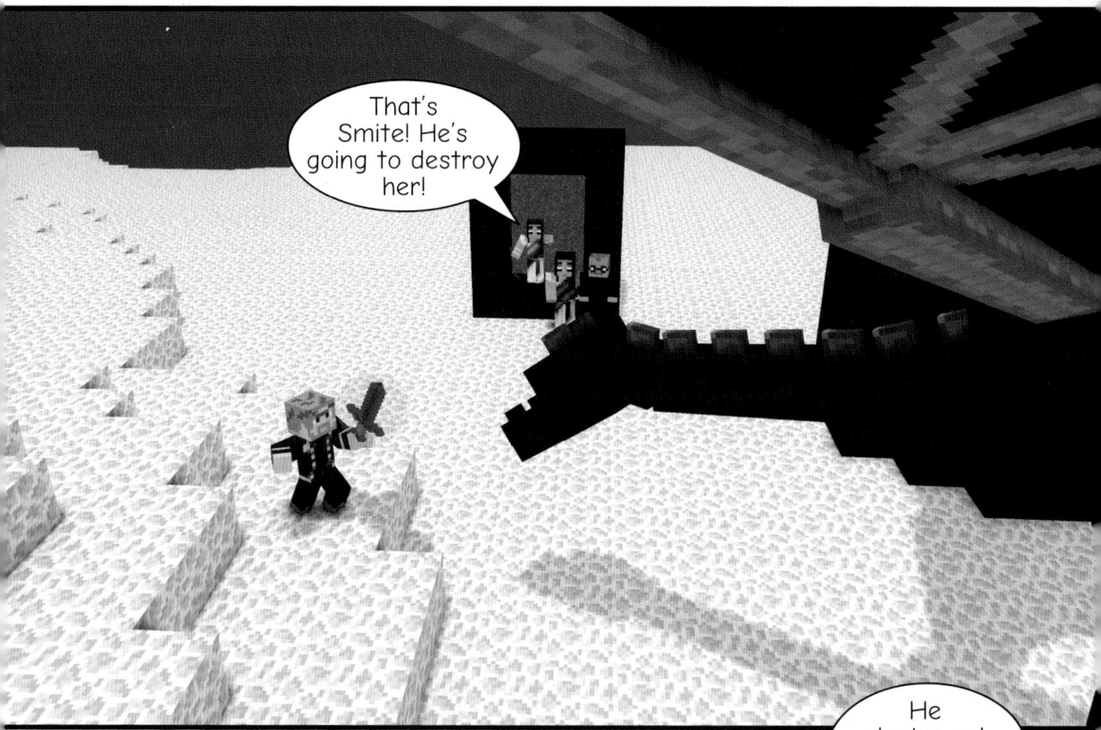

That's Smite! He's going to destroy her!

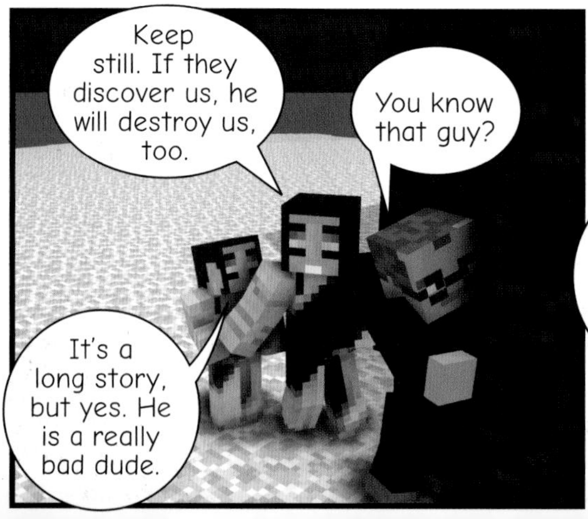

Keep still. If they discover us, he will destroy us, too.
You know that guy?
It's a long story, but yes. He is a really bad dude.

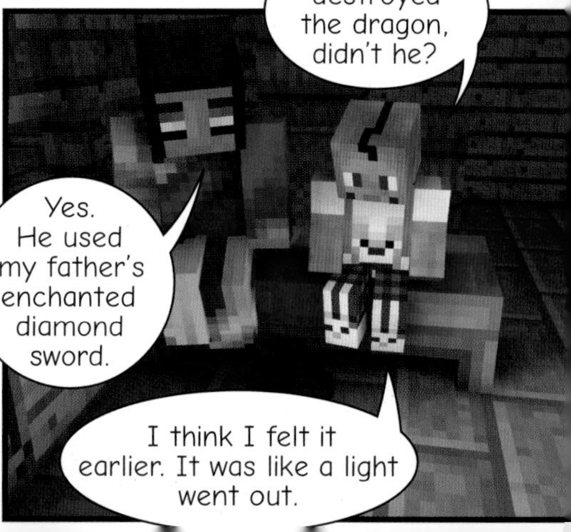

He destroyed the dragon, didn't he?
Yes. He used my father's enchanted diamond sword.
I think I felt it earlier. It was like a light went out.

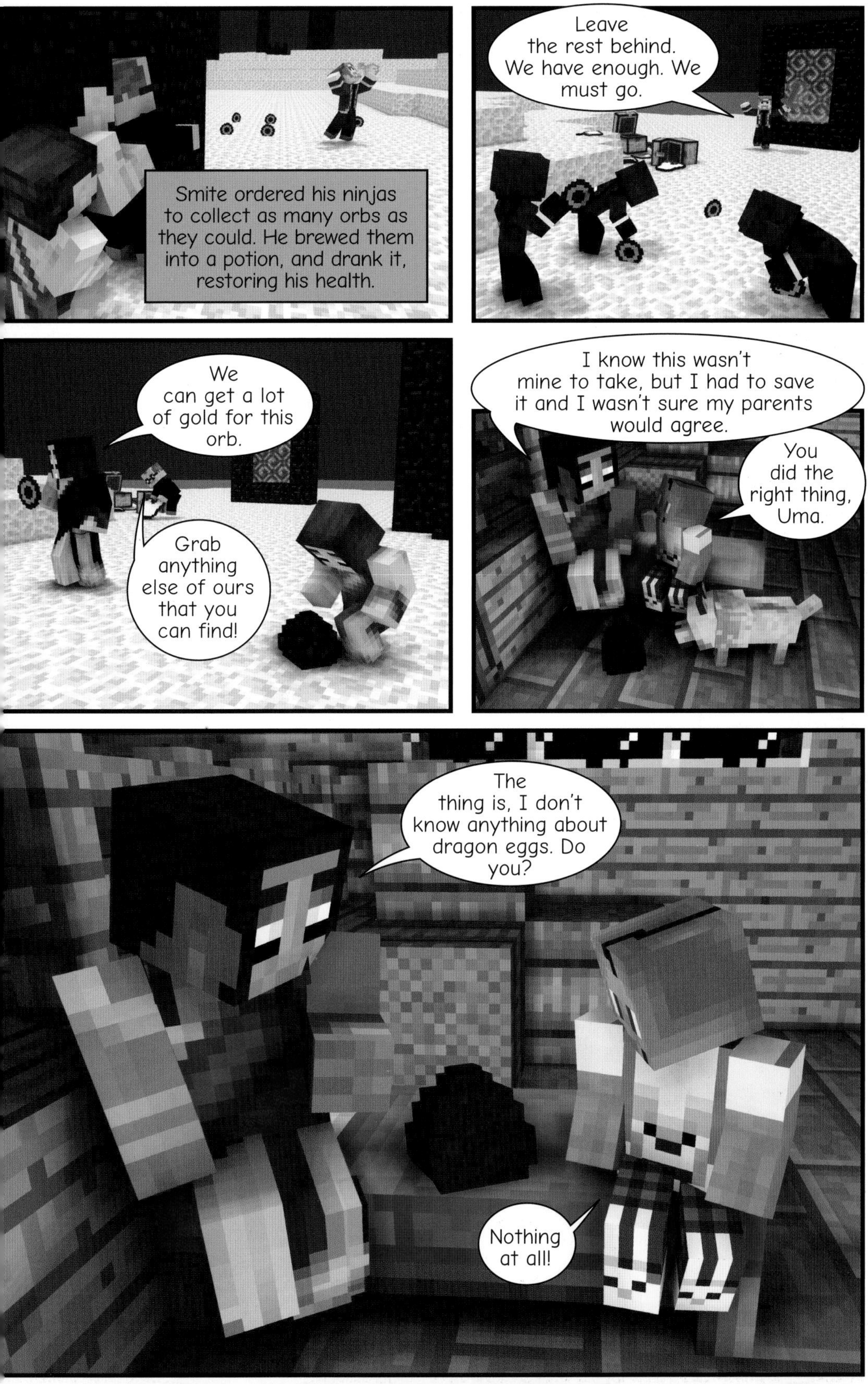
Smite ordered his ninjas to collect as many orbs as they could. He brewed them into a potion, and drank it, restoring his health.
Leave the rest behind. We have enough. We must go.
We can get a lot of gold for this orb.
Grab anything else of ours that you can find!
I know this wasn't mine to take, but I had to save it and I wasn't sure my parents would agree.
You did the right thing, Uma.
The thing is, I don't know anything about dragon eggs. Do you?
Nothing at all!

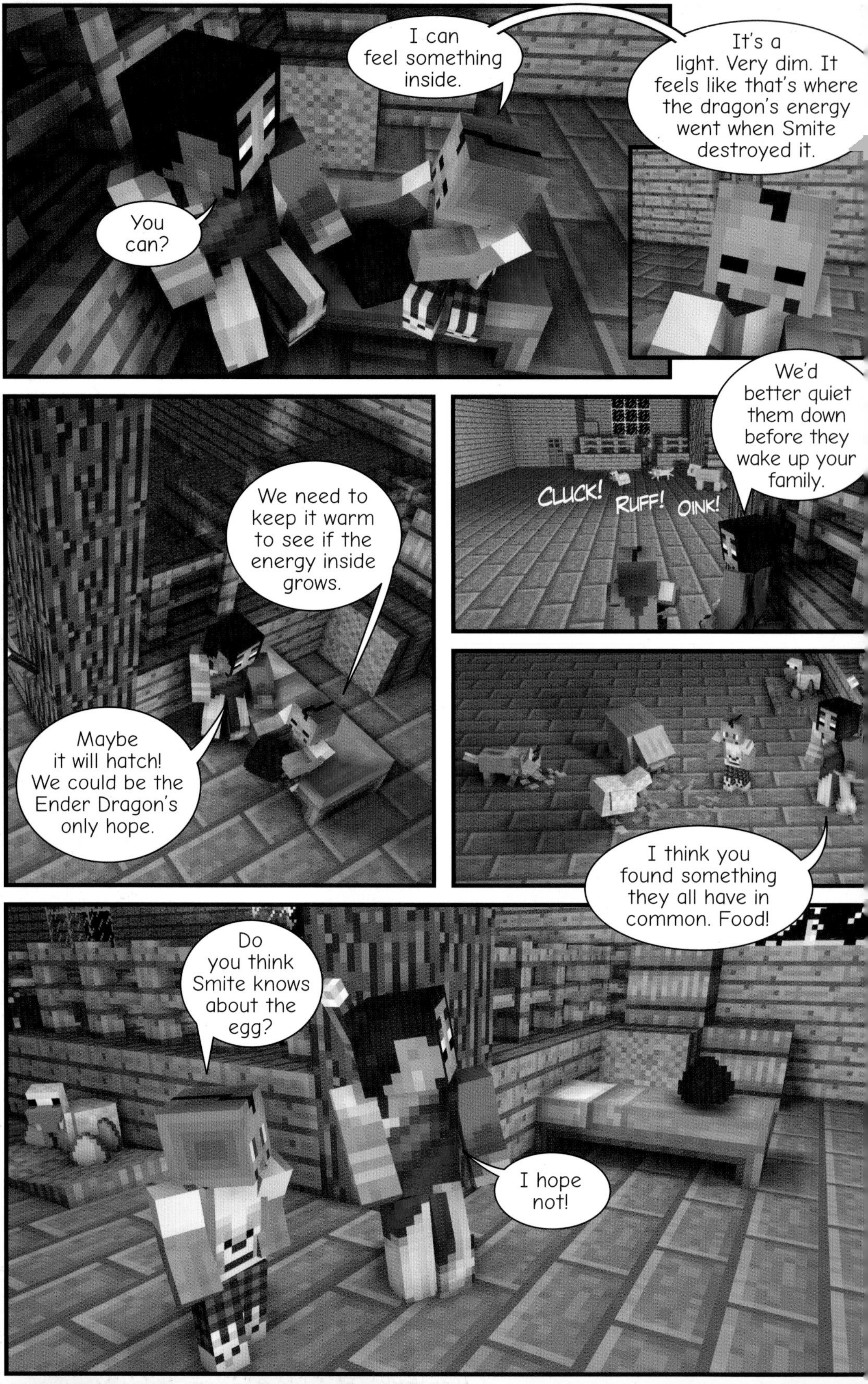

I can feel something inside.
You can?
It's a light. Very dim. It feels like that's where the dragon's energy went when Smite destroyed it.
We need to keep it warm to see if the energy inside grows.
Maybe it will hatch! We could be the Ender Dragon's only hope.
CLUCK!
RUFF!
OINK!
We'd better quiet them down before they wake up your family.
I think you found something they all have in common. Food!
Do you think Smite knows about the egg?
I hope not!

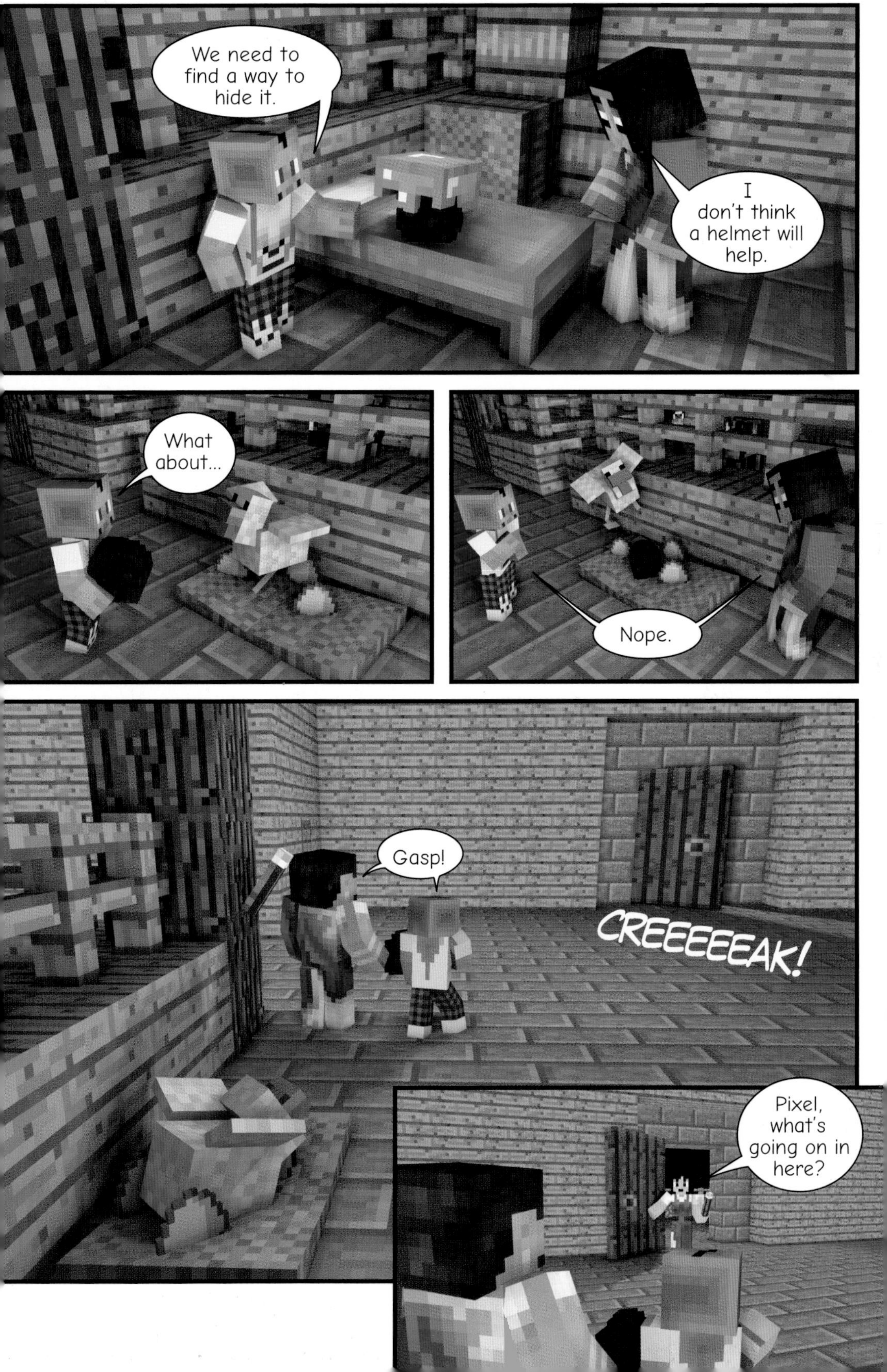
We need to find a way to hide it.
I don't think a helmet will help.
What about...
Nope.
Gasp!
CREEEEEEAK!
Pixel, what's going on in here?

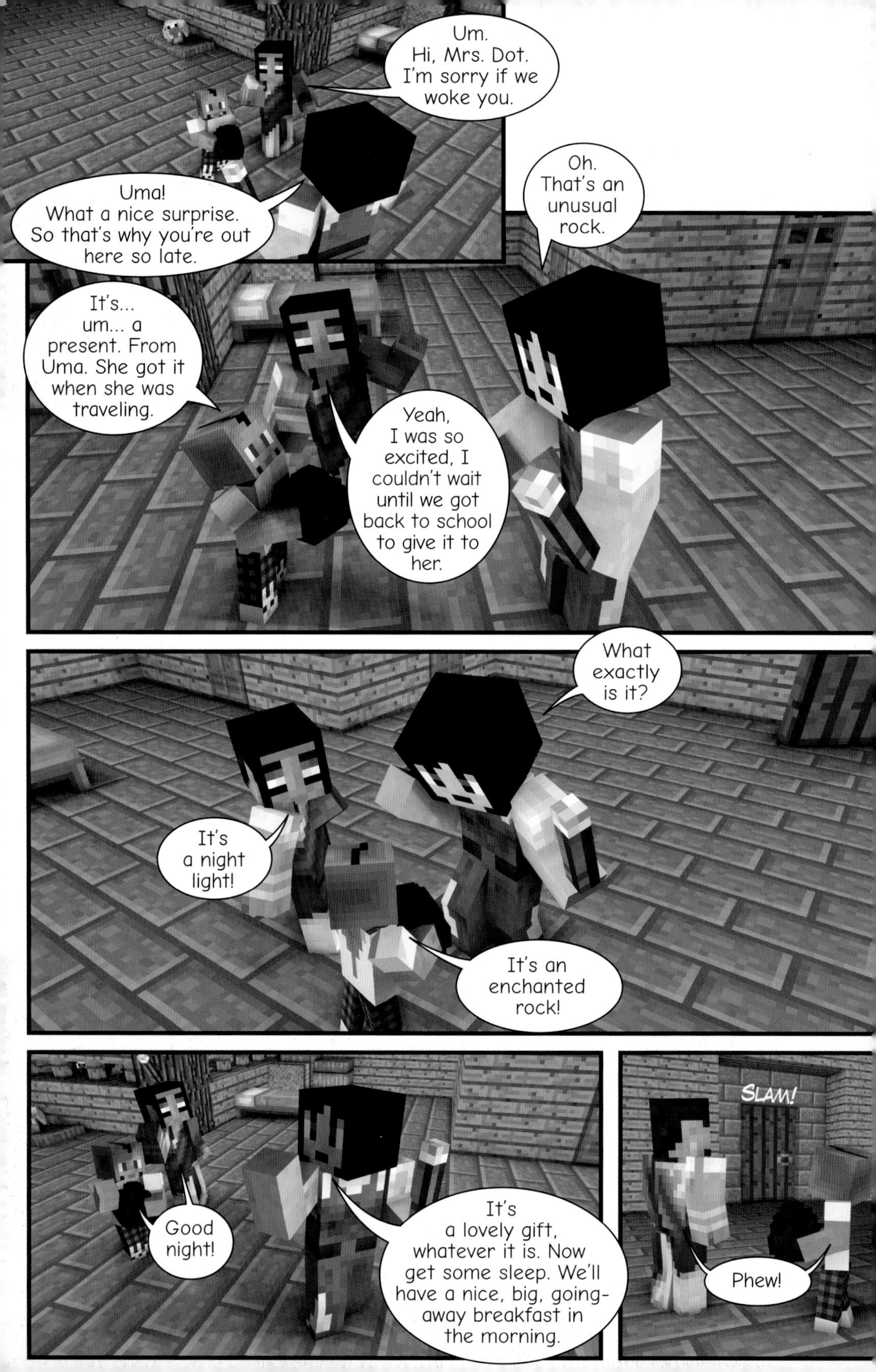
Um.
Hi, Mrs. Dot.
I'm sorry if we woke you.
Uma!
What a nice surprise.
So that's why you're out here so late.
Oh.
That's an unusual rock.
It's... um... a present. From Uma. She got it when she was traveling.
Yeah, I was so excited, I couldn't wait until we got back to school to give it to her.
What exactly is it?
It's a night light!
It's an enchanted rock!
Good night!
It's a lovely gift, whatever it is. Now get some sleep. We'll have a nice, big, going-away breakfast in the morning.
SLAM!
Phew!

CHAPTER 2

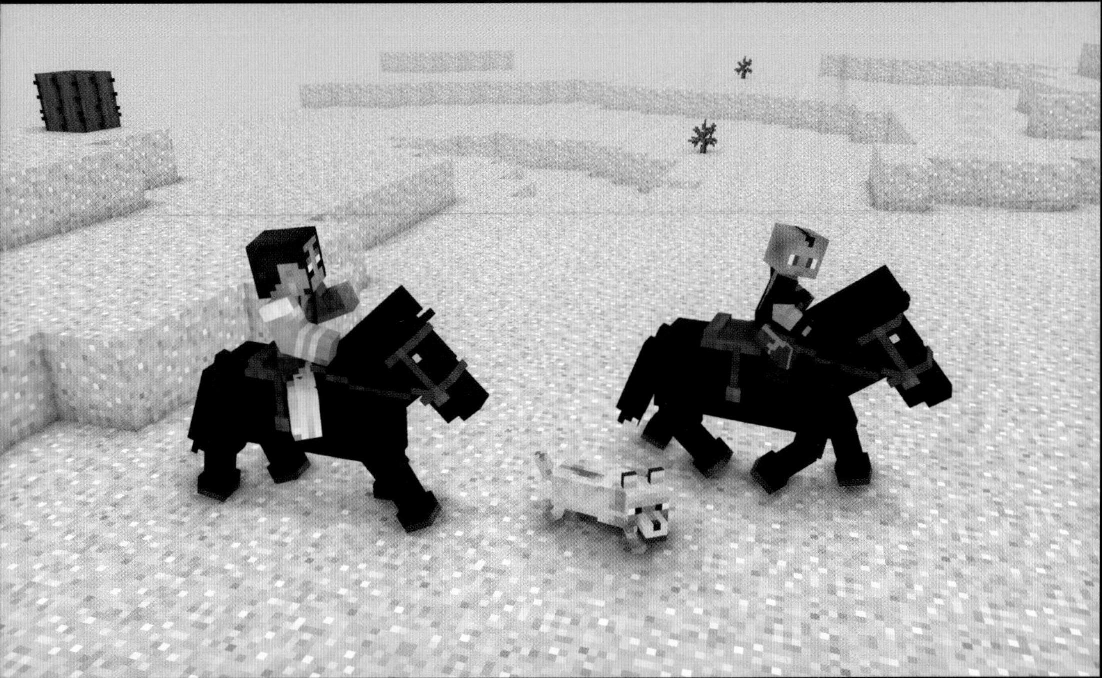

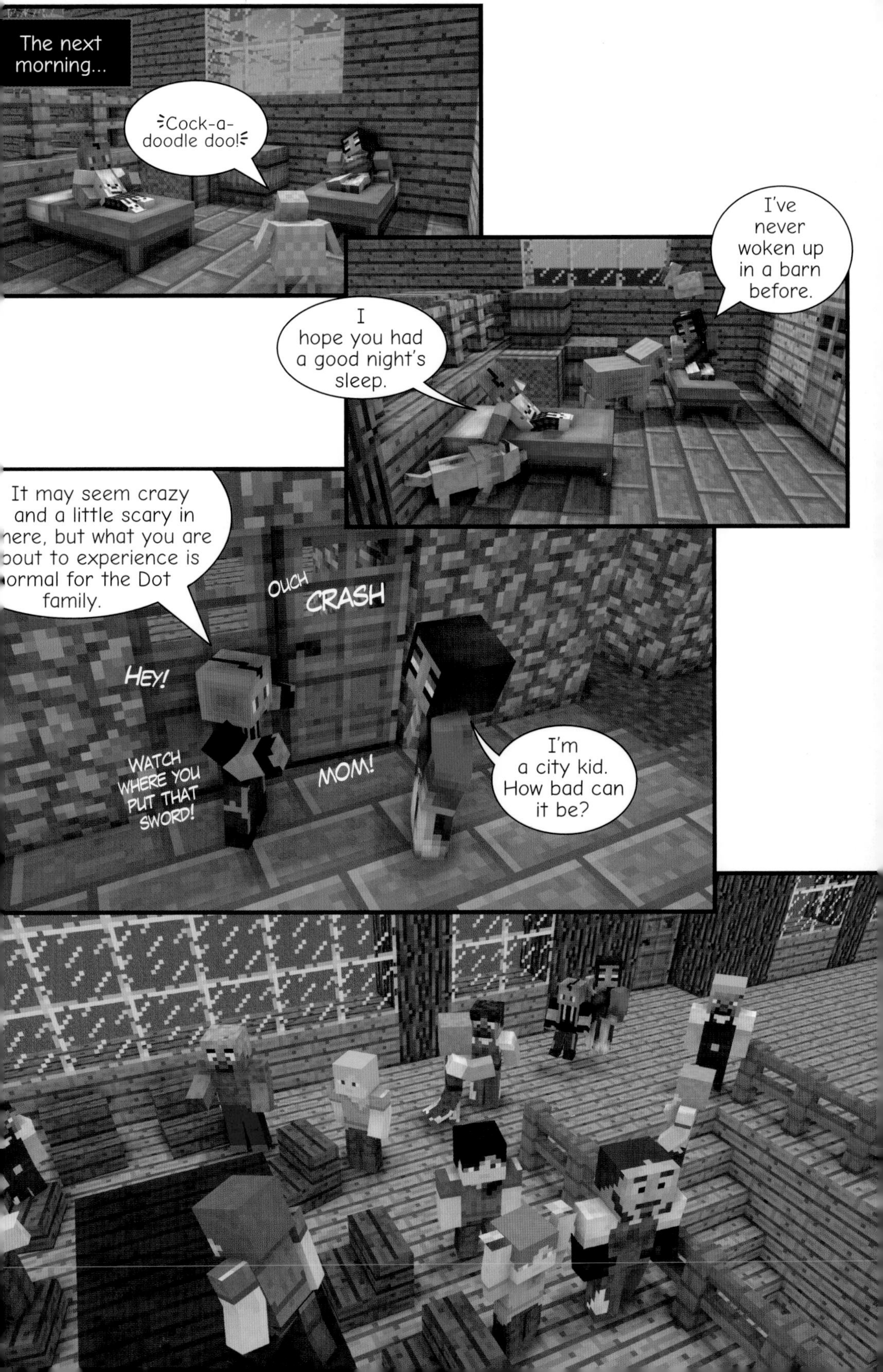
The next morning...
Cock-a-doodle doo!
I hope you had a good night's sleep.
I've never woken up in a barn before.
It may seem crazy and a little scary in here, but what you are about to experience is normal for the Dot family.
OUCH
CRASH
HEY!
WATCH WHERE YOU PUT THAT SWORD!
MOM!
I'm a city kid. How bad can it be?

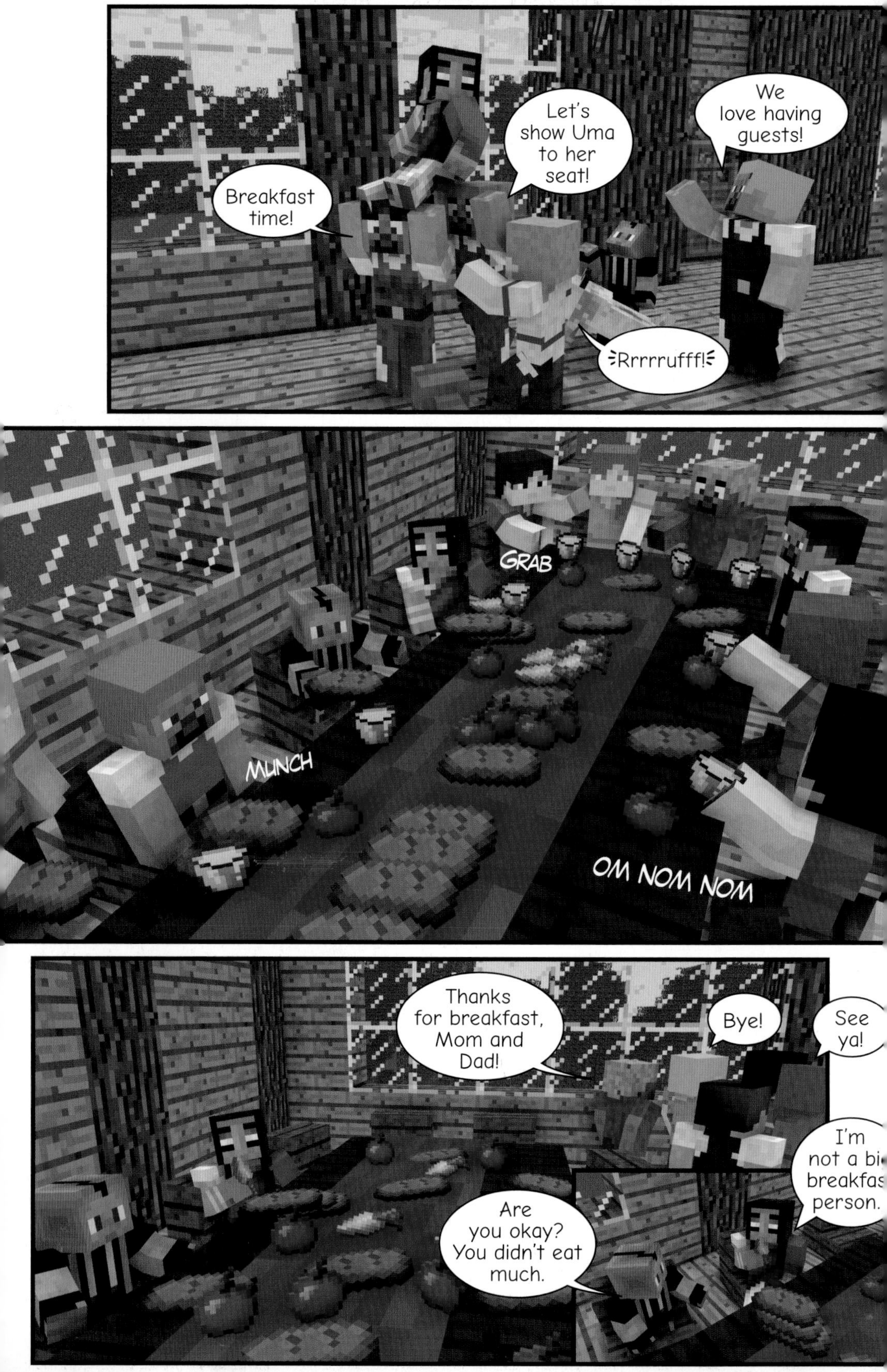
Breakfast time!
Let's show Uma to her seat!
We love having guests!
Rrrrrufff!
GRAB
MUNCH
OM NOM NOM
Thanks for breakfast, Mom and Dad!
Bye!
See ya!
Are you okay? You didn't eat much.
I'm not a bi breakfas person.

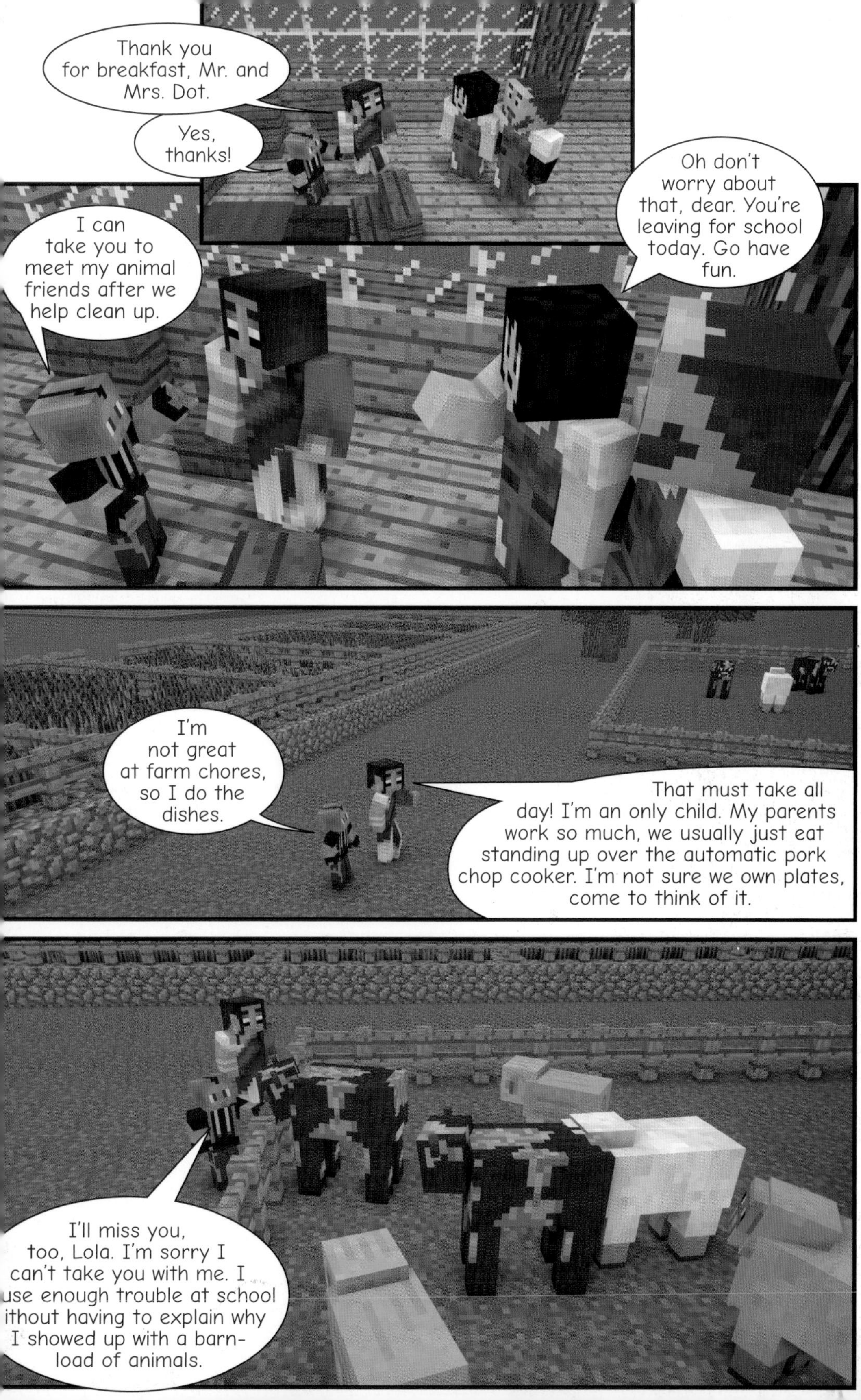
Thank you for breakfast, Mr. and Mrs. Dot.
Yes, thanks!
I can take you to meet my animal friends after we help clean up.
Oh don't worry about that, dear. You're leaving for school today. Go have fun.
I'm not great at farm chores, so I do the dishes.
That must take all day! I'm an only child. My parents work so much, we usually just eat standing up over the automatic pork chop cooker. I'm not sure we own plates, come to think of it.
I'll miss you, too, Lola. I'm sorry I can't take you with me. I use enough trouble at school ithout having to explain why I showed up with a barn-load of animals.

I can sense that your animal friends are very happy here. But they are sad that you are leaving.

That's what I figured. I envy your ability to sense emotions.

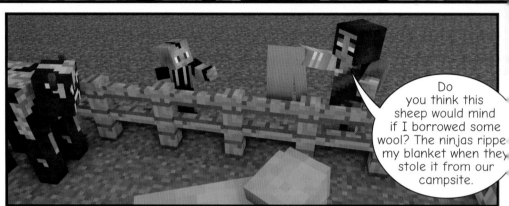

Do you think this sheep would mind if I borrowed some wool? The ninjas ripped my blanket when they stole it from our campsite.

You don't mind, do you, Vermillion?

⋜Baa baa. Baba Baaaa.⋜

She's cool with it. In fact, she's been feeling overheated lately. I was supposed to shear her last week, but I guess I forgot.

And *you* envy *my* abilities? You can talk to ANYONE!

I wonder what Tina's talent is.

We all have pretty cool talents, don't we? Like Violet's talent for enchanting. And Sky's talent for turning anything into a machine using redstone.

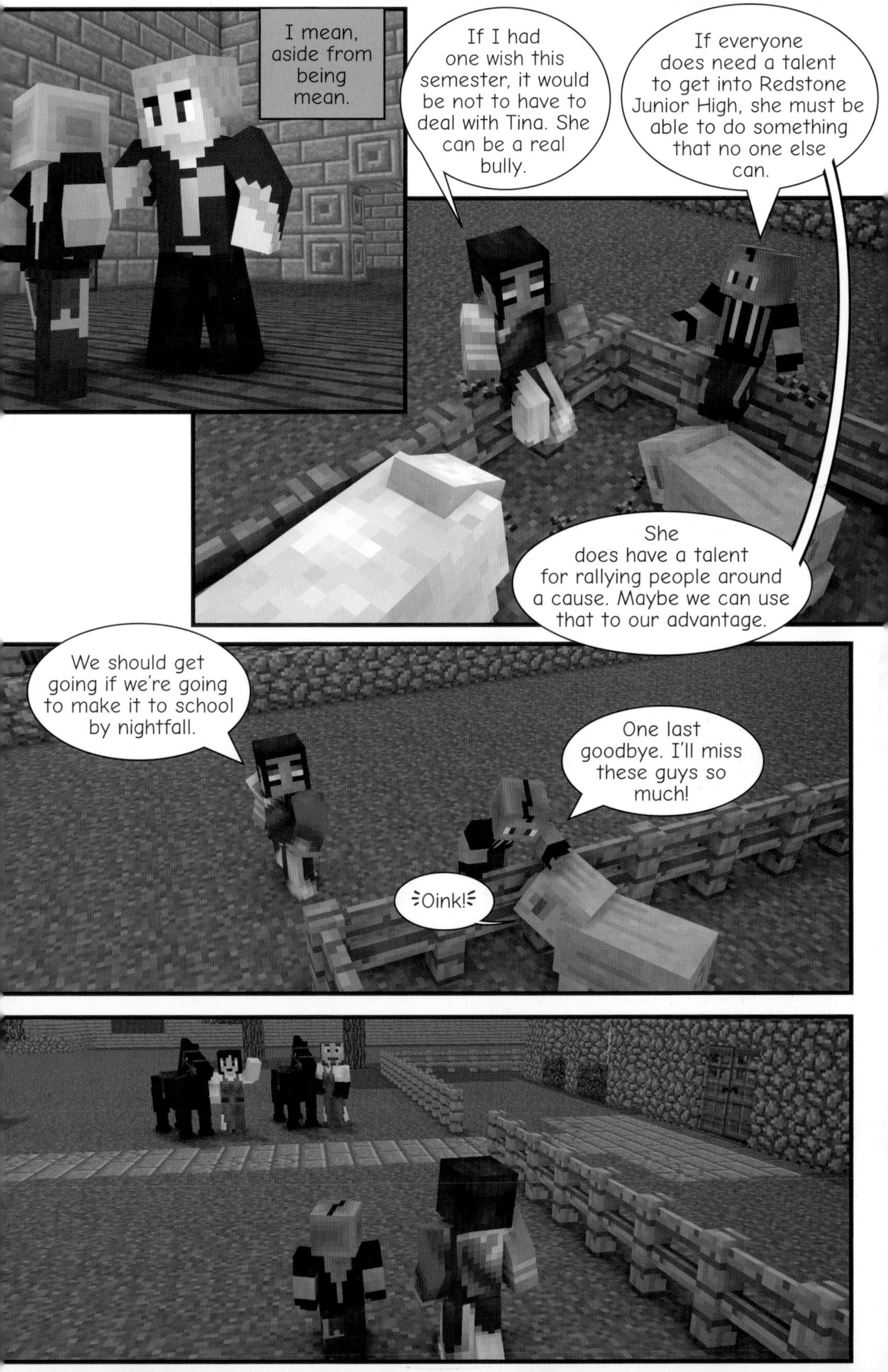

I mean, aside from being mean.
If I had one wish this semester, it would be not to have to deal with Tina. She can be a real bully.
If everyone does need a talent to get into Redstone Junior High, she must be able to do something that no one else can.
She does have a talent for rallying people around a cause. Maybe we can use that to our advantage.
We should get going if we're going to make it to school by nightfall.
One last goodbye. I'll miss these guys so much!
Oink!

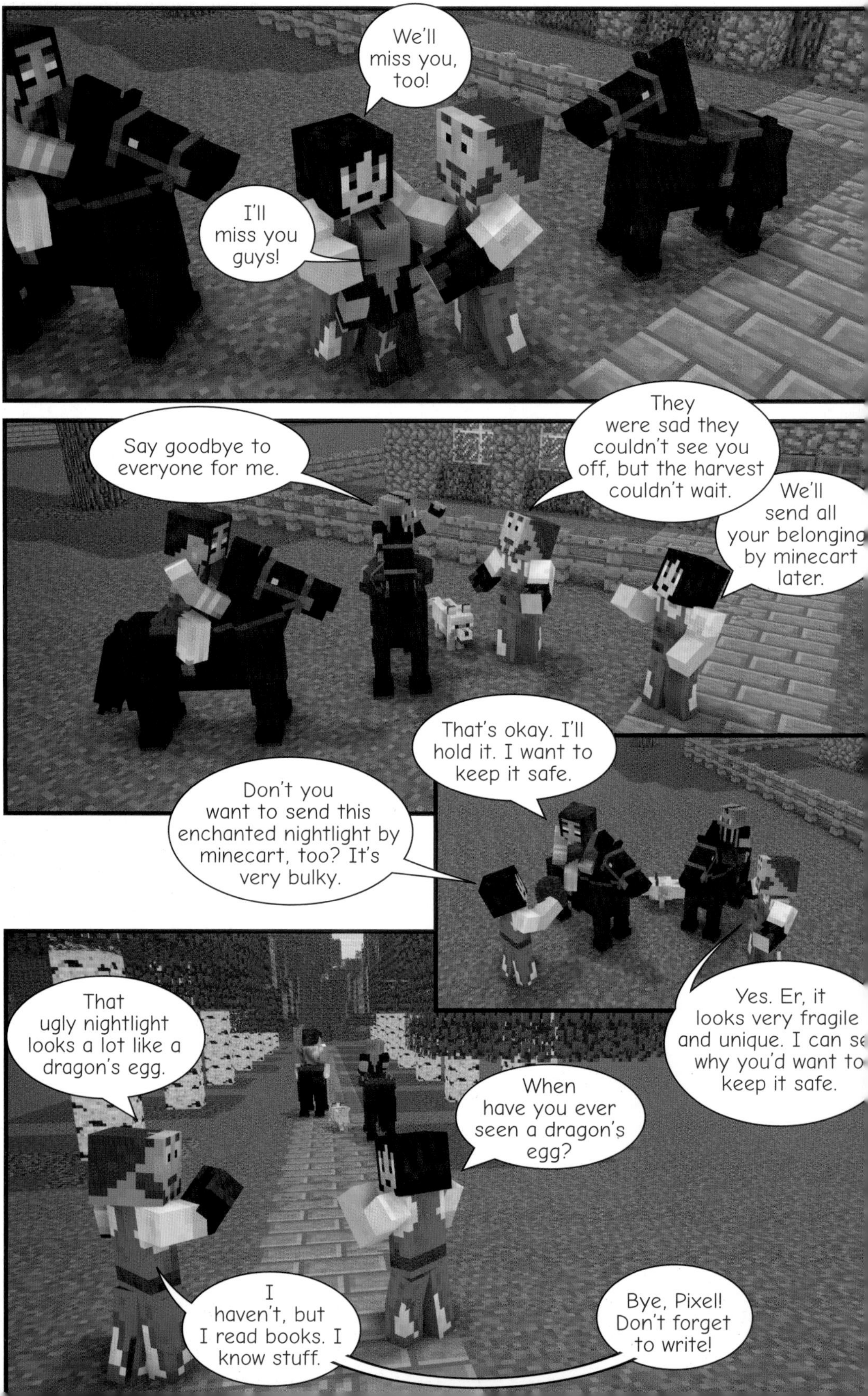

We'll miss you, too!
I'll miss you guys!
Say goodbye to everyone for me.
They were sad they couldn't see you off, but the harvest couldn't wait.
We'll send all your belonging by minecart later.
Don't you want to send this enchanted nightlight by minecart, too? It's very bulky.
That's okay. I'll hold it. I want to keep it safe.
Yes. Er, it looks very fragile and unique. I can se why you'd want to keep it safe.
That ugly nightlight looks a lot like a dragon's egg.
When have you ever seen a dragon's egg?
I haven't, but I read books. I know stuff.
Bye, Pixel! Don't forget to write!

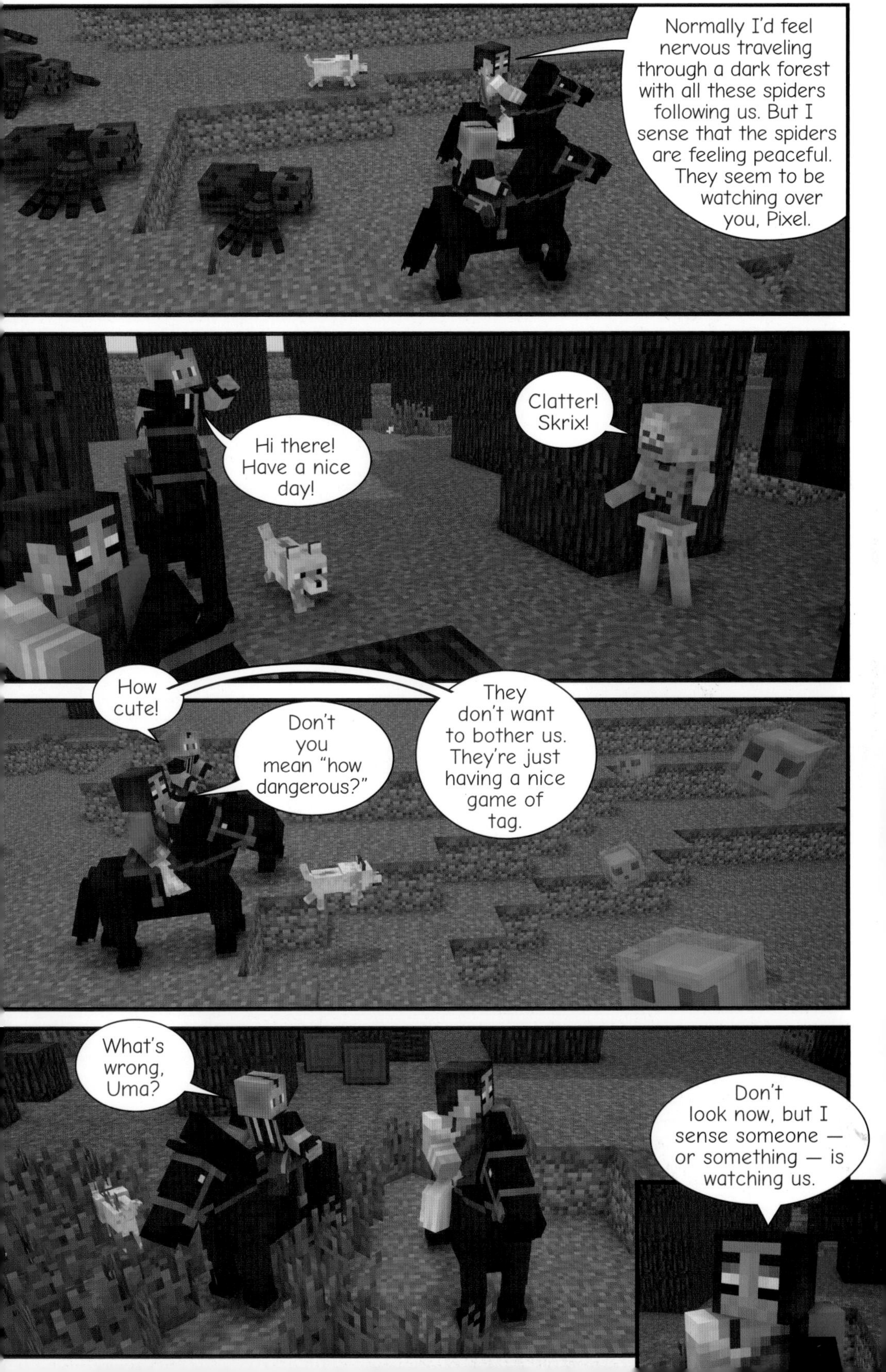
Normally I'd feel nervous traveling through a dark forest with all these spiders following us. But I sense that the spiders are feeling peaceful. They seem to be watching over you, Pixel.
Hi there! Have a nice day!
Clatter! Skrix!
How cute!
Don't you mean "how dangerous?"
They don't want to bother us. They're just having a nice game of tag.
What's wrong, Uma?
Don't look now, but I sense someone — or something — is watching us.

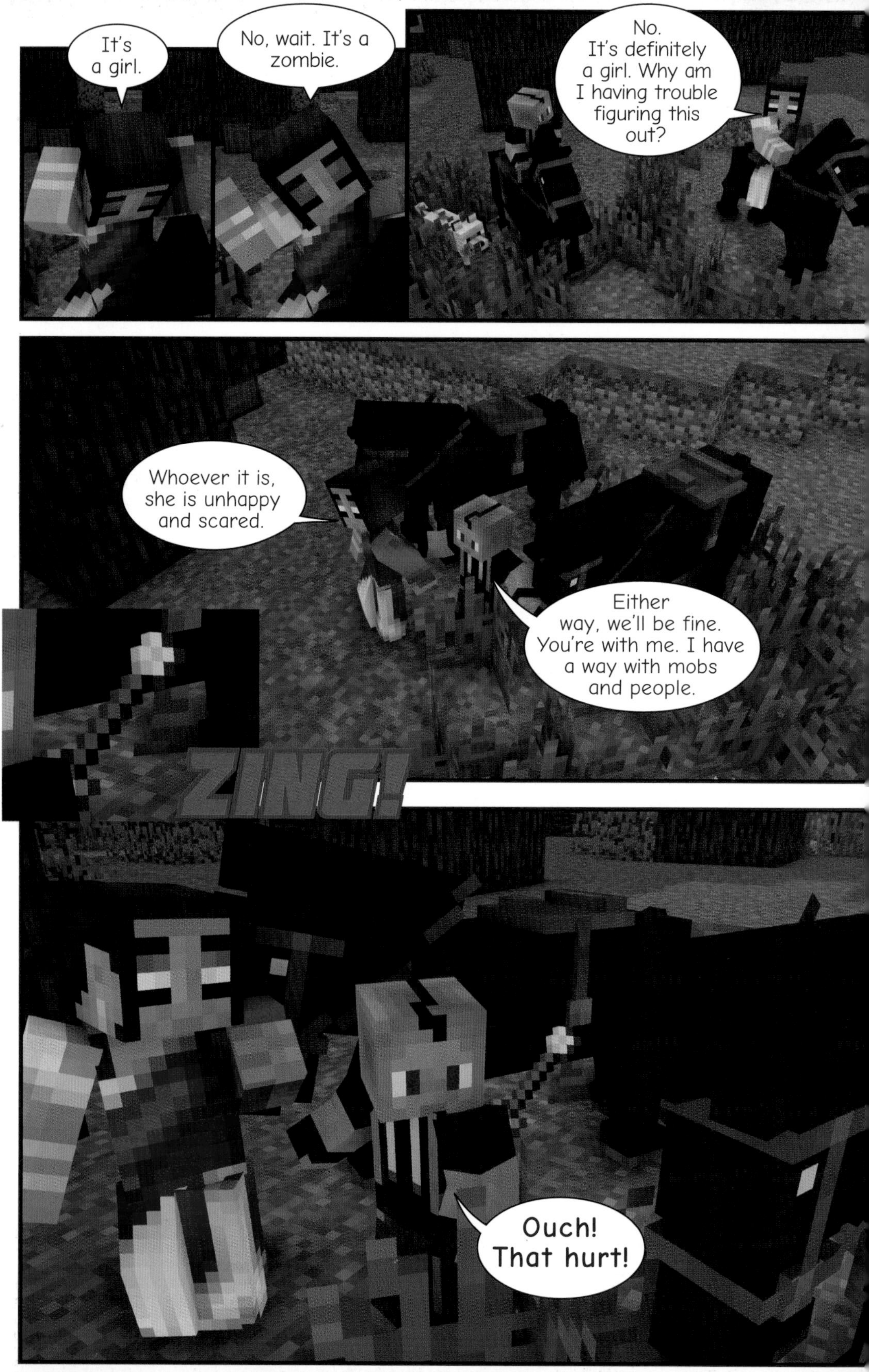
It's a girl.
No, wait. It's a zombie.
No. It's definitely a girl. Why am I having trouble figuring this out?
Whoever it is, she is unhappy and scared.
Either way, we'll be fine. You're with me. I have a way with mobs and people.
ZING!
Ouch! That hurt!

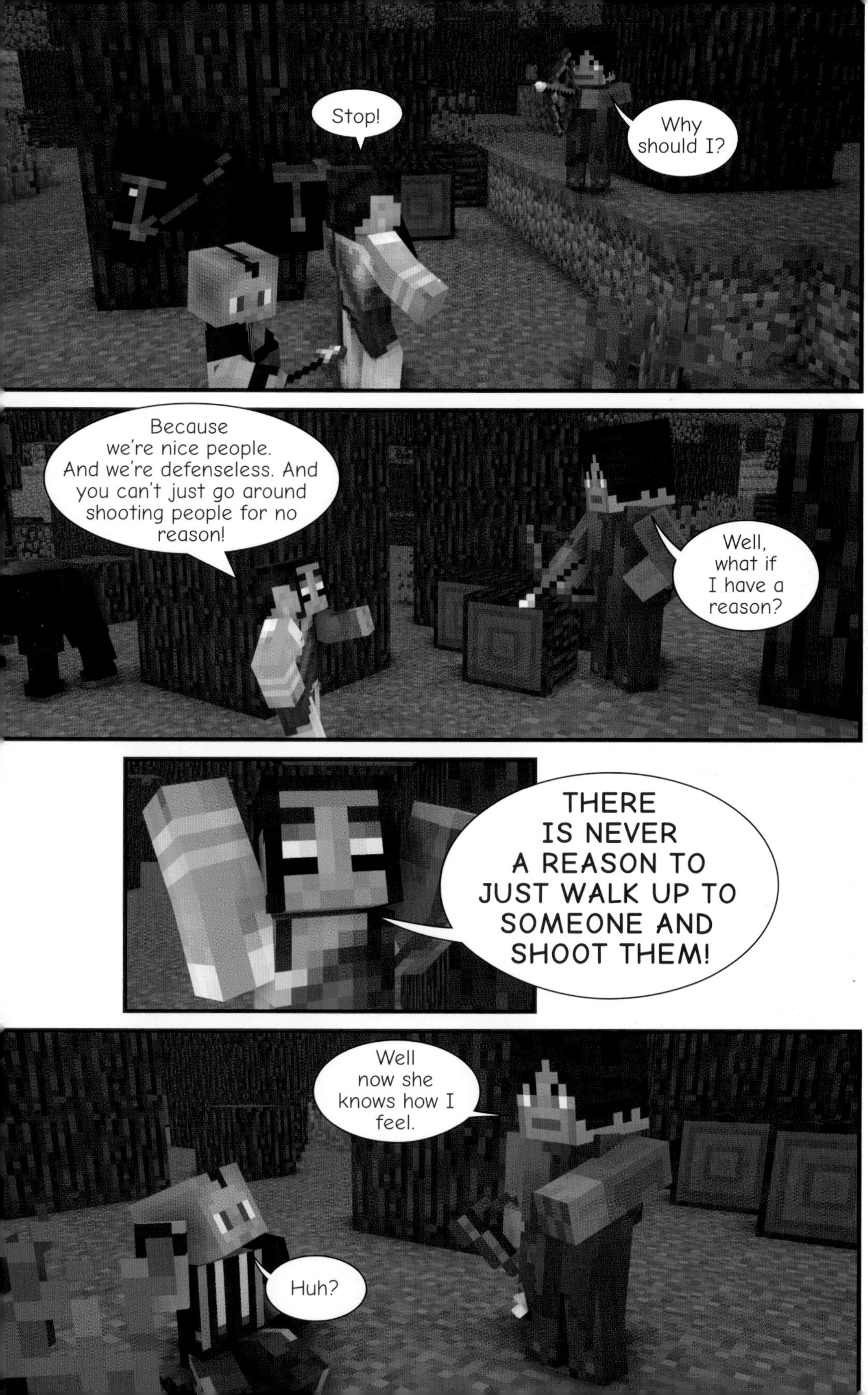
Stop!
Why should I?
Because we're nice people. And we're defenseless. And you can't just go around shooting people for no reason!
Well, what if I have a reason?
THERE IS NEVER A REASON TO JUST WALK UP TO SOMEONE AND SHOOT THEM!
Well now she knows how I feel.
Huh?

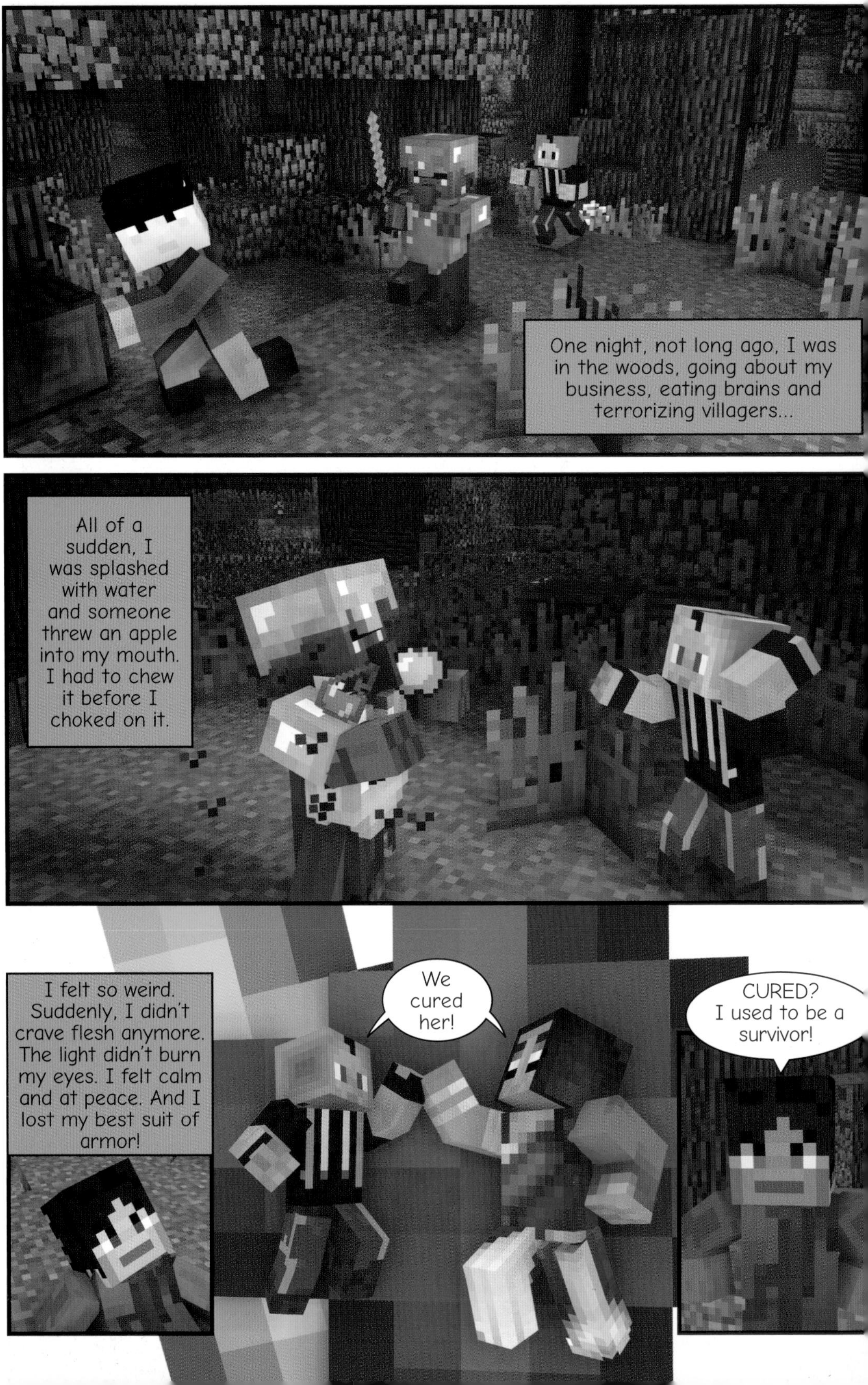

One night, not long ago, I was in the woods, going about my business, eating brains and terrorizing villagers...
All of a sudden, I was splashed with water and someone threw an apple into my mouth. I had to chew it before I choked on it.
I felt so weird. Suddenly, I didn't crave flesh anymore. The light didn't burn my eyes. I felt calm and at peace. And I lost my best suit of armor!
We cured her!
CURED? I used to be a survivor!

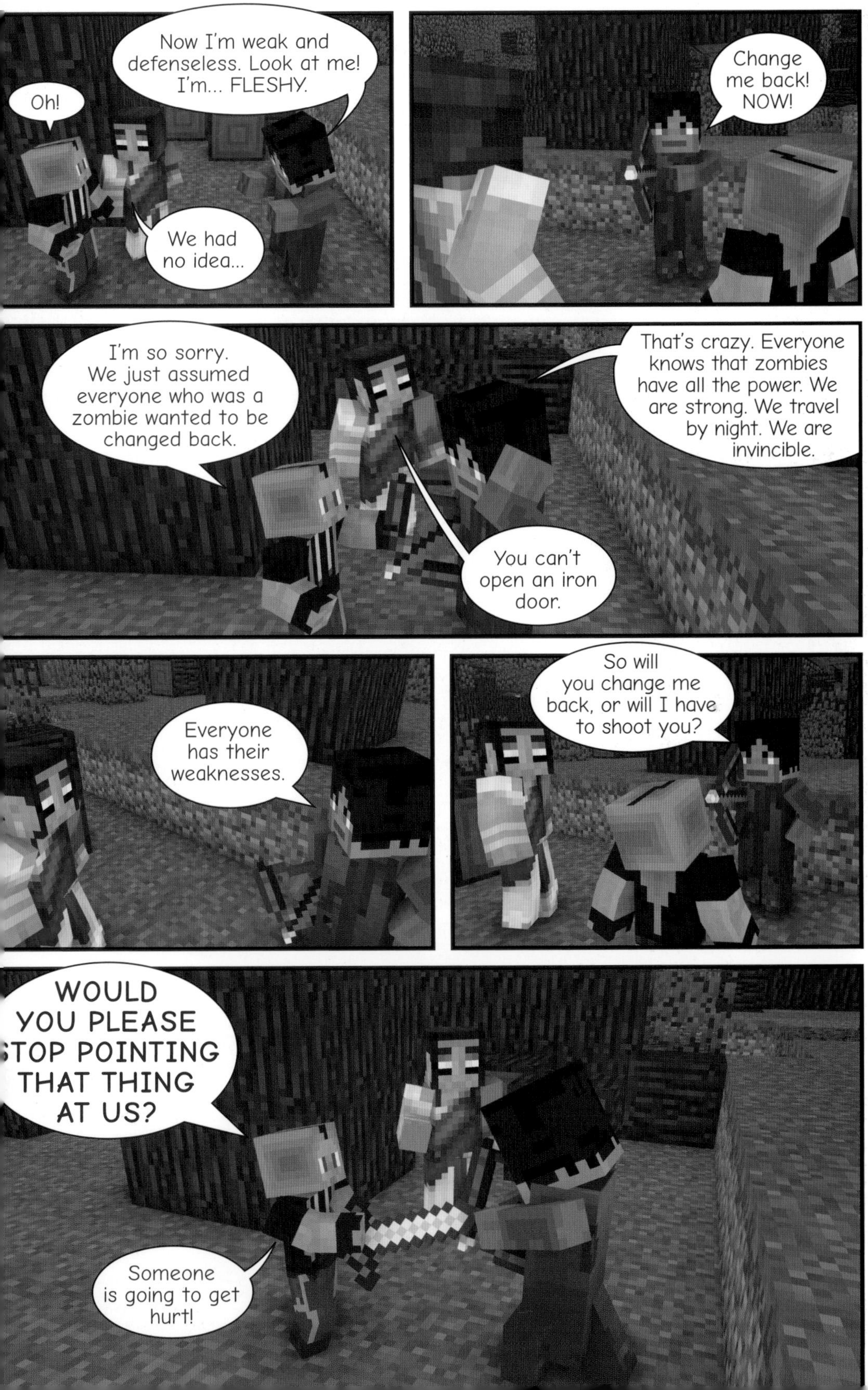
Now I'm weak and defenseless. Look at me! I'm... FLESHY.
Oh!
We had no idea...
Change me back! NOW!
I'm so sorry. We just assumed everyone who was a zombie wanted to be changed back.
That's crazy. Everyone knows that zombies have all the power. We are strong. We travel by night. We are invincible.
You can't open an iron door.
Everyone has their weaknesses.
So will you change me back, or will I have to shoot you?
WOULD YOU PLEASE STOP POINTING THAT THING AT US?
Someone is going to get hurt!

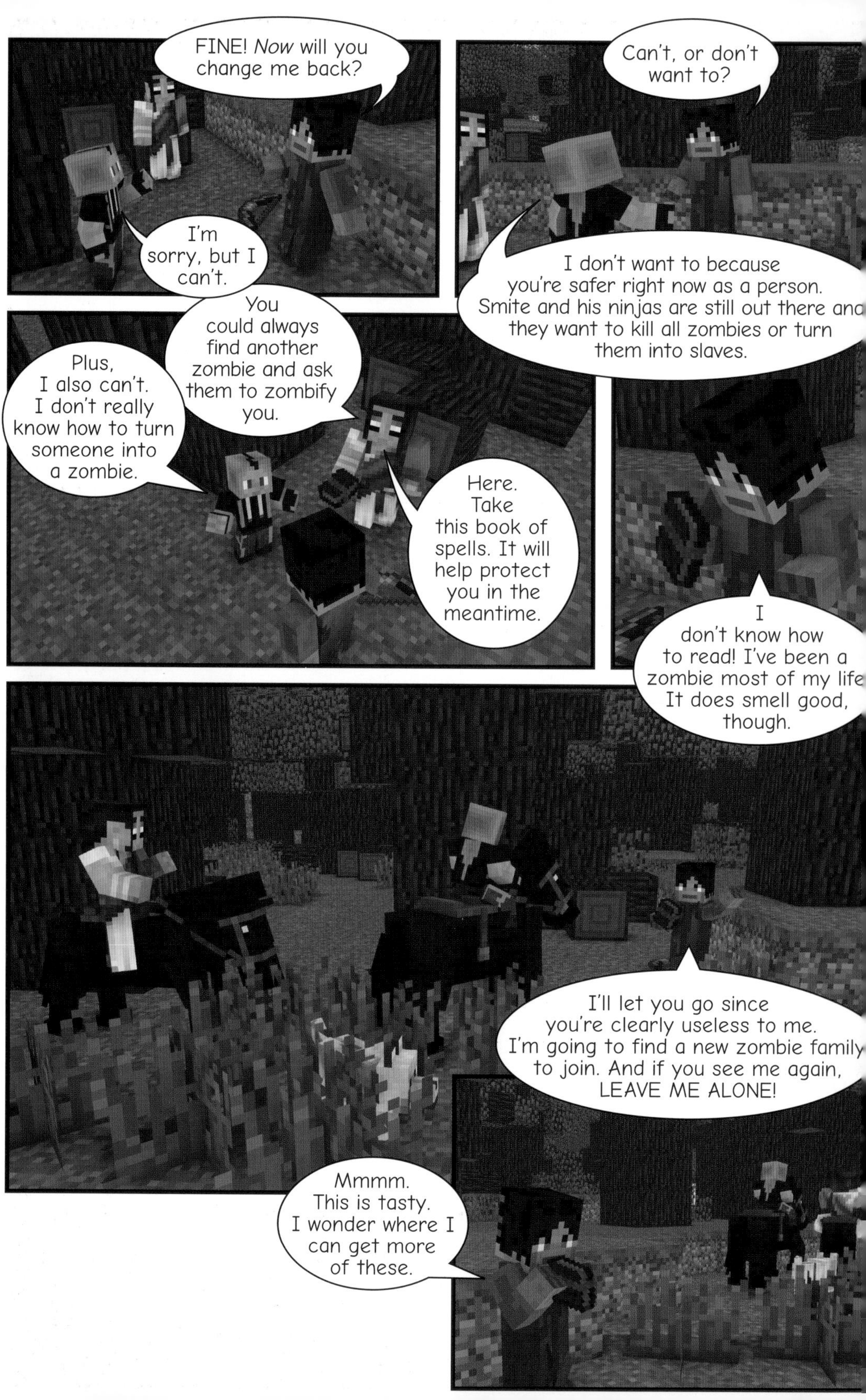

FINE! *Now* will you change me back?
I'm sorry, but I can't.
Can't, or don't want to?
I don't want to because you're safer right now as a person. Smite and his ninjas are still out there and they want to kill all zombies or turn them into slaves.
Plus, I also can't. I don't really know how to turn someone into a zombie.
You could always find another zombie and ask them to zombify you.
Here. Take this book of spells. It will help protect you in the meantime.
I don't know how to read! I've been a zombie most of my life. It does smell good, though.
I'll let you go since you're clearly useless to me. I'm going to find a new zombie family to join. And if you see me again, LEAVE ME ALONE!
Mmmm. This is tasty. I wonder where I can get more of these.

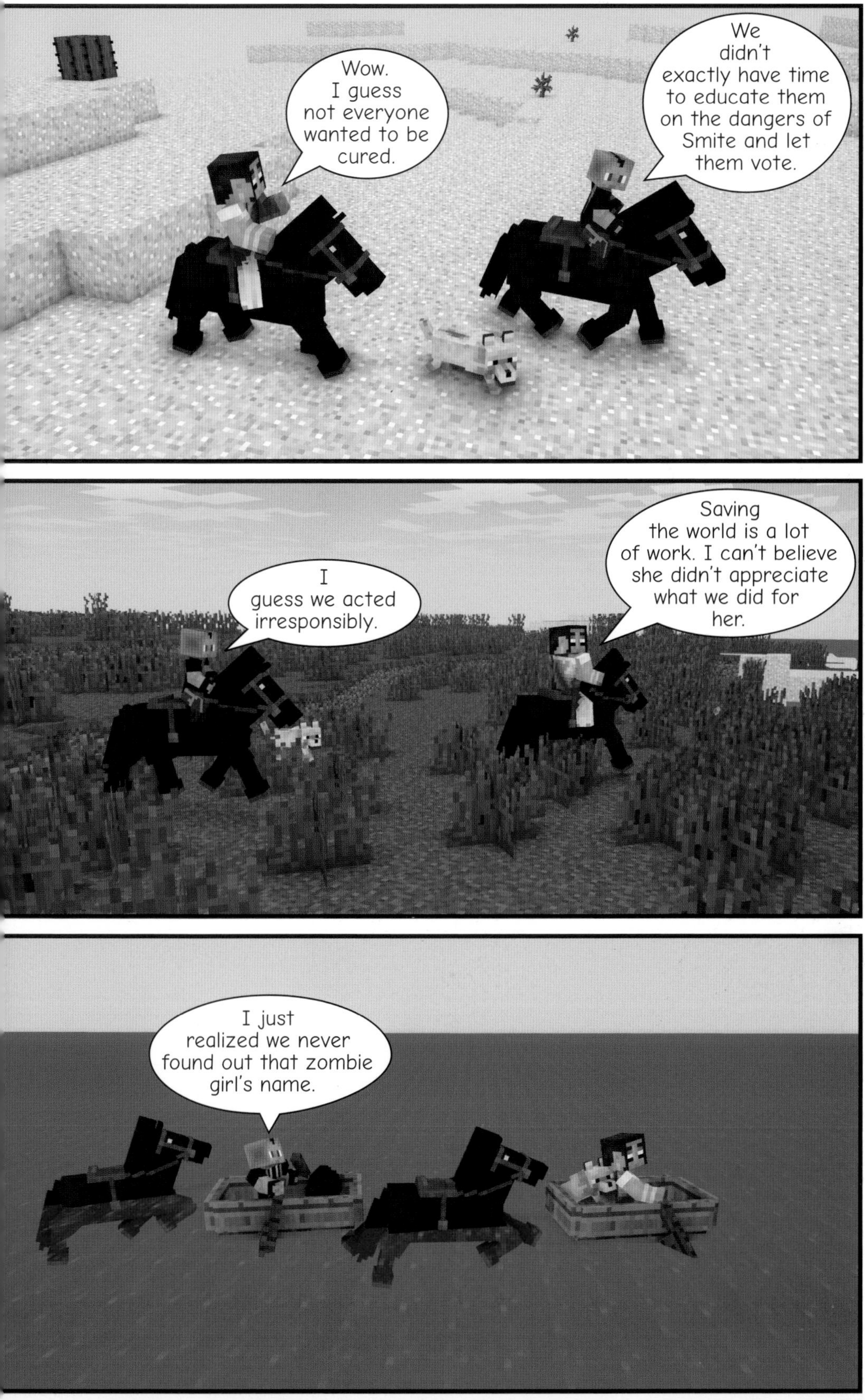
Wow. I guess not everyone wanted to be cured.
We didn't exactly have time to educate them on the dangers of Smite and let them vote.
I guess we acted irresponsibly.
Saving the world is a lot of work. I can't believe she didn't appreciate what we did for her.
I just realized we never found out that zombie girl's name.

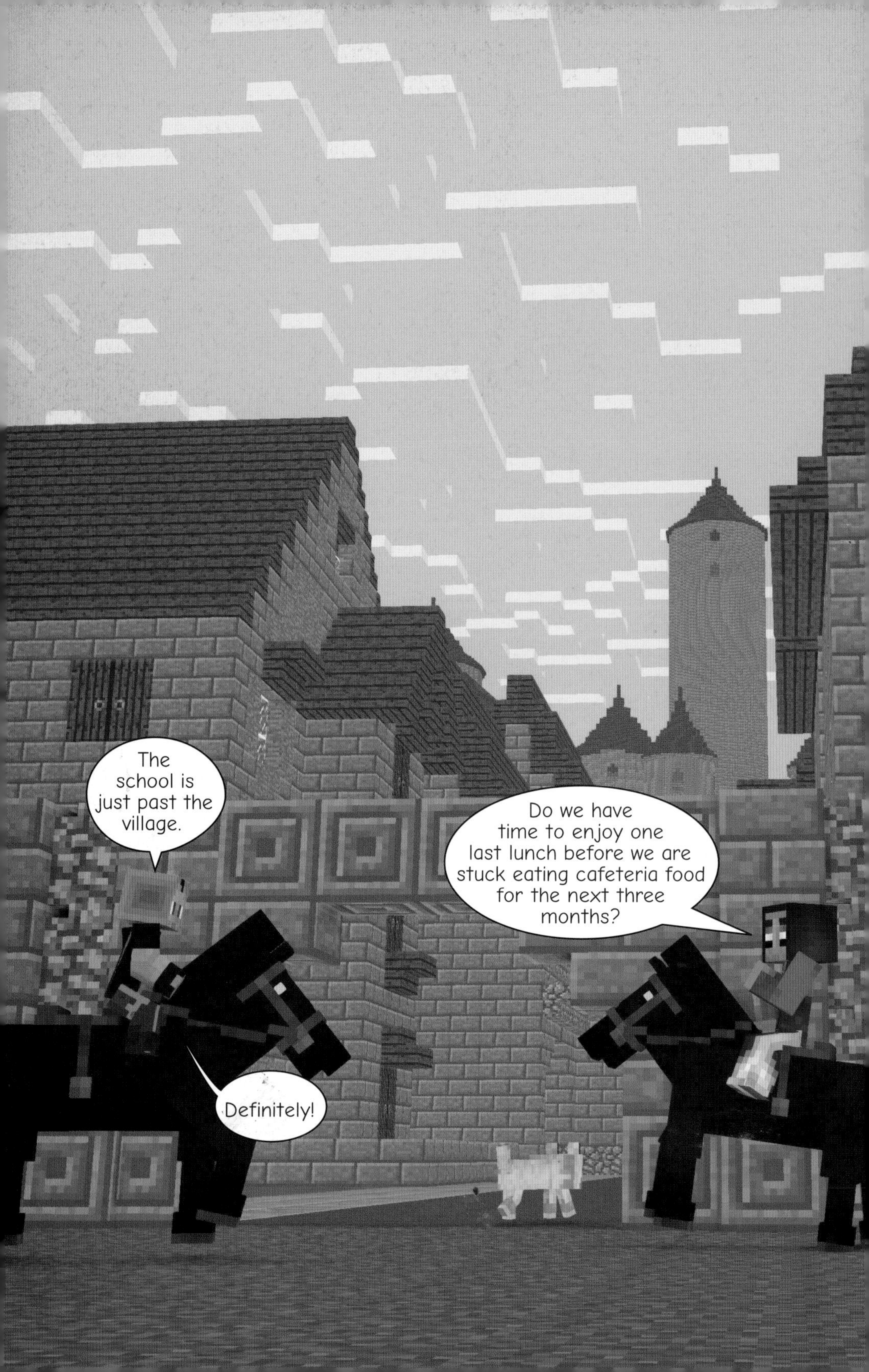
The school is just past the village.
Do we have time to enjoy one last lunch before we are stuck eating cafeteria food for the next three months?
Definitely!

CHAPTER 3

HATCHING

A PLAN

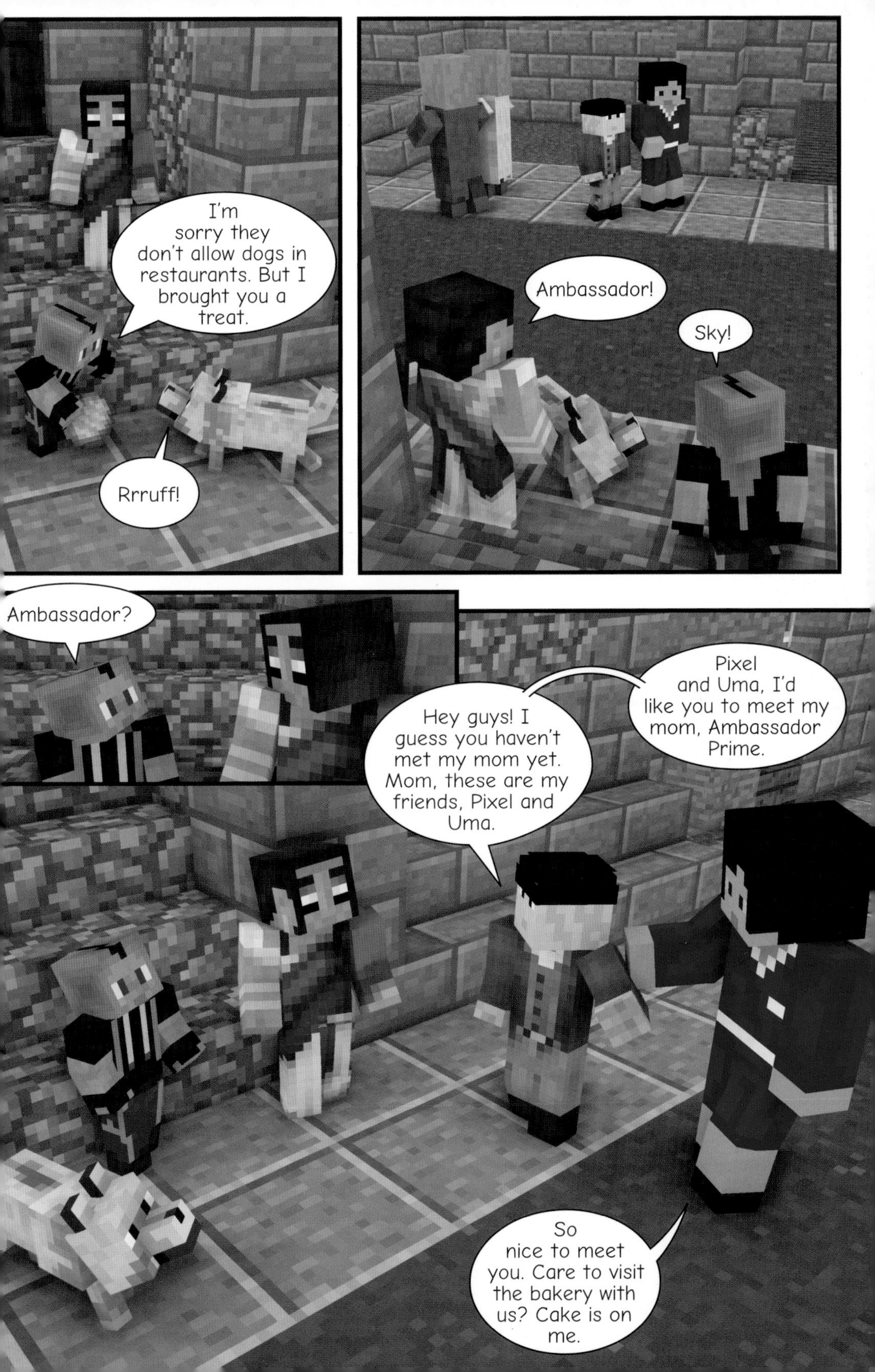
I'm sorry they don't allow dogs in restaurants. But I brought you a treat.
Rrruff!
Ambassador!
Sky!
Ambassador?
Hey guys! I guess you haven't met my mom yet. Mom, these are my friends, Pixel and Uma.
Pixel and Uma, I'd like you to meet my mom, Ambassador Prime.
So nice to meet you. Care to visit the bakery with us? Cake is on me.

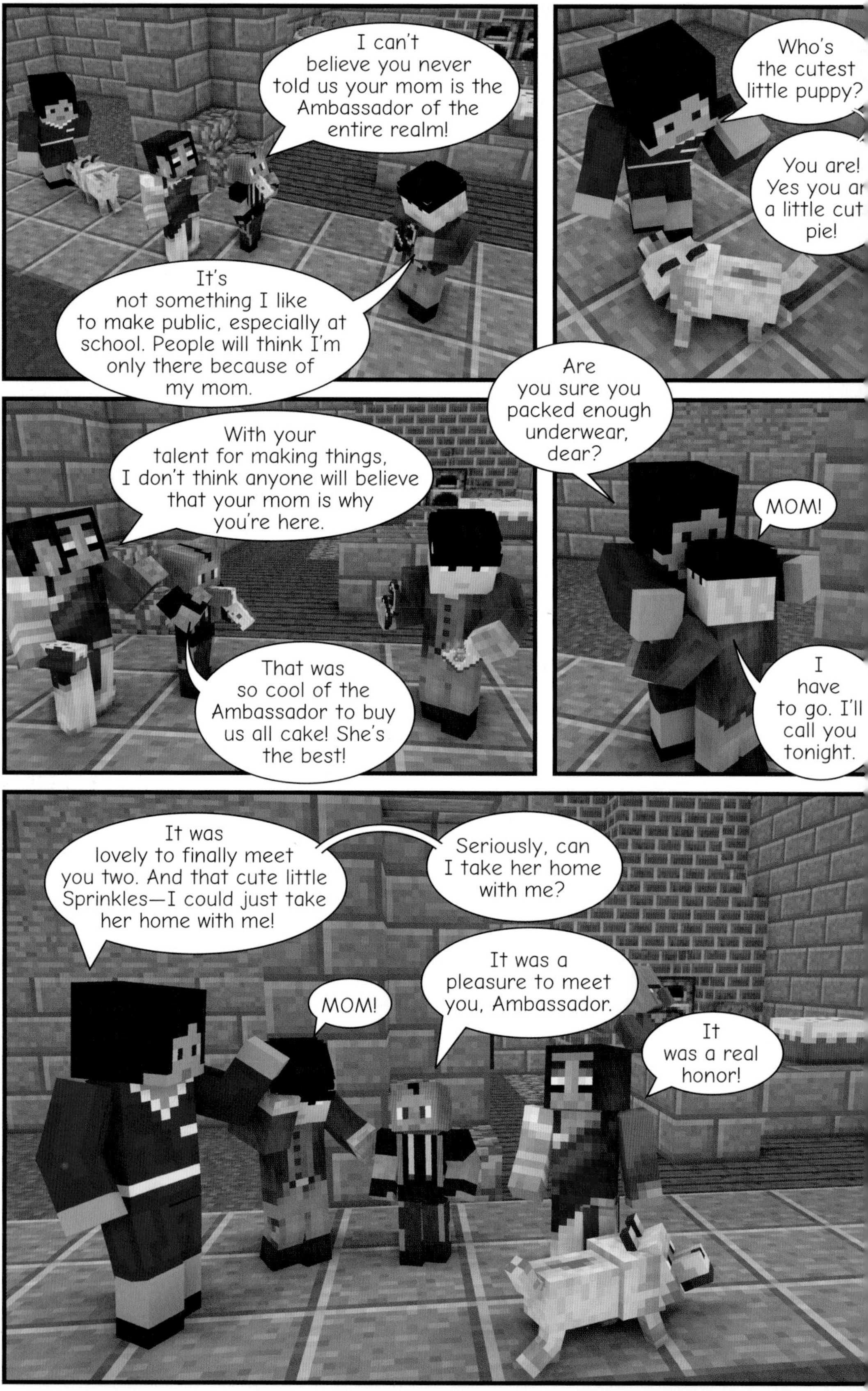

I can't believe you never told us your mom is the Ambassador of the entire realm!
It's not something I like to make public, especially at school. People will think I'm only there because of my mom.
Who's the cutest little puppy?
You are! Yes you ar a little cut pie!
With your talent for making things, I don't think anyone will believe that your mom is why you're here.
That was so cool of the Ambassador to buy us all cake! She's the best!
Are you sure you packed enough underwear, dear?
MOM!
I have to go. I'll call you tonight.
It was lovely to finally meet you two. And that cute little Sprinkles—I could just take her home with me!
Seriously, can I take her home with me?
MOM!
It was a pleasure to meet you, Ambassador.
It was a real honor!

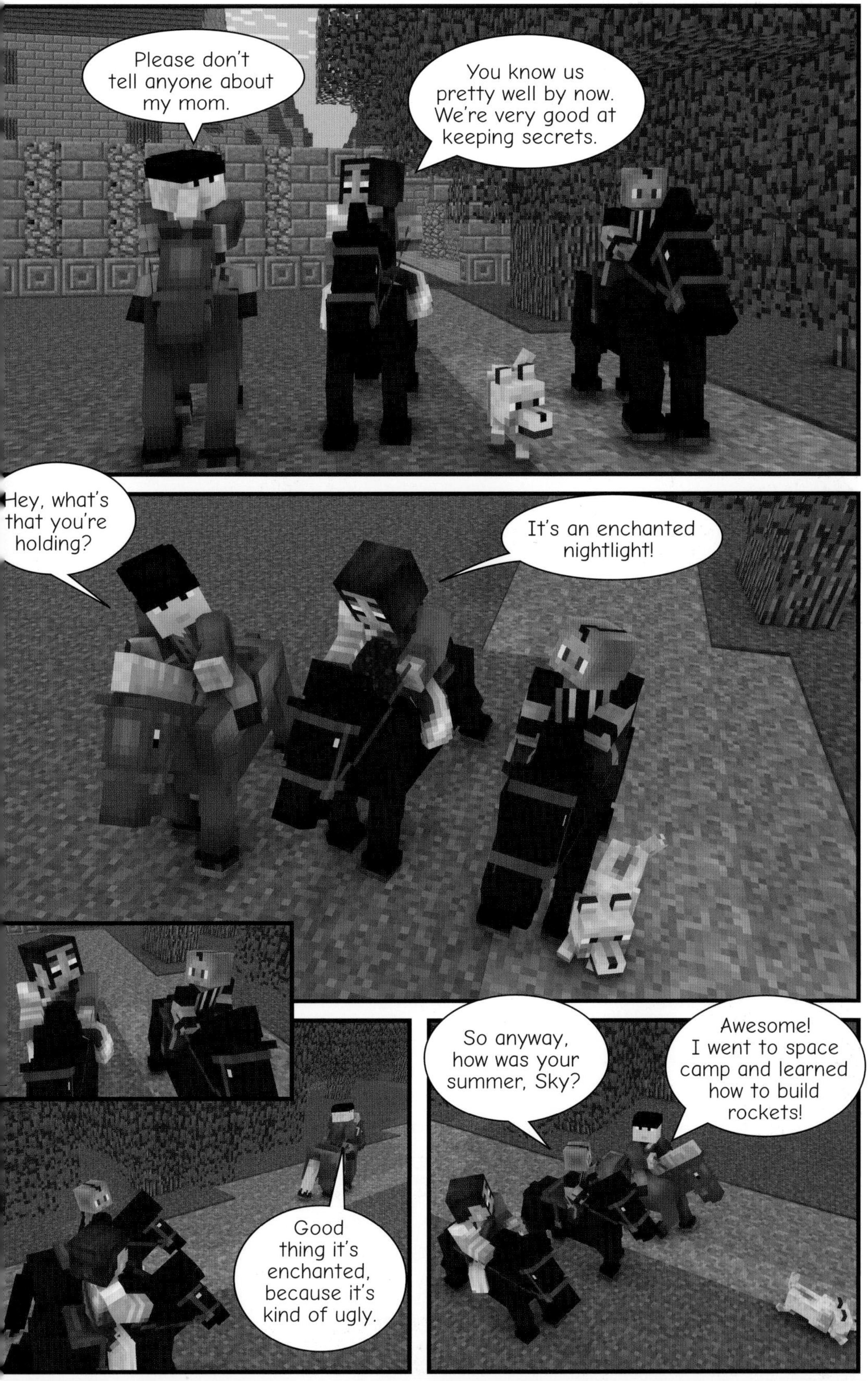
Please don't tell anyone about my mom.
You know us pretty well by now. We're very good at keeping secrets.
Hey, what's that you're holding?
It's an enchanted nightlight!
Good thing it's enchanted, because it's kind of ugly.
So anyway, how was your summer, Sky?
Awesome! I went to space camp and learned how to build rockets!

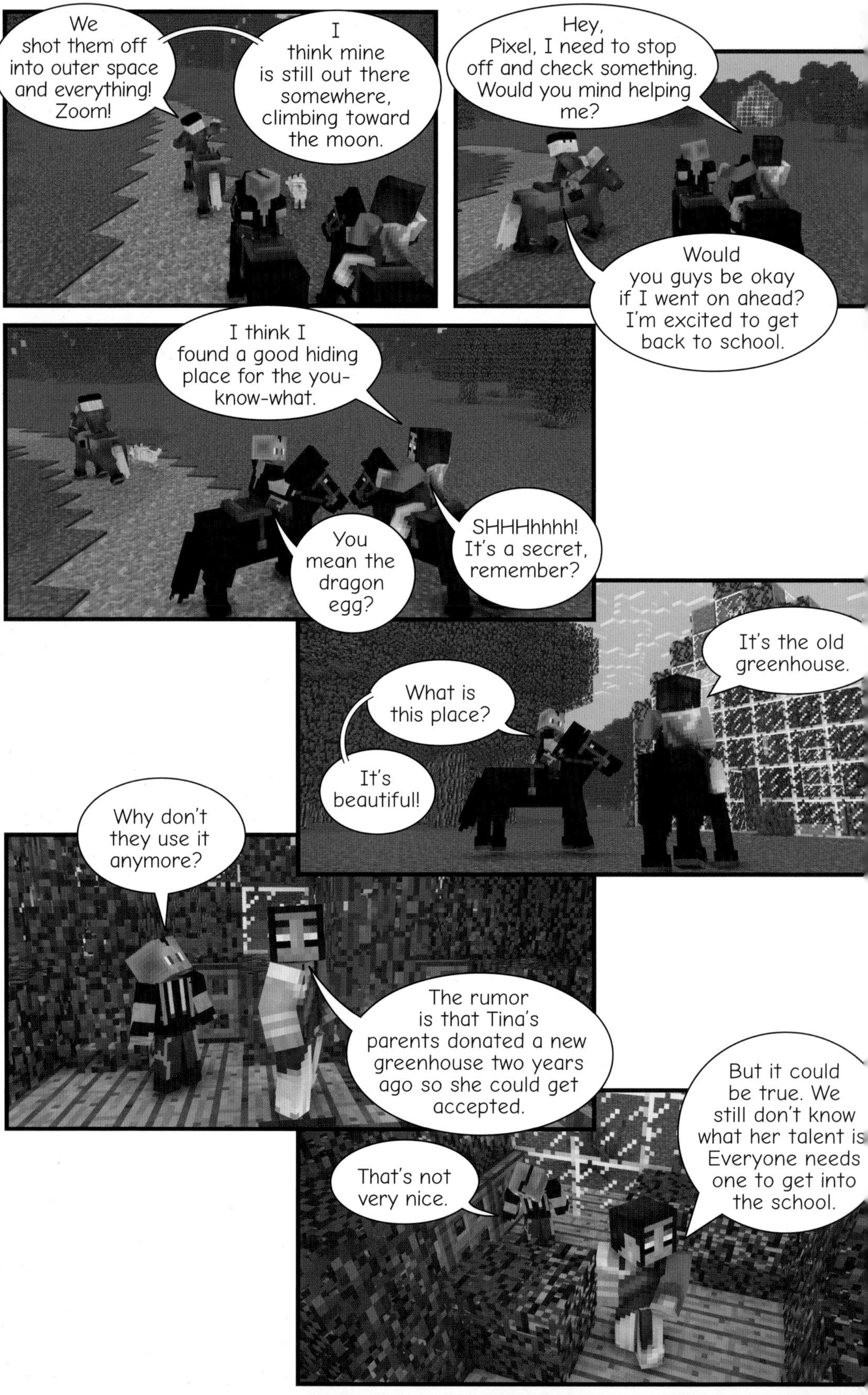
We shot them off into outer space and everything! Zoom!
I think mine is still out there somewhere, climbing toward the moon.
Hey, Pixel, I need to stop off and check something. Would you mind helping me?
Would you guys be okay if I went on ahead? I'm excited to get back to school.
I think I found a good hiding place for the you-know-what.
You mean the dragon egg?
SHHHhhhh! It's a secret, remember?
It's the old greenhouse.
What is this place?
It's beautiful!
Why don't they use it anymore?
The rumor is that Tina's parents donated a new greenhouse two years ago so she could get accepted.
That's not very nice.
But it could be true. We still don't know what her talent is
Everyone needs one to get into the school.

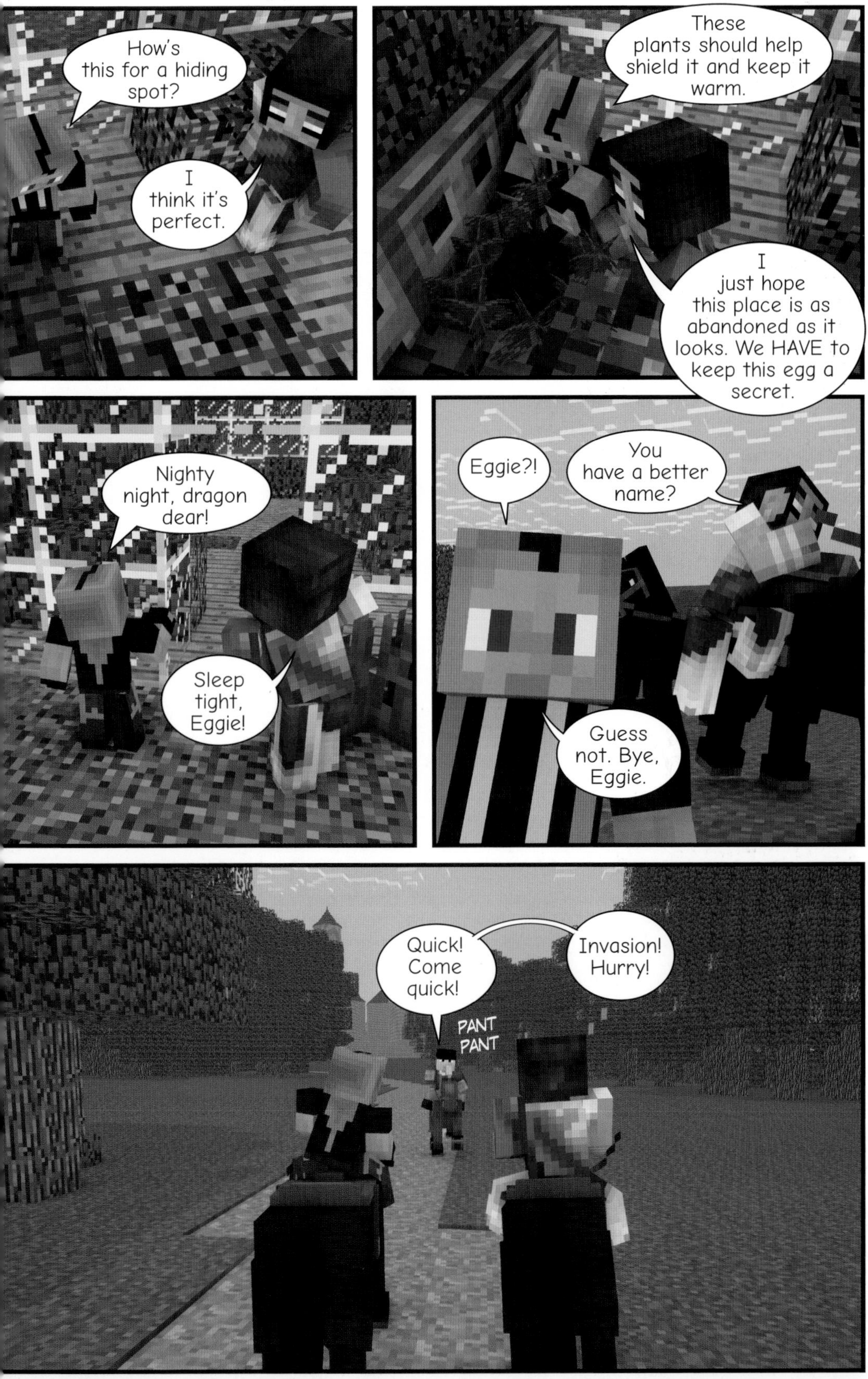
How's this for a hiding spot?
I think it's perfect.
These plants should help shield it and keep it warm.
I just hope this place is as abandoned as it looks. We HAVE to keep this egg a secret.
Nighty night, dragon dear!
Sleep tight, Eggie!
Eggie?!
You have a better name?
Guess not. Bye, Eggie.
Quick! Come quick!
Invasion! Hurry!
PANT PANT

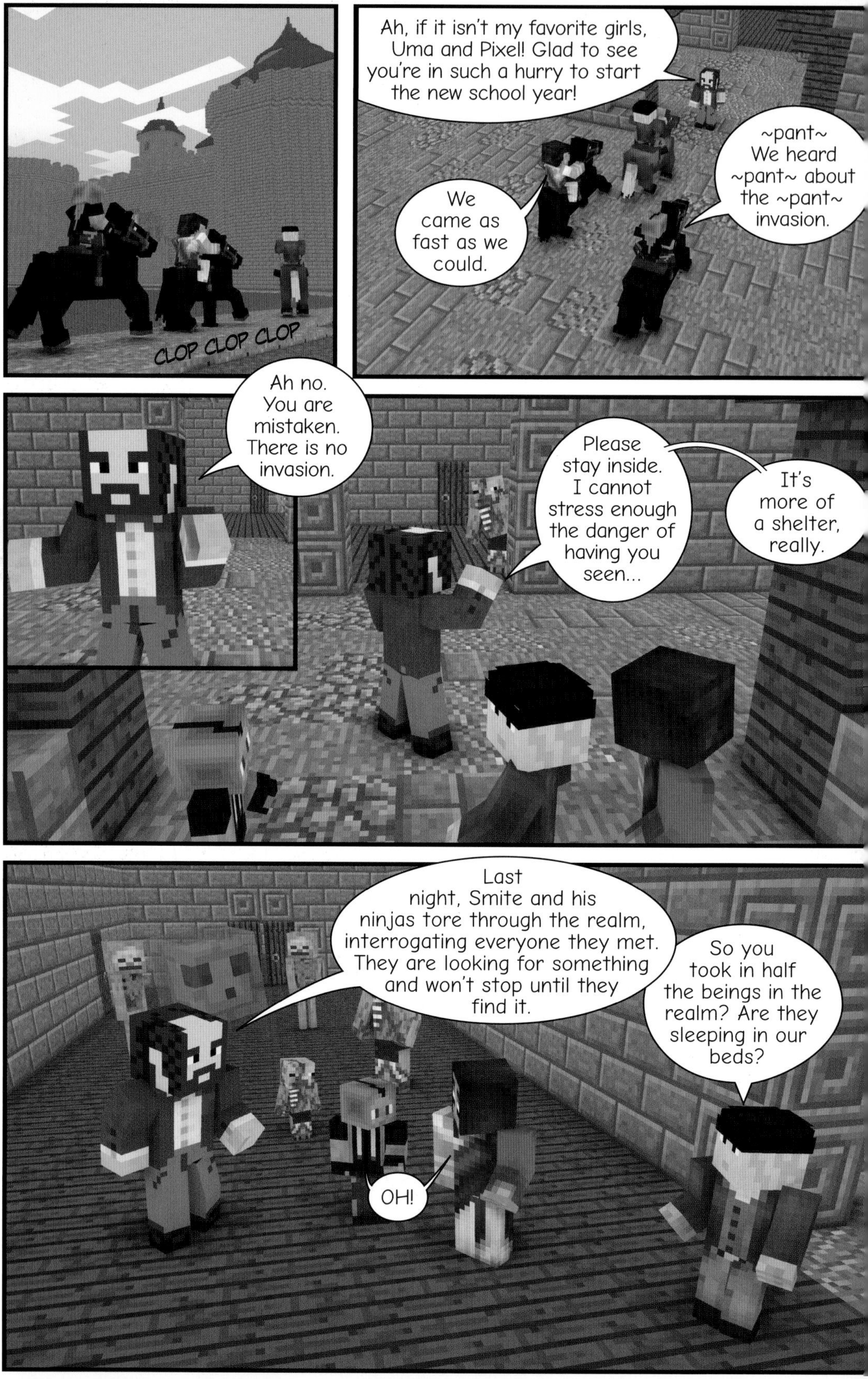
CLOP CLOP CLOP
Ah, if it isn't my favorite girls, Uma and Pixel! Glad to see you're in such a hurry to start the new school year!
We came as fast as we could.
~pant~ We heard ~pant~ about the ~pant~ invasion.
Ah no. You are mistaken. There is no invasion.
It's more of a shelter, really.
Please stay inside. I cannot stress enough the danger of having you seen...
Last night, Smite and his ninjas tore through the realm, interrogating everyone they met. They are looking for something and won't stop until they find it.
So you took in half the beings in the realm? Are they sleeping in our beds?
OH!

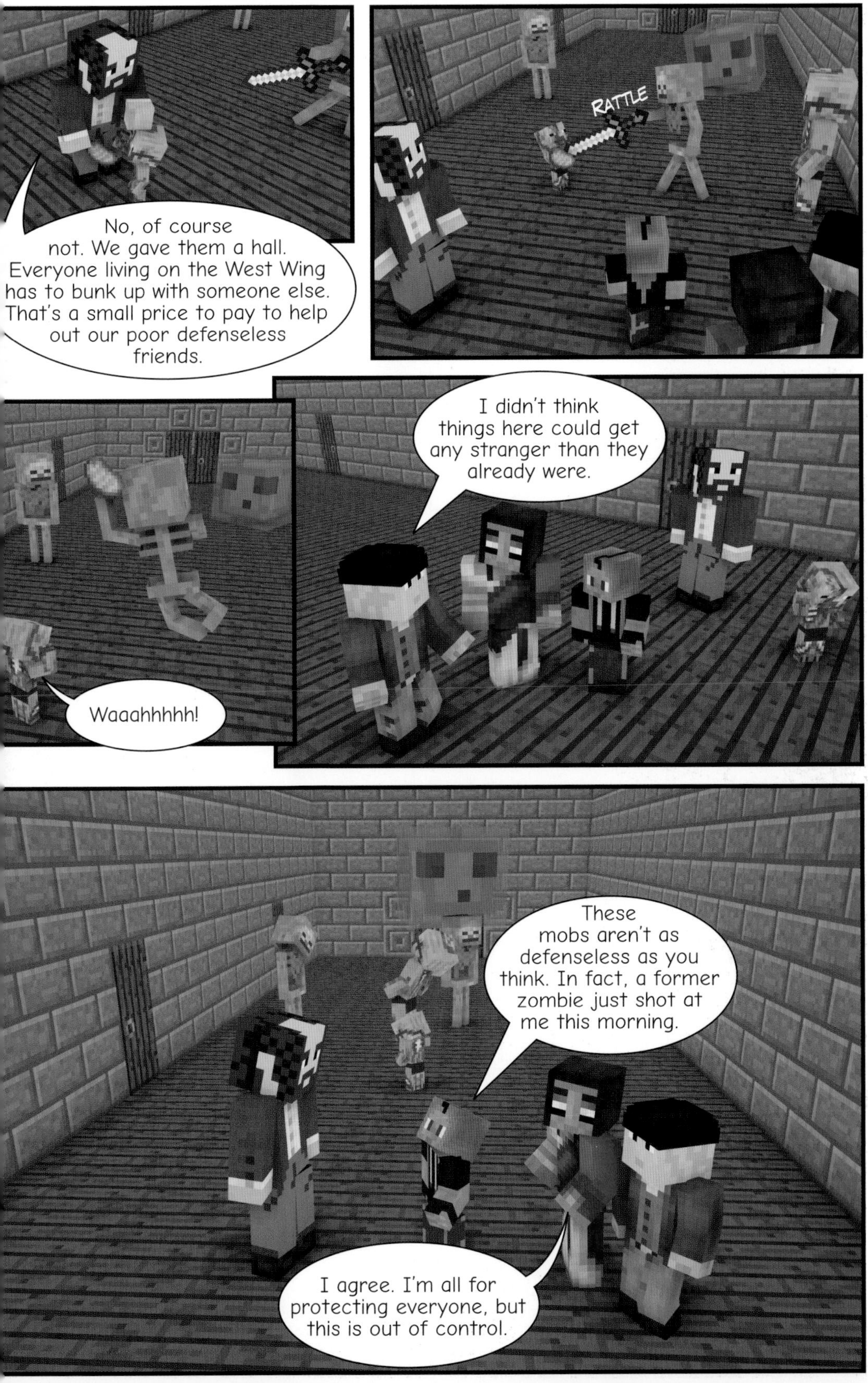
No, of course not. We gave them a hall. Everyone living on the West Wing has to bunk up with someone else. That's a small price to pay to help out our poor defenseless friends.
RATTLE
Waaahhhhh!
I didn't think things here could get any stranger than they already were.
These mobs aren't as defenseless as you think. In fact, a former zombie just shot at me this morning.
I agree. I'm all for protecting everyone, but this is out of control.

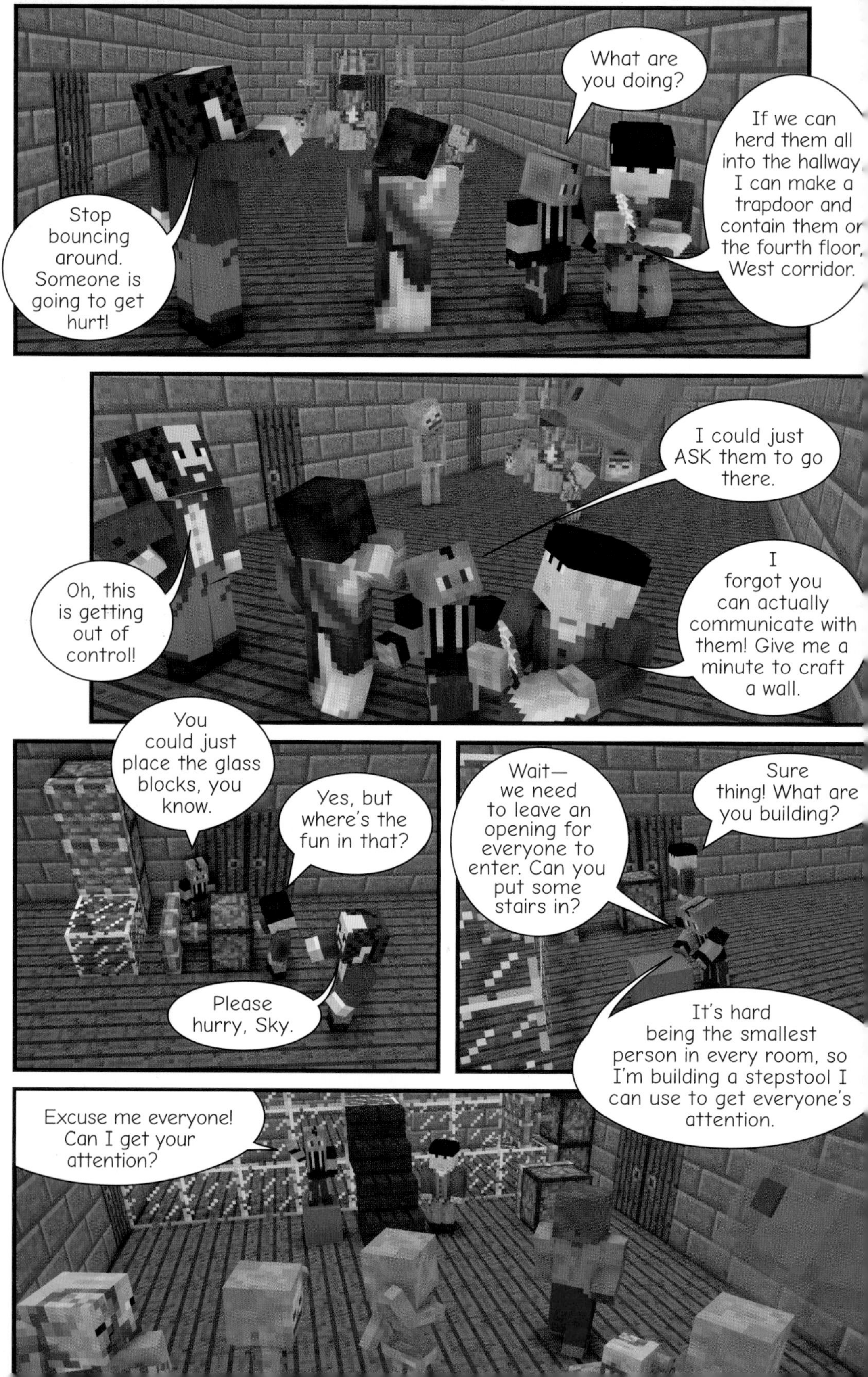
What are you doing?
If we can herd them all into the hallway, I can make a trapdoor and contain them on the fourth floor, West corridor.
Stop bouncing around. Someone is going to get hurt!
I could just ASK them to go there.
Oh, this is getting out of control!
I forgot you can actually communicate with them! Give me a minute to craft a wall.
You could just place the glass blocks, you know.
Yes, but where's the fun in that?
Please hurry, Sky.
Wait— we need to leave an opening for everyone to enter. Can you put some stairs in?
Sure thing! What are you building?
It's hard being the smallest person in every room, so I'm building a stepstool I can use to get everyone's attention.
Excuse me everyone! Can I get your attention?

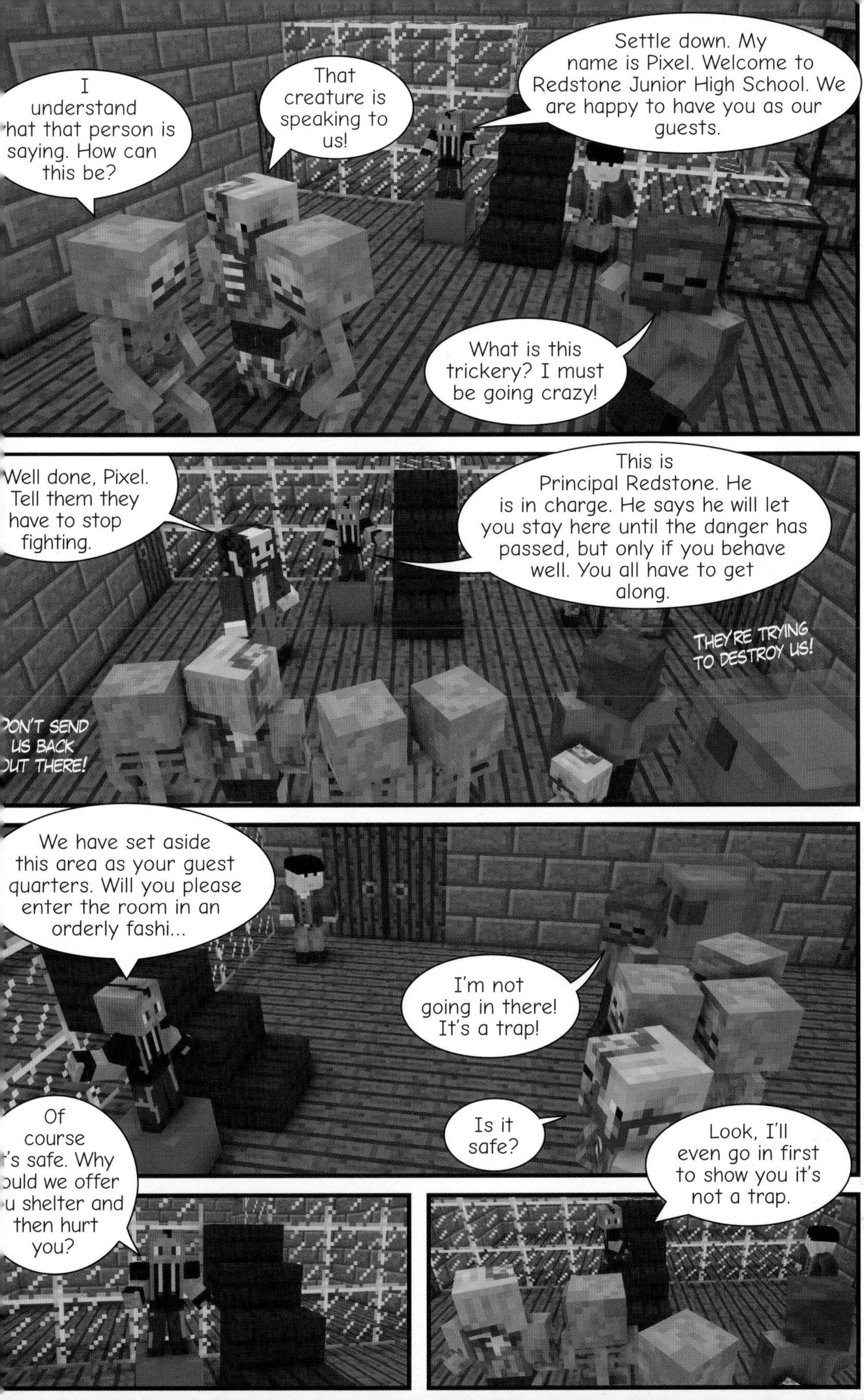
I understand
hat that person is saying. How can this be?
That creature is speaking to us!
Settle down. My name is Pixel. Welcome to Redstone Junior High School. We are happy to have you as our guests.
What is this trickery? I must be going crazy!
Well done, Pixel. Tell them they have to stop fighting.
This is Principal Redstone. He is in charge. He says he will let you stay here until the danger has passed, but only if you behave well. You all have to get along.
THEY'RE TRYING TO DESTROY US!
ON'T SEND US BACK
UT THERE!
We have set aside this area as your guest quarters. Will you please enter the room in an orderly fashi...
I'm not going in there! It's a trap!
Is it safe?
Of course
's safe. Why
uld we offer
u shelter and then hurt you?
Look, I'll even go in first to show you it's not a trap.

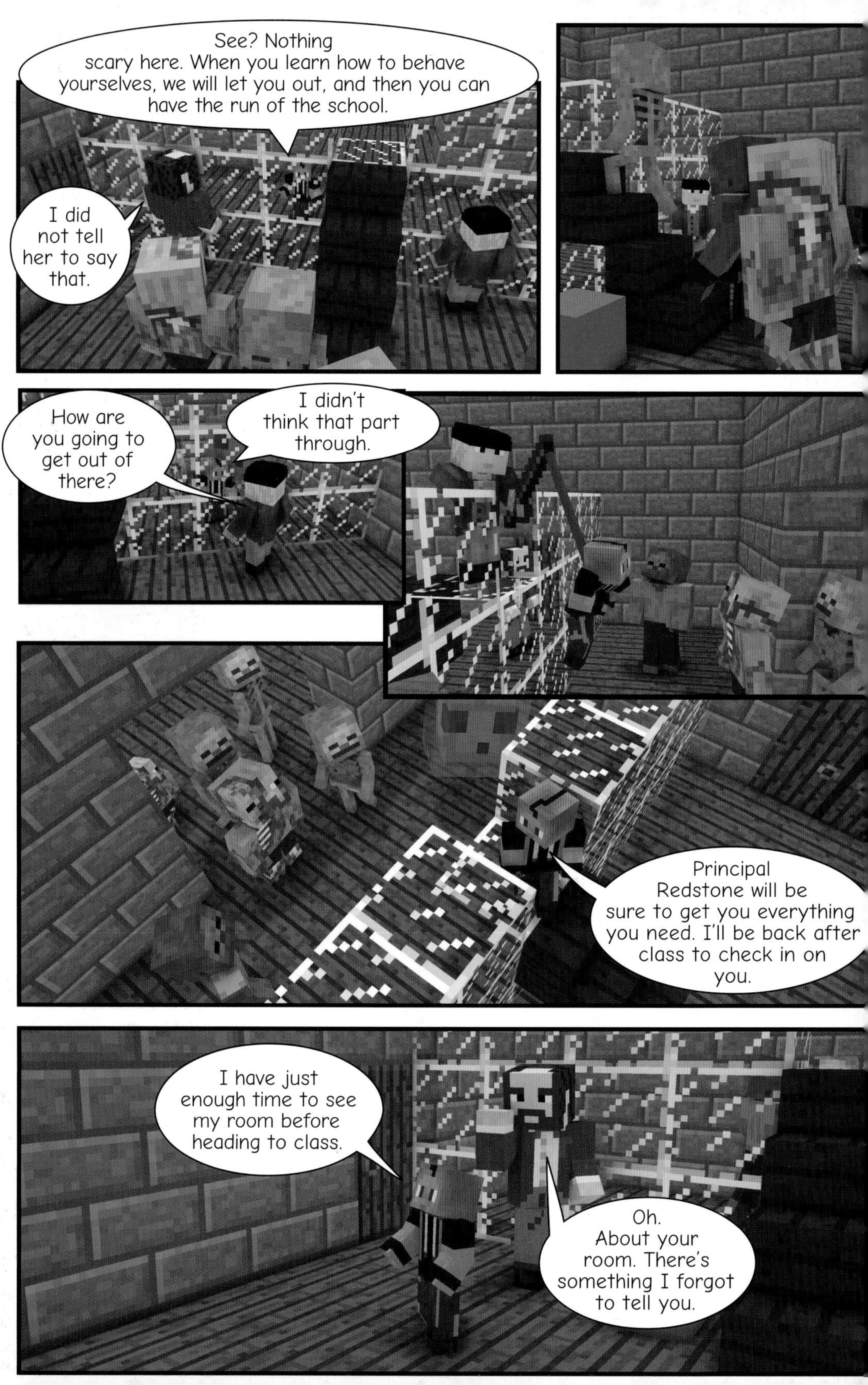
See? Nothing scary here. When you learn how to behave yourselves, we will let you out, and then you can have the run of the school.
I did not tell her to say that.
How are you going to get out of there?
I didn't think that part through.
Principal Redstone will be sure to get you everything you need. I'll be back after class to check in on you.
I have just enough time to see my room before heading to class.
Oh. About your room. There's something I forgot to tell you.

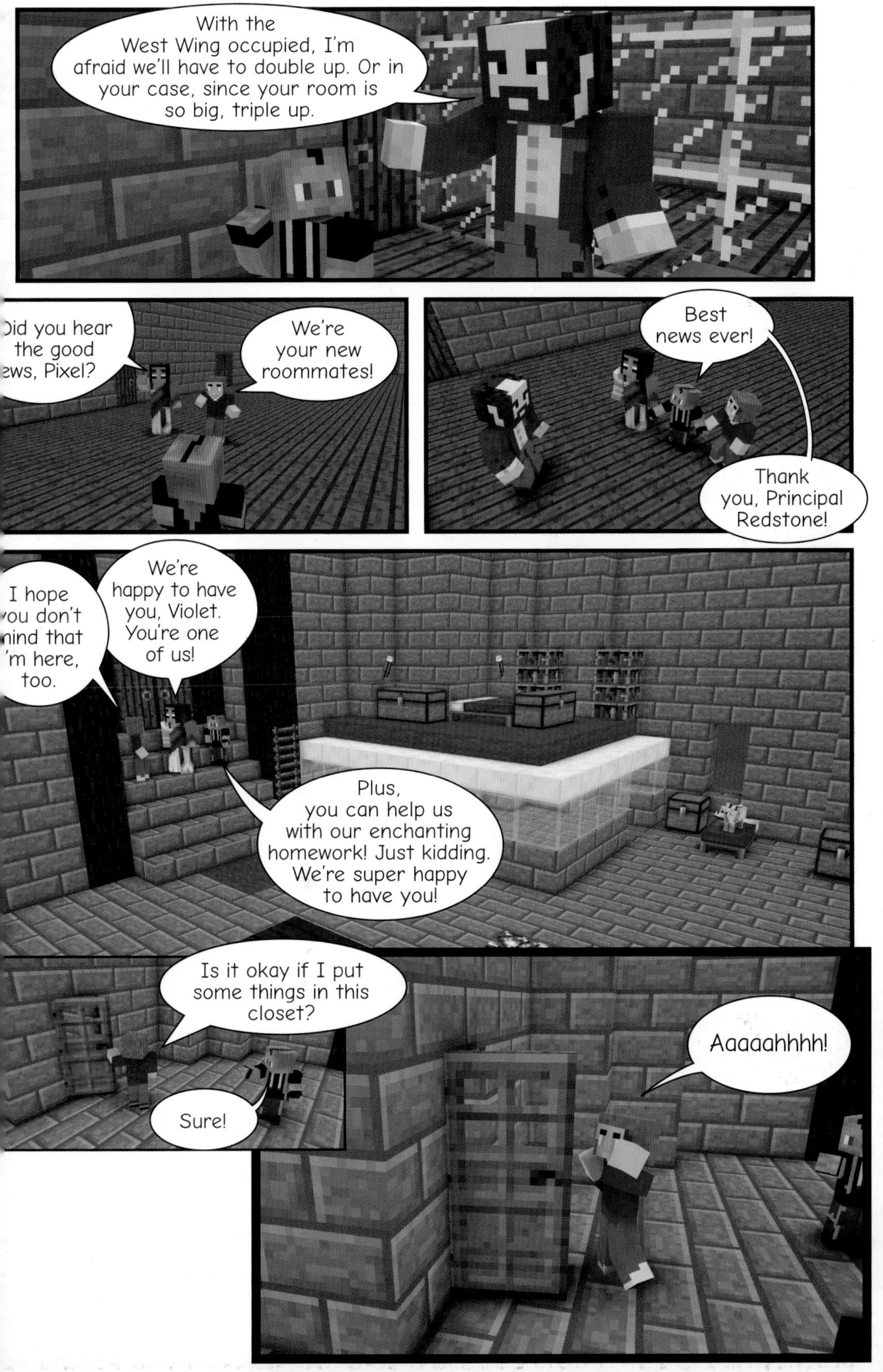
With the West Wing occupied, I'm afraid we'll have to double up. Or in your case, since your room is so big, triple up.
Did you hear the good ews, Pixel?
We're your new roommates!
Best news ever!
Thank you, Principal Redstone!
I hope ou don't nind that 'm here, too.
We're happy to have you, Violet. You're one of us!
Plus, you can help us with our enchanting homework! Just kidding. We're super happy to have you!
Is it okay if I put some things in this closet?
Sure!
Aaaaahhhh!

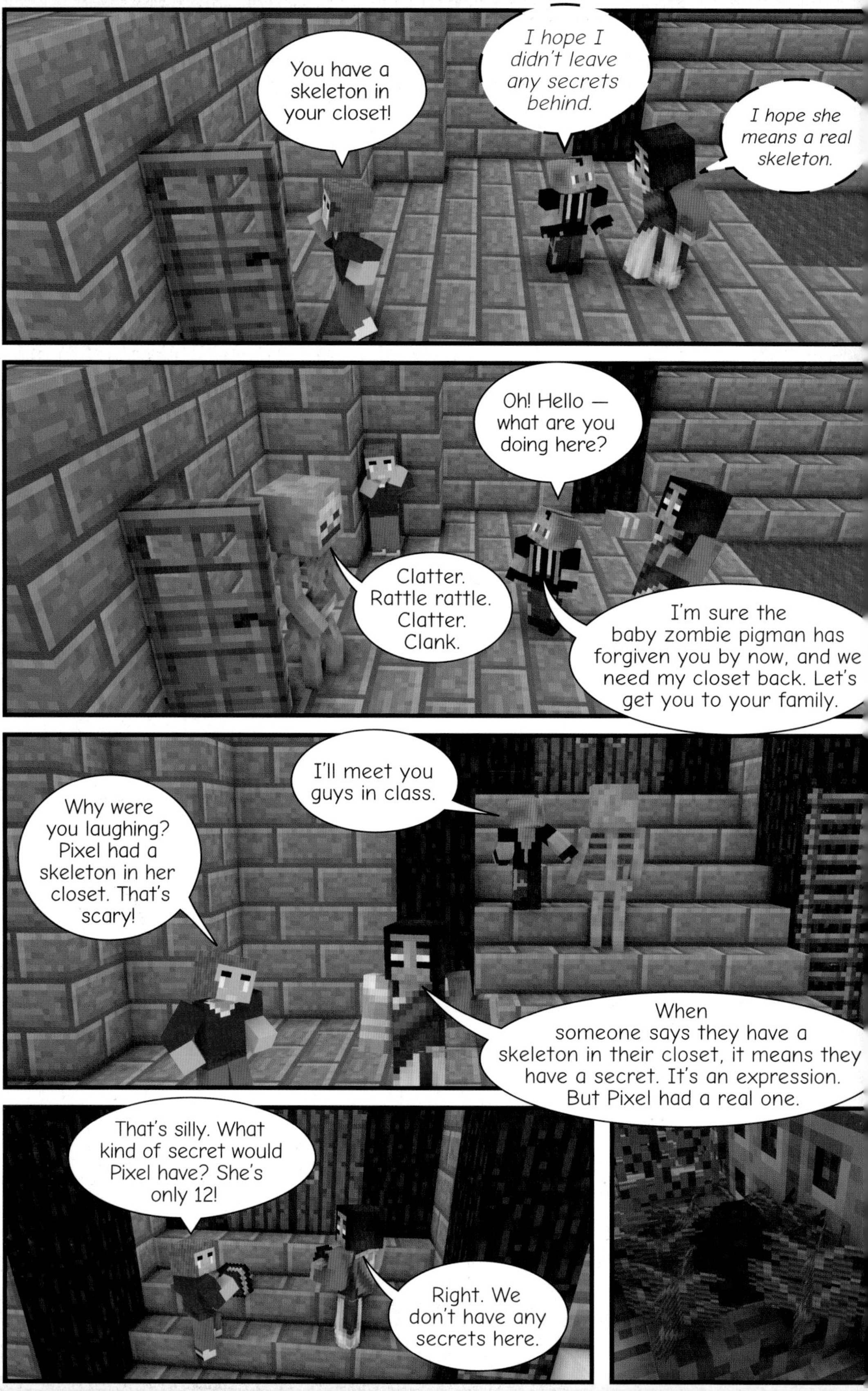
You have a skeleton in your closet!
I hope I didn't leave any secrets behind.
I hope she means a real skeleton.
Oh! Hello — what are you doing here?
Clatter. Rattle rattle. Clatter. Clank.
I'm sure the baby zombie pigman has forgiven you by now, and we need my closet back. Let's get you to your family.
Why were you laughing? Pixel had a skeleton in her closet. That's scary!
I'll meet you guys in class.
When someone says they have a skeleton in their closet, it means they have a secret. It's an expression. But Pixel had a real one.
That's silly. What kind of secret would Pixel have? She's only 12!
Right. We don't have any secrets here.

CHAPTER 4

CHICKENS AND
FRAIDY CATS

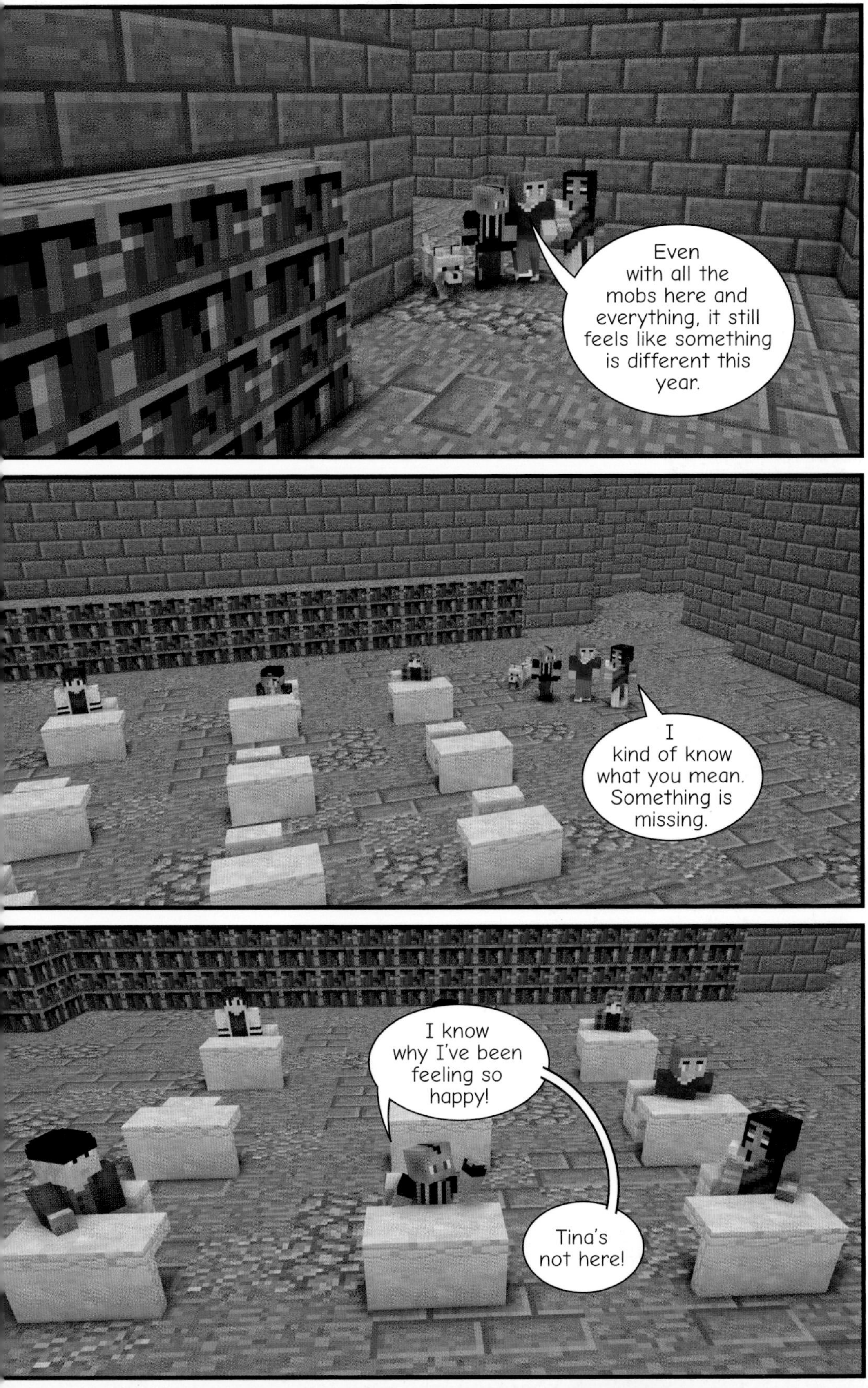
Even with all the mobs here and everything, it still feels like something is different this year.
I kind of know what you mean. Something is missing.
I know why I've been feeling so happy!
Tina's not here!

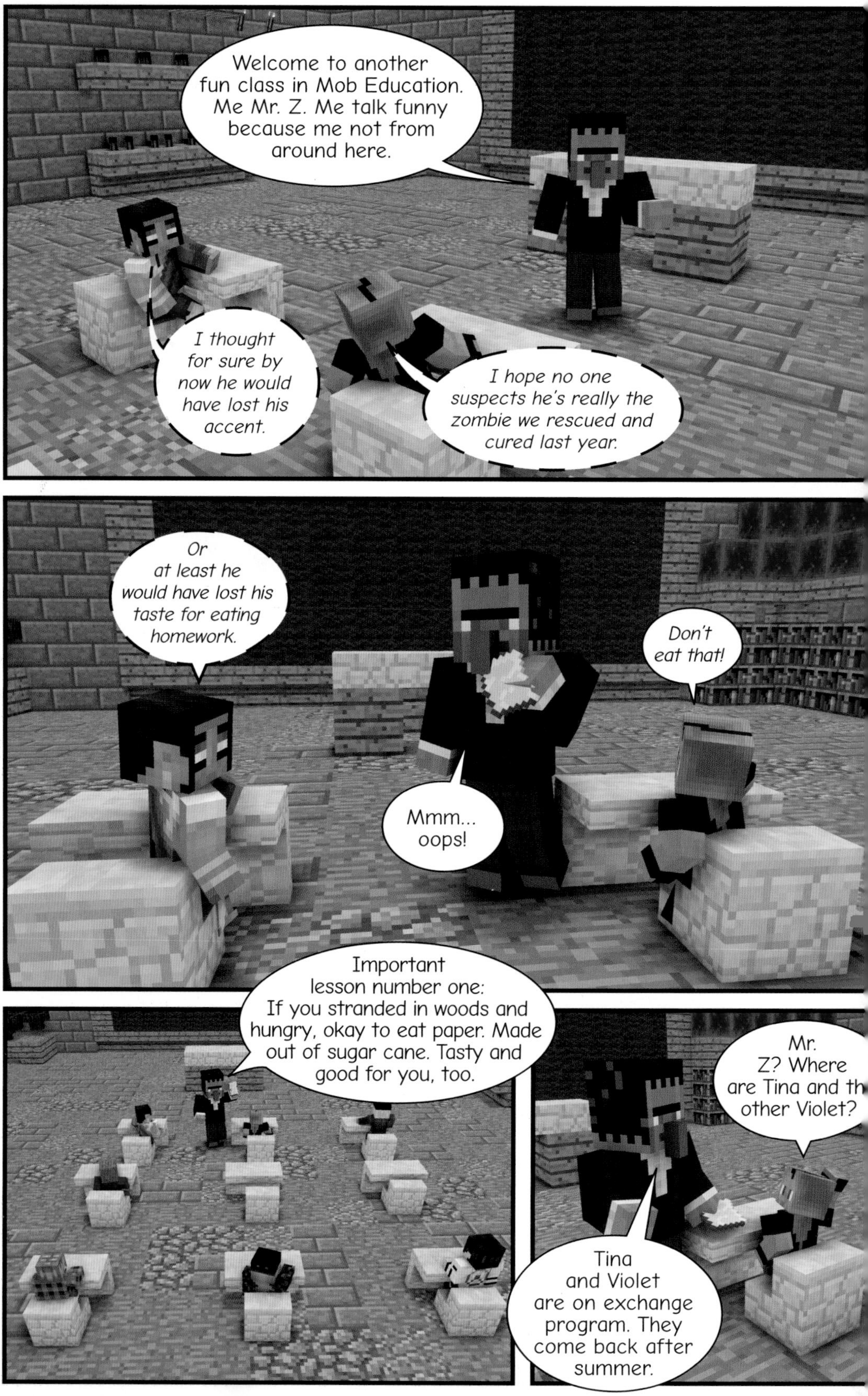
Welcome to another fun class in Mob Education. Me Mr. Z. Me talk funny because me not from around here.
I thought for sure by now he would have lost his accent.
I hope no one suspects he's really the zombie we rescued and cured last year.
Or at least he would have lost his taste for eating homework.
Don't eat that!
Mmm... oops!
Important lesson number one: If you stranded in woods and hungry, okay to eat paper. Made out of sugar cane. Tasty and good for you, too.
Mr. Z? Where are Tina and th
other Violet?
Tina and Violet are on exchange program. They come back after summer.

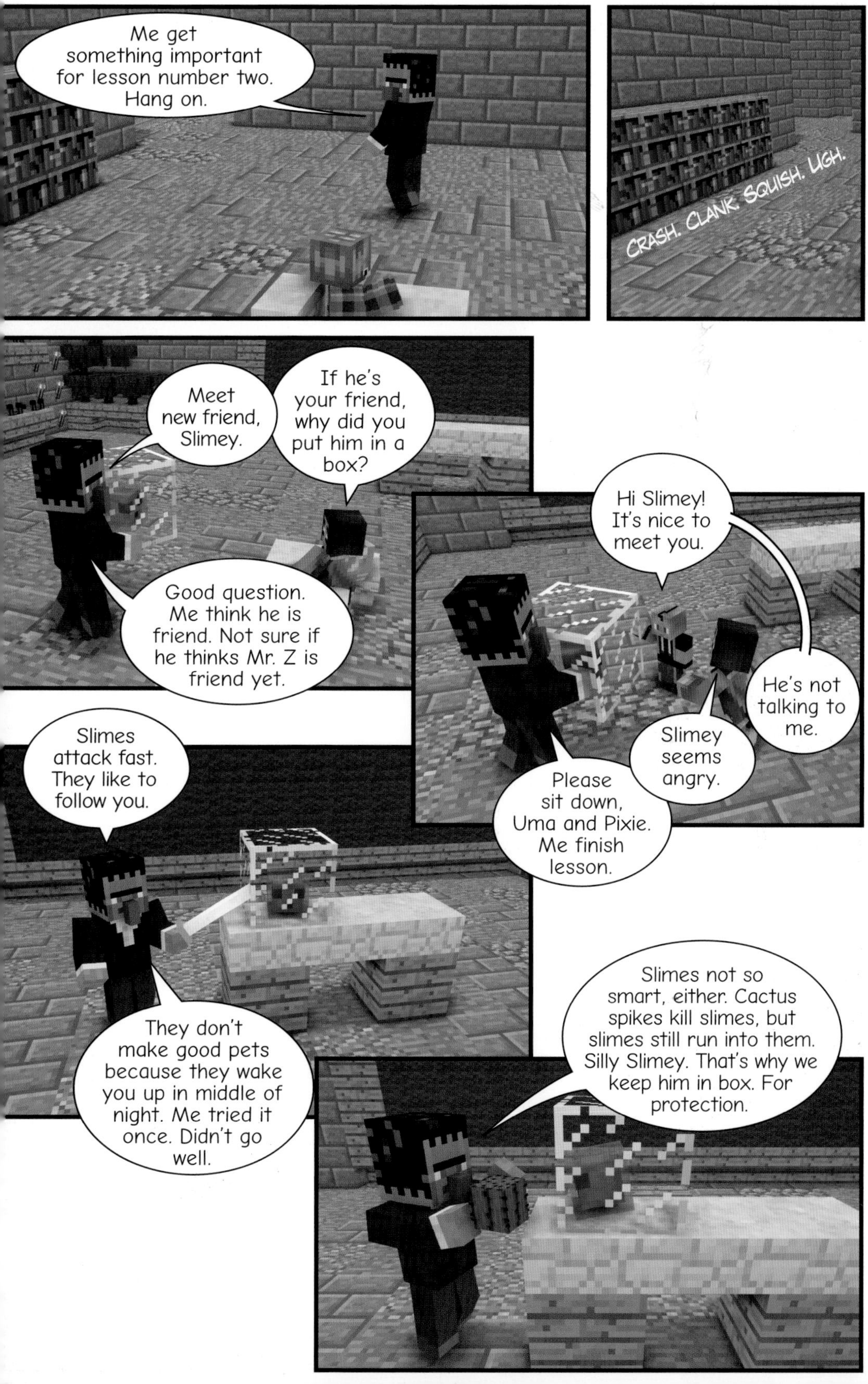
Me get something important for lesson number two. Hang on.
CRASH. CLANK. SQUISH. UGH.
Meet new friend, Slimey.
If he's your friend, why did you put him in a box?
Good question. Me think he is friend. Not sure if he thinks Mr. Z is friend yet.
Hi Slimey! It's nice to meet you.
He's not talking to me.
Slimey seems angry.
Please sit down, Uma and Pixie. Me finish lesson.
Slimes attack fast. They like to follow you.
They don't make good pets because they wake you up in middle of night. Me tried it once. Didn't go well.
Slimes not so smart, either. Cactus spikes kill slimes, but slimes still run into them. Silly Slimey. That's why we keep him in box. For protection.

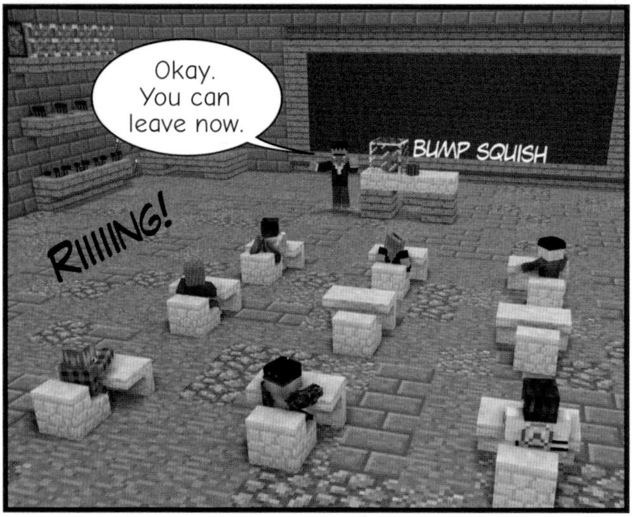
Okay. You can leave now.
BUMP SQUISH
RIIIING!

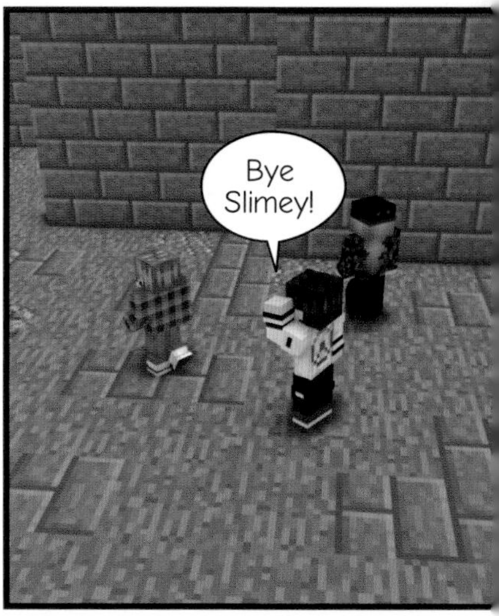
Bye Slimey!

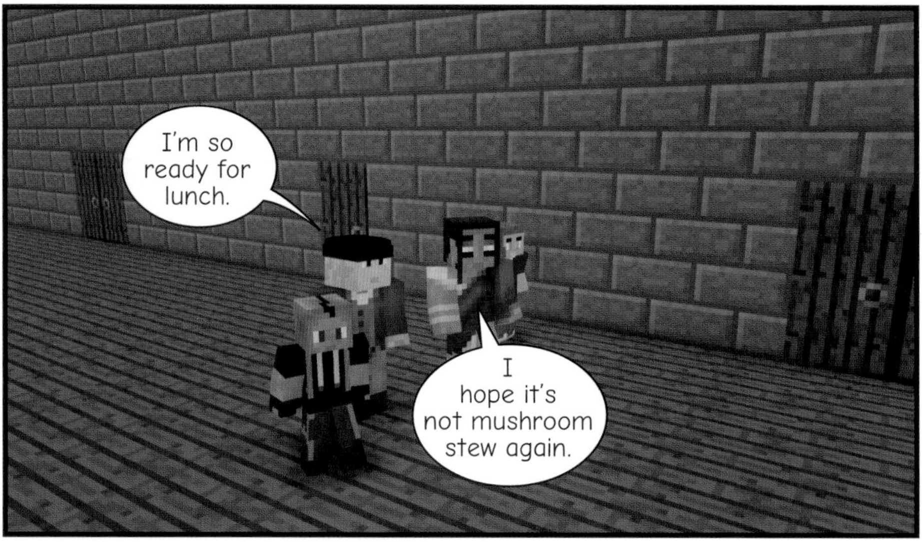
I'm so ready for lunch.
I hope it's not mushroom stew again.

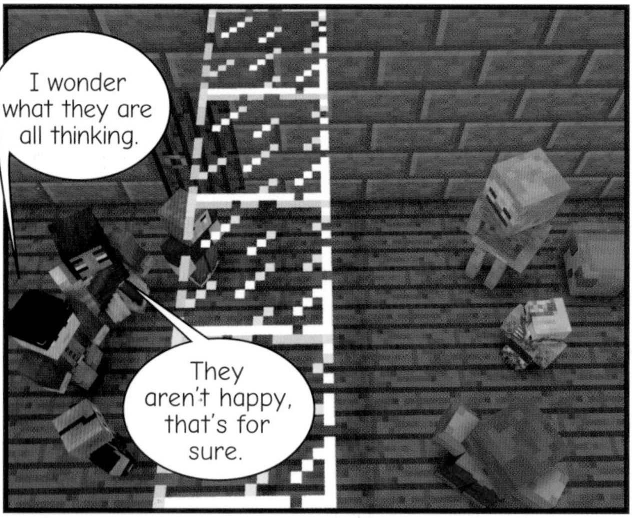
I wonder what they are all thinking.
They aren't happy, that's for sure.

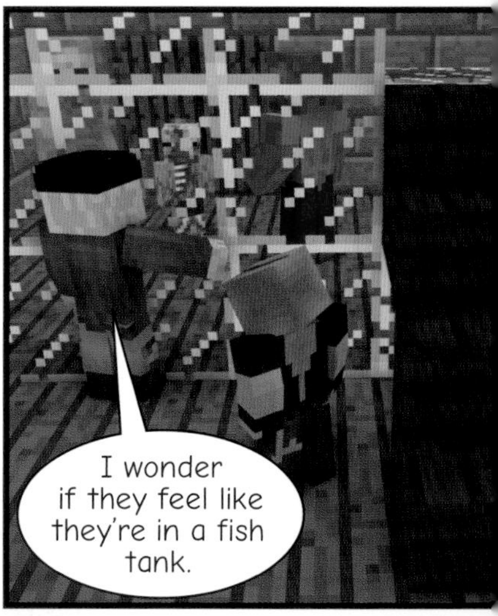
I wonder if they feel like they're in a fish tank.

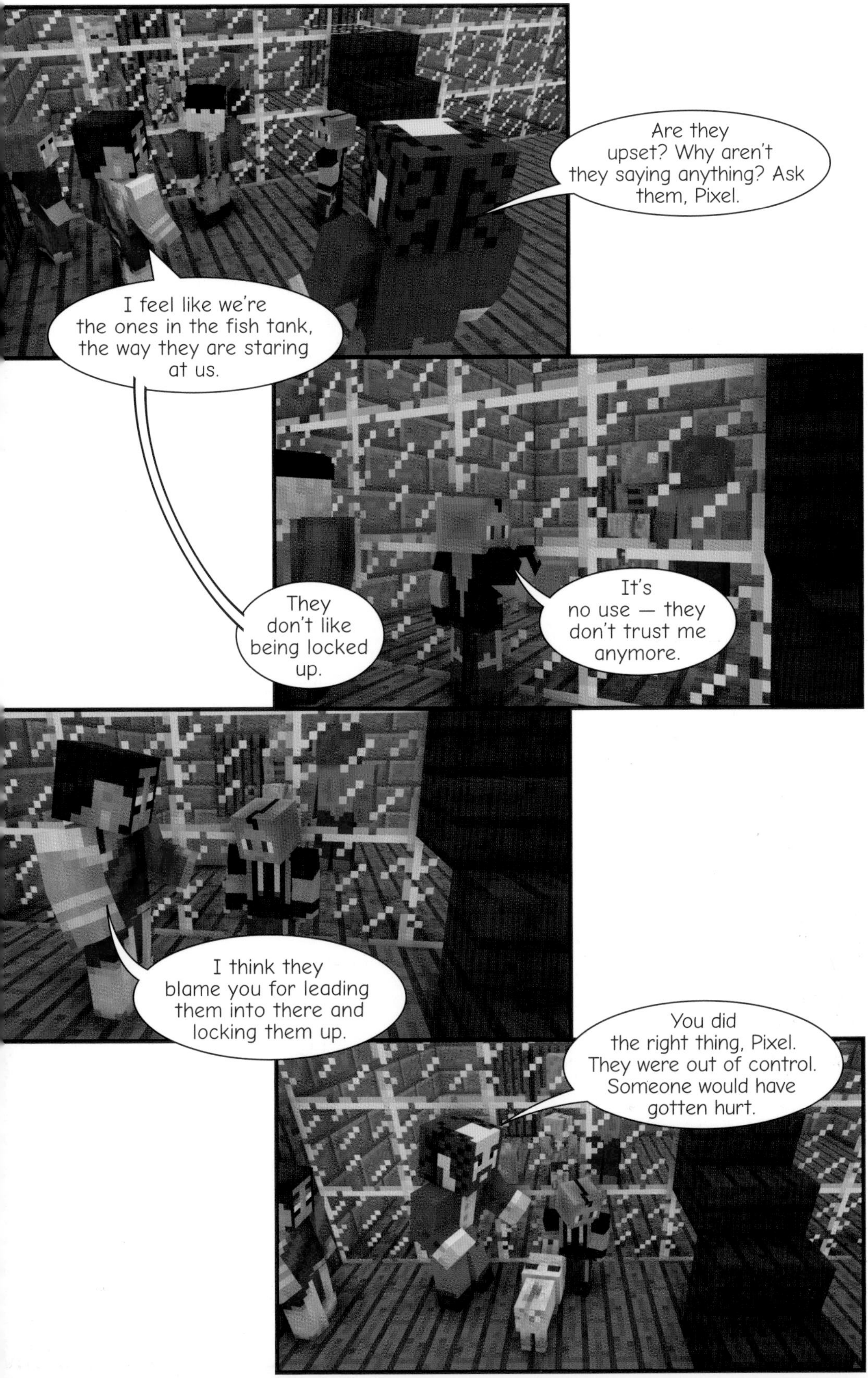

Are they upset? Why aren't they saying anything? Ask them, Pixel.
I feel like we're the ones in the fish tank, the way they are staring at us.
They don't like being locked up.
It's no use — they don't trust me anymore.
I think they blame you for leading them into there and locking them up.
You did the right thing, Pixel. They were out of control. Someone would have gotten hurt.

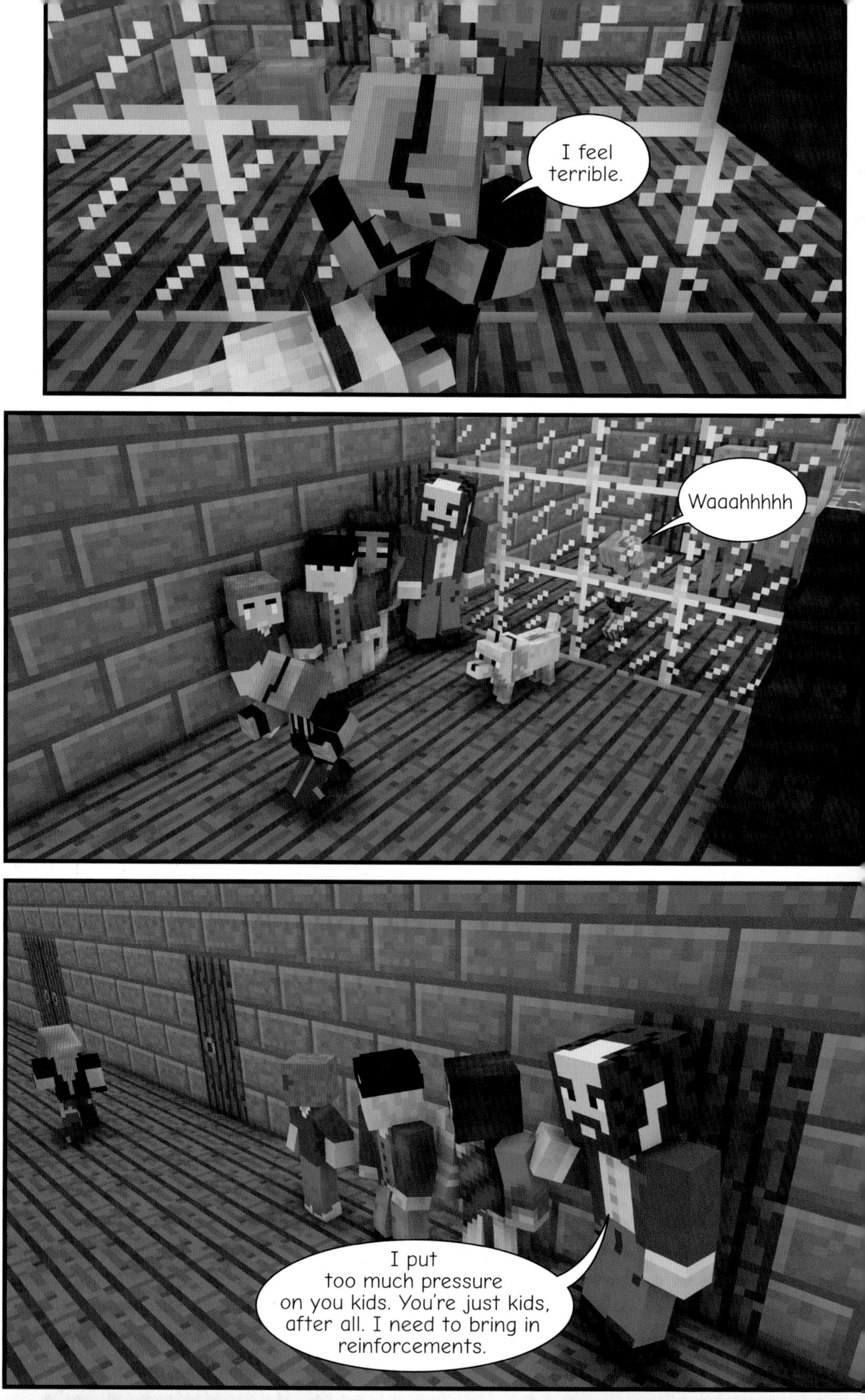
I feel terrible.
Waaahhhhh
I put too much pressure on you kids. You're just kids, after all. I need to bring in reinforcements.

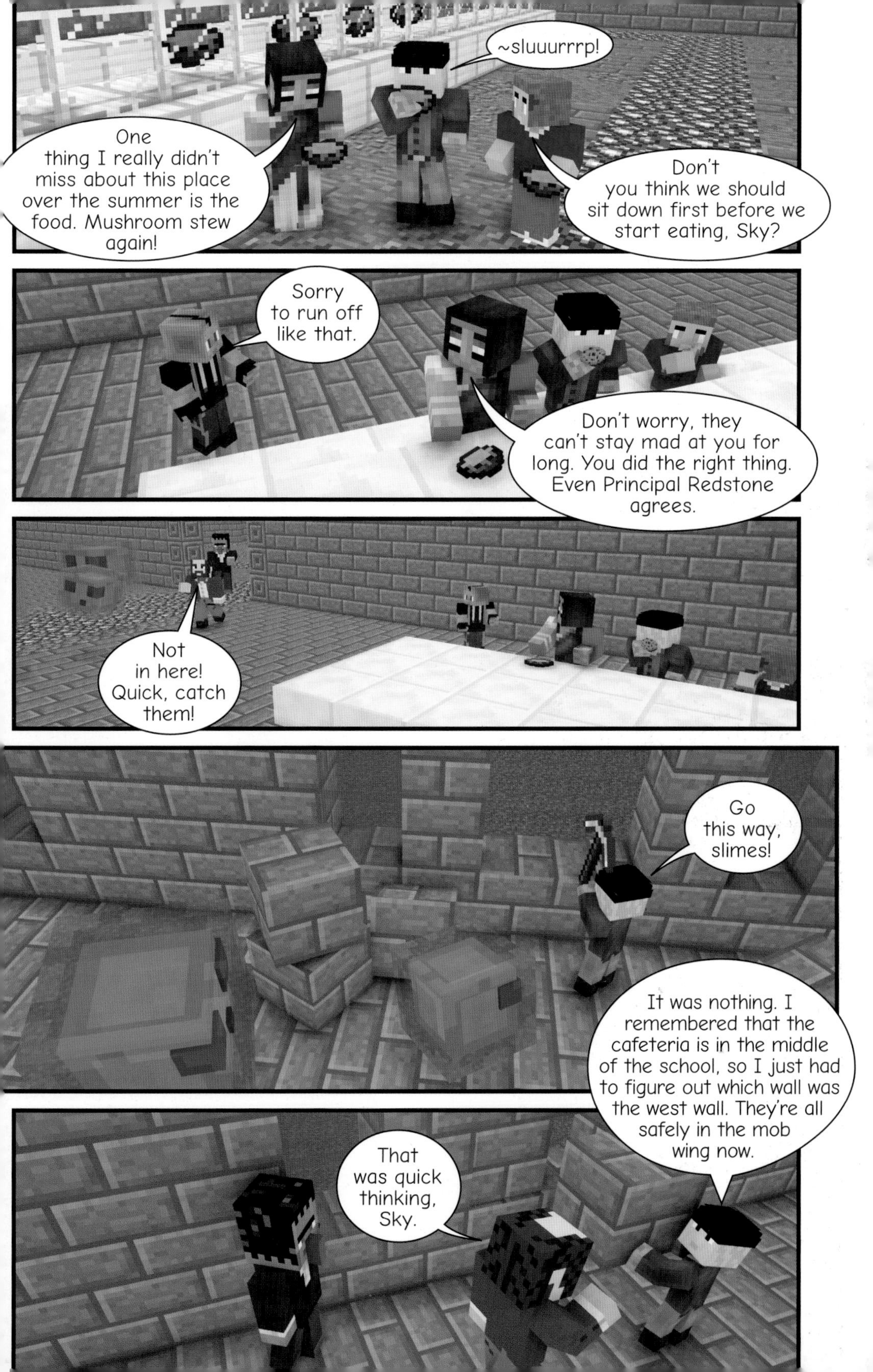
~sluuurrrp!
One thing I really didn't miss about this place over the summer is the food. Mushroom stew again!
Don't you think we should sit down first before we start eating, Sky?
Sorry to run off like that.
Don't worry, they can't stay mad at you for long. You did the right thing. Even Principal Redstone agrees.
Not in here! Quick, catch them!
Go this way, slimes!
That was quick thinking, Sky.
It was nothing. I remembered that the cafeteria is in the middle of the school, so I just had to figure out which wall was the west wall. They're all safely in the mob wing now.

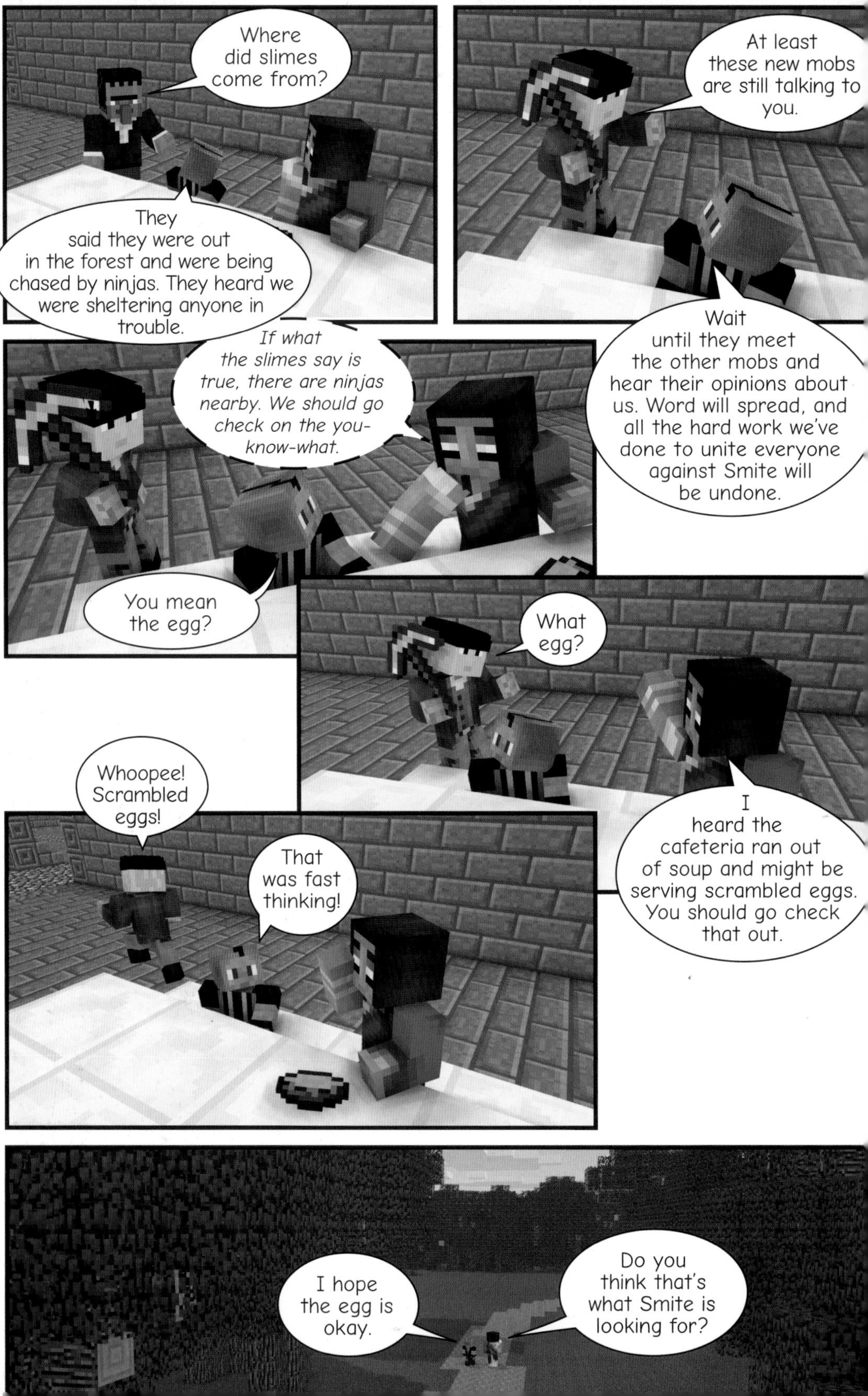
Where did slimes come from?
They said they were out in the forest and were being chased by ninjas. They heard we were sheltering anyone in trouble.
At least these new mobs are still talking to you.
Wait until they meet the other mobs and hear their opinions about us. Word will spread, and all the hard work we've done to unite everyone against Smite will be undone.
If what the slimes say is true, there are ninjas nearby. We should go check on the you-know-what.
You mean the egg?
What egg?
I heard the cafeteria ran out of soup and might be serving scrambled eggs. You should go check that out.
Whoopee! Scrambled eggs!
That was fast thinking!
I hope the egg is okay.
Do you think that's what Smite is looking for?

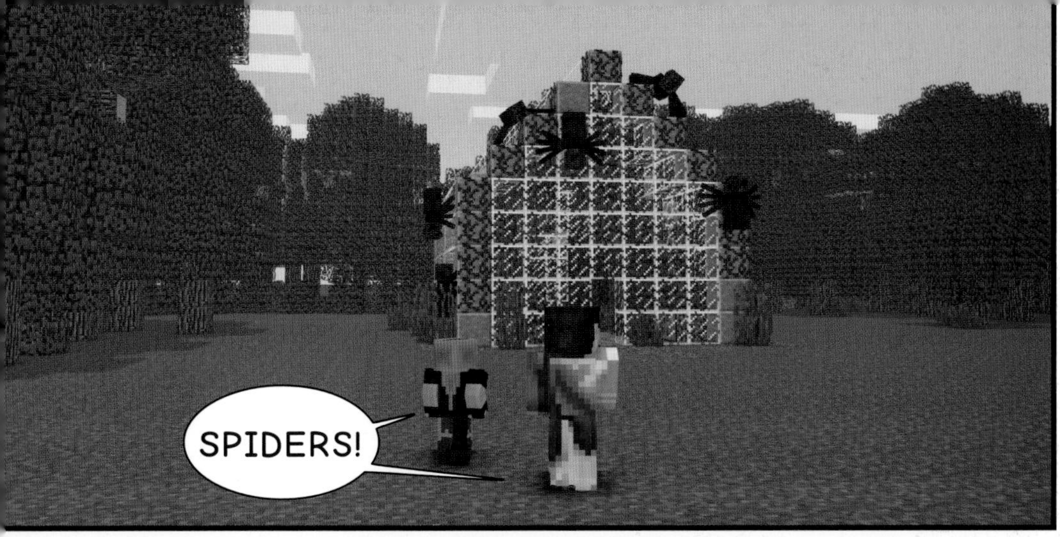
SPIDERS!

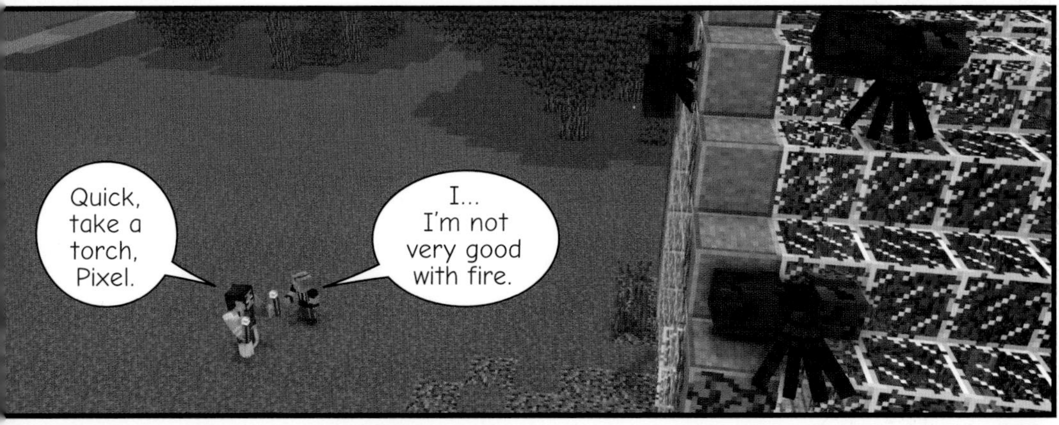
Quick, take a torch, Pixel.
I... I'm not very good with fire.

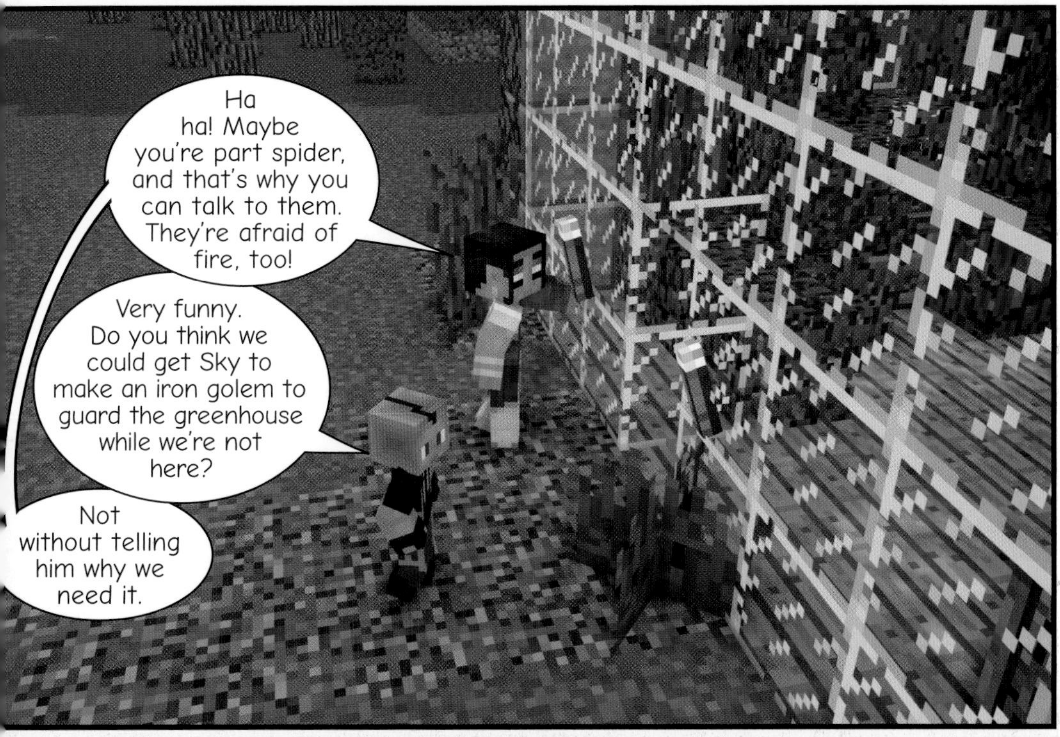
Ha ha! Maybe you're part spider, and that's why you can talk to them. They're afraid of fire, too!
Very funny. Do you think we could get Sky to make an iron golem to guard the greenhouse while we're not here?
Not without telling him why we need it.

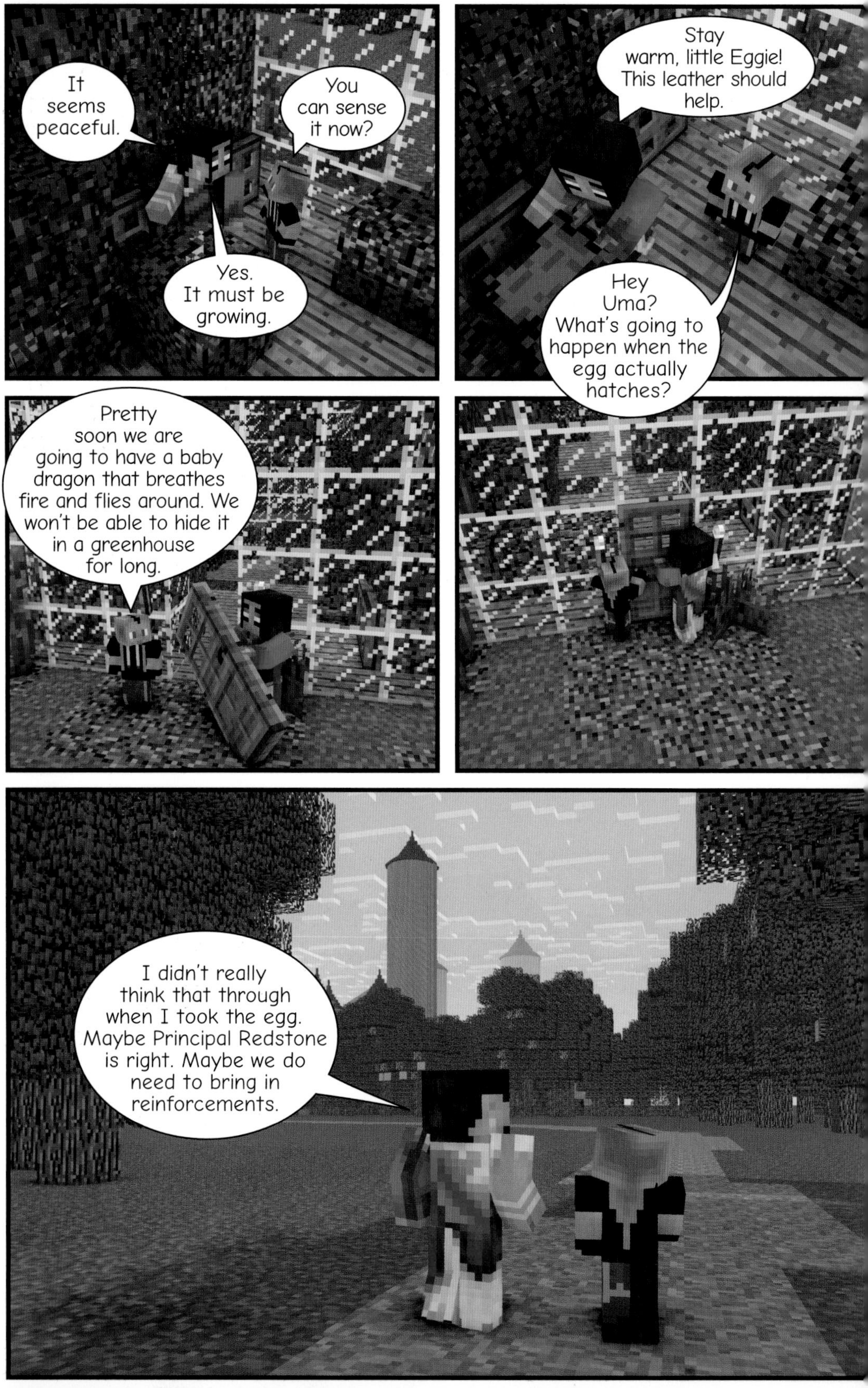

It seems peaceful.
You can sense it now?
Yes. It must be growing.
Stay warm, little Eggie! This leather should help.
Hey Uma? What's going to happen when the egg actually hatches?
Pretty soon we are going to have a baby dragon that breathes fire and flies around. We won't be able to hide it in a greenhouse for long.
I didn't really think that through when I took the egg. Maybe Principal Redstone is right. Maybe we do need to bring in reinforcements.

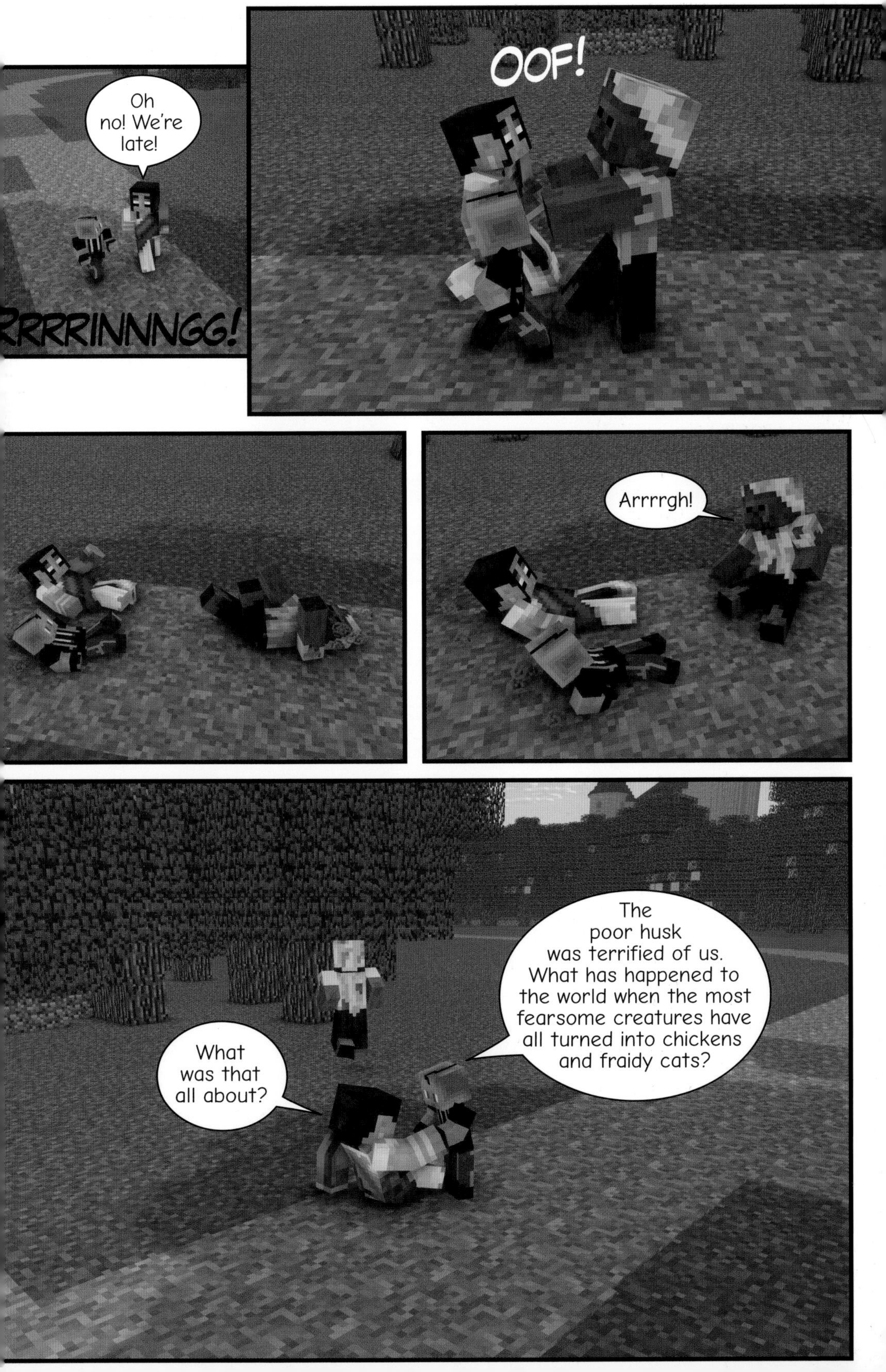
Oh no! We're late!
RRRRINNNGG!
OOF!
Arrrrgh!
What was that all about?
The poor husk was terrified of us. What has happened to the world when the most fearsome creatures have all turned into chickens and fraidy cats?

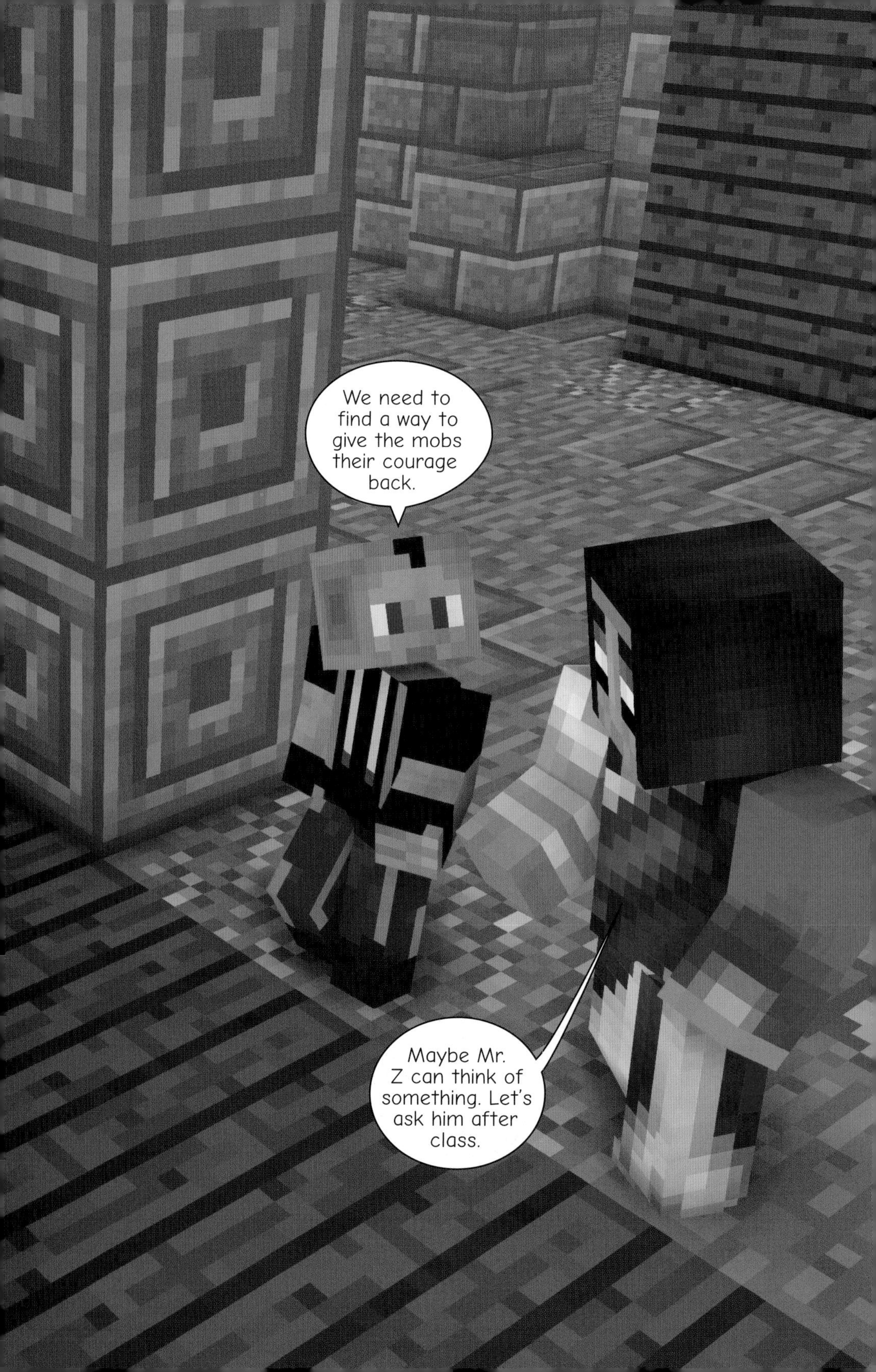
We need to find a way to give the mobs their courage back.
Maybe Mr. Z can think of something. Let's ask him after class.

CHAPTER 5

FRIGHT SCHOOL

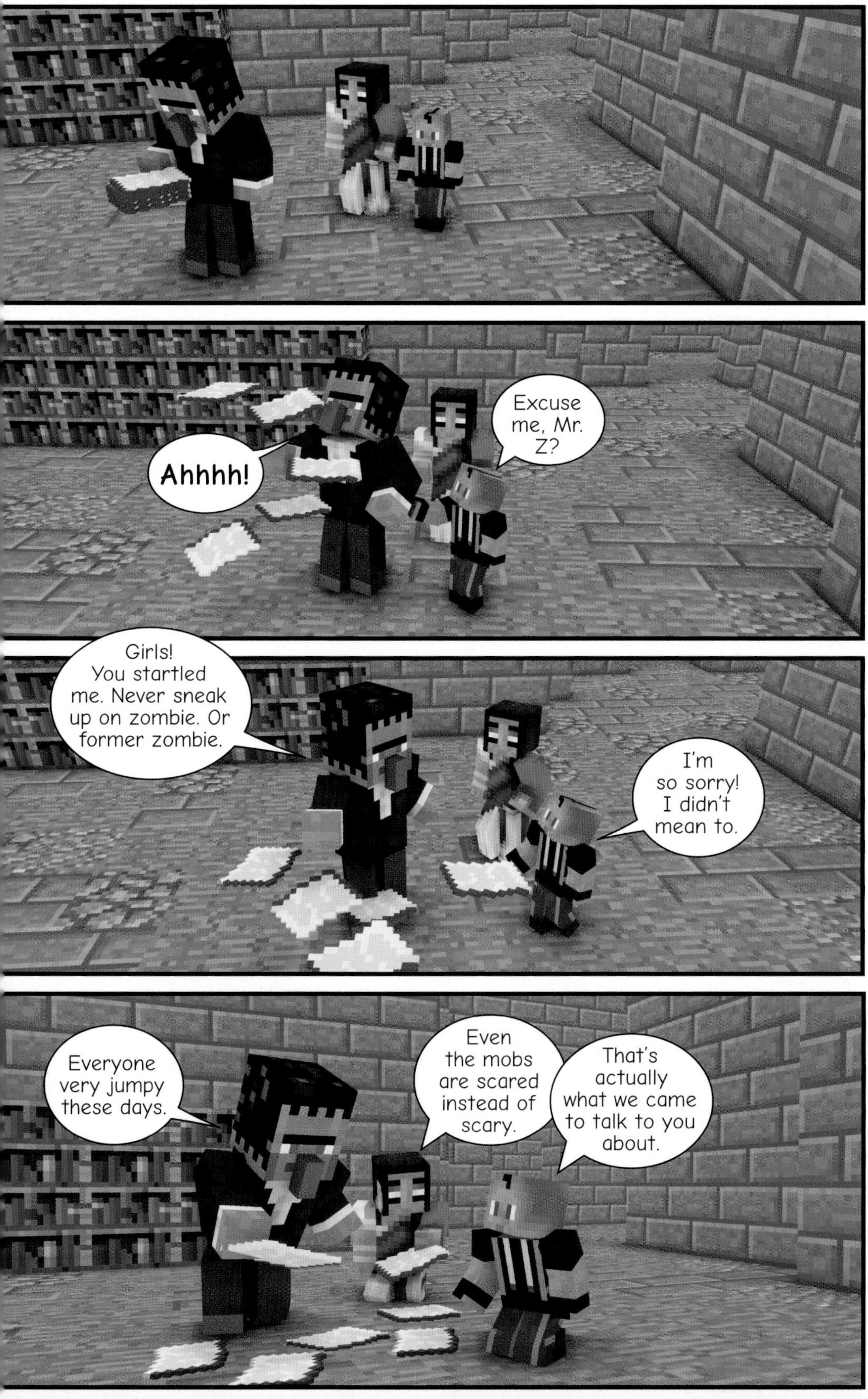
Ahhhh!
Excuse me, Mr. Z?
Girls! You startled me. Never sneak up on zombie. Or former zombie.
I'm so sorry! I didn't mean to.
Everyone very jumpy these days.
Even the mobs are scared instead of scary.
That's actually what we came to talk to you about.

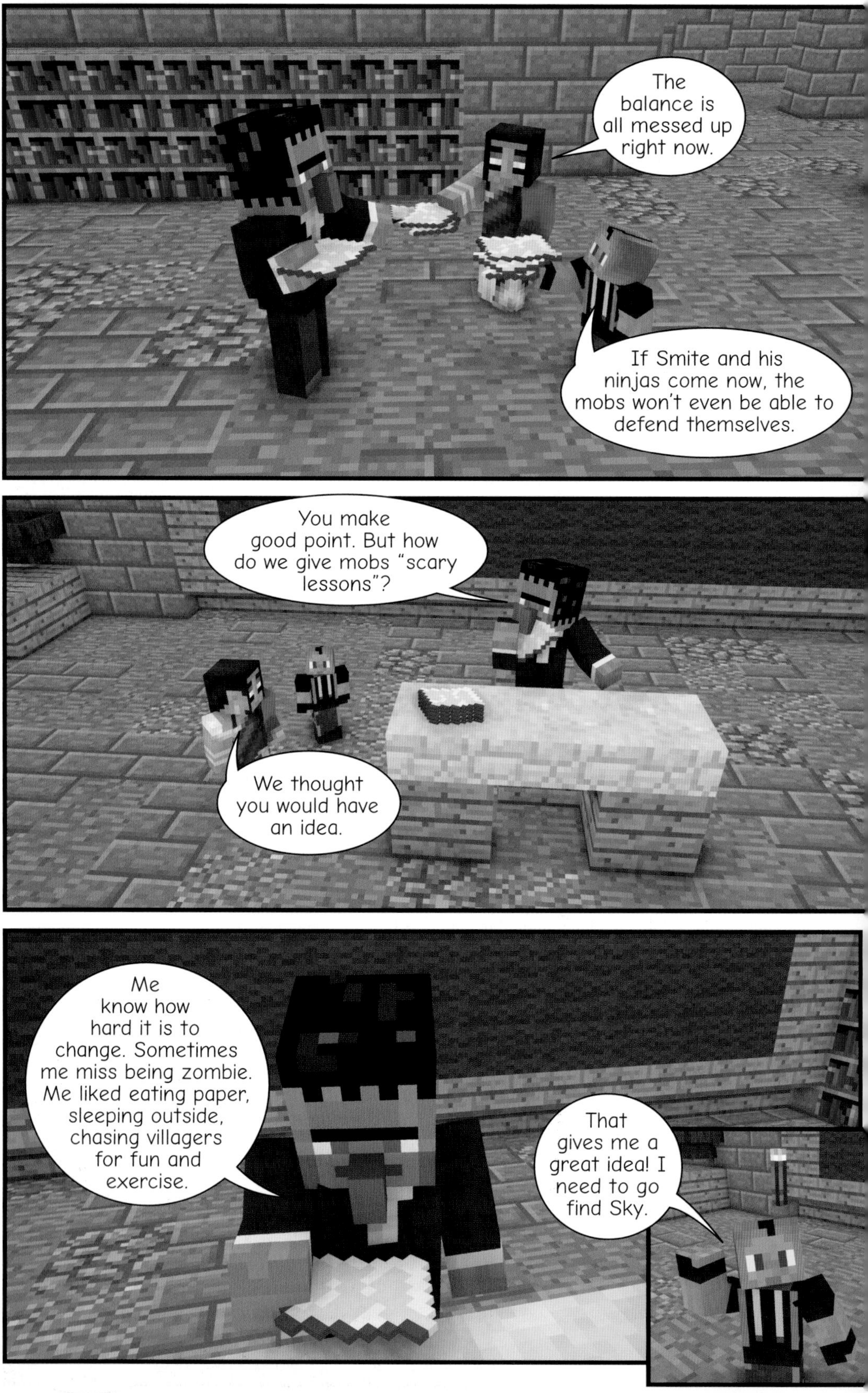
The balance is all messed up right now.
If Smite and his ninjas come now, the mobs won't even be able to defend themselves.
You make good point. But how do we give mobs "scary lessons"?
We thought you would have an idea.
Me know how hard it is to change. Sometimes me miss being zombie. Me liked eating paper, sleeping outside, chasing villagers for fun and exercise.
That gives me a great idea! I need to go find Sky.

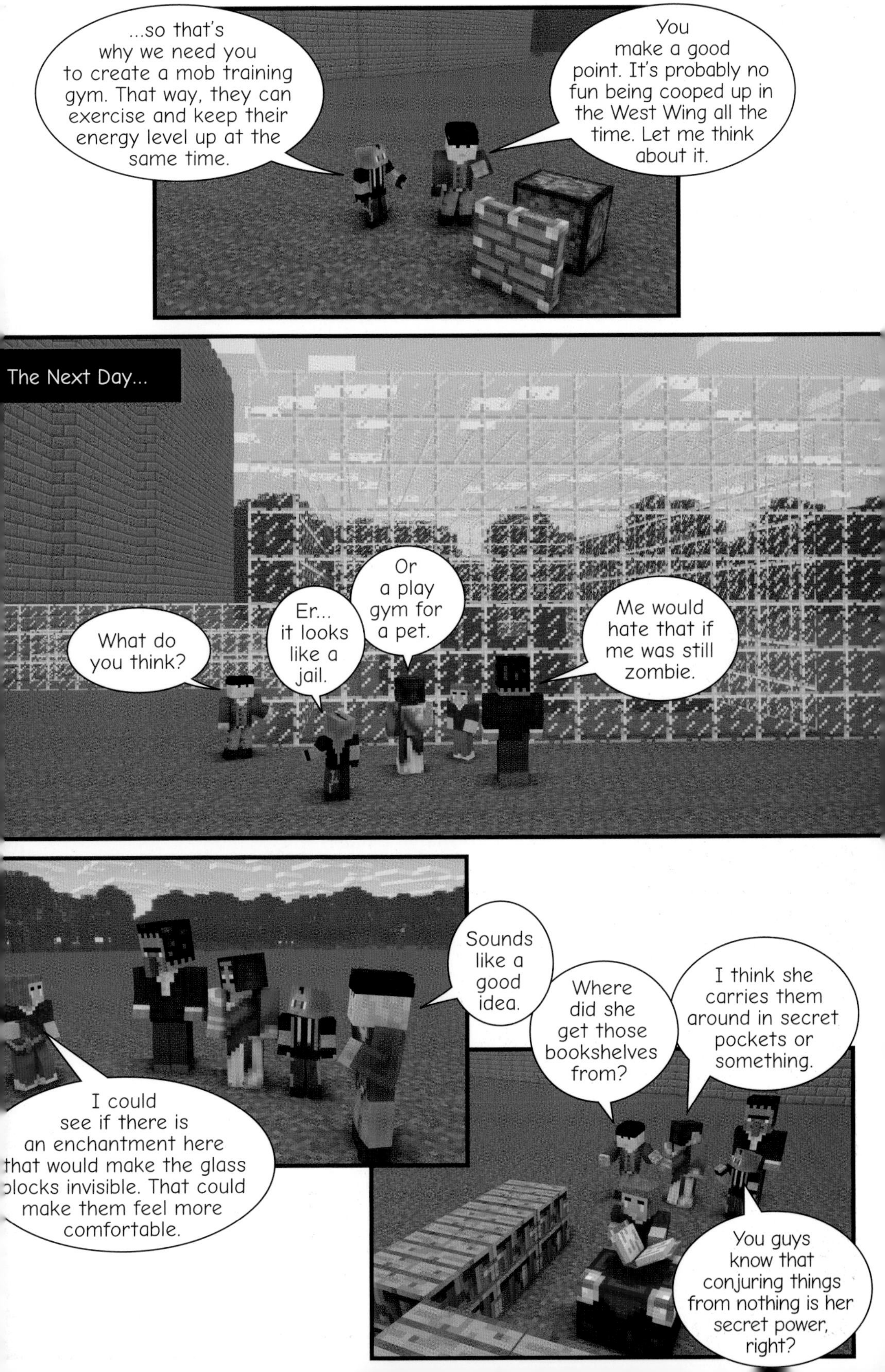
...so that's why we need you to create a mob training gym. That way, they can exercise and keep their energy level up at the same time.
You make a good point. It's probably no fun being cooped up in the West Wing all the time. Let me think about it.
The Next Day...
What do you think?
Er... it looks like a jail.
Or a play gym for a pet.
Me would hate that if me was still zombie.
I could see if there is an enchantment here that would make the glass blocks invisible. That could make them feel more comfortable.
Sounds like a good idea.
Where did she get those bookshelves from?
I think she carries them around in secret pockets or something.
You guys know that conjuring things from nothing is her secret power, right?

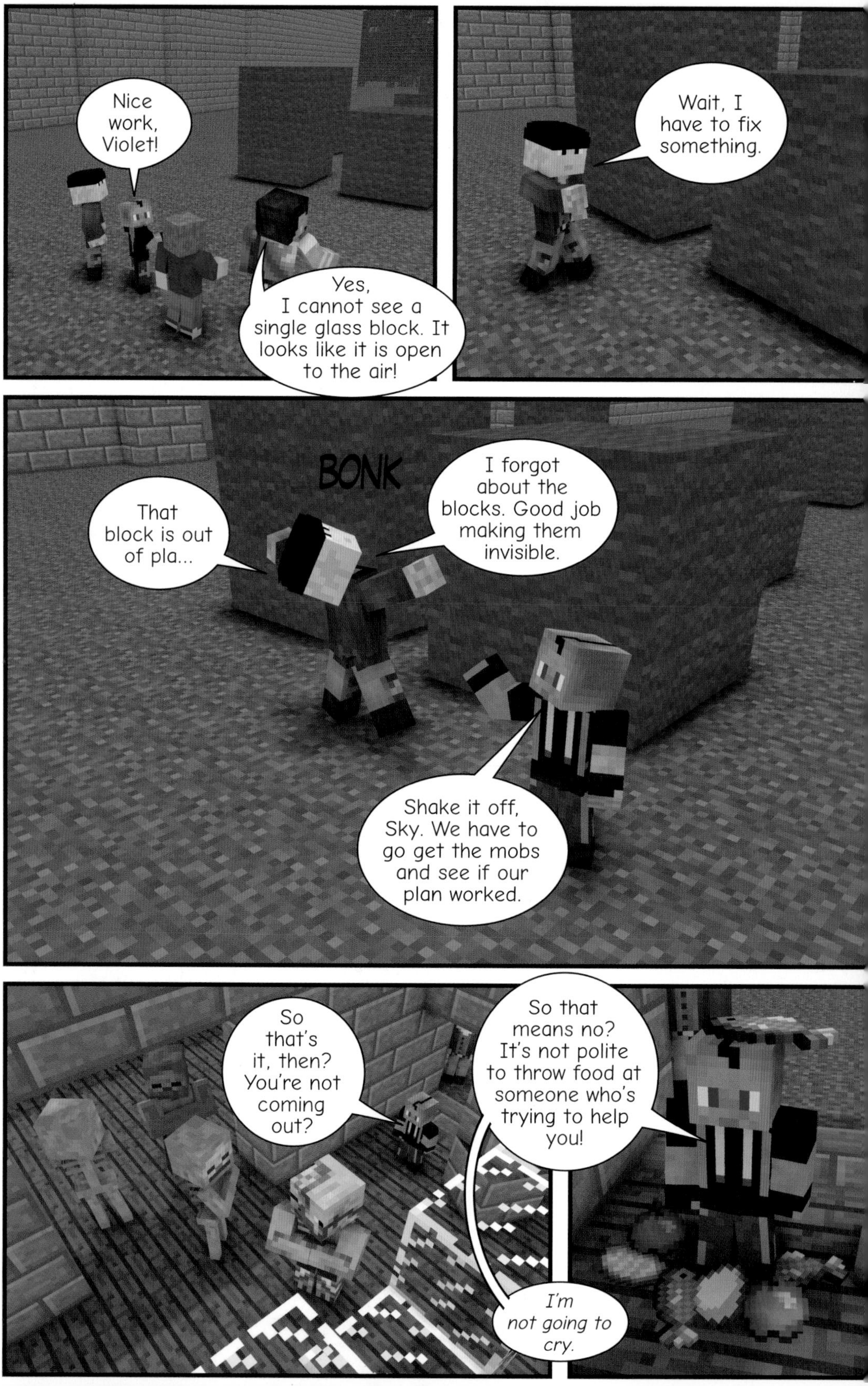

Nice work, Violet!
Yes, I cannot see a single glass block. It looks like it is open to the air!
Wait, I have to fix something.
BONK
That block is out of pla...
I forgot about the blocks. Good job making them invisible.
Shake it off, Sky. We have to go get the mobs and see if our plan worked.
So that's it, then? You're not coming out?
So that means no? It's not polite to throw food at someone who's trying to help you!
I'm not going to cry.

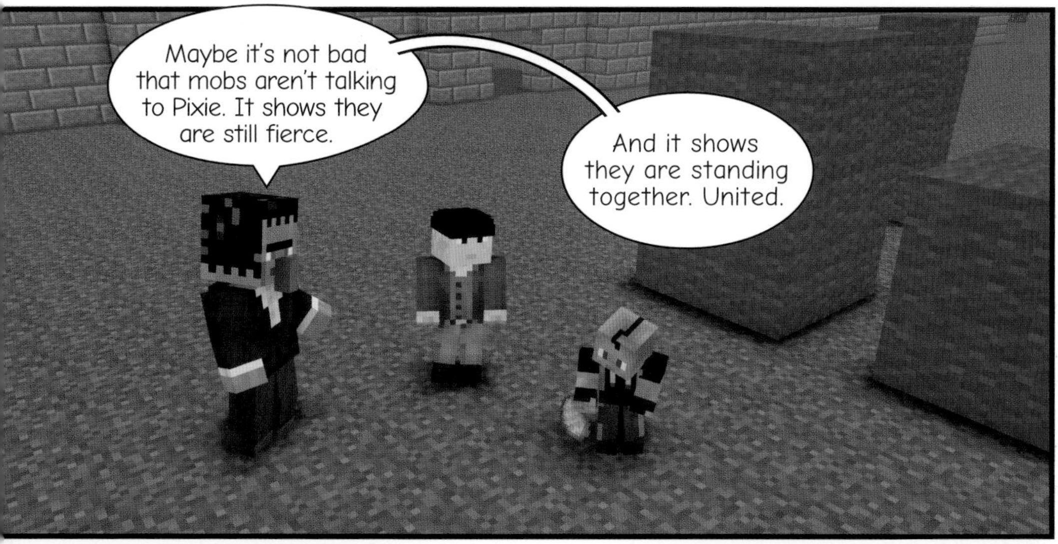
Maybe it's not bad that mobs aren't talking to Pixie. It shows they are still fierce.
And it shows they are standing together. United.

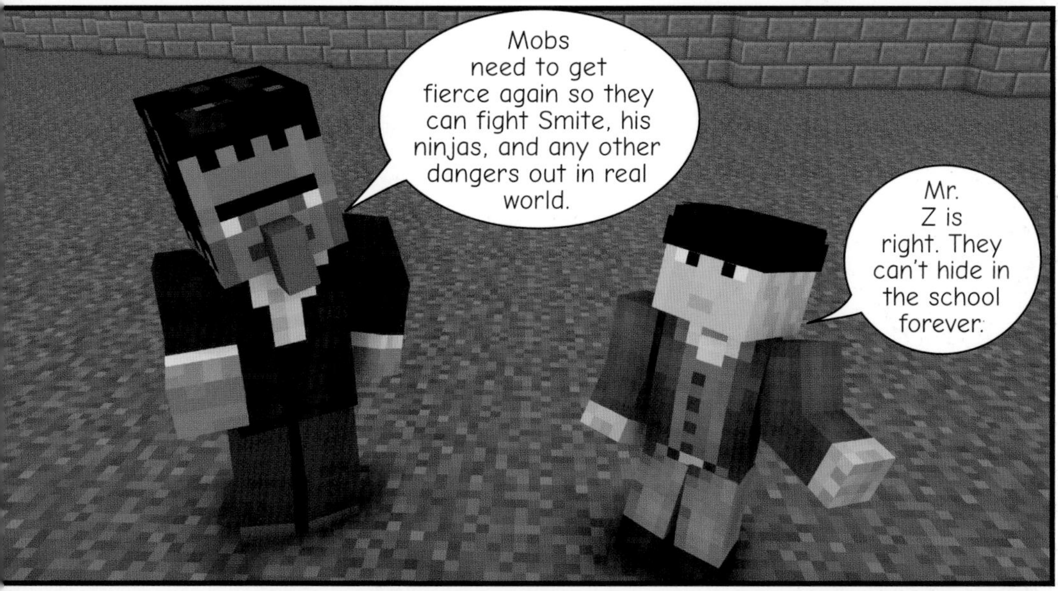
Mobs need to get fierce again so they can fight Smite, his ninjas, and any other dangers out in real world.
Mr. Z is right. They can't hide in the school forever.

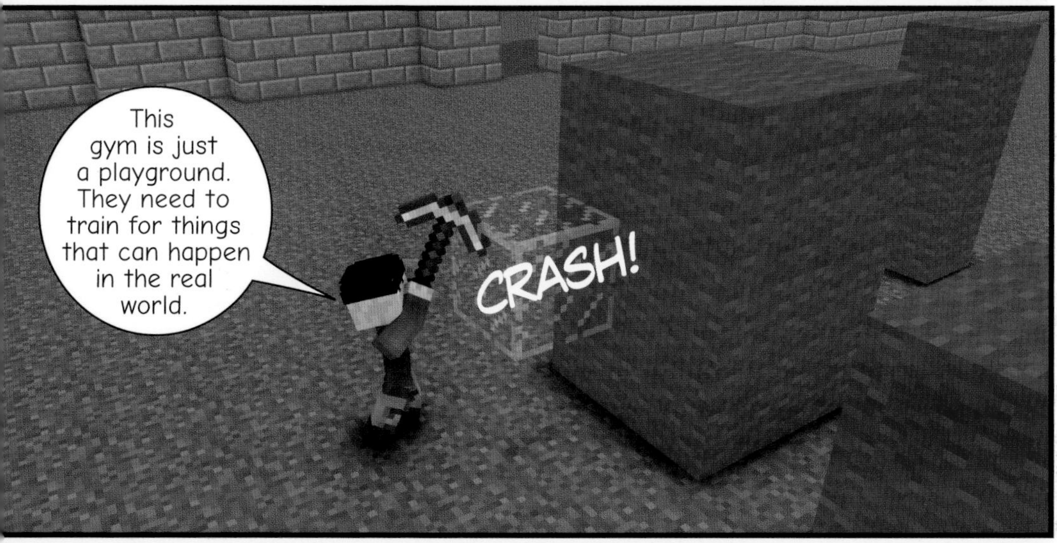
This gym is just a playground. They need to train for things that can happen in the real world.
CRASH!

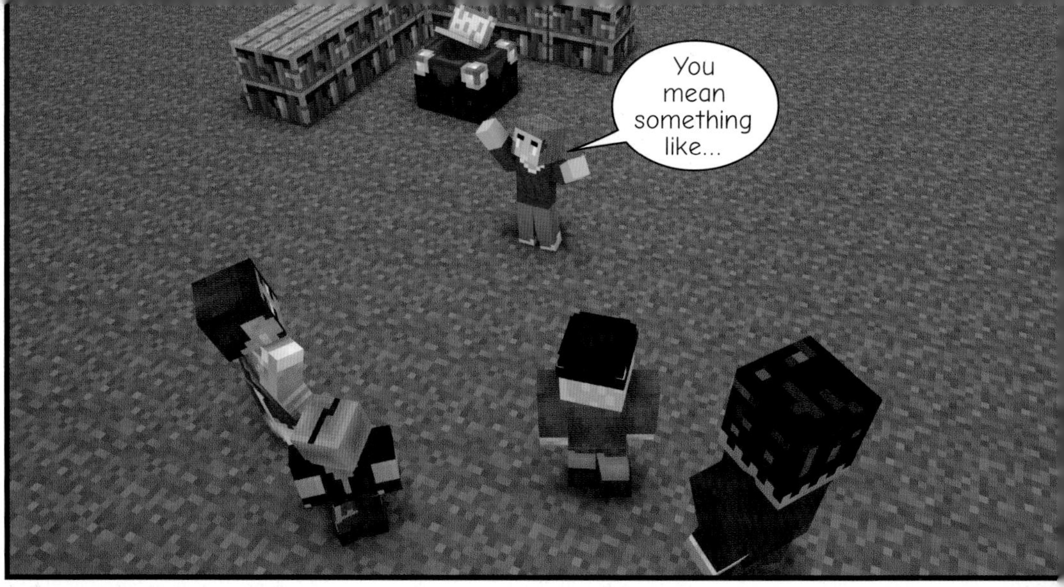
You mean something like...

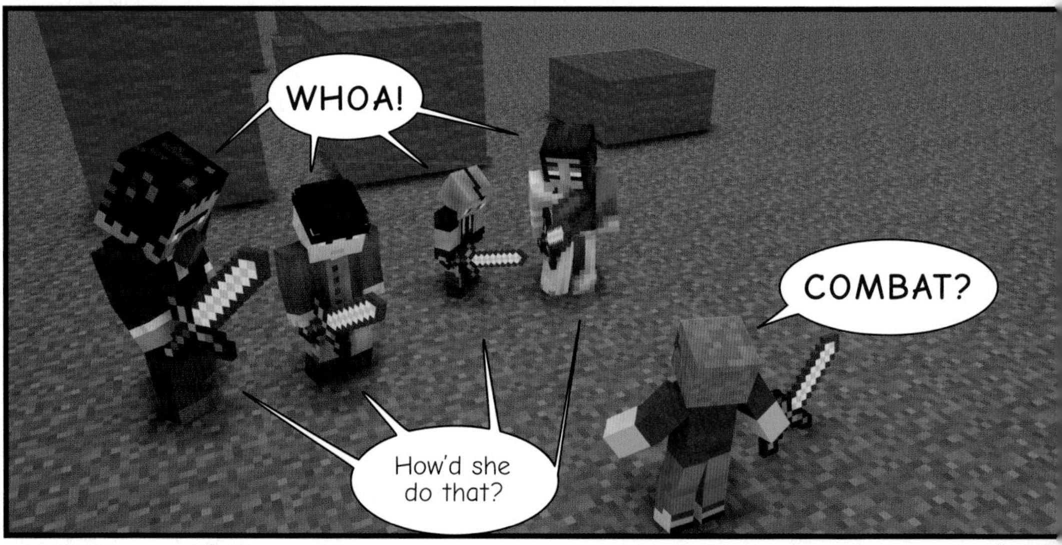
WHOA!
COMBAT?
How'd she do that?

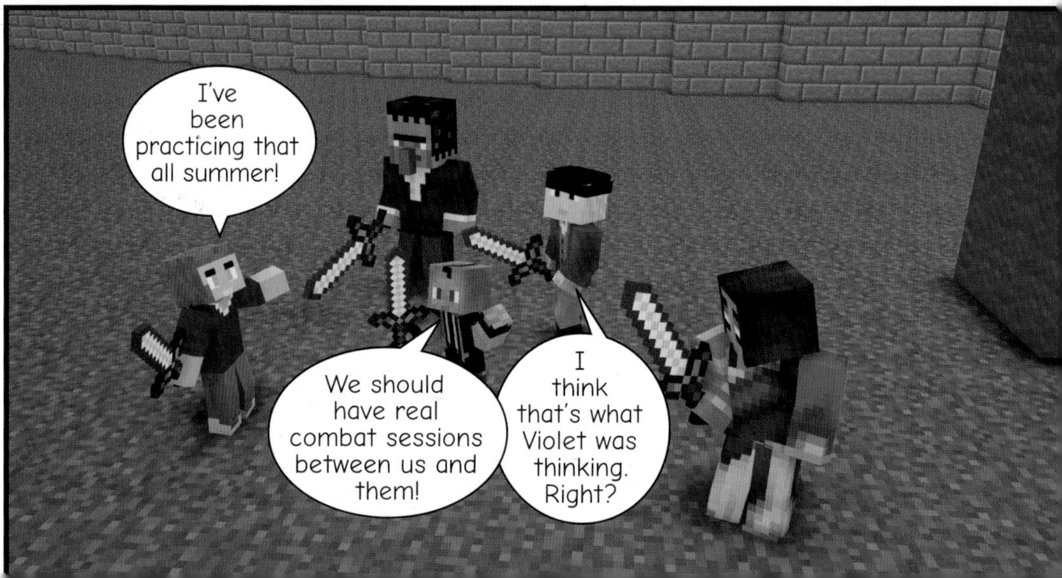
I've been practicing that all summer!
We should have real combat sessions between us and them!
I think that's what Violet was thinking. Right?

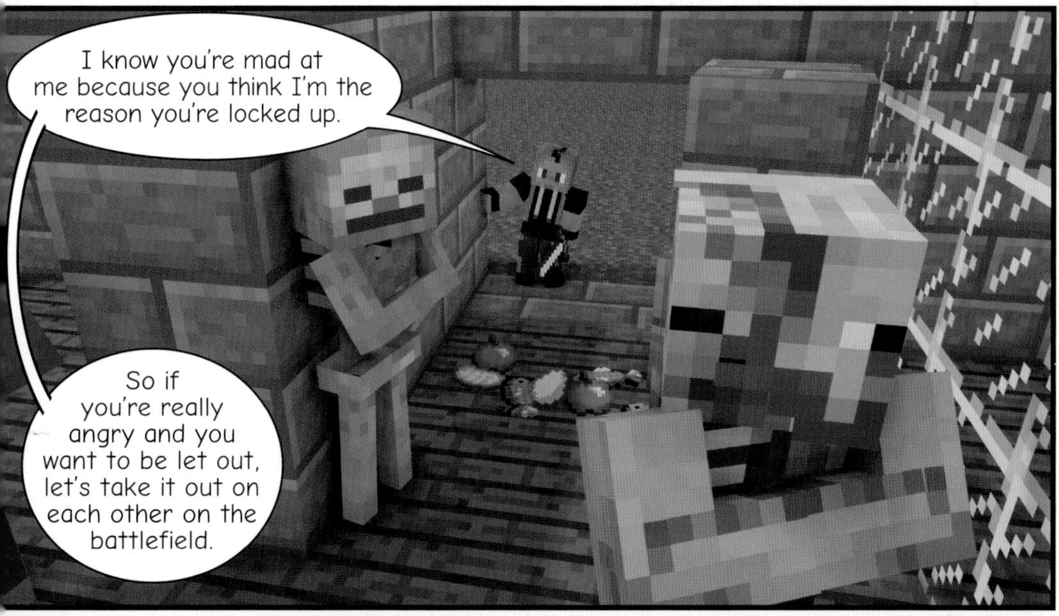
I know you're mad at me because you think I'm the reason you're locked up.
So if you're really angry and you want to be let out, let's take it out on each other on the battlefield.

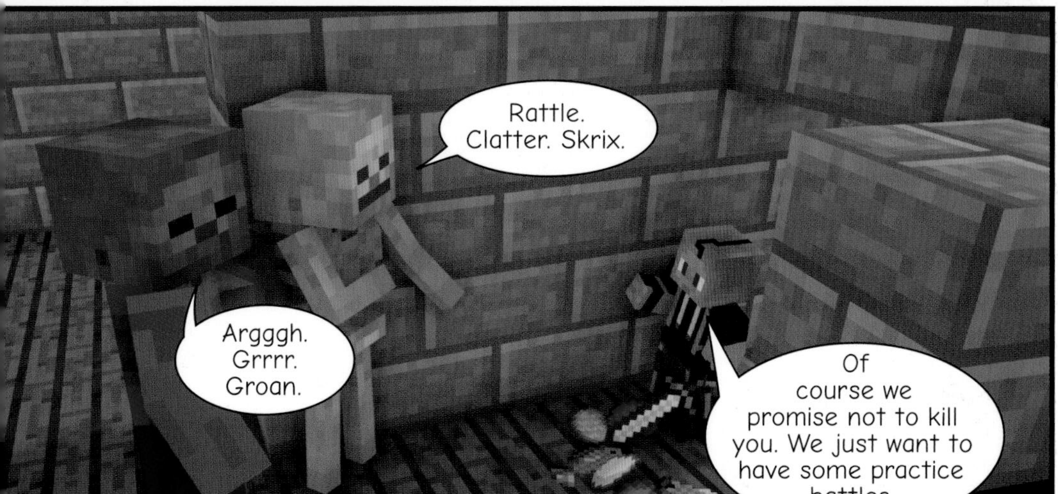
Rattle. Clatter. Skrix.
Argggh. Grrrr. Groan.
Of course we promise not to kill you. We just want to have some practice battles.

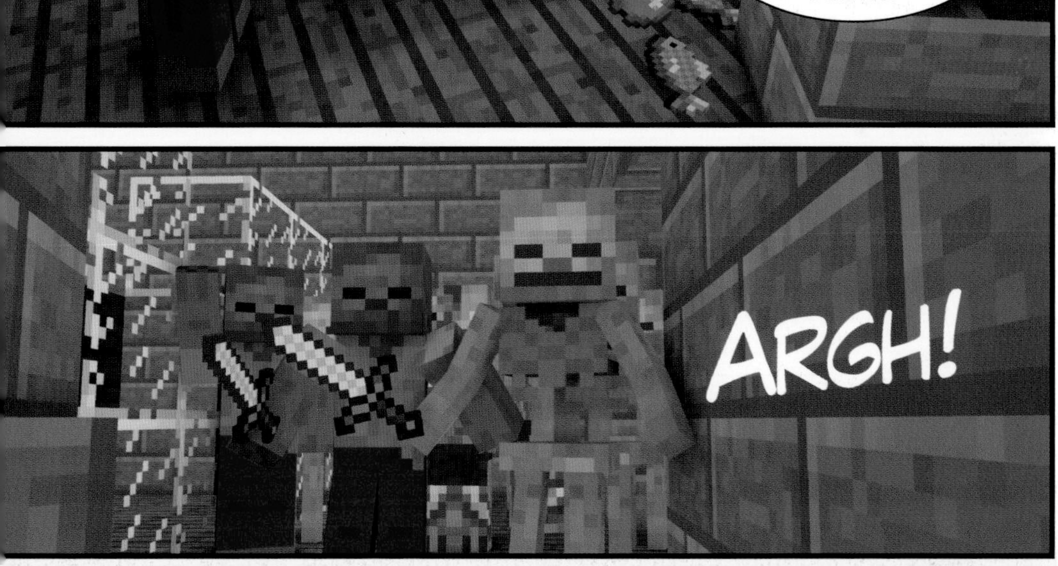
ARGH!

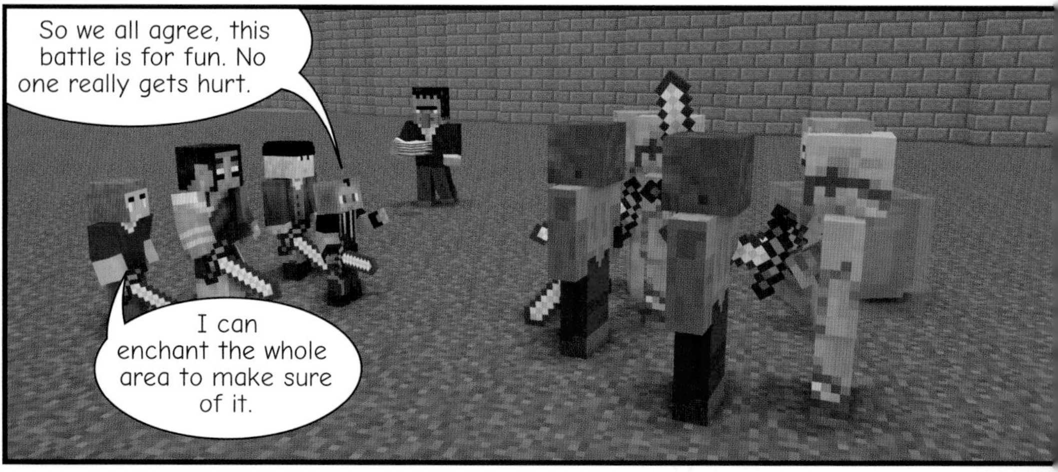
So we all agree, this battle is for fun. No one really gets hurt.
I can enchant the whole area to make sure of it.

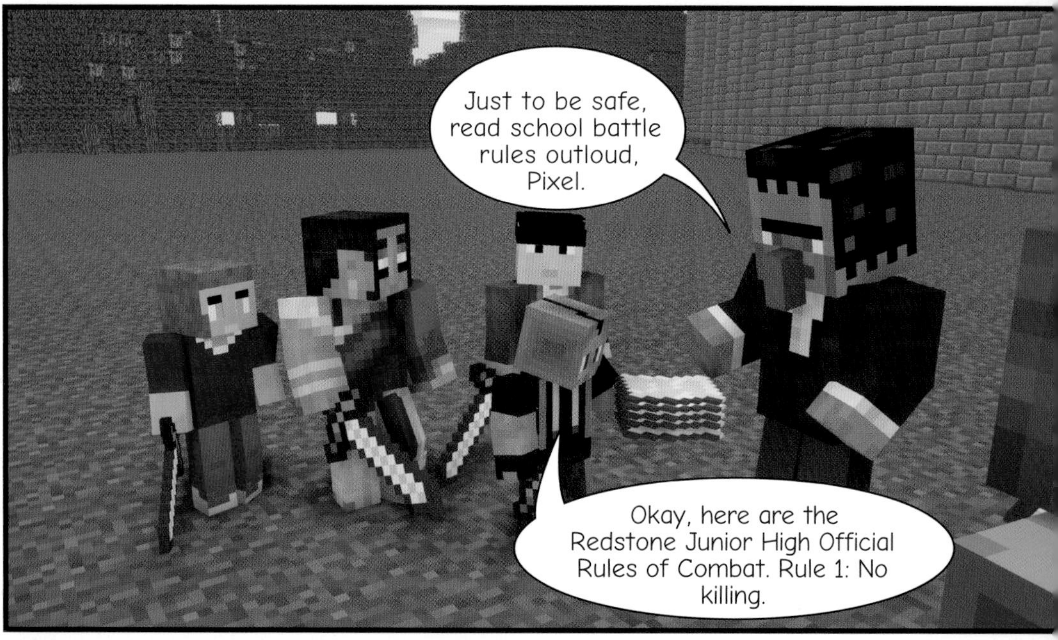
Just to be safe, read school battle rules outloud, Pixel.
Okay, here are the Redstone Junior High Official Rules of Combat. Rule 1: No killing.

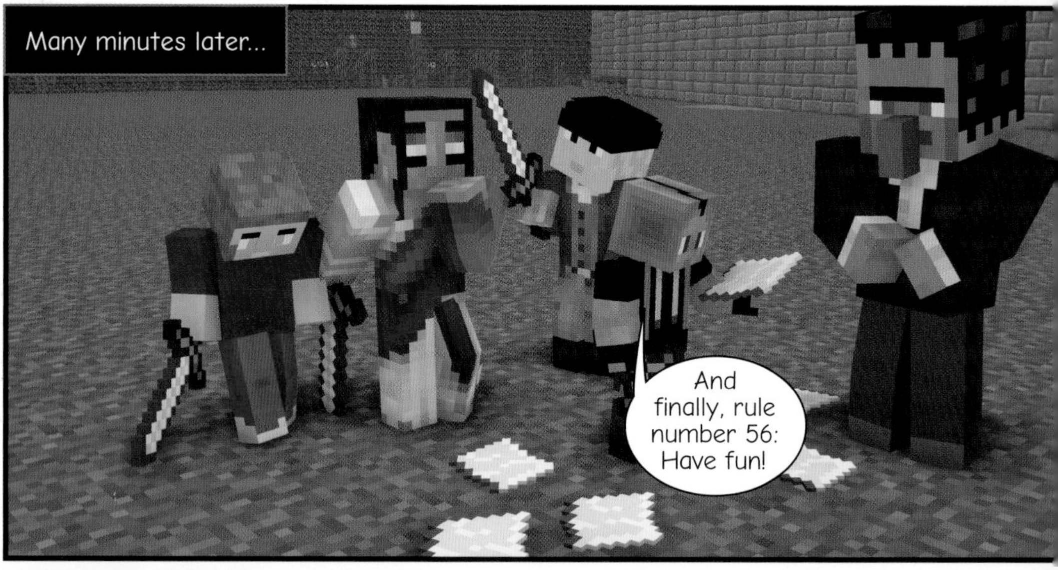
Many minutes later...
And finally, rule number 56: Have fun!

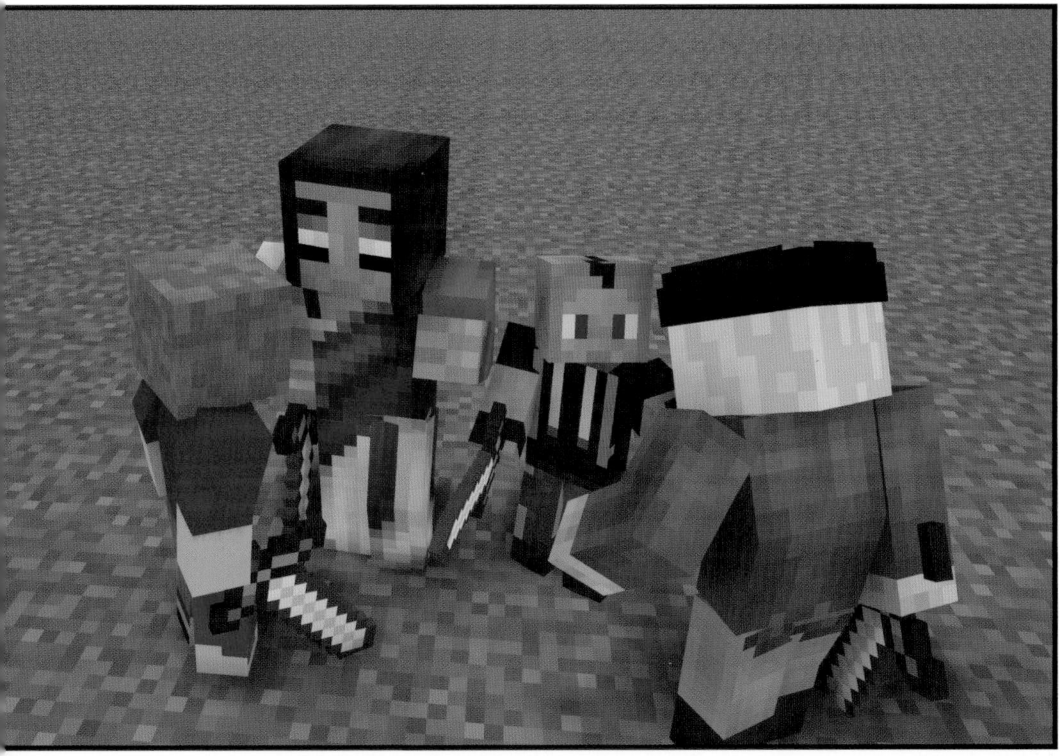

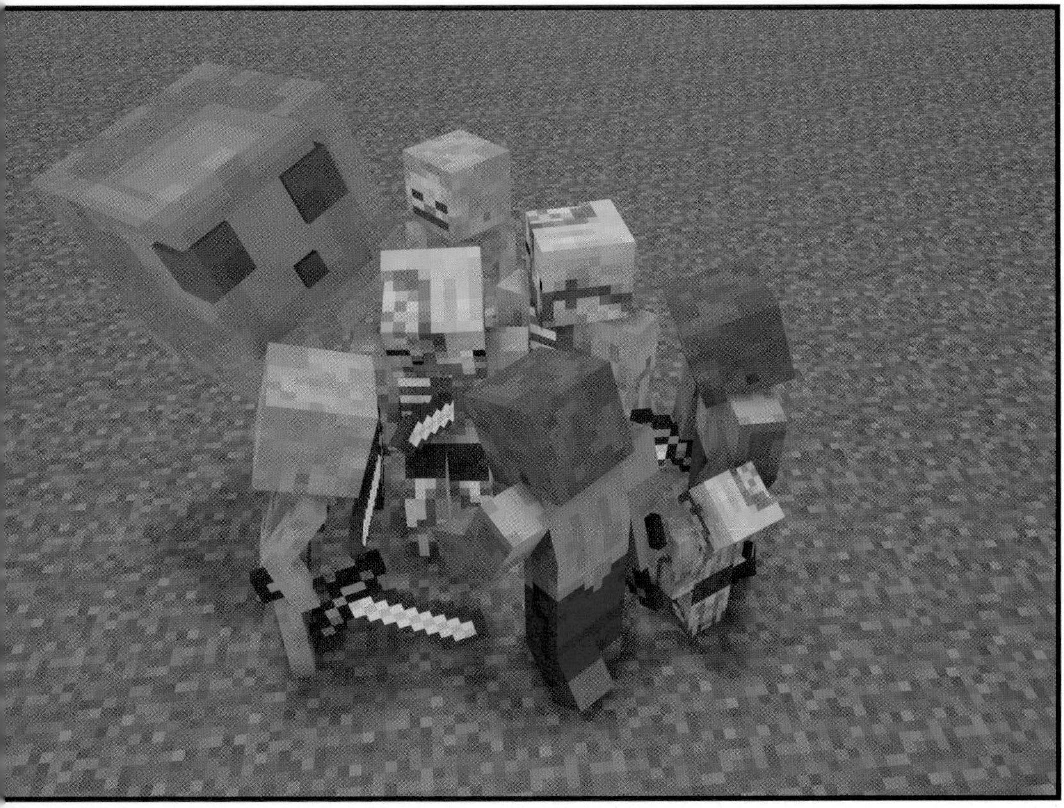

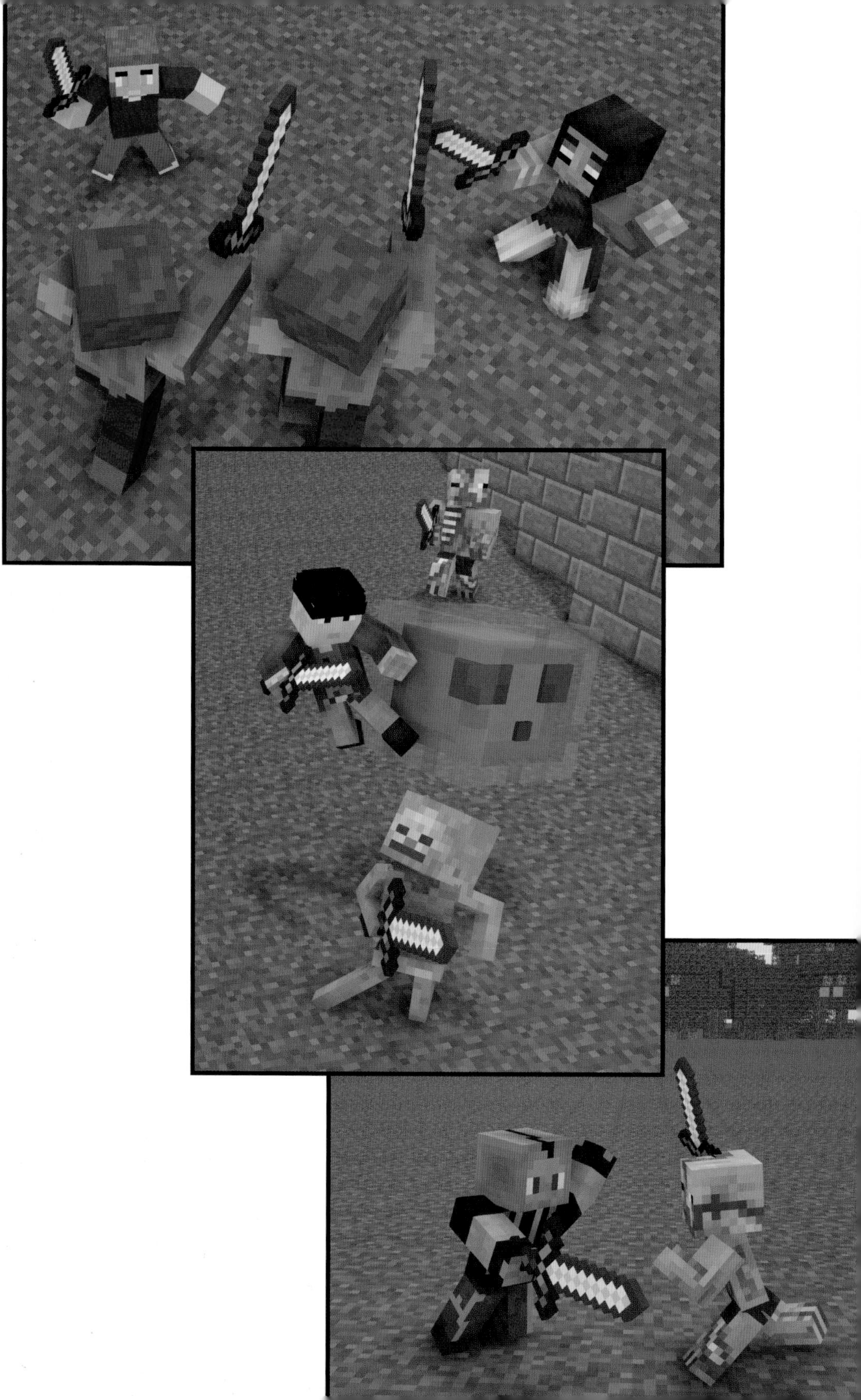

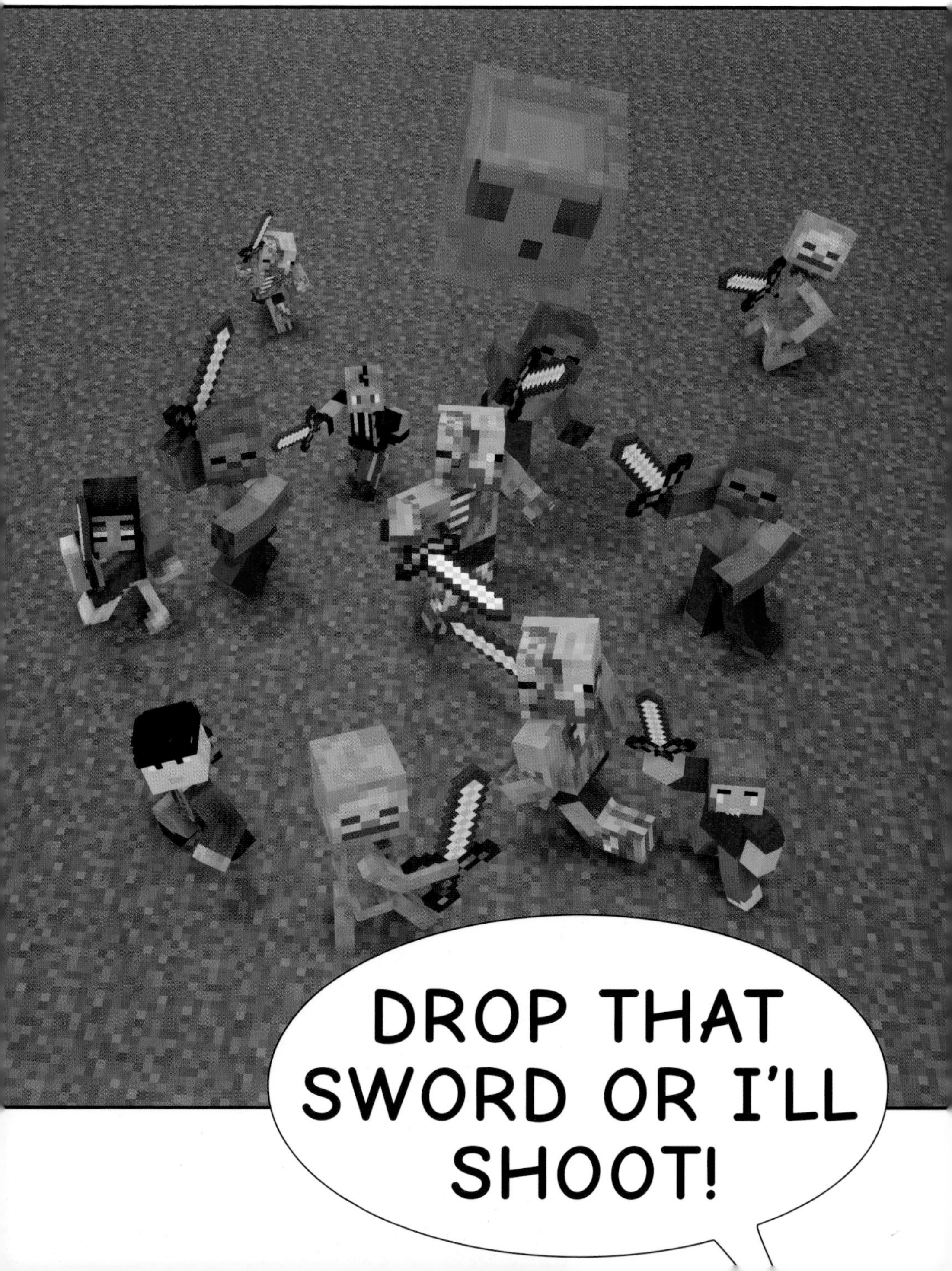
DROP THAT SWORD OR I'LL SHOOT!

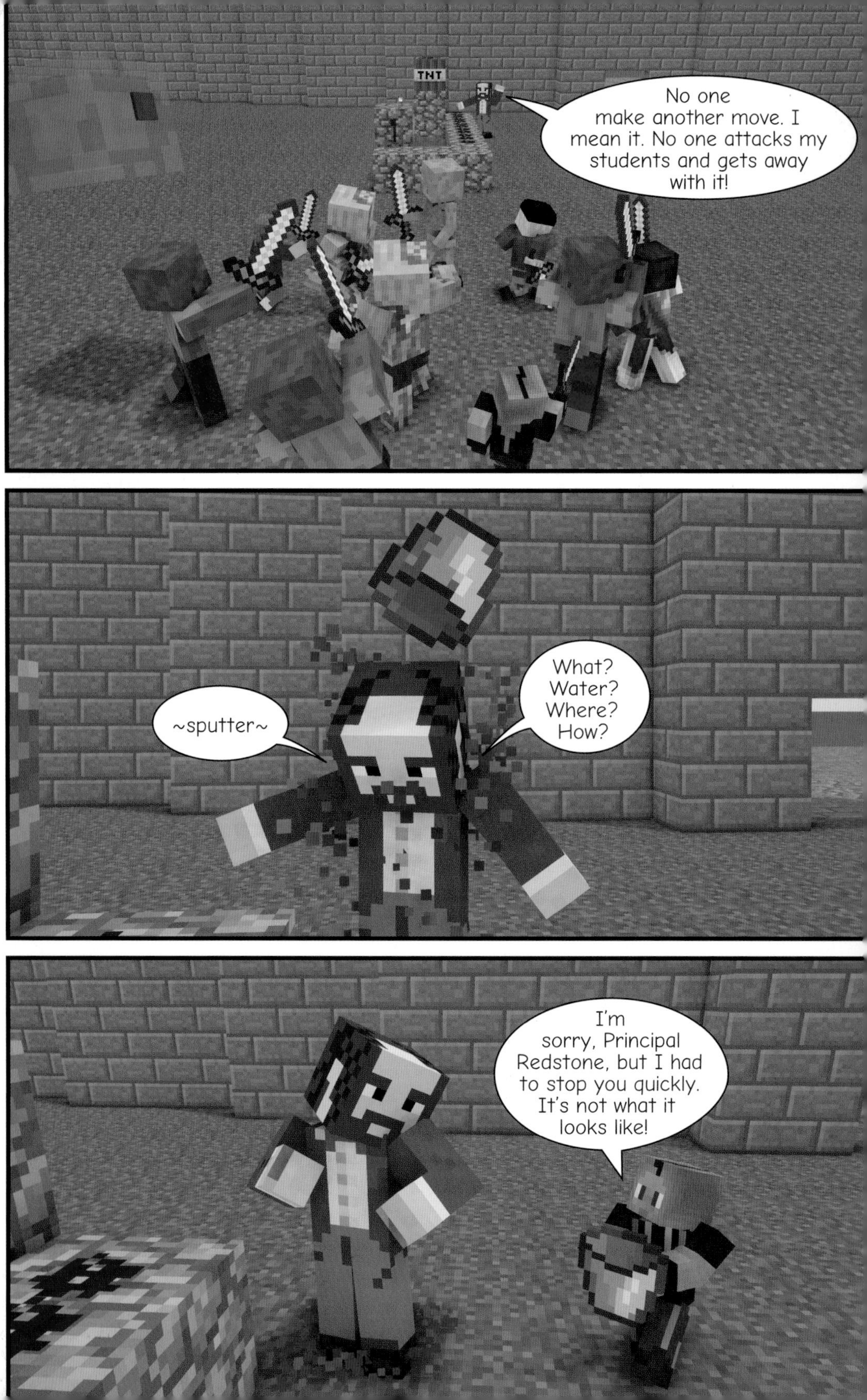
No one make another move. I mean it. No one attacks my students and gets away with it!
~sputter~
What? Water? Where? How?
I'm sorry, Principal Redstone, but I had to stop you quickly. It's not what it looks like!

CHAPTER 6

BREAKING THROUGH WALLS

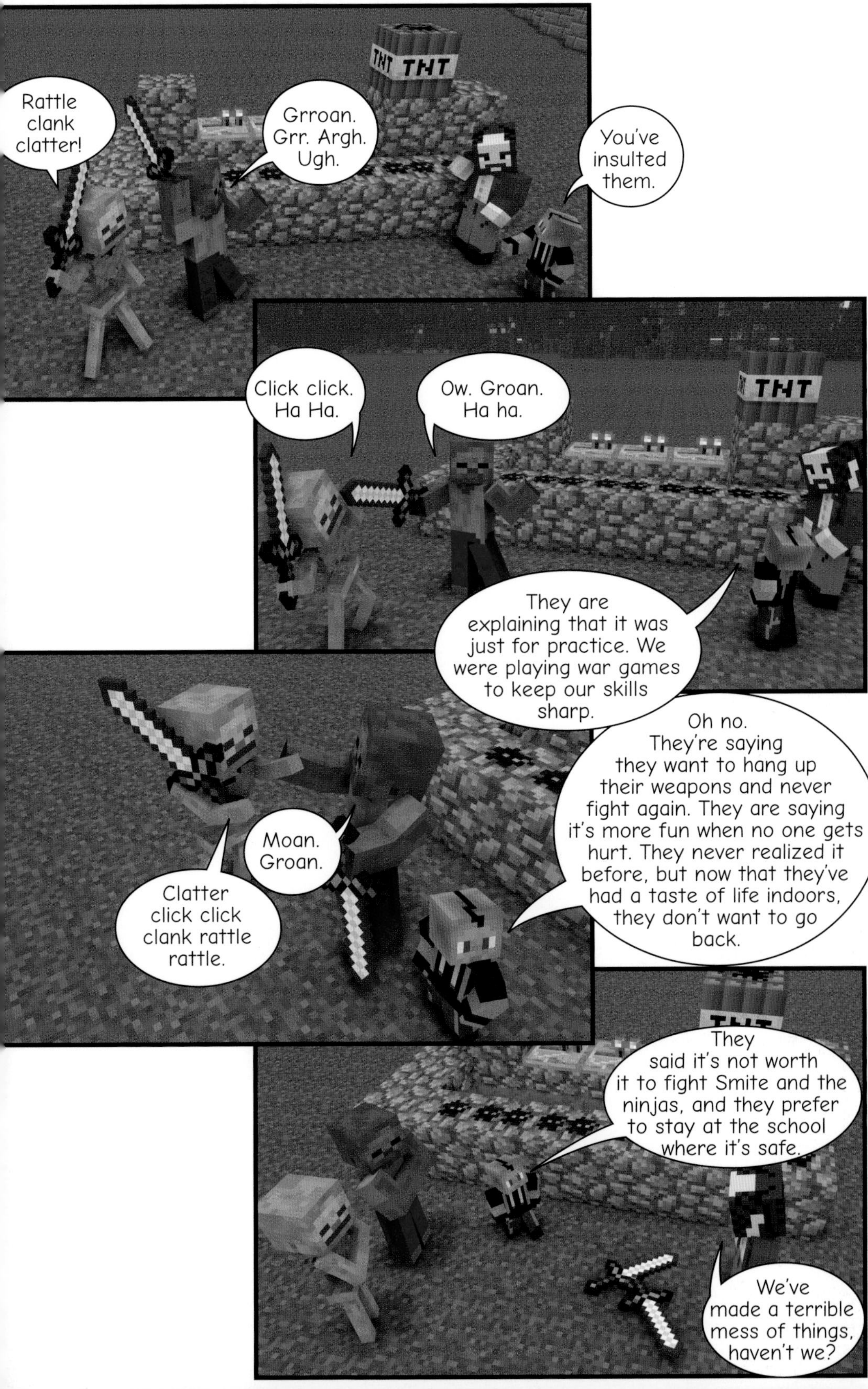

Rattle clank clatter!
Grroan. Grr. Argh. Ugh.
You've insulted them.
Click click. Ha Ha.
Ow. Groan. Ha ha.
They are explaining that it was just for practice. We were playing war games to keep our skills sharp.
Moan. Groan.
Clatter click click clank rattle rattle.
Oh no. They're saying they want to hang up their weapons and never fight again. They are saying it's more fun when no one gets hurt. They never realized it before, but now that they've had a taste of life indoors, they don't want to go back.
They said it's not worth it to fight Smite and the ninjas, and they prefer to stay at the school where it's safe.
We've made a terrible mess of things, haven't we?

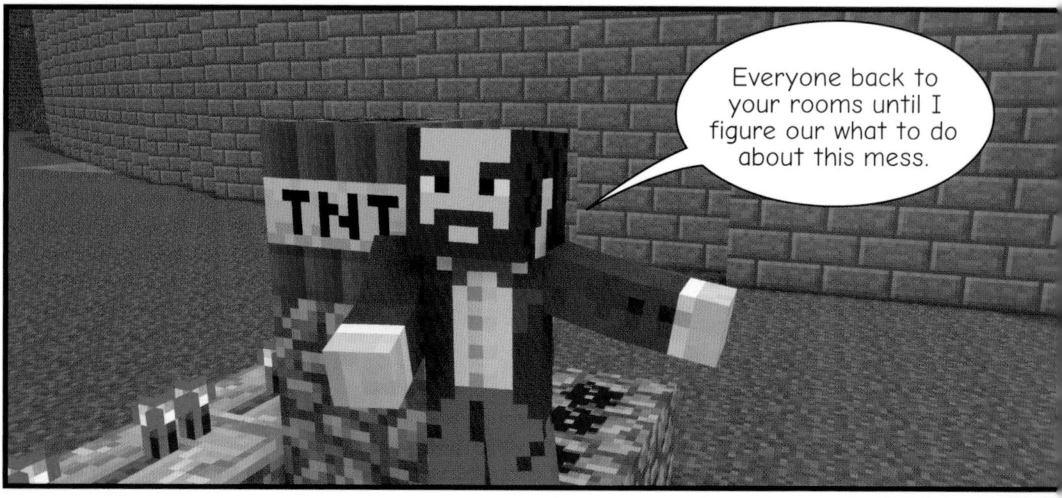
TNT
Everyone back to your rooms until I figure our what to do about this mess.

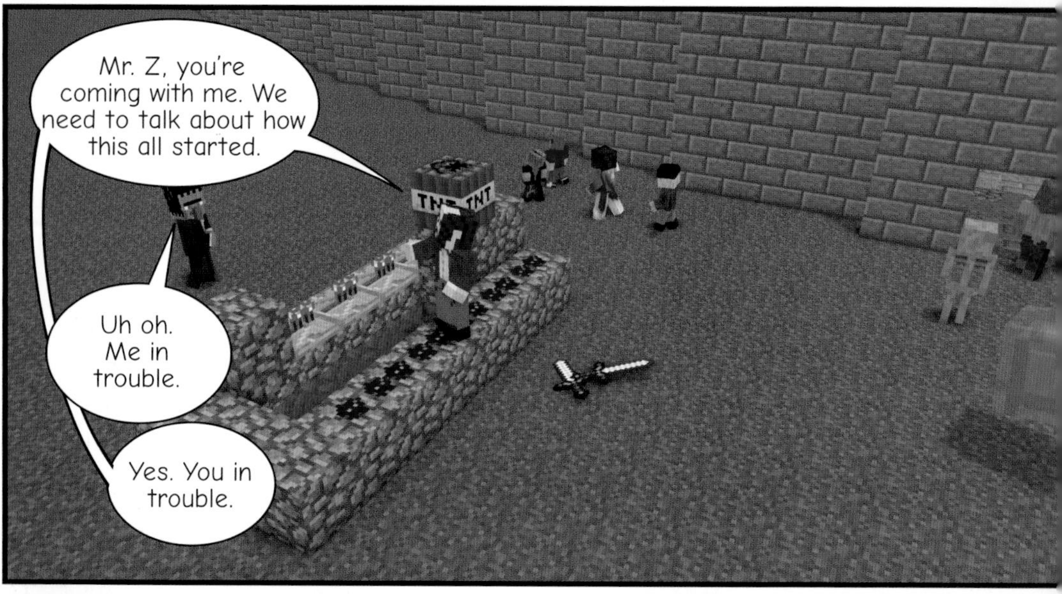
Mr. Z, you're coming with me. We need to talk about how this all started.
Uh oh. Me in trouble.
Yes. You in trouble.

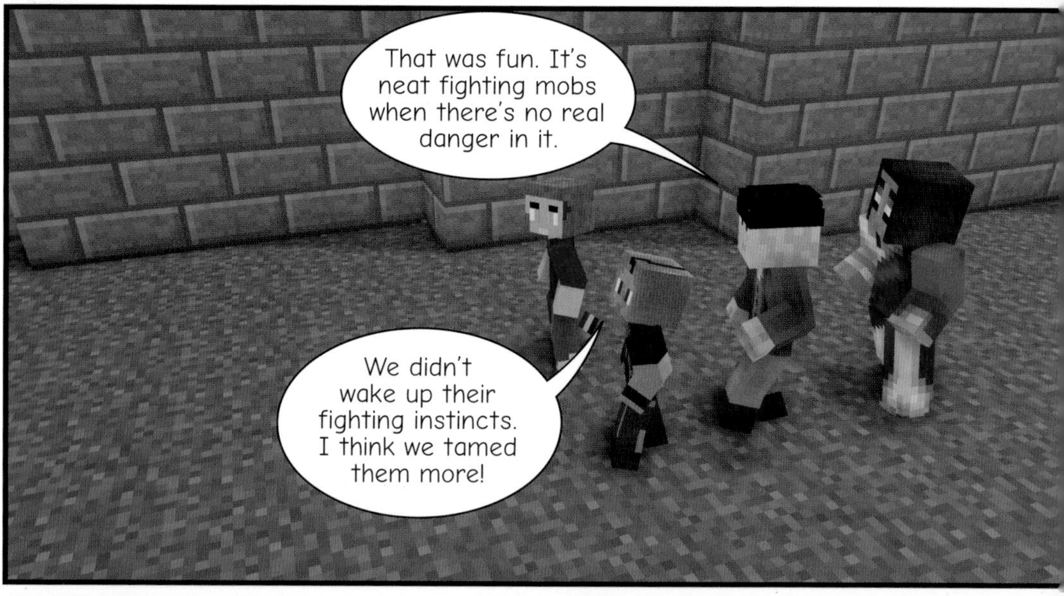
That was fun. It's neat fighting mobs when there's no real danger in it.
We didn't wake up their fighting instincts. I think we tamed them more!

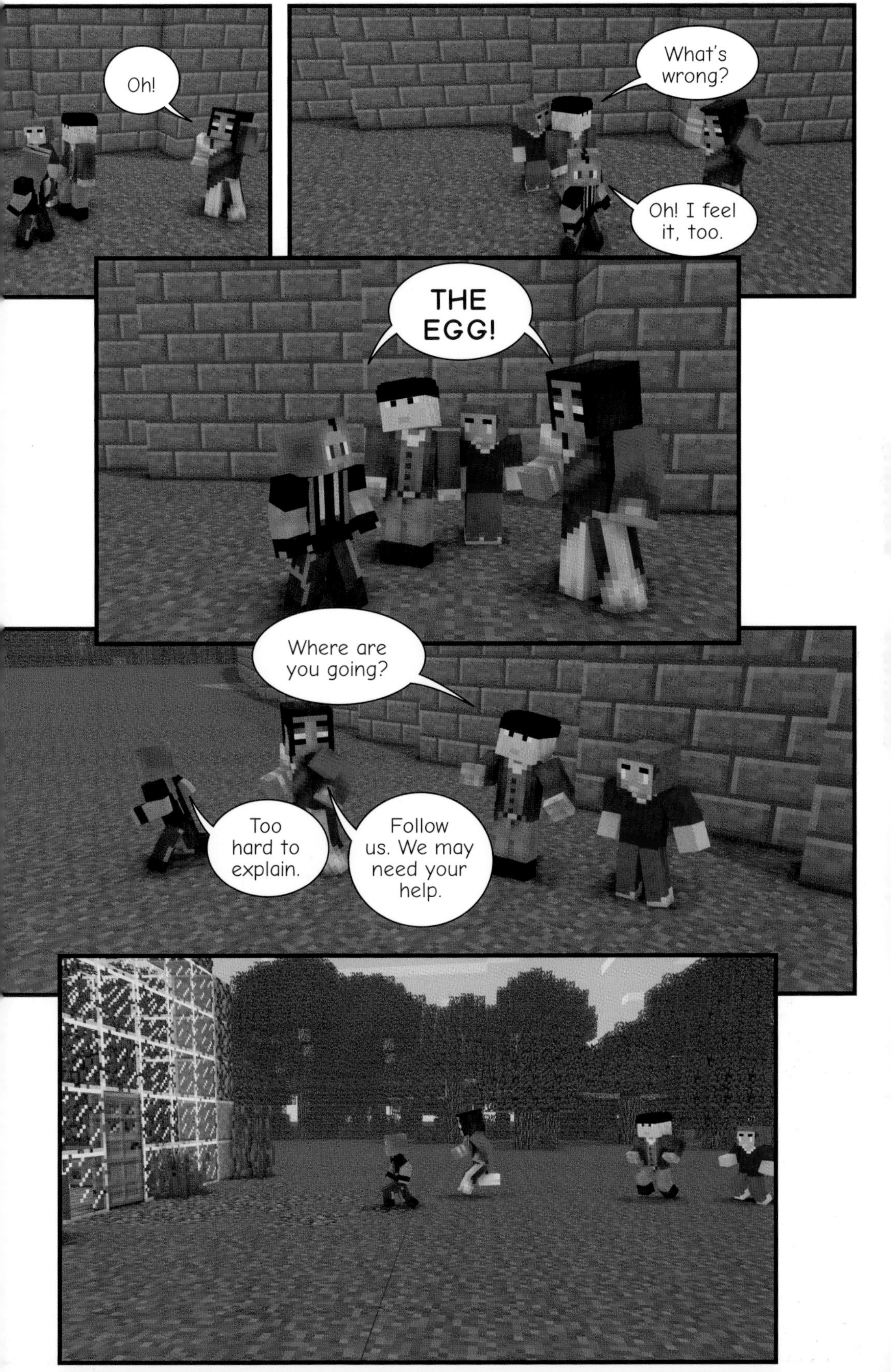
Oh!
What's wrong?
Oh! I feel it, too.
THE EGG!
Where are you going?
Too hard to explain.
Follow us. We may need your help.

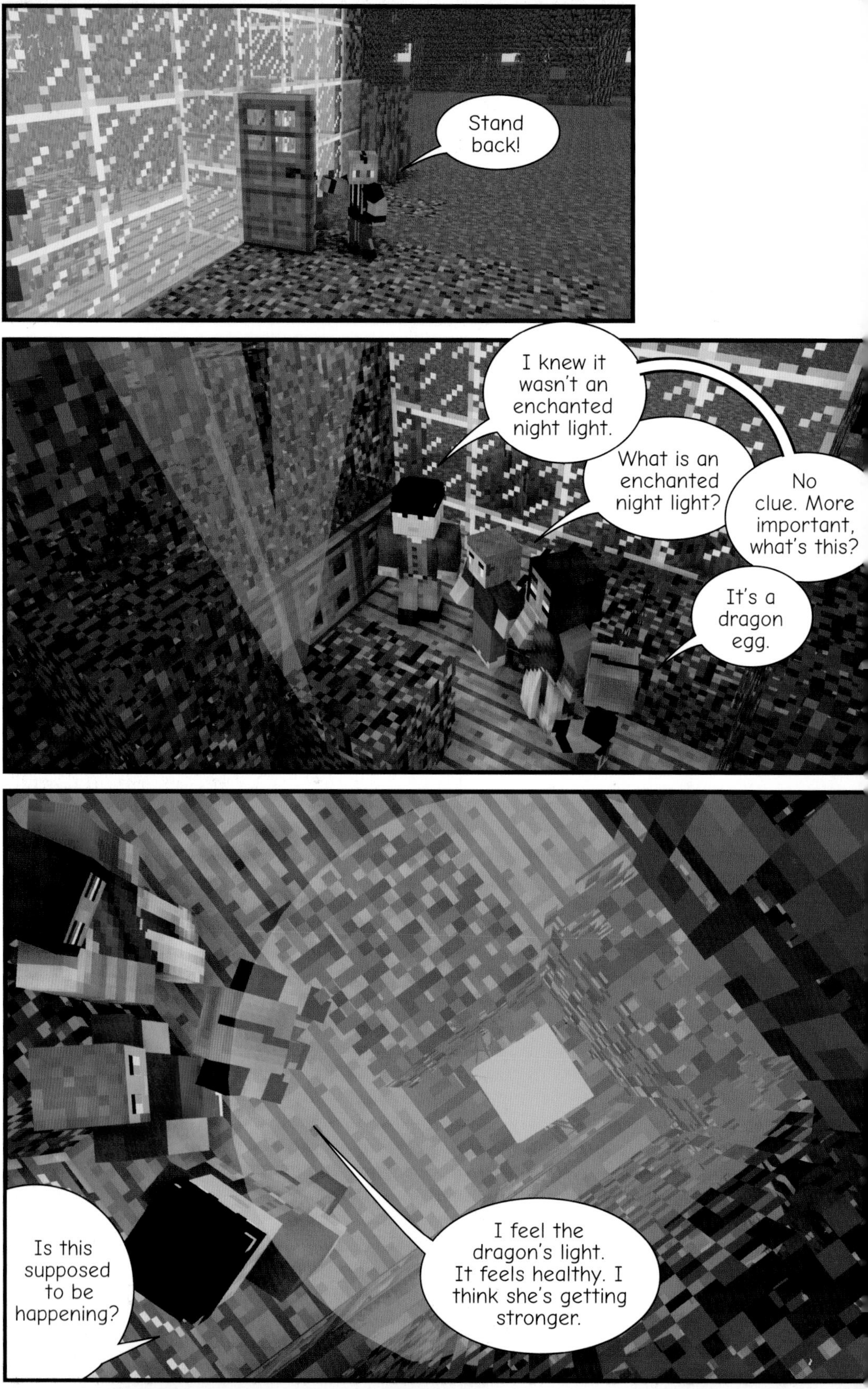
Stand back!
I knew it wasn't an enchanted night light.
What is an enchanted night light?
No clue. More important, what's this?
It's a dragon egg.
Is this supposed to be happening?
I feel the dragon's light. It feels healthy. I think she's getting stronger.

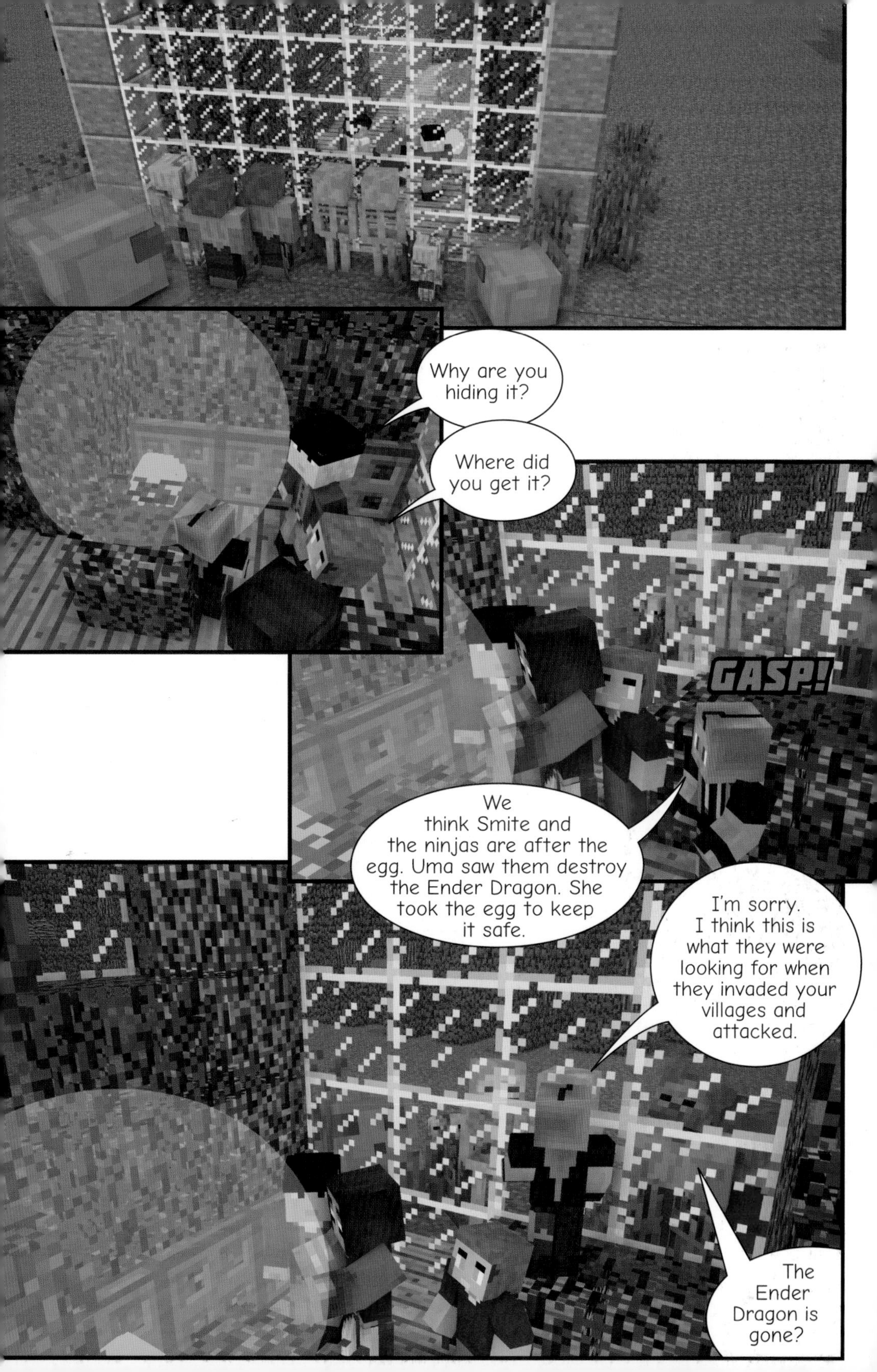
Why are you hiding it?
Where did you get it?
GASP!
We think Smite and the ninjas are after the egg. Uma saw them destroy the Ender Dragon. She took the egg to keep it safe.
I'm sorry. I think this is what they were looking for when they invaded your villages and attacked.
The Ender Dragon is gone?

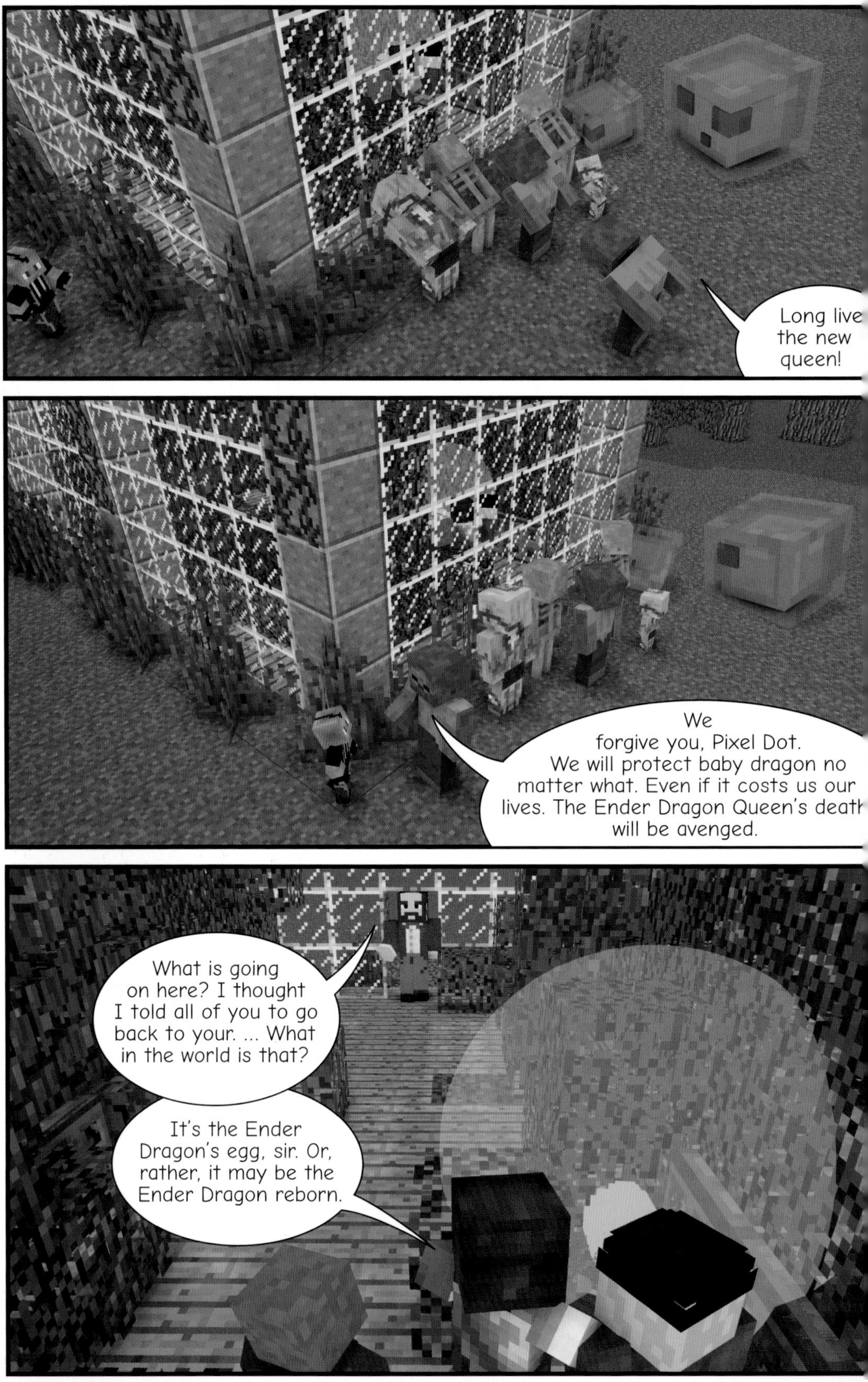
Long live the new queen!
We forgive you, Pixel Dot. We will protect baby dragon no matter what. Even if it costs us our lives. The Ender Dragon Queen's death will be avenged.
What is going on here? I thought I told all of you to go back to your. ... What in the world is that?
It's the Ender Dragon's egg, sir. Or, rather, it may be the Ender Dragon reborn.

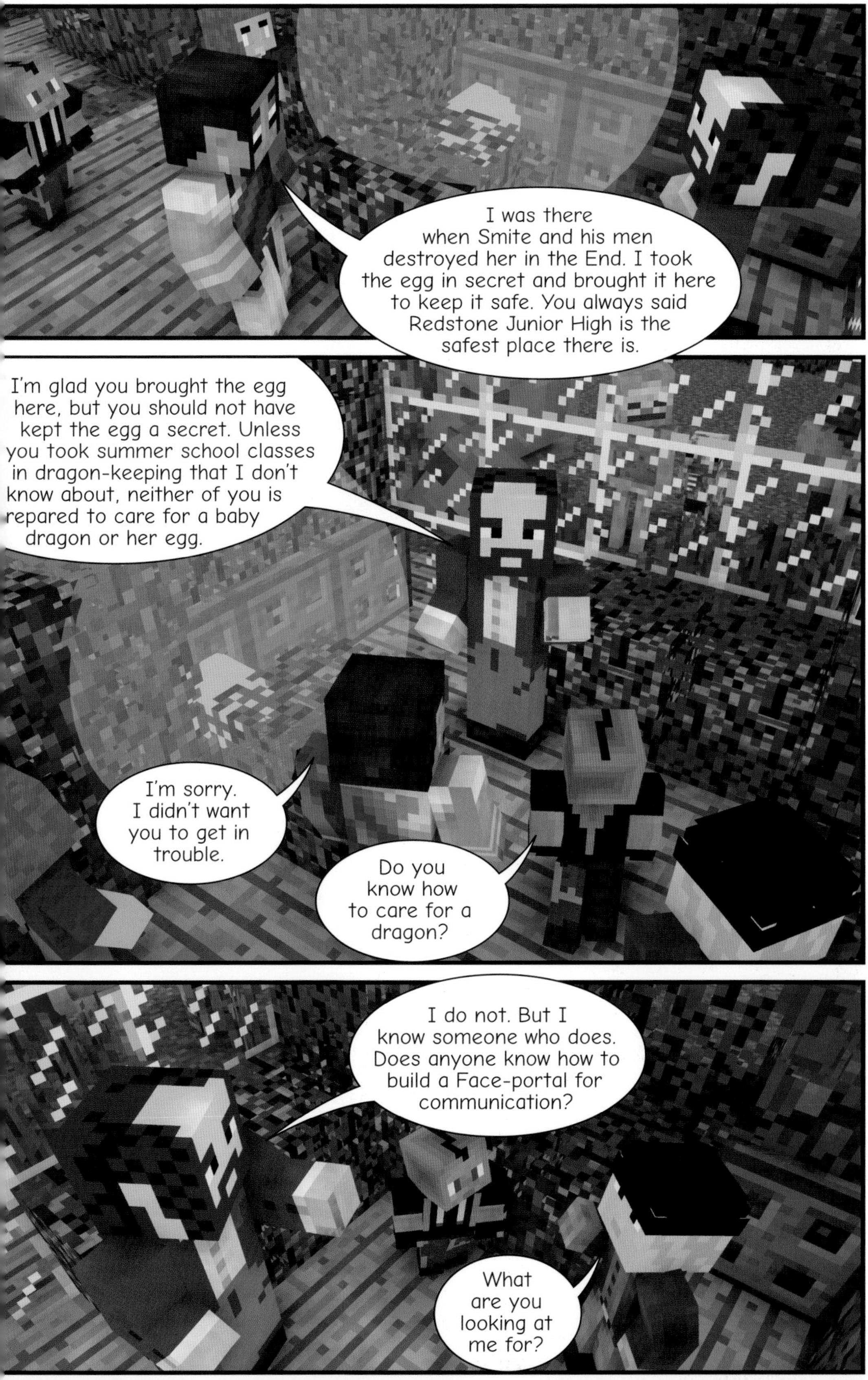

I was there when Smite and his men destroyed her in the End. I took the egg in secret and brought it here to keep it safe. You always said Redstone Junior High is the safest place there is.
I'm glad you brought the egg here, but you should not have kept the egg a secret. Unless you took summer school classes in dragon-keeping that I don't know about, neither of you is repared to care for a baby dragon or her egg.
I'm sorry. I didn't want you to get in trouble.
Do you know how to care for a dragon?
I do not. But I know someone who does. Does anyone know how to build a Face-portal for communication?
What are you looking at me for?

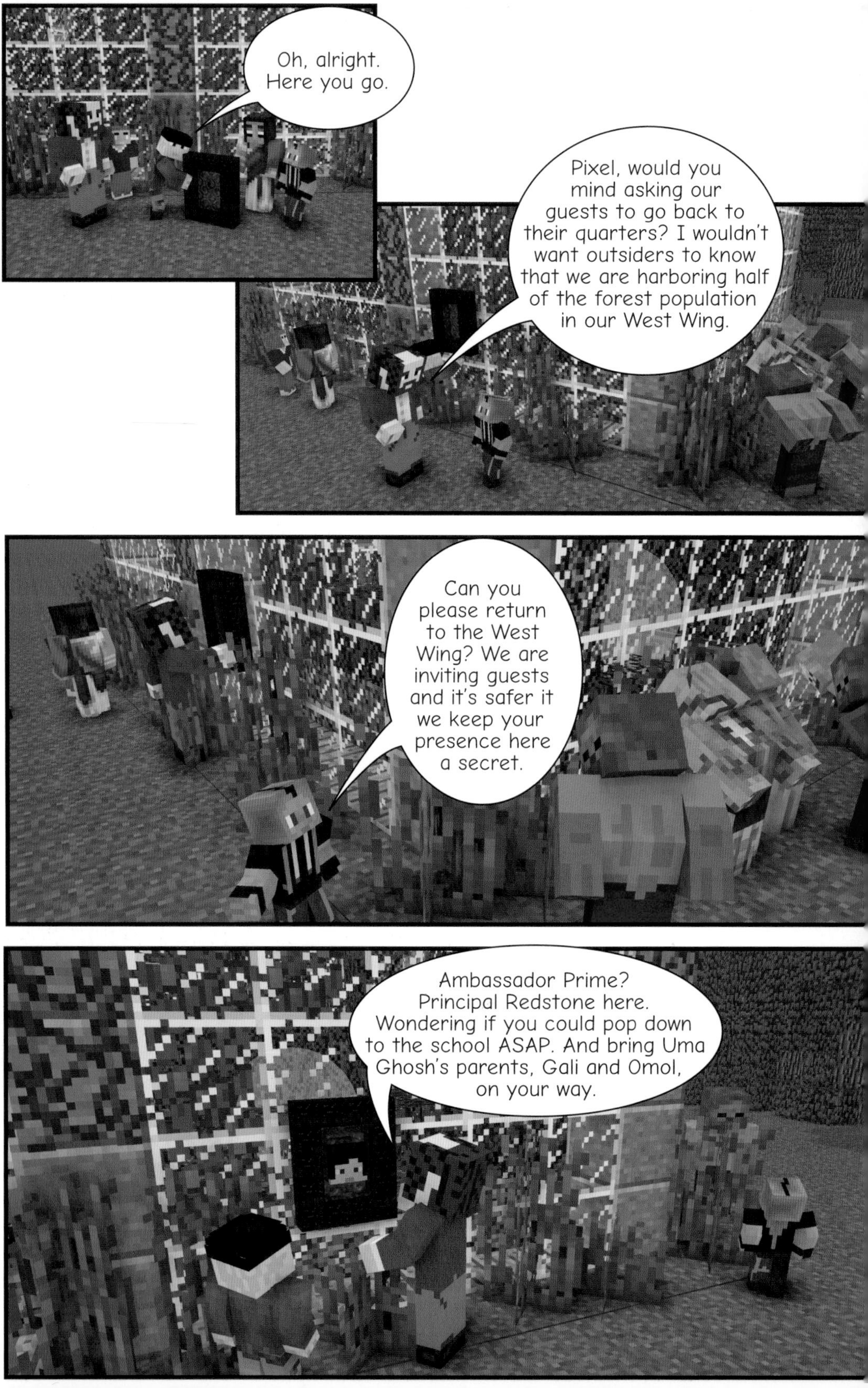
Oh, alright. Here you go.
Pixel, would you mind asking our guests to go back to their quarters? I wouldn't want outsiders to know that we are harboring half of the forest population in our West Wing.
Can you please return to the West Wing? We are inviting guests and it's safer it we keep your presence here a secret.
Ambassador Prime? Principal Redstone here. Wondering if you could pop down to the school ASAP. And bring Uma Ghosh's parents, Gali and Omol, on your way.

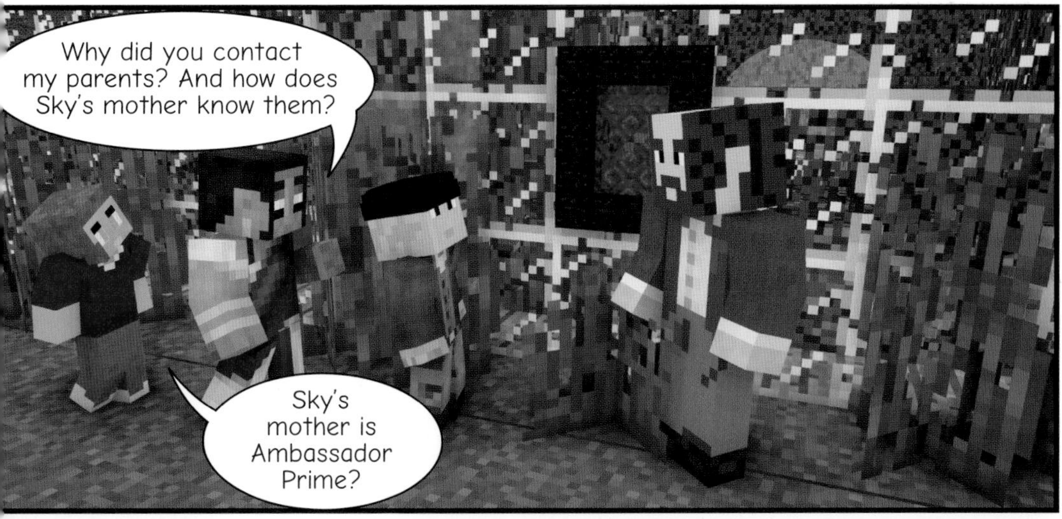
Why did you contact my parents? And how does Sky's mother know them?
Sky's mother is Ambassador Prime?

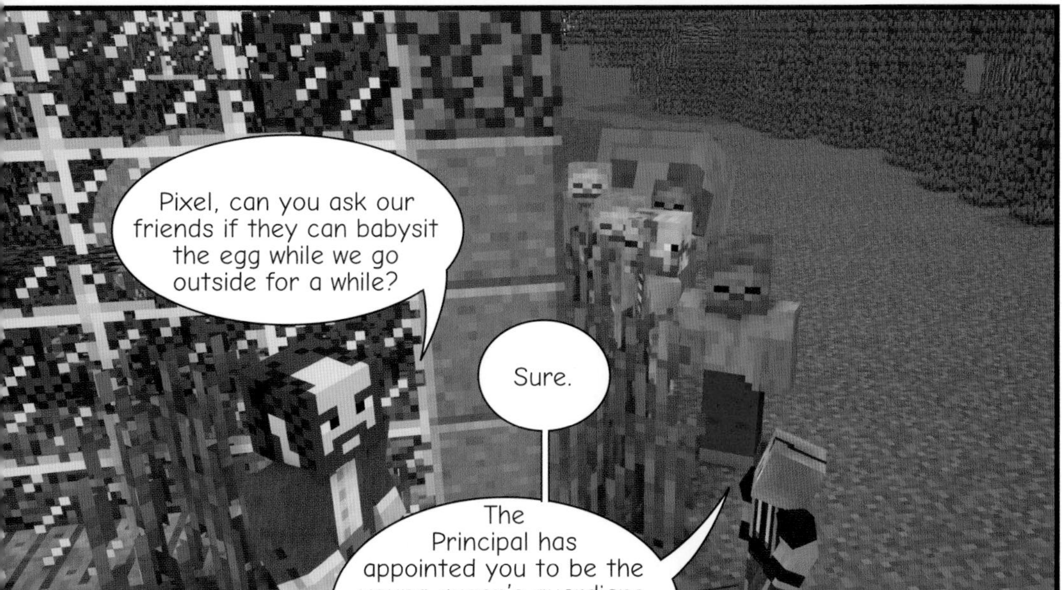
Pixel, can you ask our friends if they can babysit the egg while we go outside for a while?
Sure.
The Principal has appointed you to be the young queen's guardians. Please watch over the egg in the greenhouse, and let me know if there is any trouble.

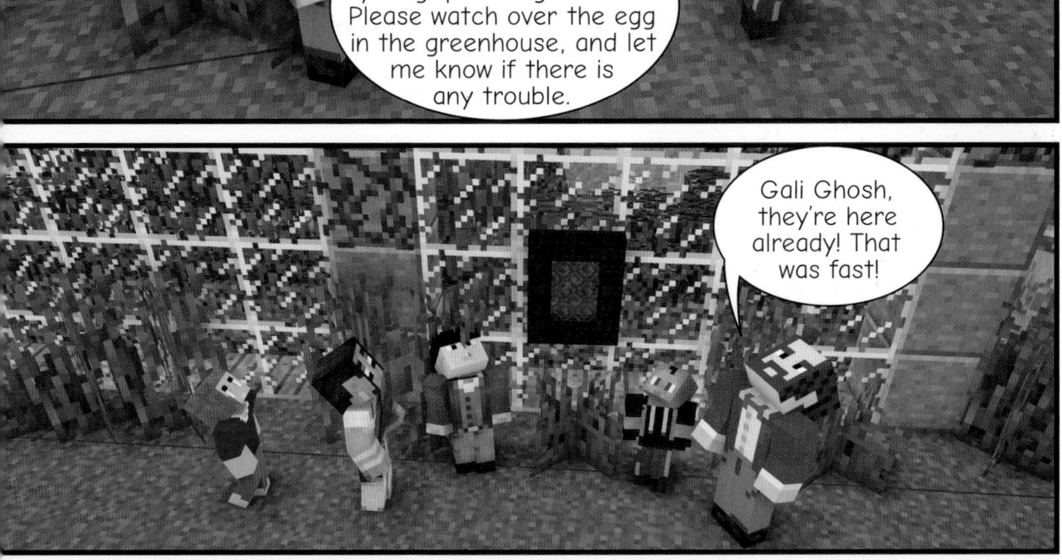
Gali Ghosh, they're here already! That was fast!

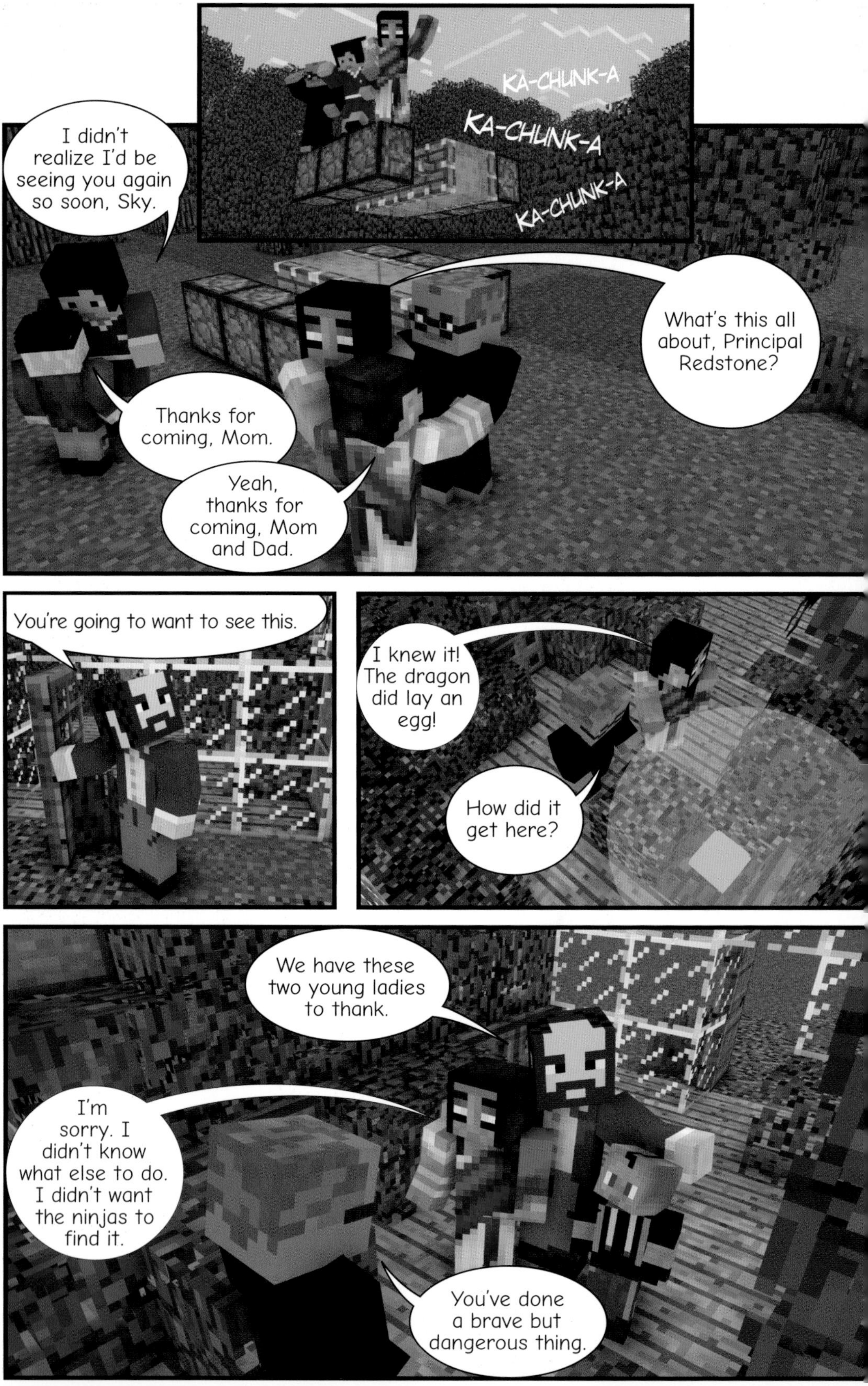
KA-CHUNK-A
KA-CHUNK-A
KA-CHUNK-A
I didn't realize I'd be seeing you again so soon, Sky.
What's this all about, Principal Redstone?
Thanks for coming, Mom.
Yeah, thanks for coming, Mom and Dad.
You're going to want to see this.
I knew it! The dragon did lay an egg!
How did it get here?
We have these two young ladies to thank.
I'm sorry. I didn't know what else to do. I didn't want the ninjas to find it.
You've done a brave but dangerous thing.

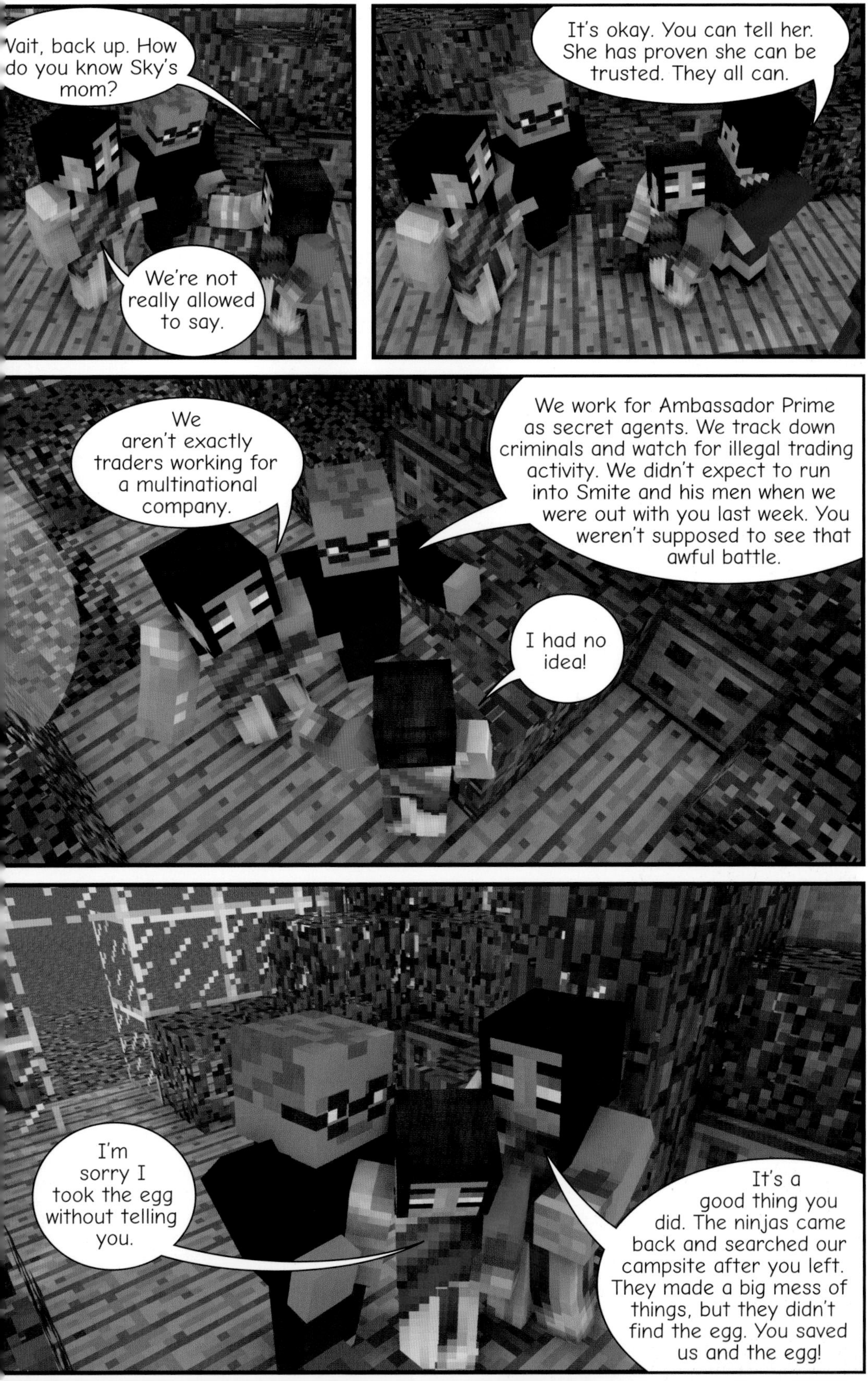
Vait, back up. How do you know Sky's mom?
We're not really allowed to say.
It's okay. You can tell her. She has proven she can be trusted. They all can.
We aren't exactly traders working for a multinational company.
We work for Ambassador Prime as secret agents. We track down criminals and watch for illegal trading activity. We didn't expect to run into Smite and his men when we were out with you last week. You weren't supposed to see that awful battle.
I had no idea!
I'm sorry I took the egg without telling you.
It's a good thing you did. The ninjas came back and searched our campsite after you left. They made a big mess of things, but they didn't find the egg. You saved us and the egg!

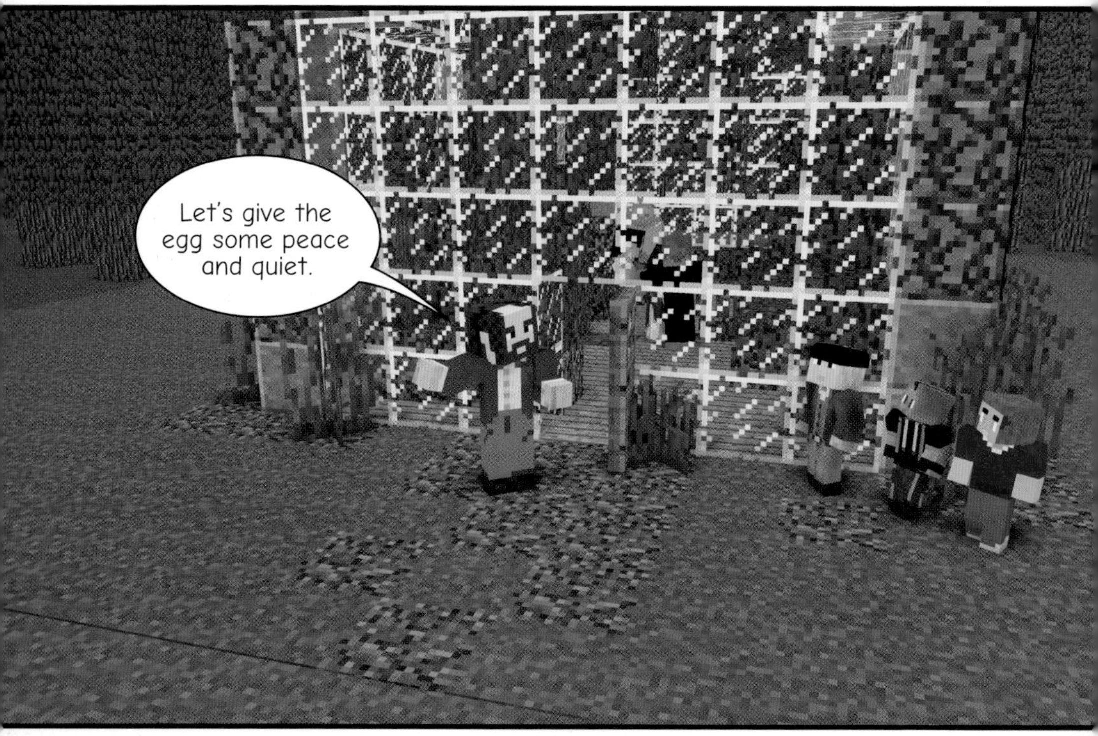
Let's give the egg some peace and quiet.

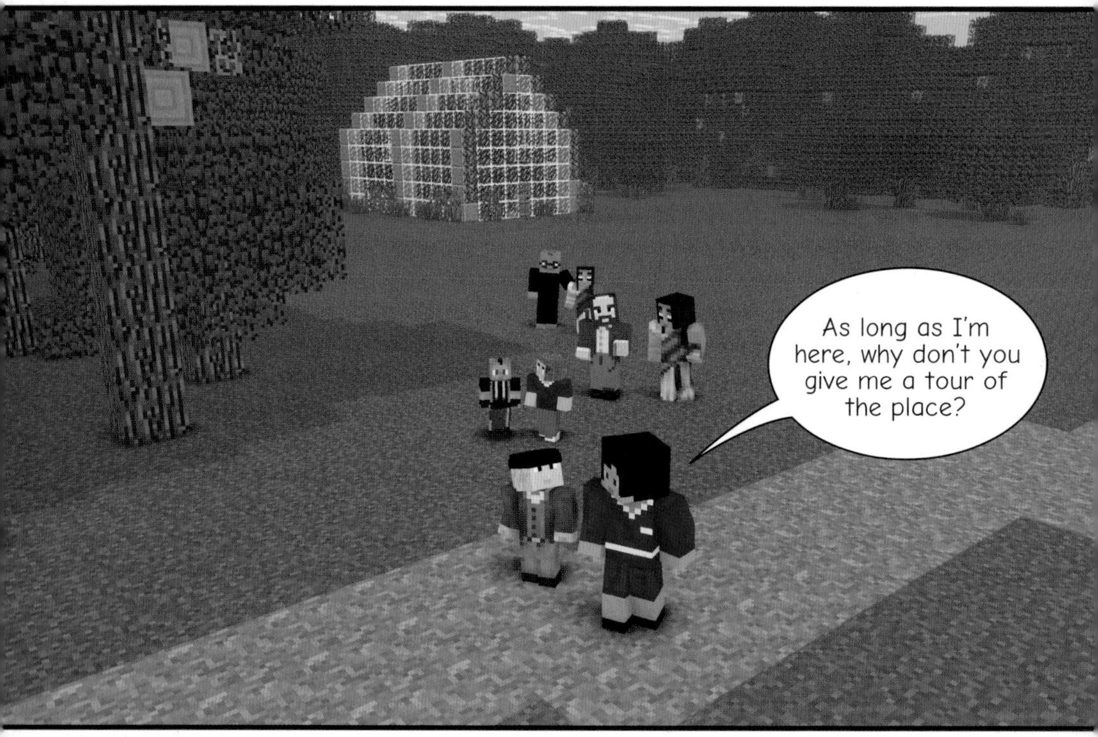
As long as I'm here, why don't you give me a tour of the place?

CHAPTER 7

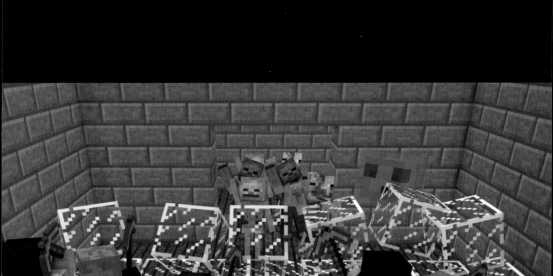

A COMMON
ENEMY

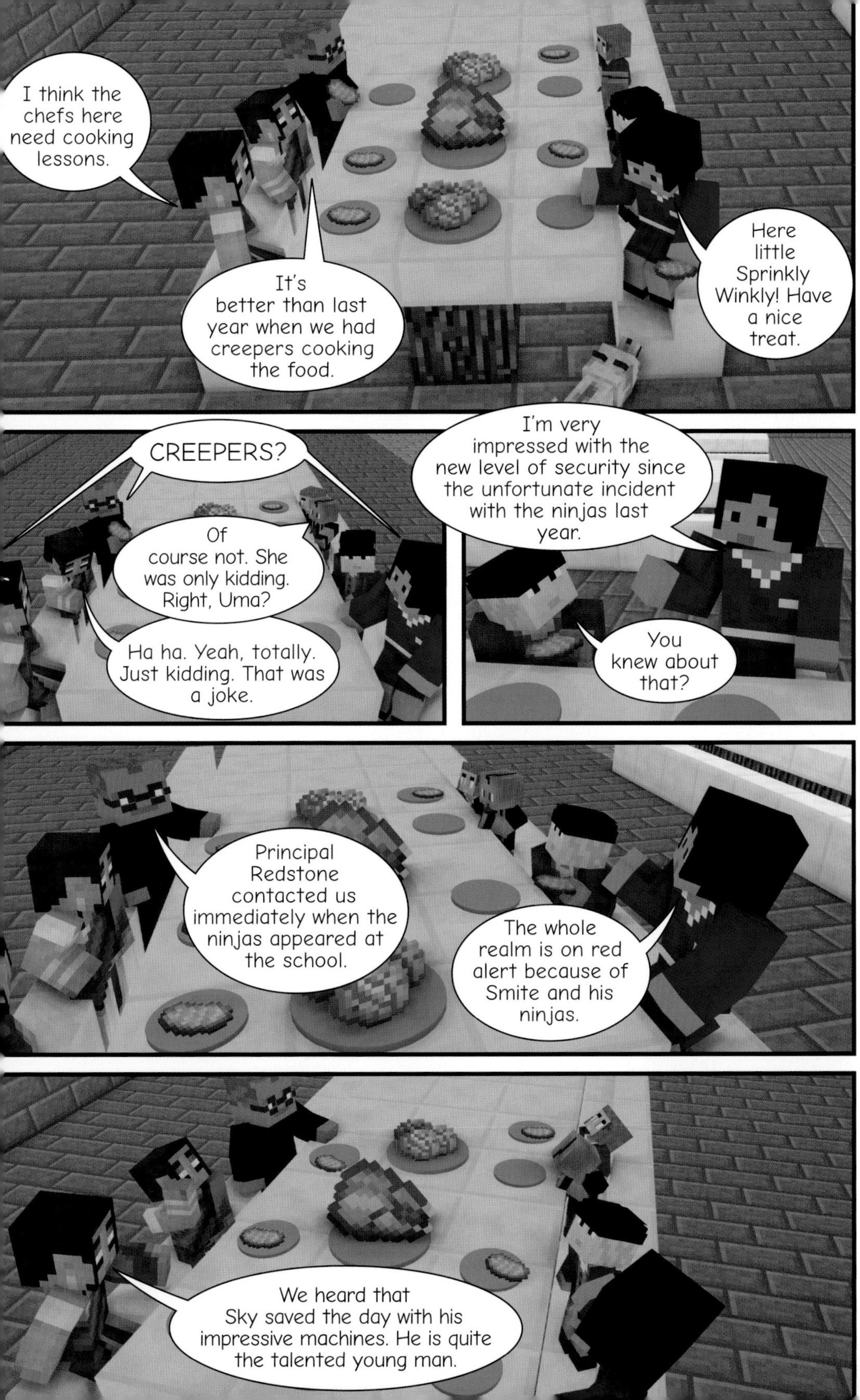
I think the chefs here need cooking lessons.
It's better than last year when we had creepers cooking the food.
Here little Sprinkly Winkly! Have a nice treat.
CREEPERS?
Of course not. She was only kidding. Right, Uma?
Ha ha. Yeah, totally. Just kidding. That was a joke.
I'm very impressed with the new level of security since the unfortunate incident with the ninjas last year.
You knew about that?
Principal Redstone contacted us immediately when the ninjas appeared at the school.
The whole realm is on red alert because of Smite and his ninjas.
We heard that Sky saved the day with his impressive machines. He is quite the talented young man.

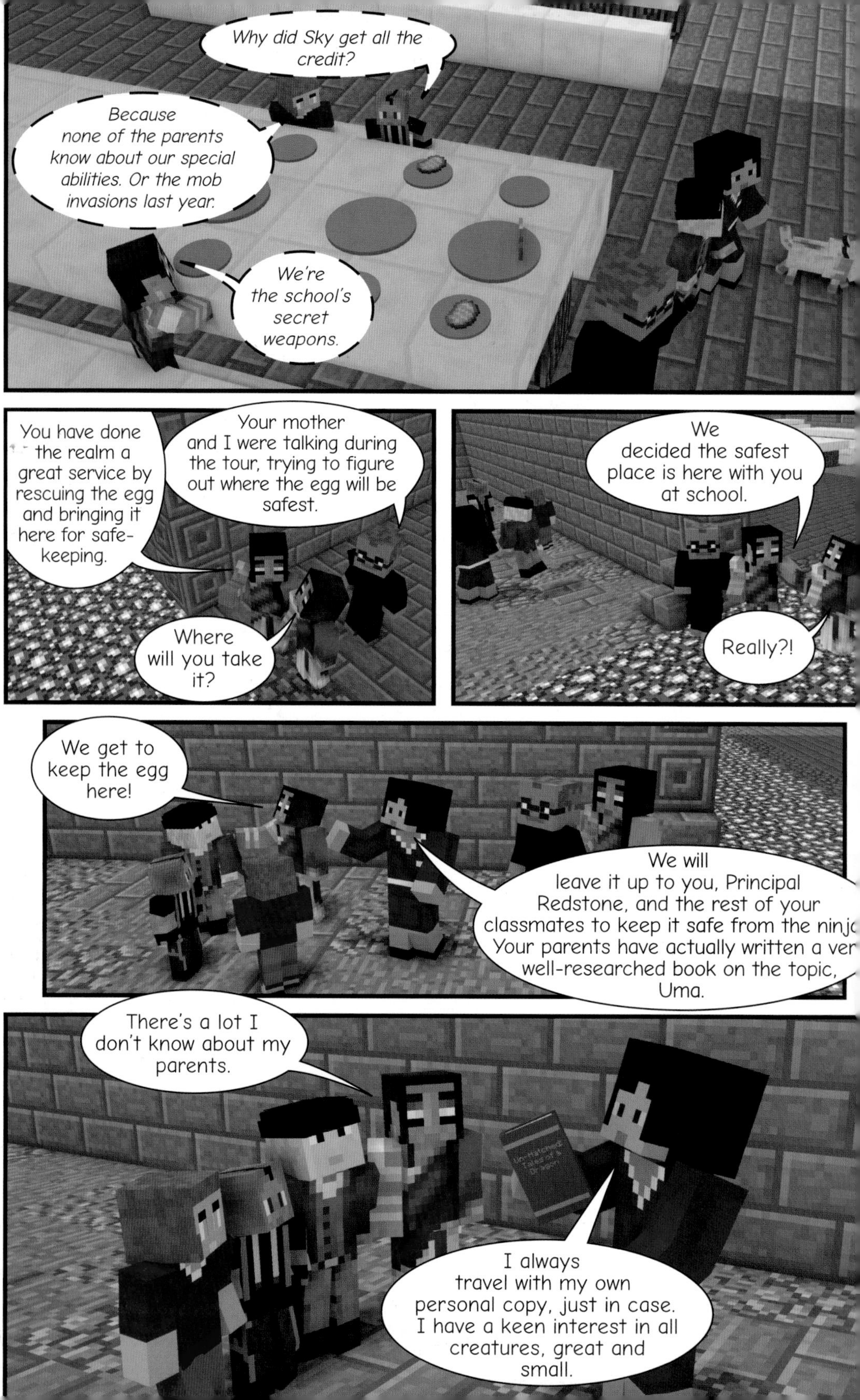
Why did Sky get all the credit?
Because none of the parents know about our special abilities. Or the mob invasions last year.
We're the school's secret weapons.
You have done the realm a great service by rescuing the egg and bringing it here for safe-keeping.
Your mother and I were talking during the tour, trying to figure out where the egg will be safest.
Where will you take it?
We decided the safest place is here with you at school.
Really?!
We get to keep the egg here!
We will leave it up to you, Principal Redstone, and the rest of your classmates to keep it safe from the ninj
Your parents have actually written a ver
well-researched book on the topic, Uma.
There's a lot I don't know about my parents.
I always travel with my own personal copy, just in case. I have a keen interest in all creatures, great and small.

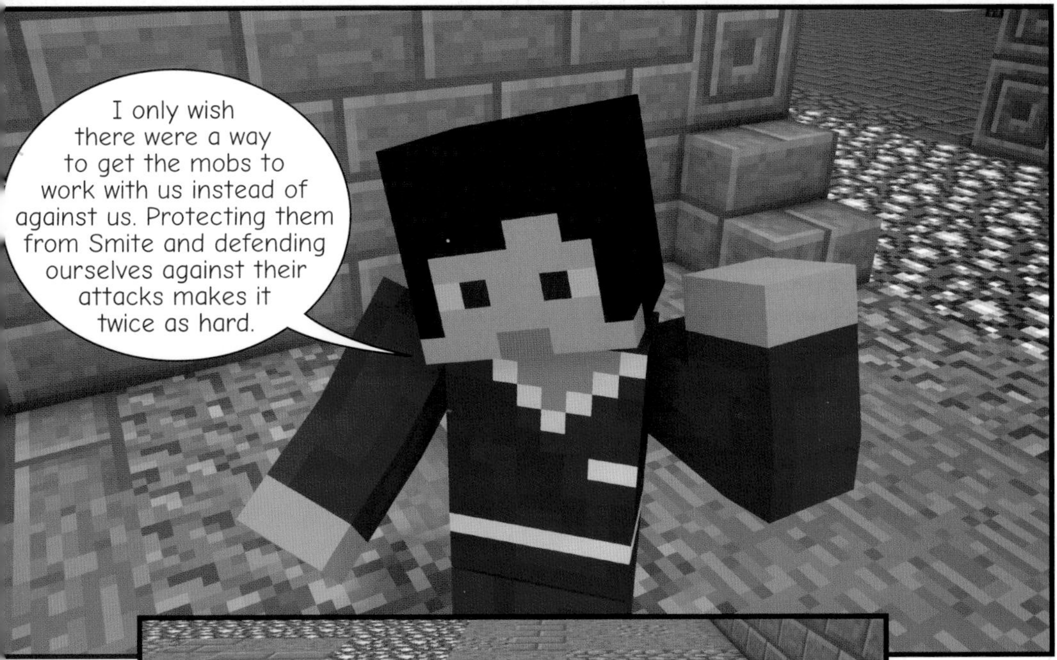
I only wish there were a way to get the mobs to work with us instead of against us. Protecting them from Smite and defending ourselves against their attacks makes it twice as hard.

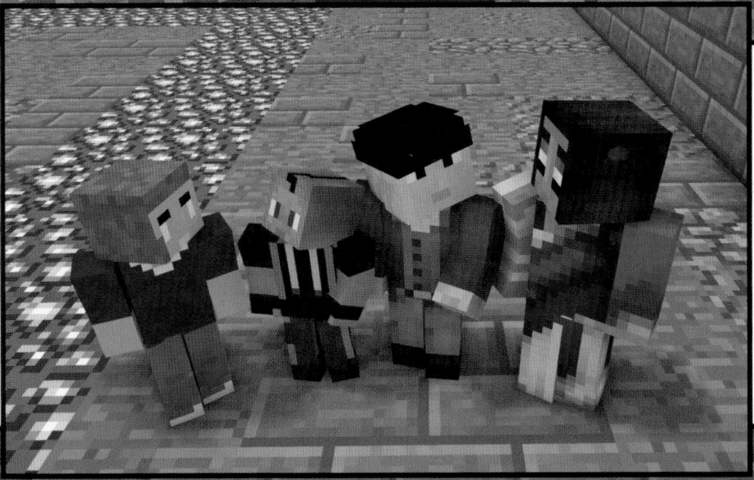

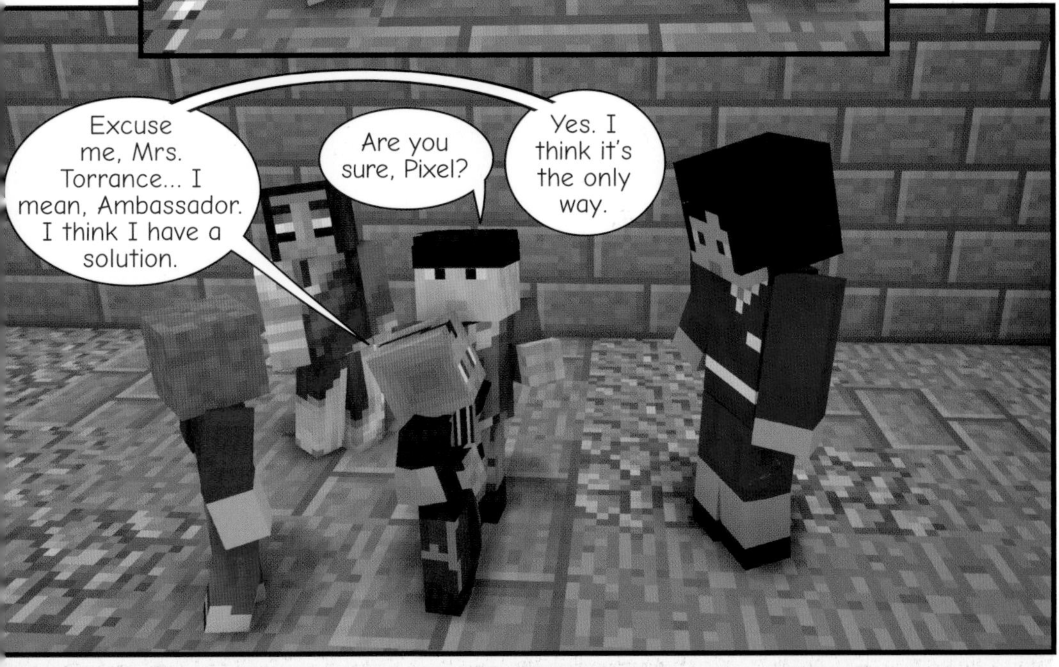
Excuse me, Mrs. Torrance... I mean, Ambassador. I think I have a solution.
Are you sure, Pixel?
Yes. I think it's the only way.

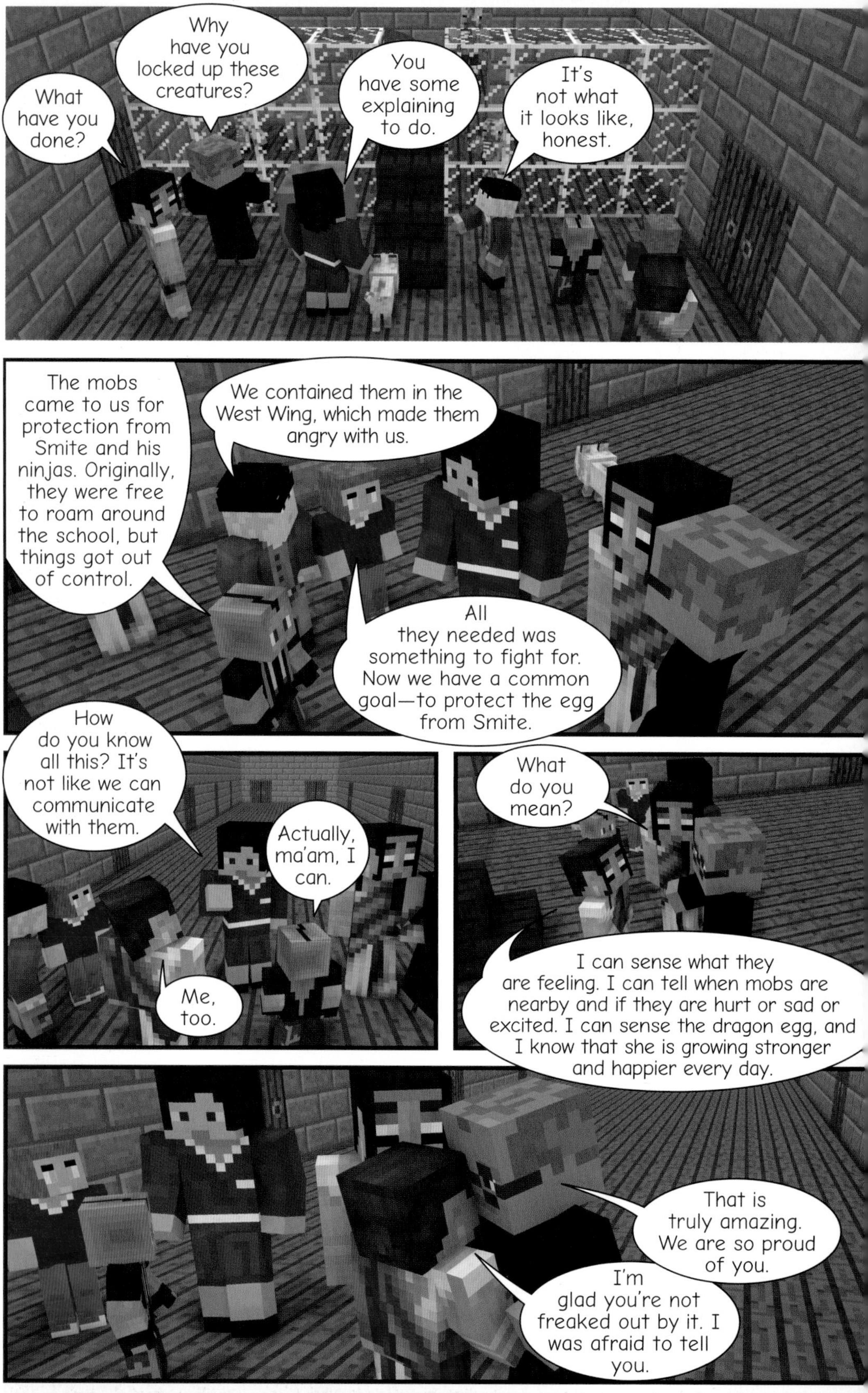
What have you done?
Why have you locked up these creatures?
You have some explaining to do.
It's not what it looks like, honest.
The mobs came to us for protection from Smite and his ninjas. Originally, they were free to roam around the school, but things got out of control.
We contained them in the West Wing, which made them angry with us.
All they needed was something to fight for. Now we have a common goal—to protect the egg from Smite.
How do you know all this? It's not like we can communicate with them.
Actually, ma'am, I can.
Me, too.
What do you mean?
I can sense what they are feeling. I can tell when mobs are nearby and if they are hurt or sad or excited. I can sense the dragon egg, and I know that she is growing stronger and happier every day.
That is truly amazing. We are so proud of you.
I'm glad you're not freaked out by it. I was afraid to tell you.

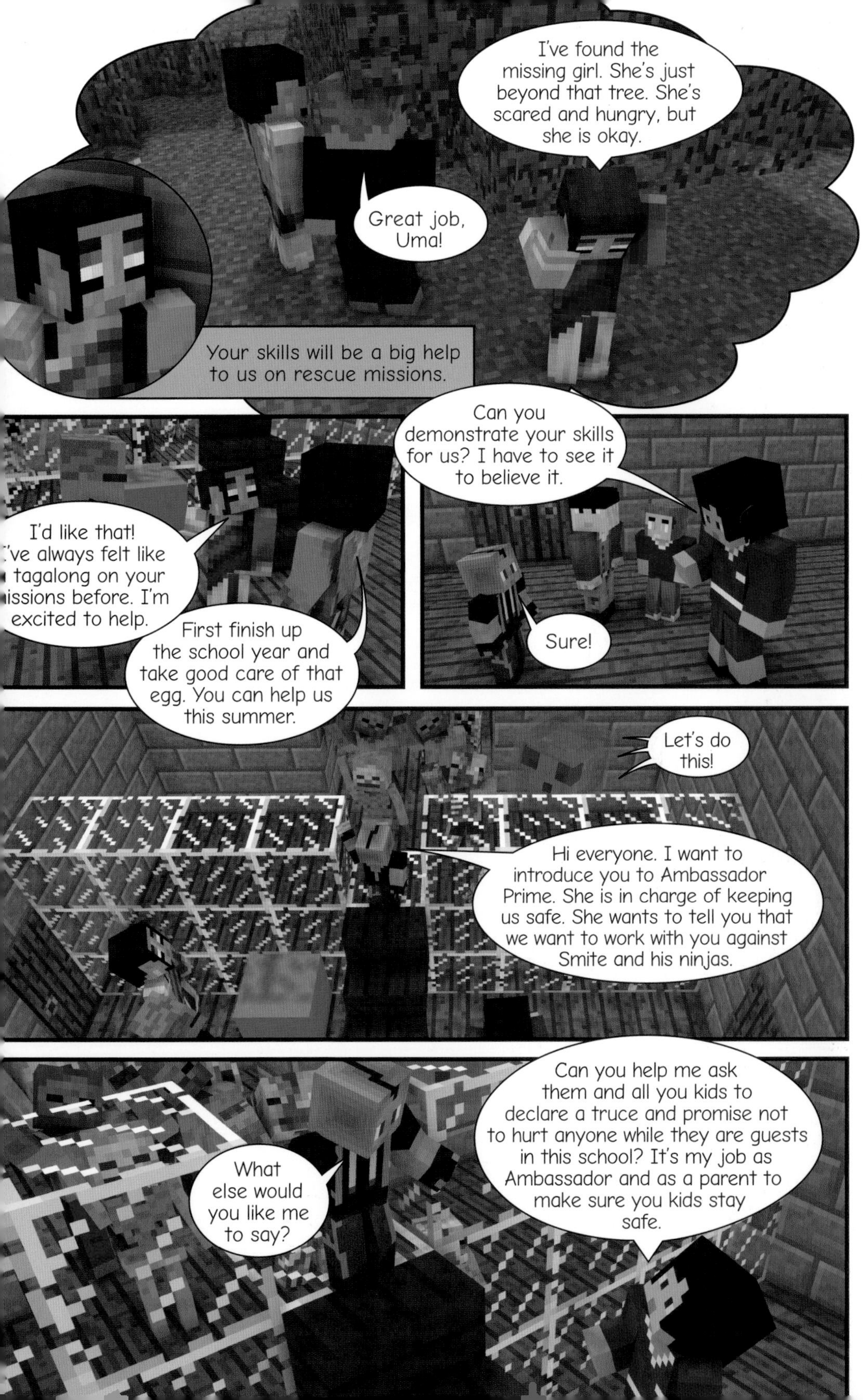
I've found the missing girl. She's just beyond that tree. She's scared and hungry, but she is okay.
Great job, Uma!
Your skills will be a big help to us on rescue missions.
I'd like that! 've always felt like tagalong on your issions before. I'm excited to help.
First finish up the school year and take good care of that egg. You can help us this summer.
Can you demonstrate your skills for us? I have to see it to believe it.
Sure!
Let's do this!
Hi everyone. I want to introduce you to Ambassador Prime. She is in charge of keeping us safe. She wants to tell you that we want to work with you against Smite and his ninjas.
What else would you like me to say?
Can you help me ask them and all you kids to declare a truce and promise not to hurt anyone while they are guests in this school? It's my job as Ambassador and as a parent to make sure you kids stay safe.

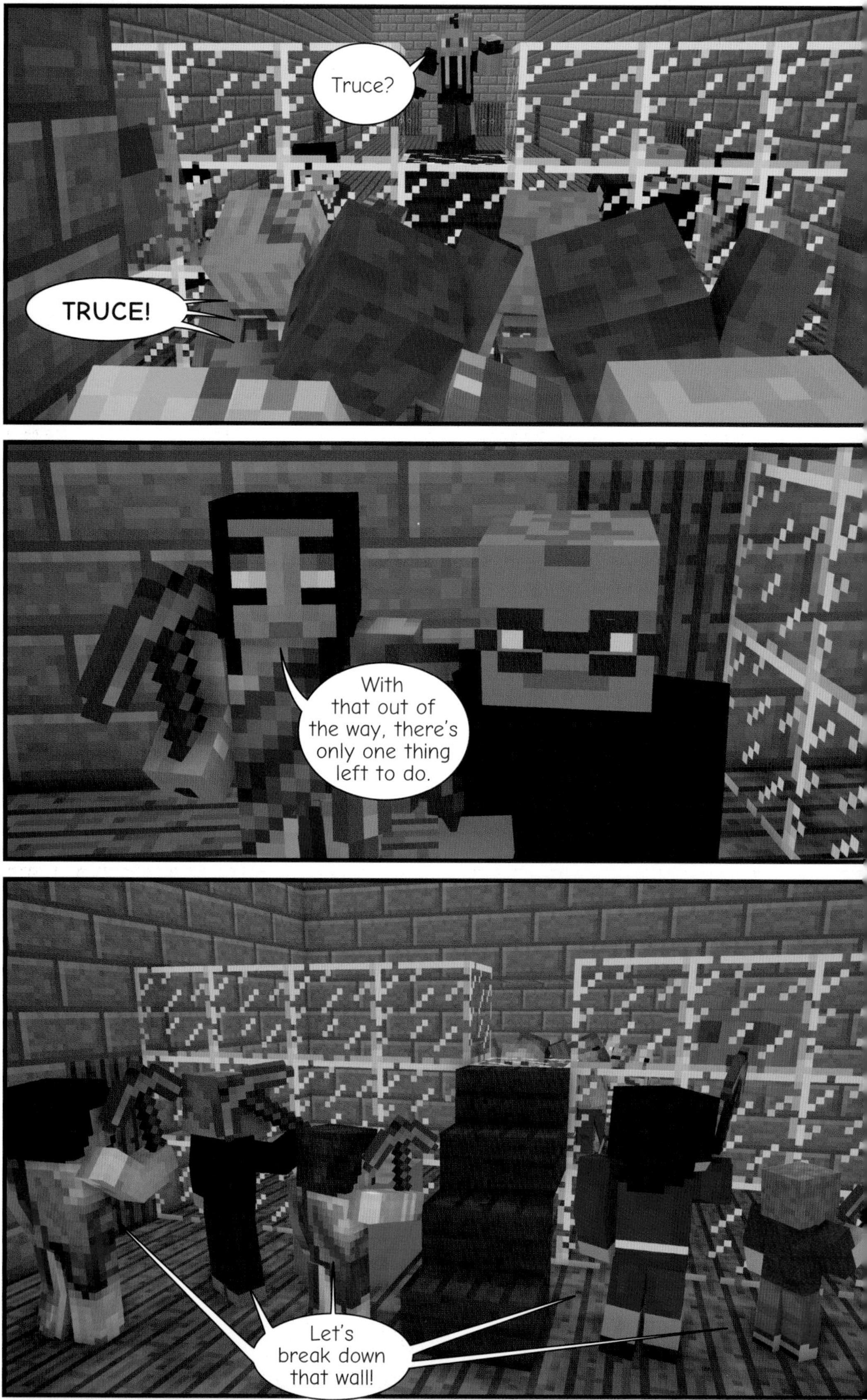
Truce?
TRUCE!
With that out of the way, there's only one thing left to do.
Let's break down that wall!

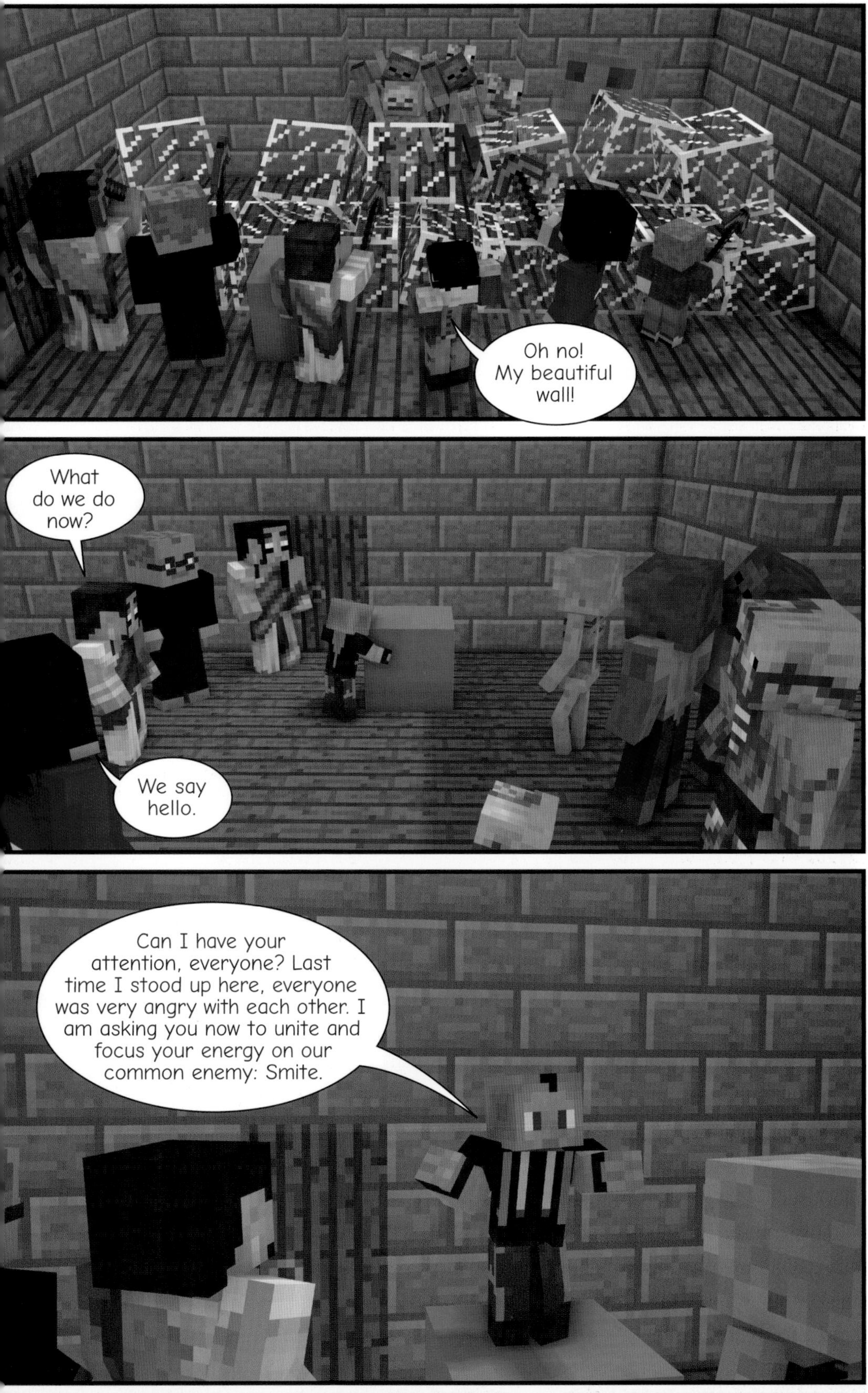
Oh no! My beautiful wall!
What do we do now?
We say hello.
Can I have your attention, everyone? Last time I stood up here, everyone was very angry with each other. I am asking you now to unite and focus your energy on our common enemy: Smite.

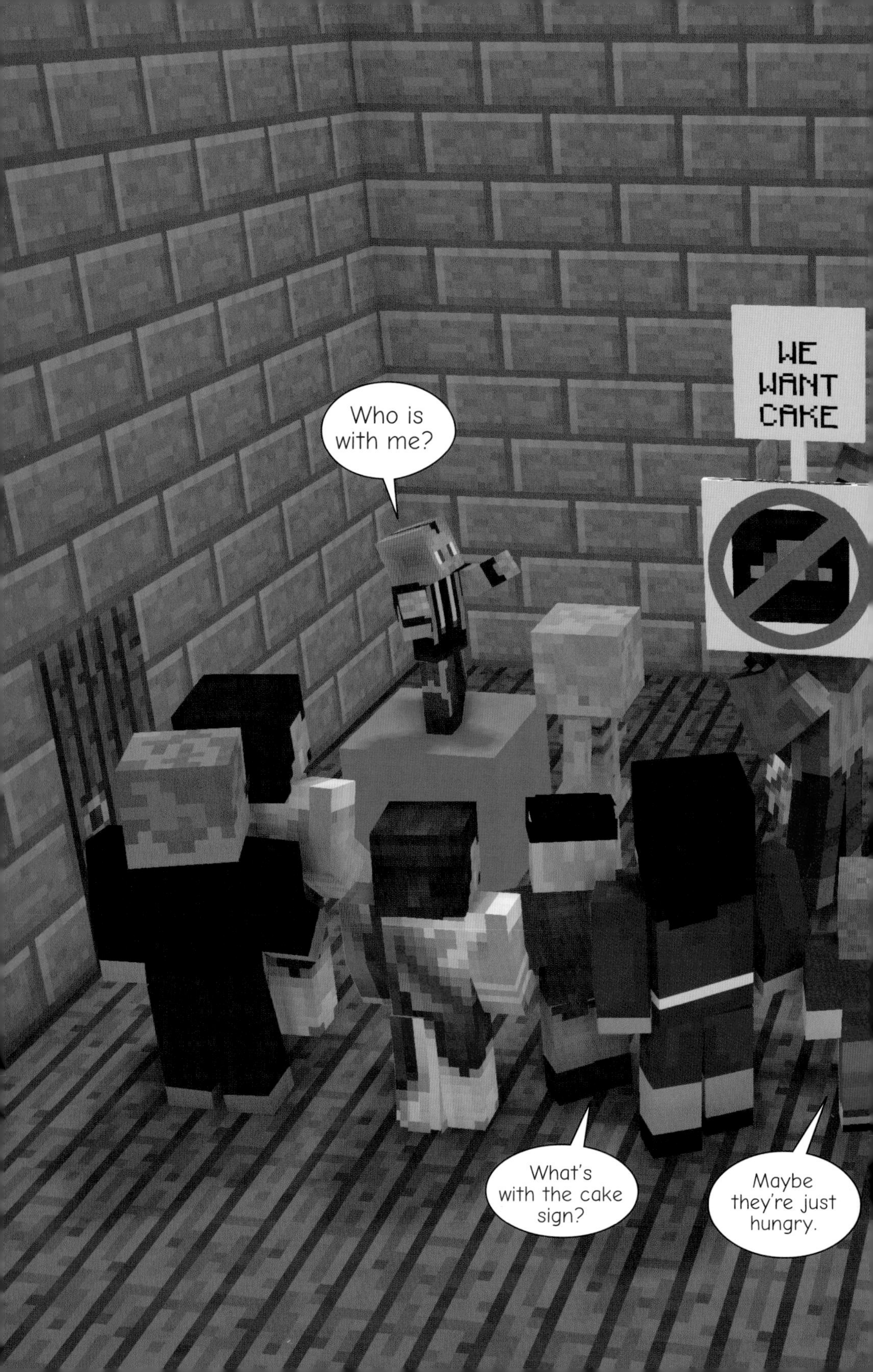
WE WANT CAKE
Who is with me?
What's with the cake sign?
Maybe they're just hungry.

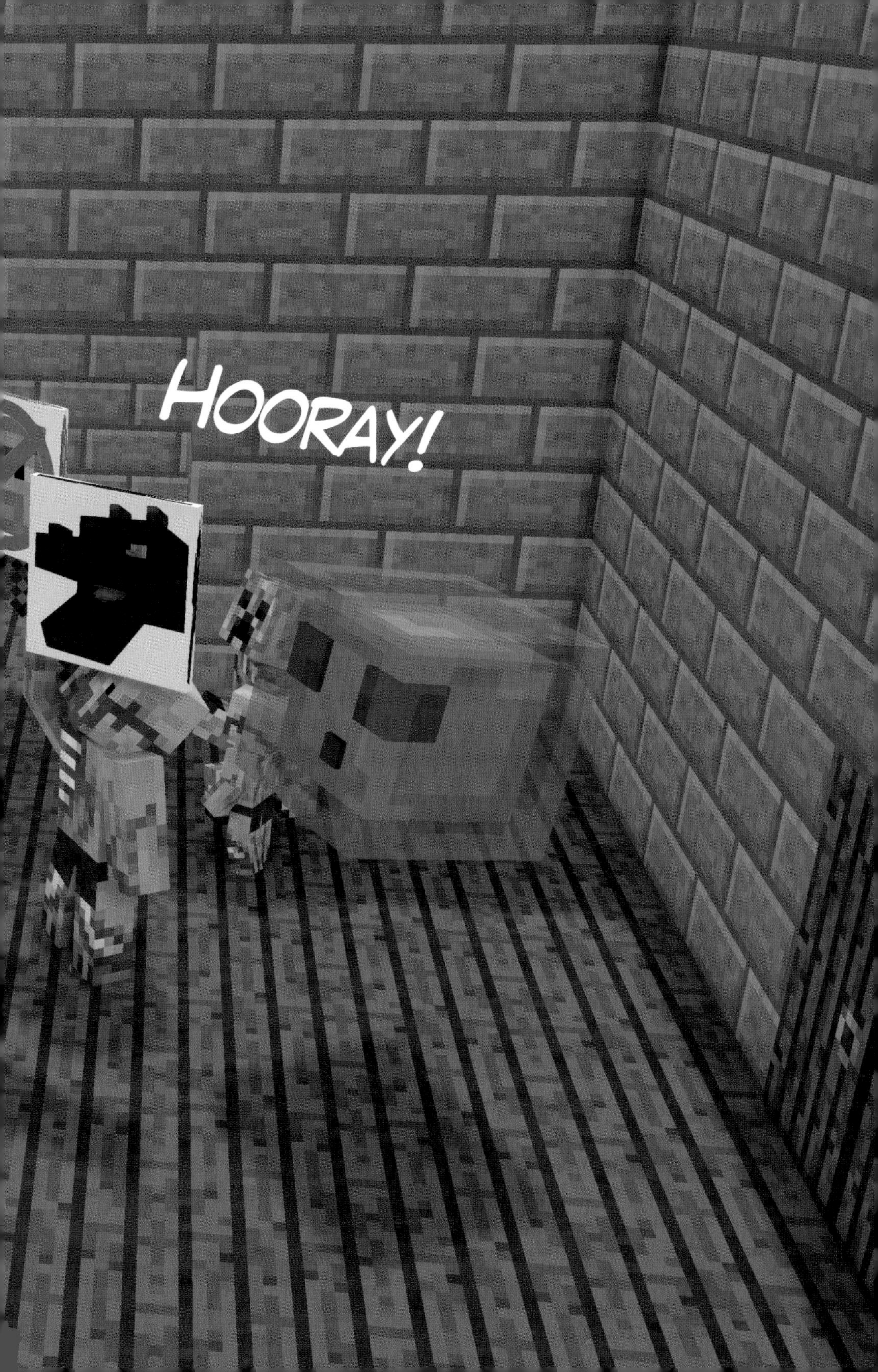
HOORAY!

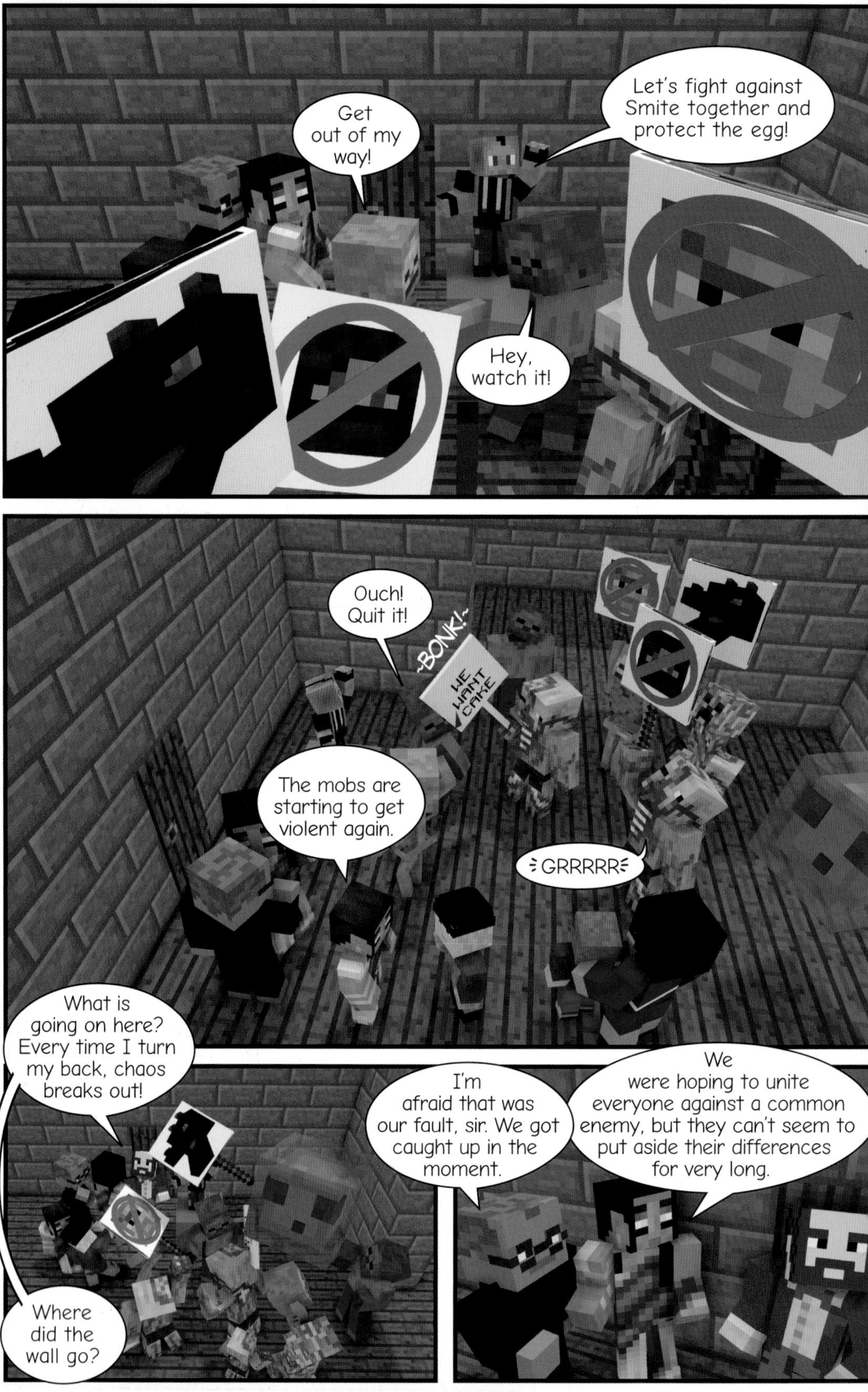
Get out of my way!
Let's fight against Smite together and protect the egg!
Hey, watch it!
Ouch! Quit it!
~BONK!~
WE WANT CAKE
The mobs are starting to get violent again.
GRRRRR
What is going on here? Every time I turn my back, chaos breaks out!
Where did the wall go?
I'm afraid that was our fault, sir. We got caught up in the moment.
We were hoping to unite everyone against a common enemy, but they can't seem to put aside their differences for very long.

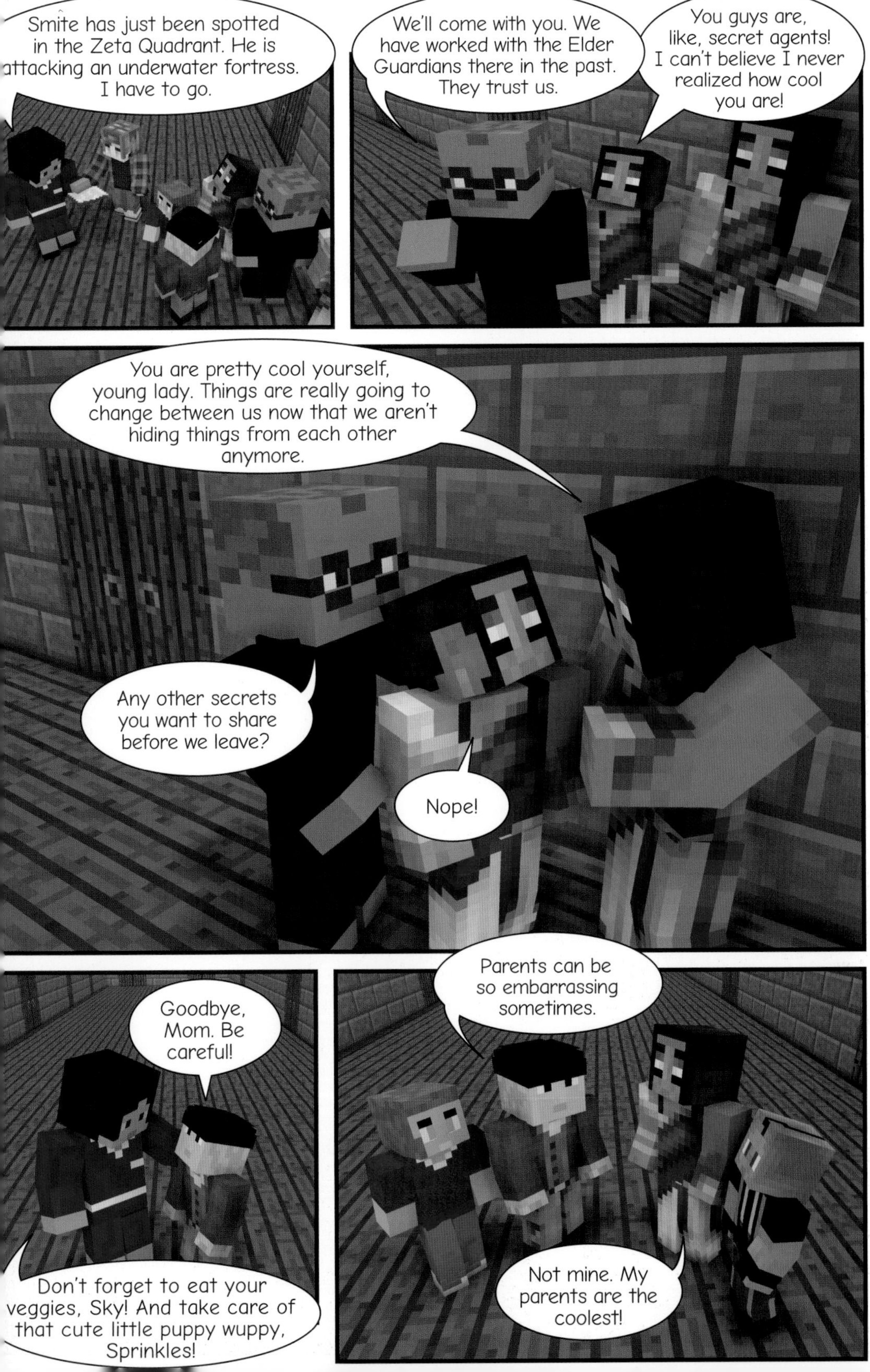
Smite has just been spotted in the Zeta Quadrant. He is attacking an underwater fortress. I have to go.
We'll come with you. We have worked with the Elder Guardians there in the past. They trust us.
You guys are, like, secret agents! I can't believe I never realized how cool you are!
You are pretty cool yourself, young lady. Things are really going to change between us now that we aren't hiding things from each other anymore.
Any other secrets you want to share before we leave?
Nope!
Goodbye, Mom. Be careful!
Don't forget to eat your veggies, Sky! And take care of that cute little puppy wuppy, Sprinkles!
Parents can be so embarrassing sometimes.
Not mine. My parents are the coolest!

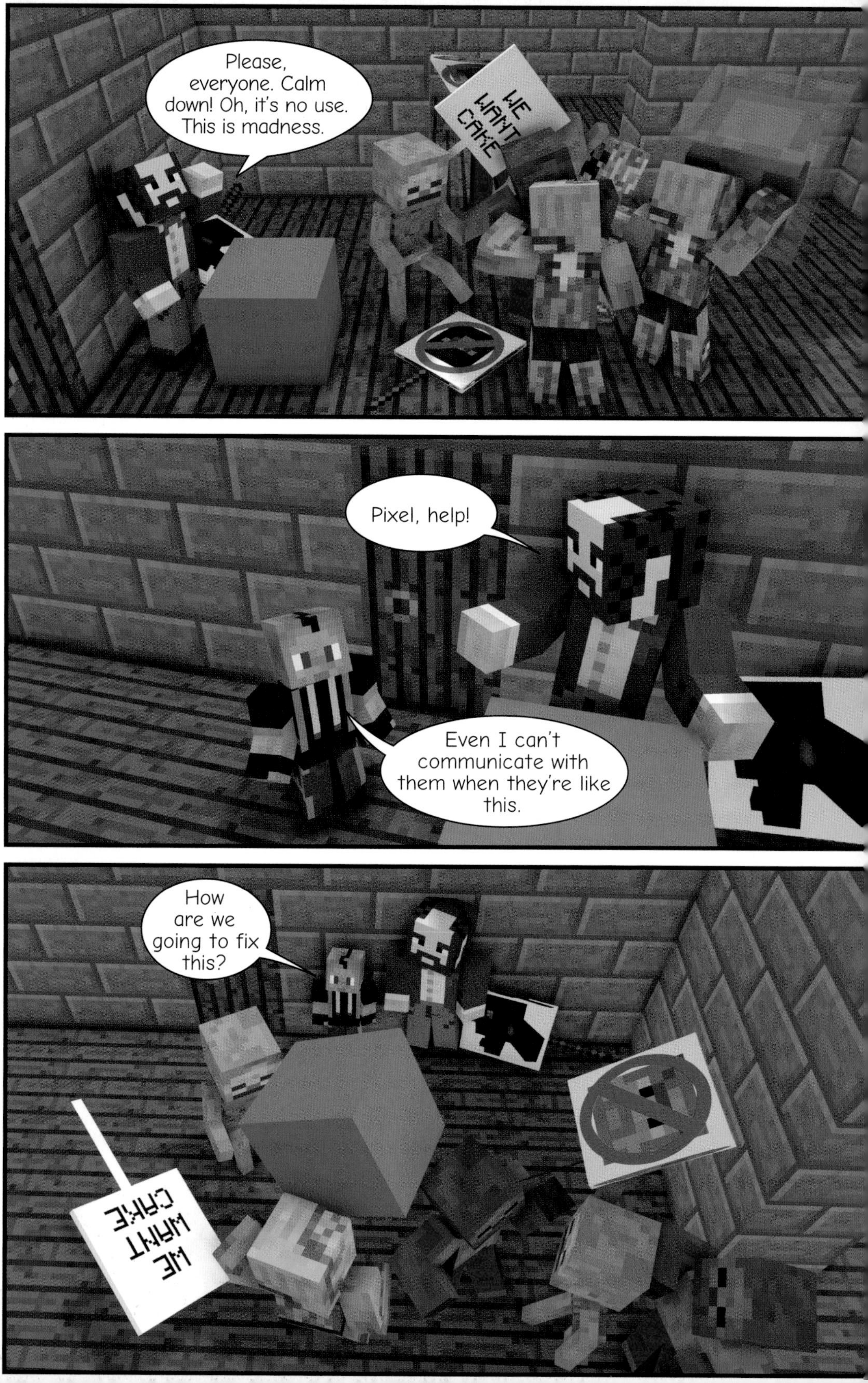
Please, everyone. Calm down! Oh, it's no use. This is madness.
WE WANT CAKE
Pixel, help!
Even I can't communicate with them when they're like this.
How are we going to fix this?
WE WANT CAKE

CHAPTER 8

TEAM
BUILDING

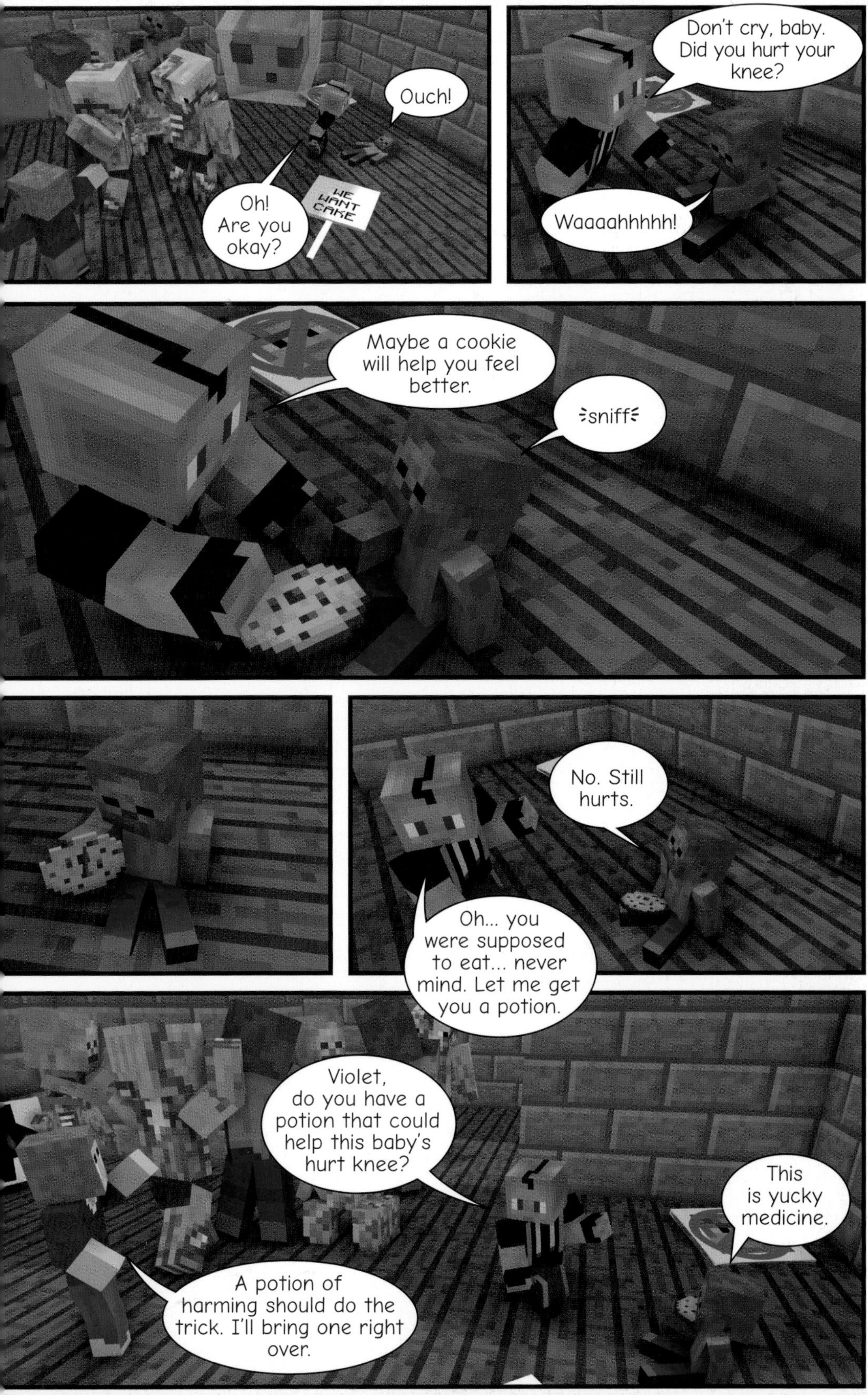
Ouch!
Oh! Are you okay?
WE WANT CAKE
Don't cry, baby. Did you hurt your knee?
Waaaahhhhh!
Maybe a cookie will help you feel better.
sniff
No. Still hurts.
Oh... you were supposed to eat... never mind. Let me get you a potion.
Violet, do you have a potion that could help this baby's hurt knee?
A potion of harming should do the trick. I'll bring one right over.
This is yucky medicine.

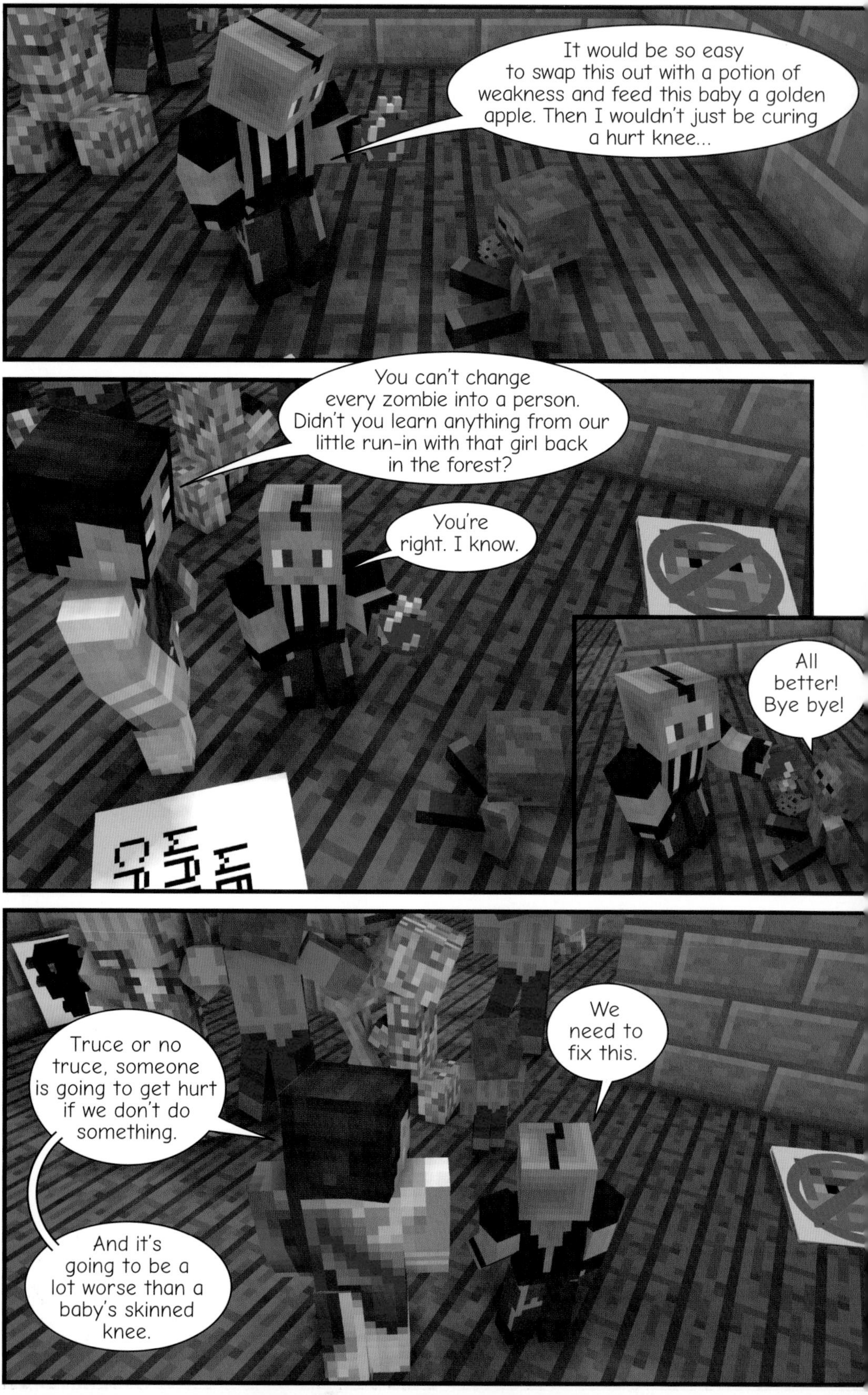
It would be so easy to swap this out with a potion of weakness and feed this baby a golden apple. Then I wouldn't just be curing a hurt knee...
You can't change every zombie into a person. Didn't you learn anything from our little run-in with that girl back in the forest?
You're right. I know.
All better! Bye bye!
Truce or no truce, someone is going to get hurt if we don't do something.
And it's going to be a lot worse than a baby's skinned knee.
We need to fix this.

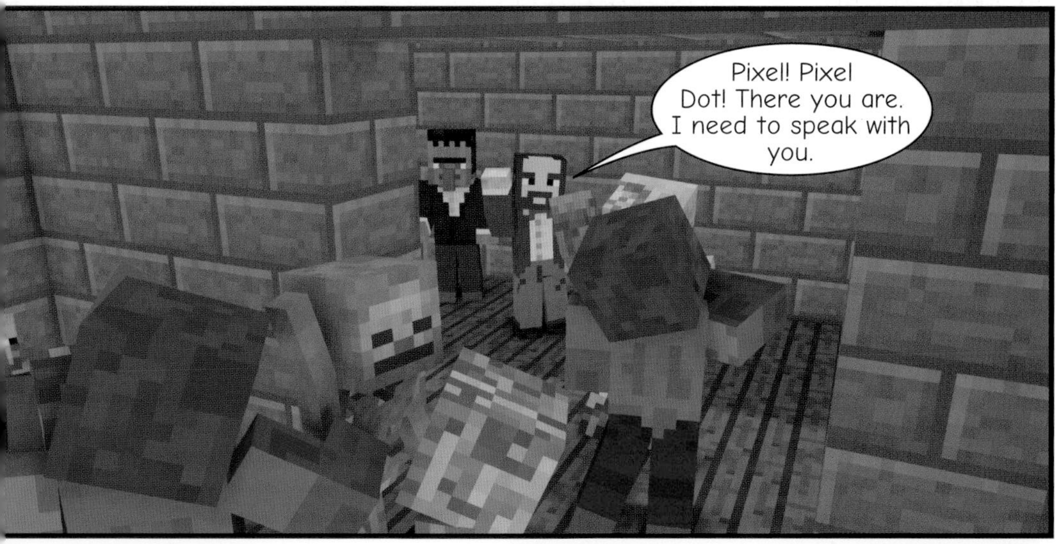
Pixel! Pixel
Dot! There you are. I need to speak with you.

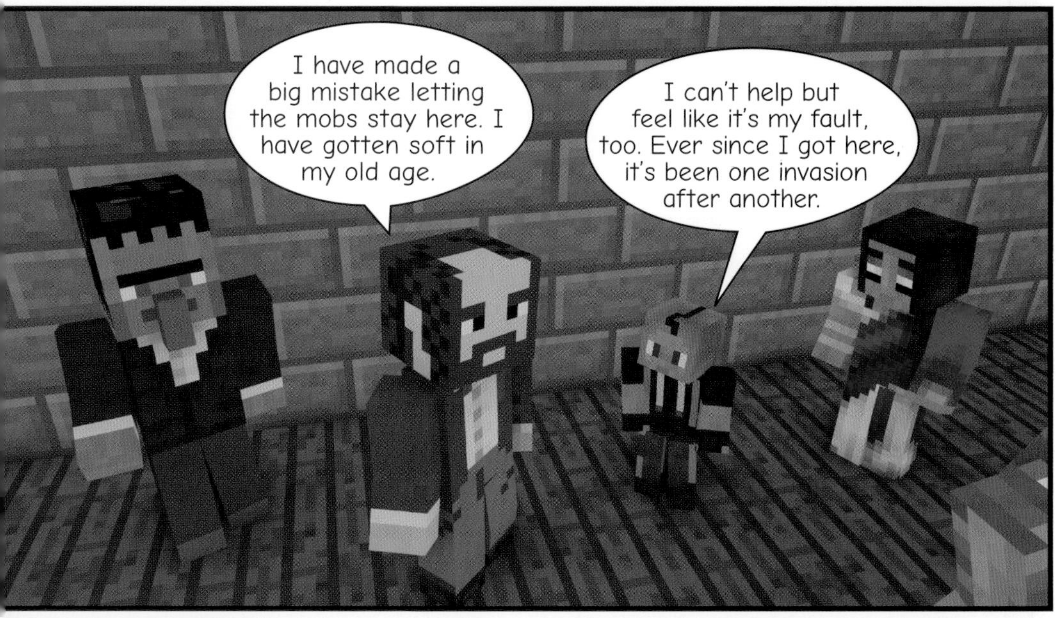
I have made a big mistake letting the mobs stay here. I have gotten soft in my old age.
I can't help but feel like it's my fault, too. Ever since I got here, it's been one invasion after another.

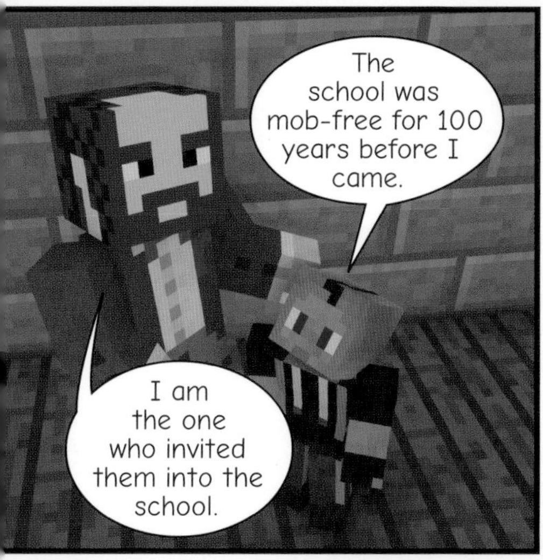
The school was mob-free for 100 years before I came.
I am the one who invited them into the school.

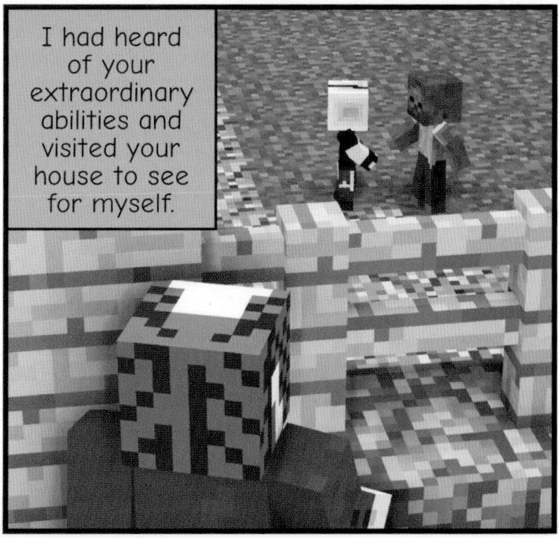
I had heard of your extraordinary abilities and visited your house to see for myself.

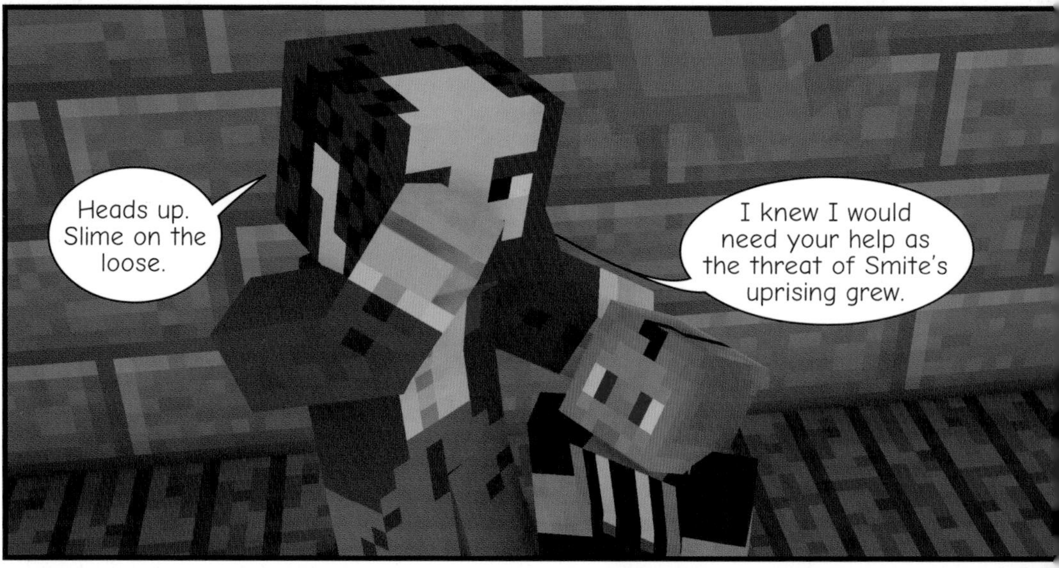
Heads up. Slime on the loose.
I knew I would need your help as the threat of Smite's uprising grew.

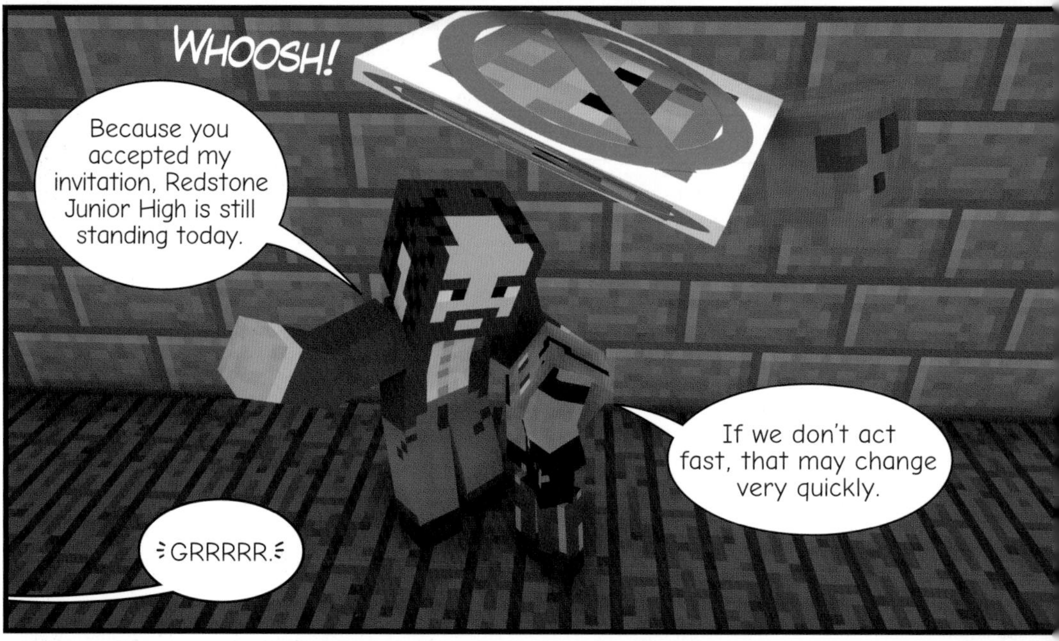
WHOOSH!
Because you accepted my invitation, Redstone Junior High is still standing today.
If we don't act fast, that may change very quickly.
GRRRRR.

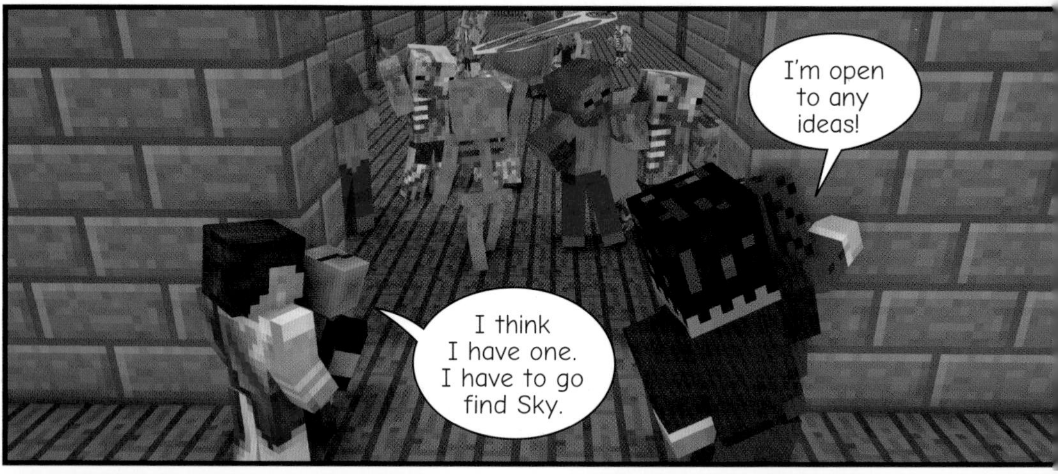
I'm open to any ideas!
I think I have one. I have to go find Sky.

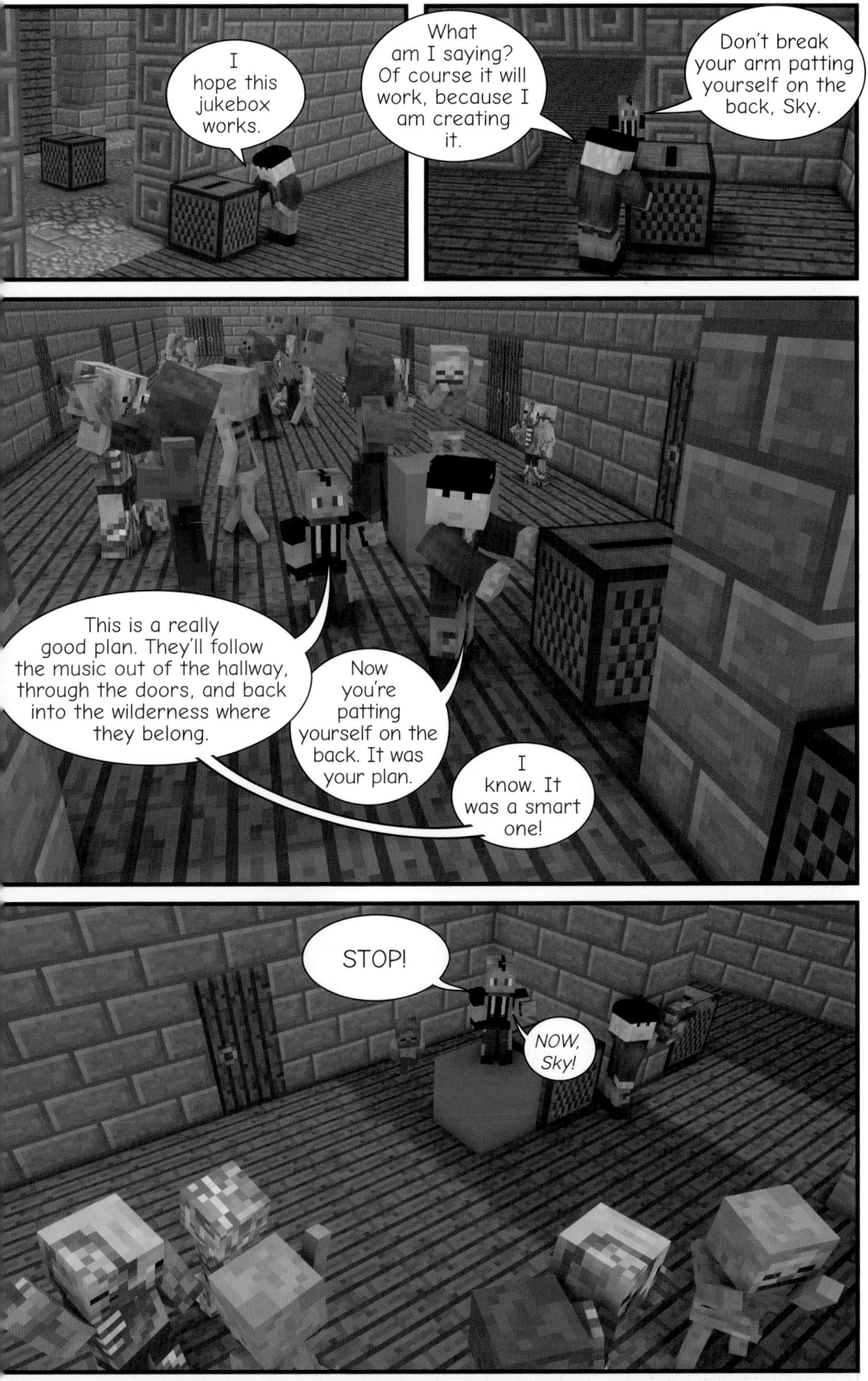
I hope this jukebox works.
What am I saying? Of course it will work, because I am creating it.
Don't break your arm patting yourself on the back, Sky.
This is a really good plan. They'll follow the music out of the hallway, through the doors, and back into the wilderness where they belong.
Now you're patting yourself on the back. It was your plan.
I know. It was a smart one!
STOP!
NOW, Sky!

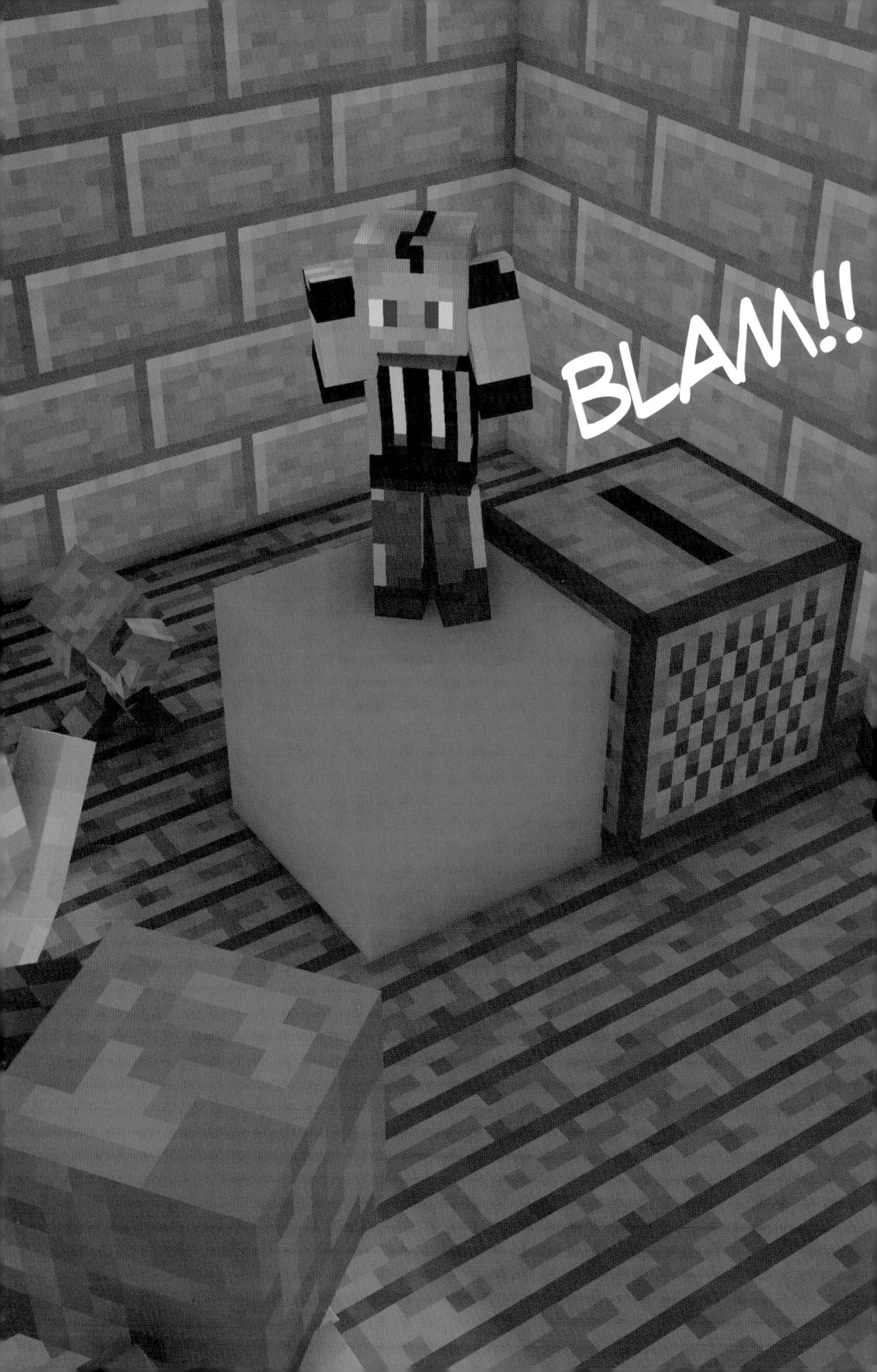
BLAM!!

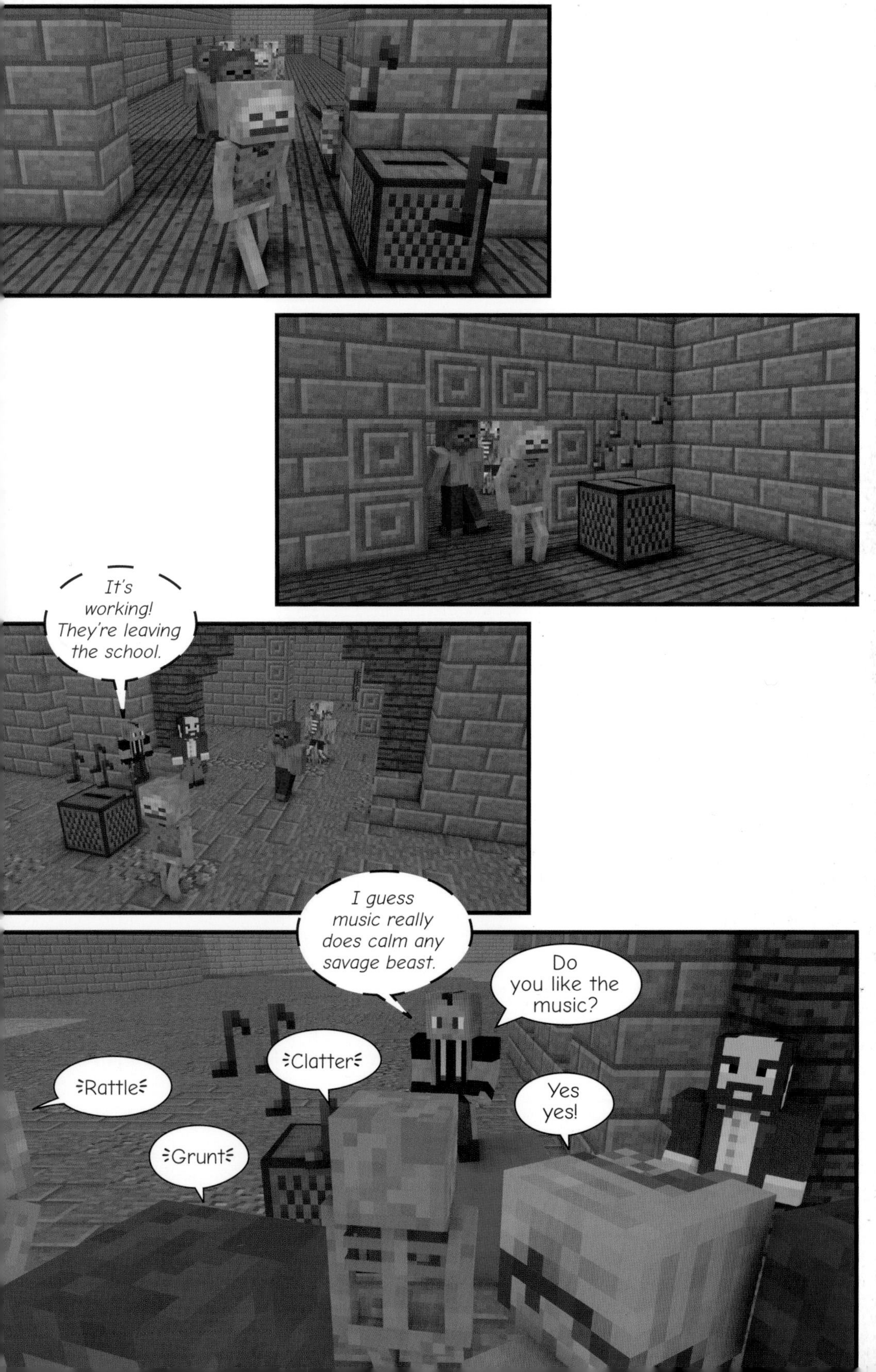
It's working! They're leaving the school.
I guess music really does calm any savage beast.
Do you like the music?
Clatter
Rattle
Yes yes!
Grunt

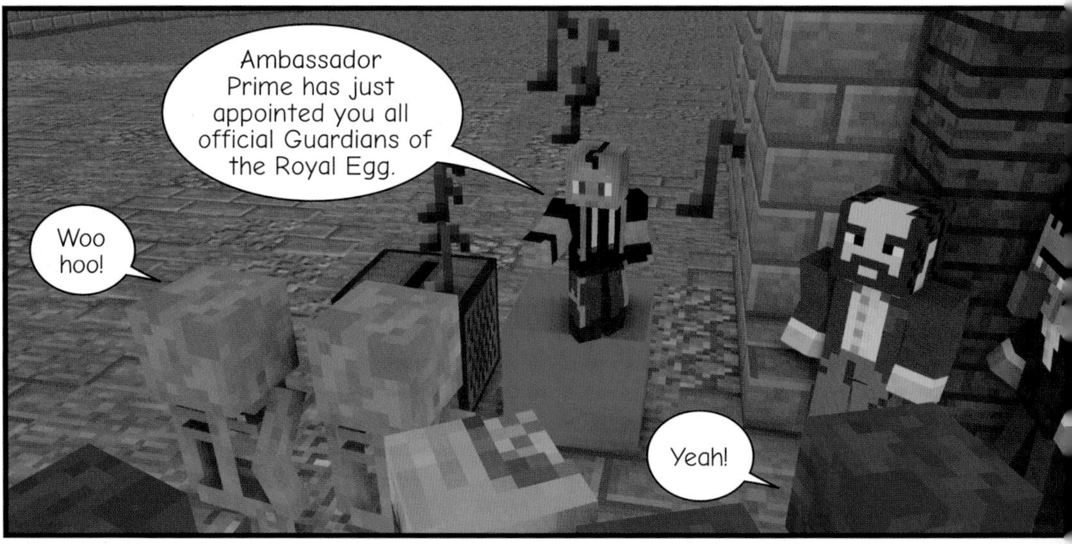
Ambassador Prime has just appointed you all official Guardians of the Royal Egg.
Woo hoo!
Yeah!

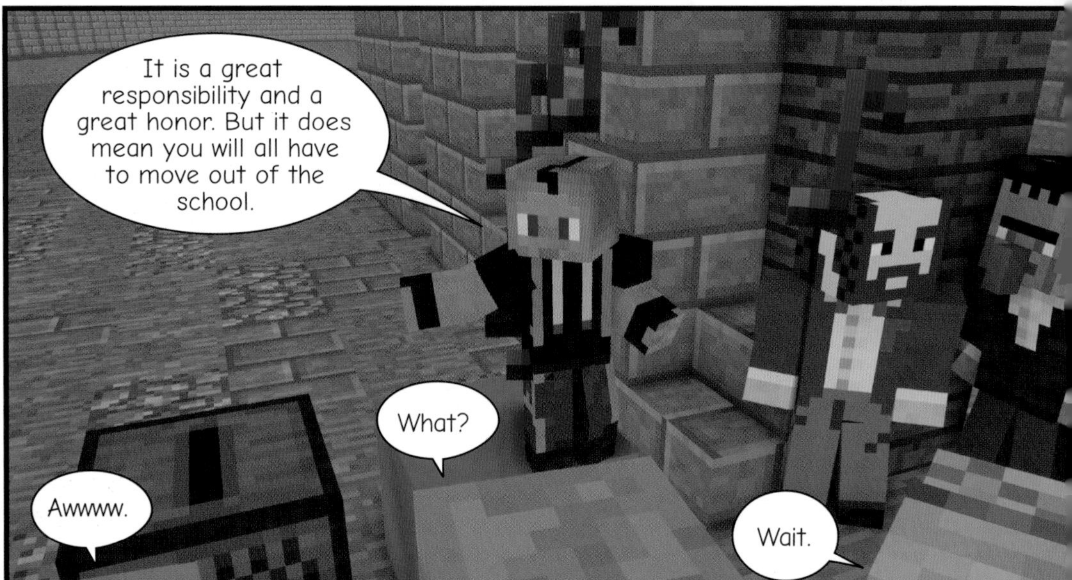
It is a great responsibility and a great honor. But it does mean you will all have to move out of the school.
What?
Awwww.
Wait.

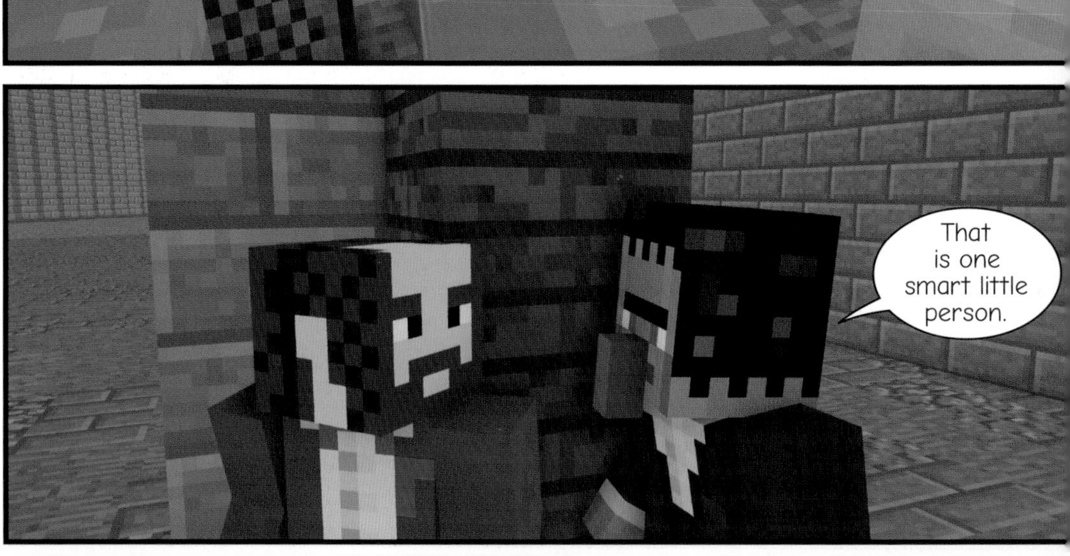
That is one smart little person.

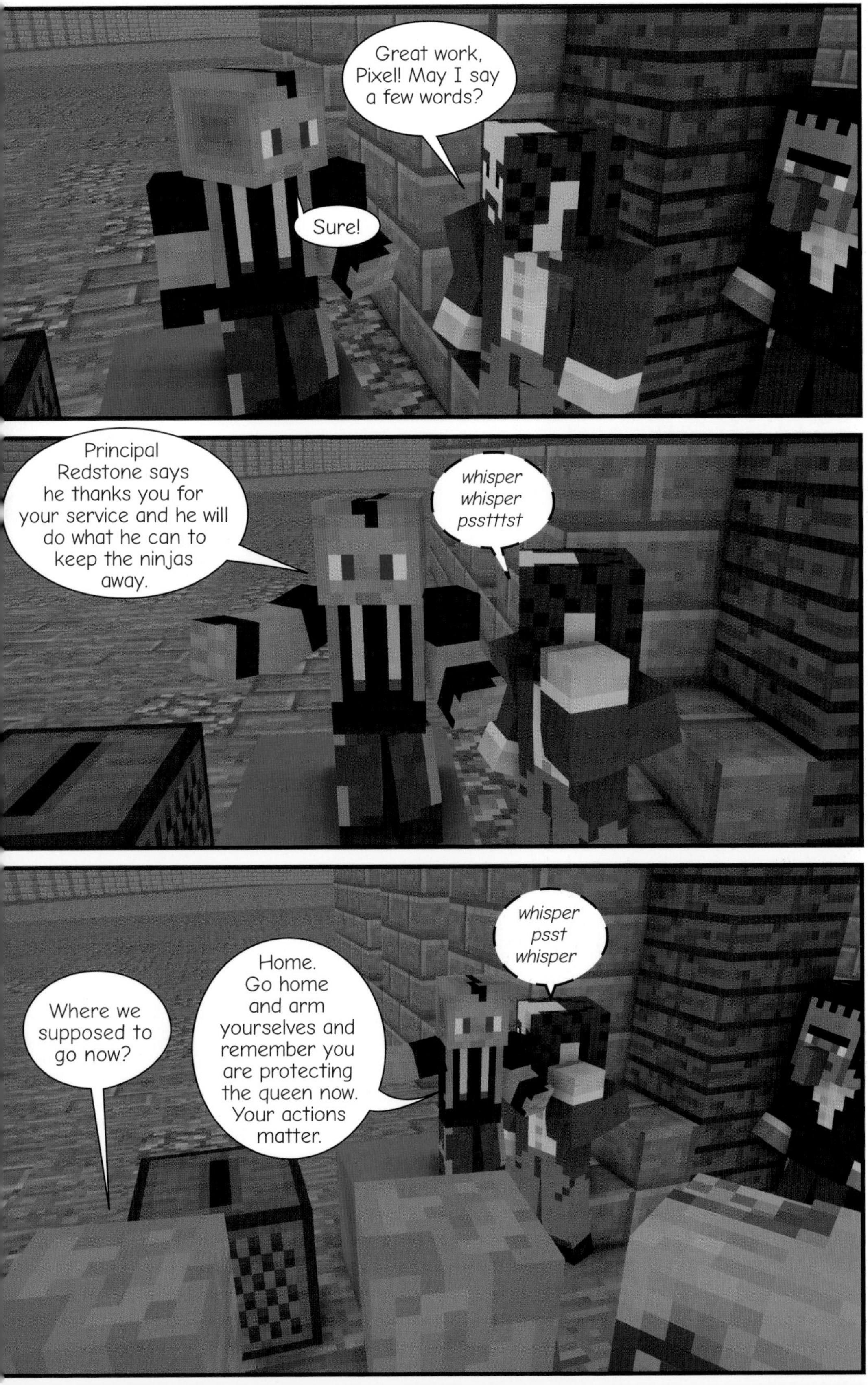

Great work, Pixel! May I say a few words?
Sure!
Principal Redstone says he thanks you for your service and he will do what he can to keep the ninjas away.
whisper whisper pssttst
Where we supposed to go now?
Home. Go home and arm yourselves and remember you are protecting the queen now. Your actions matter.
whisper psst whisper

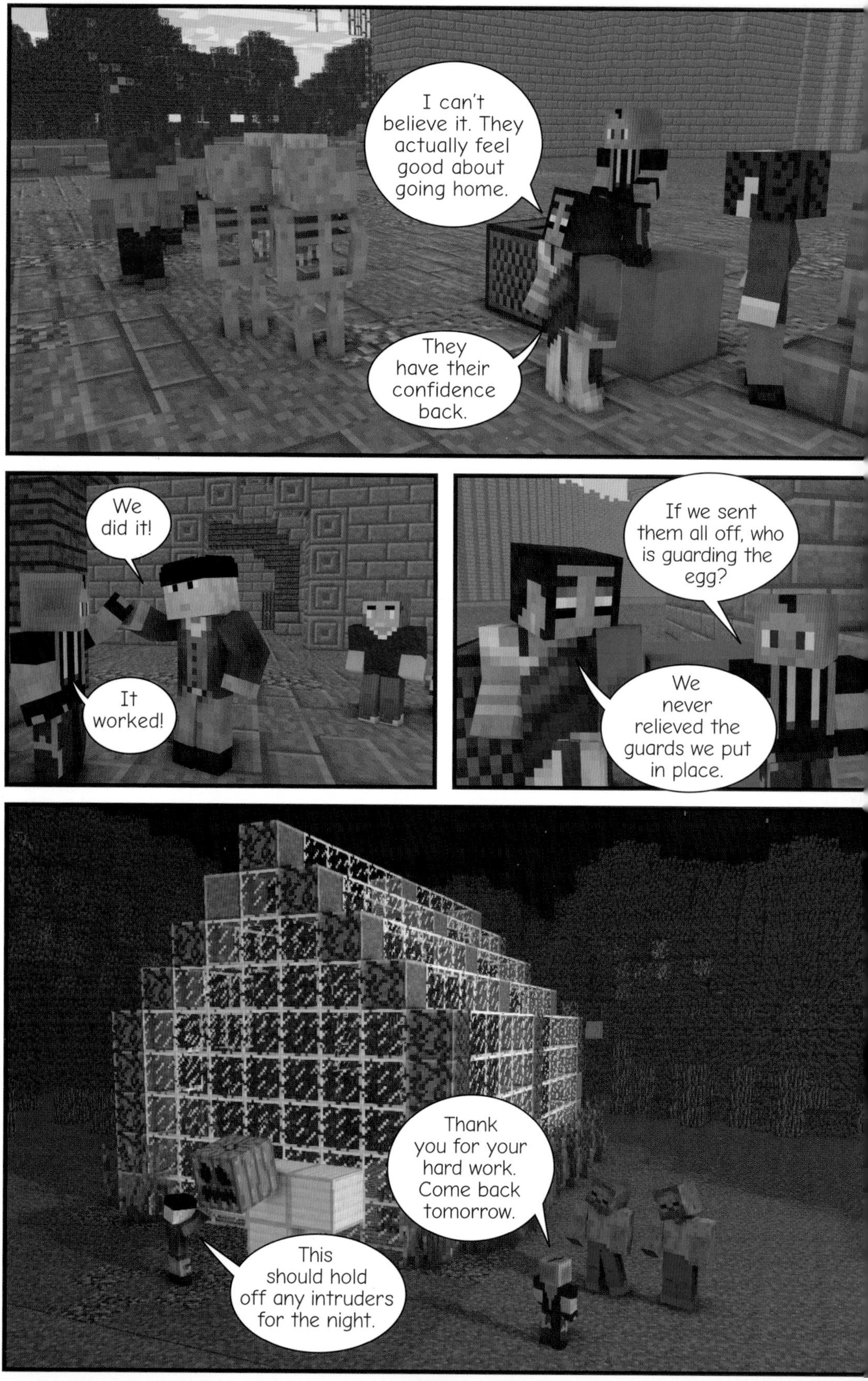
I can't believe it. They actually feel good about going home.
They have their confidence back.
We did it!
It worked!
If we sent them all off, who is guarding the egg?
We never relieved the guards we put in place.
Thank you for your hard work. Come back tomorrow.
This should hold off any intruders for the night.

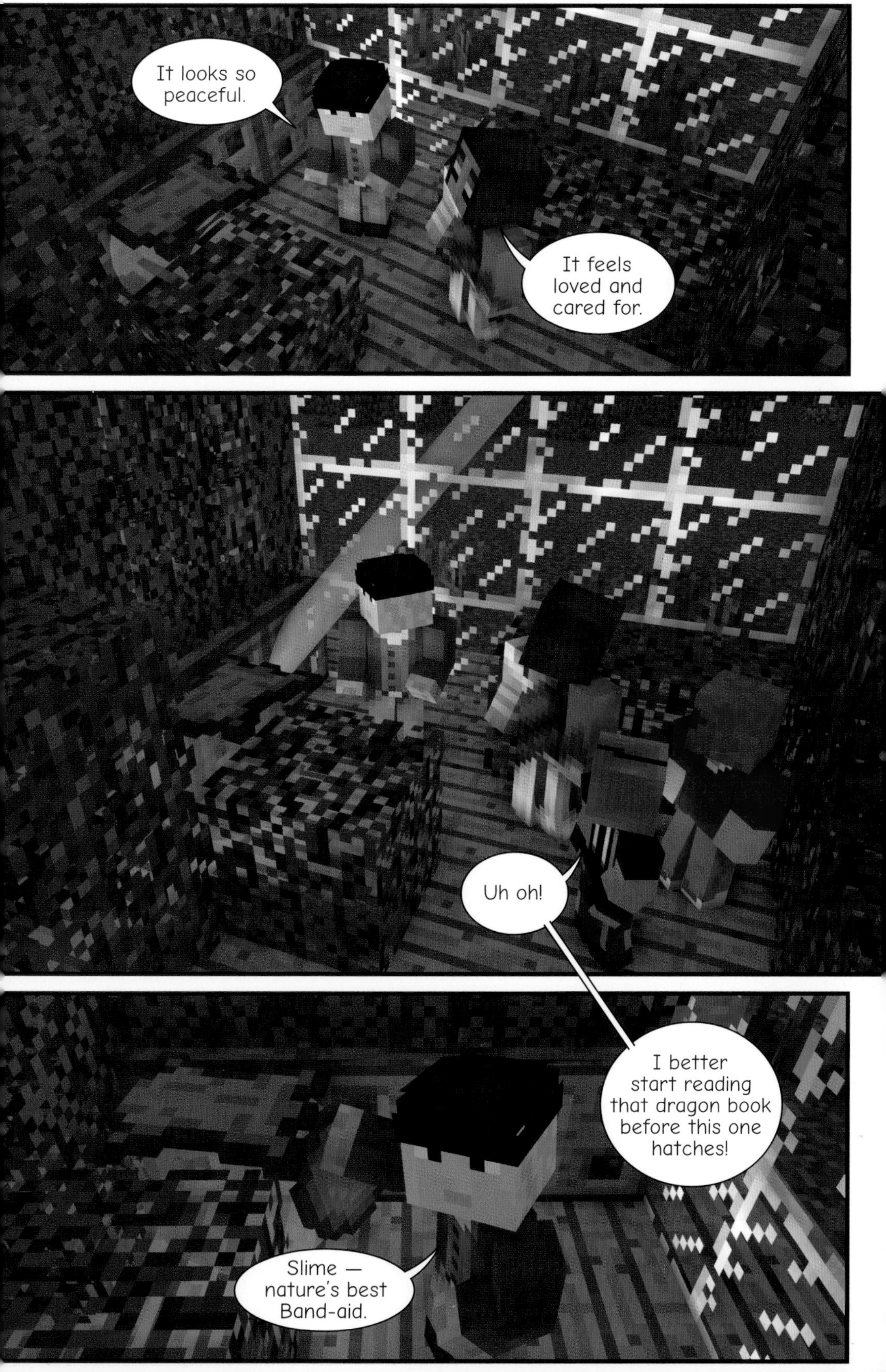
It looks so peaceful.
It feels loved and cared for.
Uh oh!
I better start reading that dragon book before this one hatches!
Slime — nature's best Band-aid.

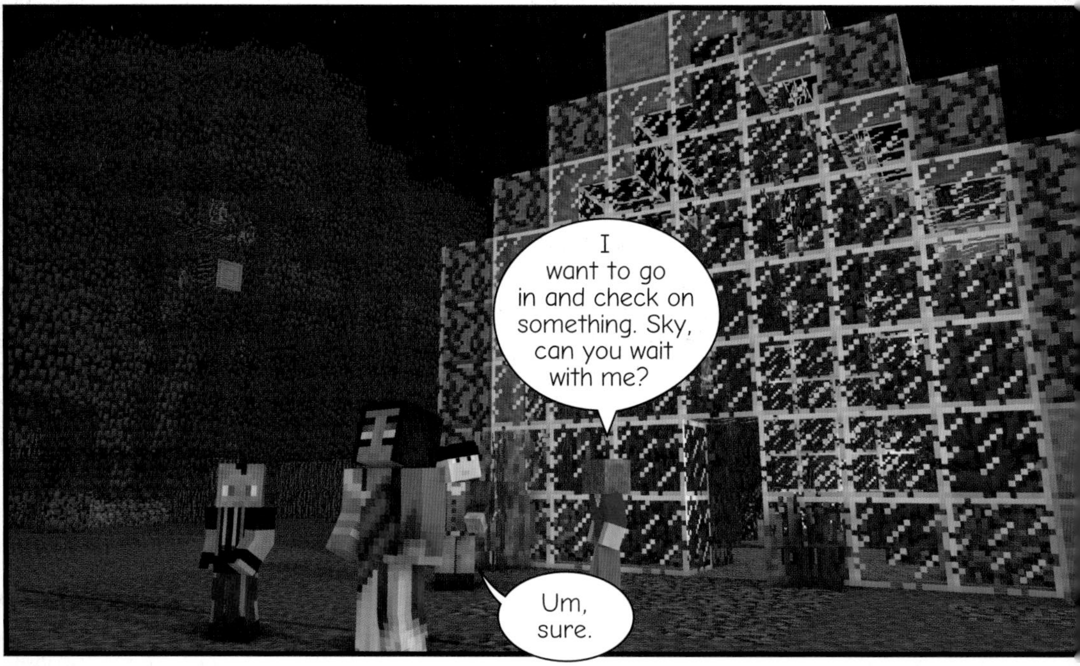
I want to go in and check on something. Sky, can you wait with me?
Um, sure.

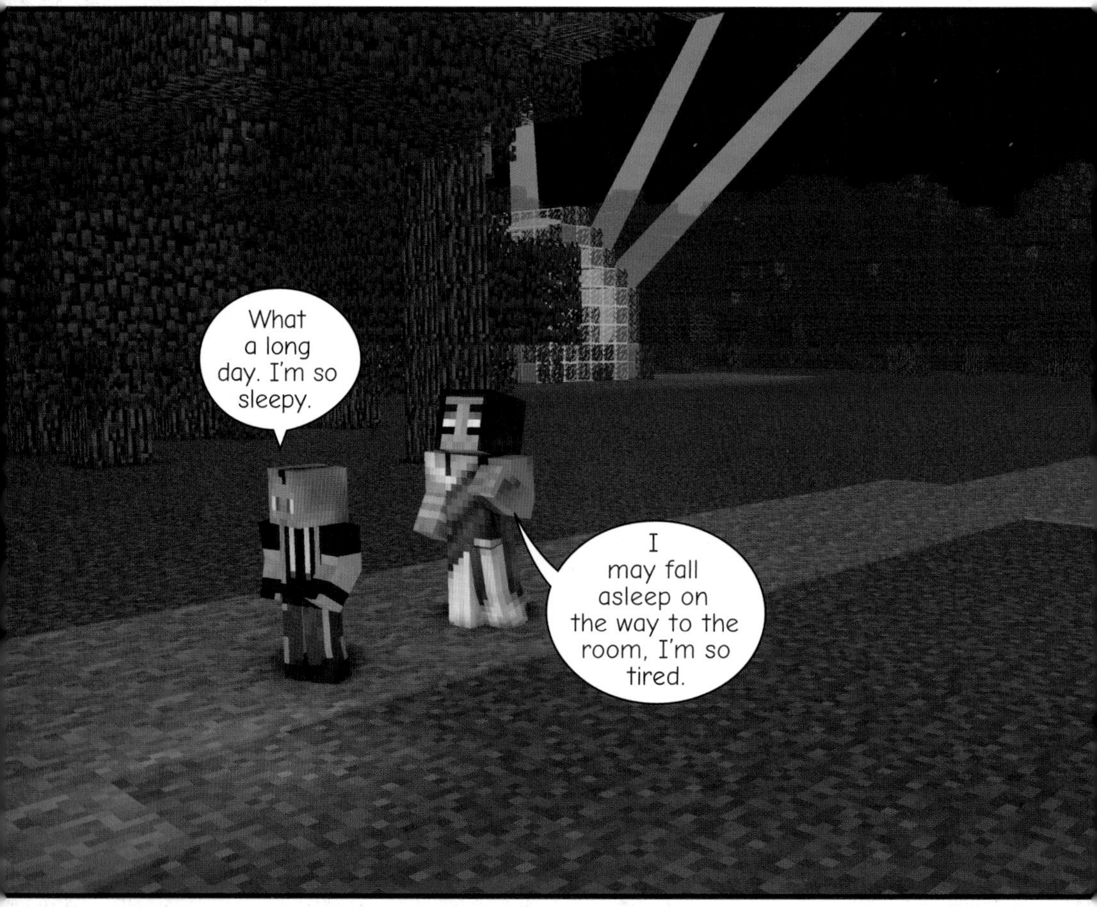
What a long day. I'm so sleepy.
I may fall asleep on the way to the room, I'm so tired.

CHAPTER 9

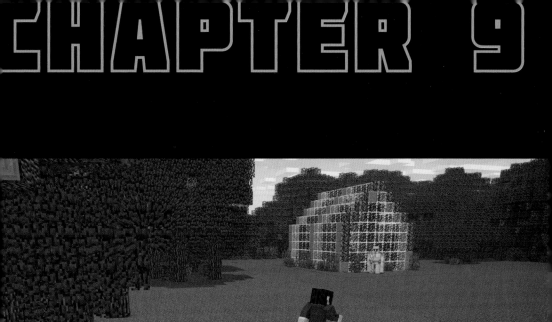

EGG-TASTROPHE!

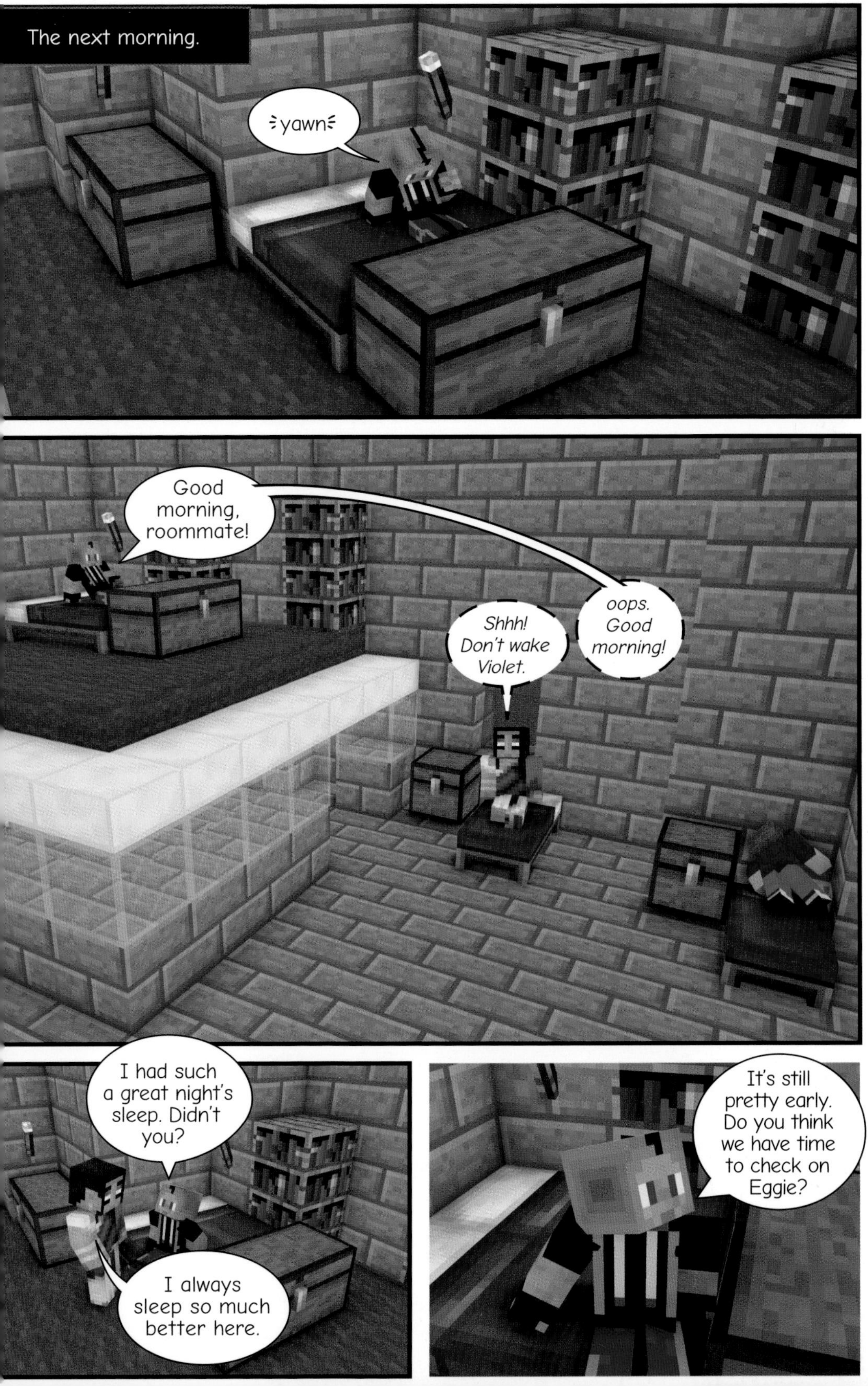

The next morning.
yawn
Good morning, roommate!
Shhh! Don't wake Violet.
oops. Good morning!
I had such a great night's sleep. Didn't you?
I always sleep so much better here.
It's still pretty early. Do you think we have time to check on Eggie?

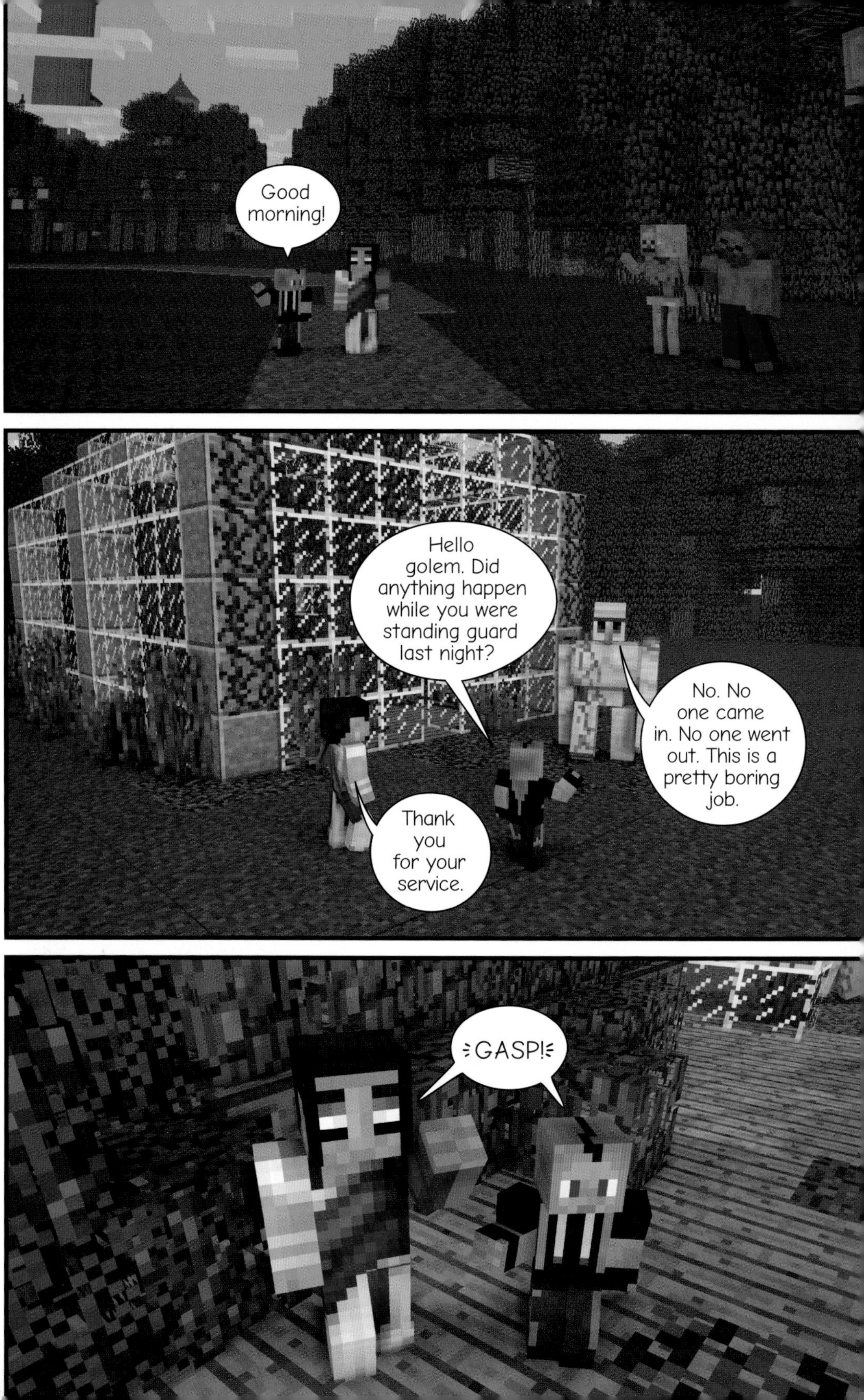
Good morning!
Hello golem. Did anything happen while you were standing guard last night?
No. No one came in. No one went out. This is a pretty boring job.
Thank you for your service.
GASP!

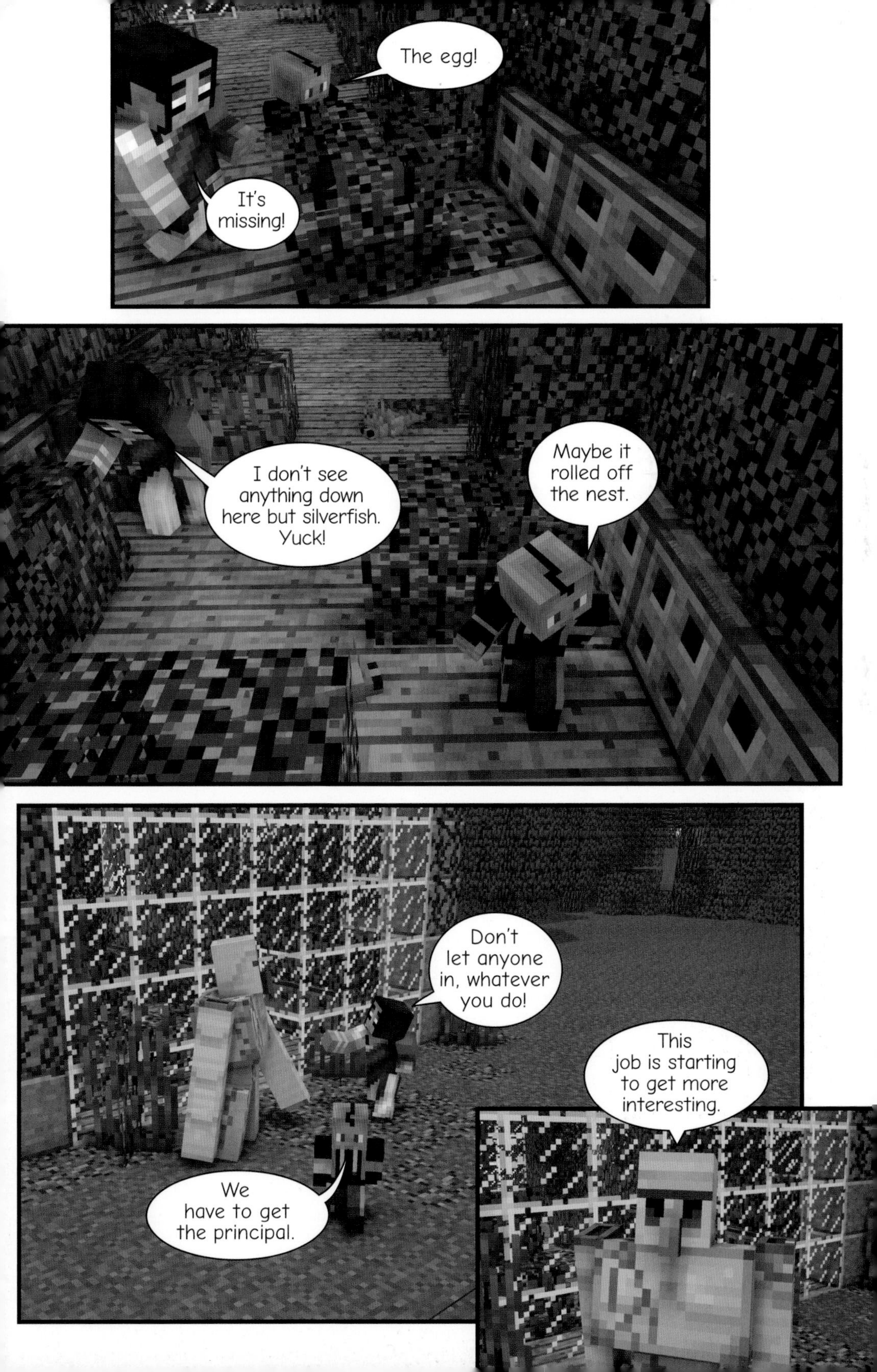
The egg!
It's missing!
I don't see anything down here but silverfish. Yuck!
Maybe it rolled off the nest.
Don't let anyone in, whatever you do!
We have to get the principal.
This job is starting to get more interesting.

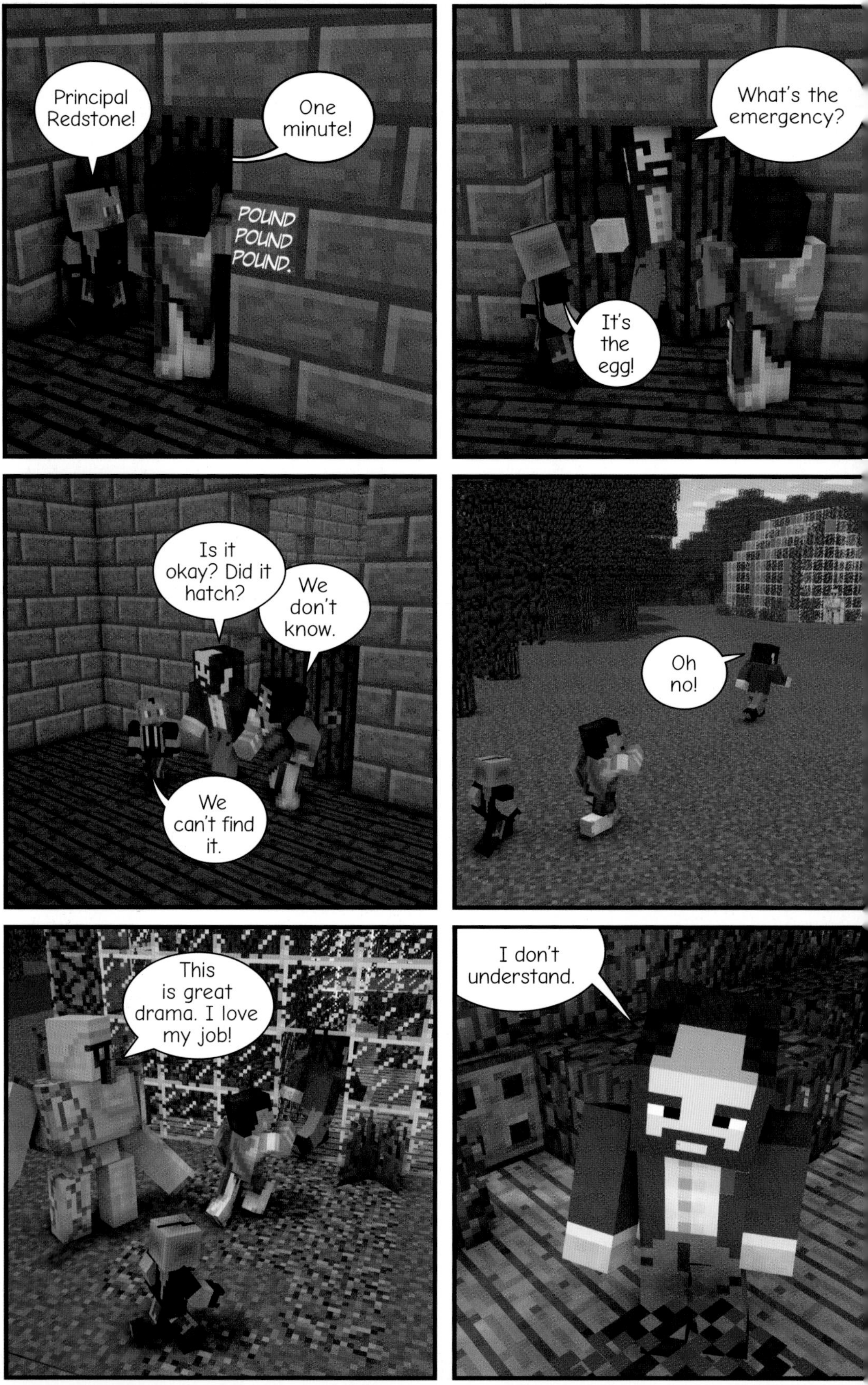

Principal Redstone!
One minute!
POUND POUND POUND.
What's the emergency?
It's the egg!
Is it okay? Did it hatch?
We don't know.
We can't find it.
Oh no!
This is great drama. I love my job!
I don't understand.

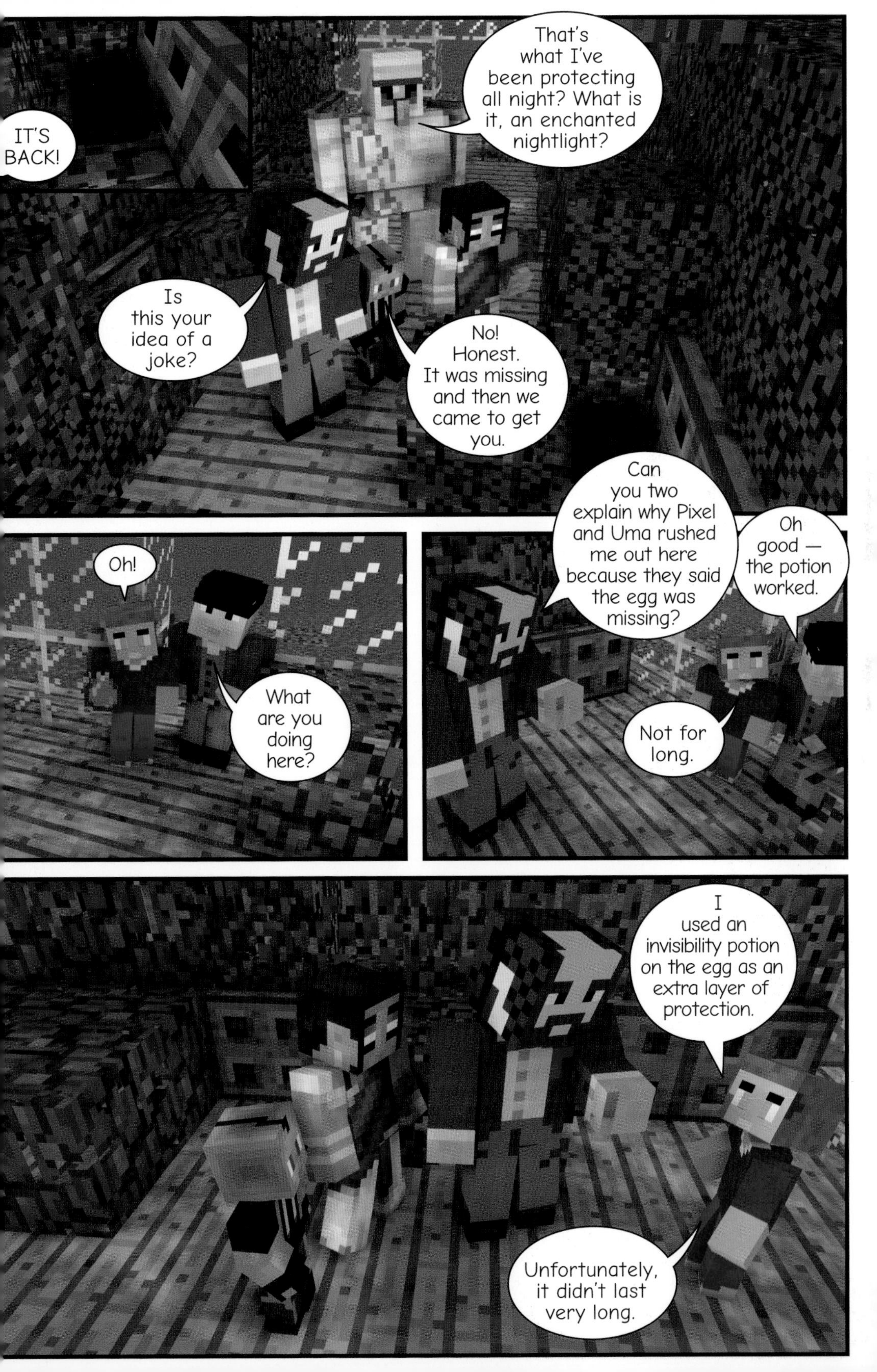
IT'S BACK!
That's what I've been protecting all night? What is it, an enchanted nightlight?
Is this your idea of a joke?
No! Honest. It was missing and then we came to get you.
Oh!
What are you doing here?
Can you two explain why Pixel and Uma rushed me out here because they said the egg was missing?
Oh good — the potion worked.
Not for long.
I used an invisibility potion on the egg as an extra layer of protection.
Unfortunately, it didn't last very long.

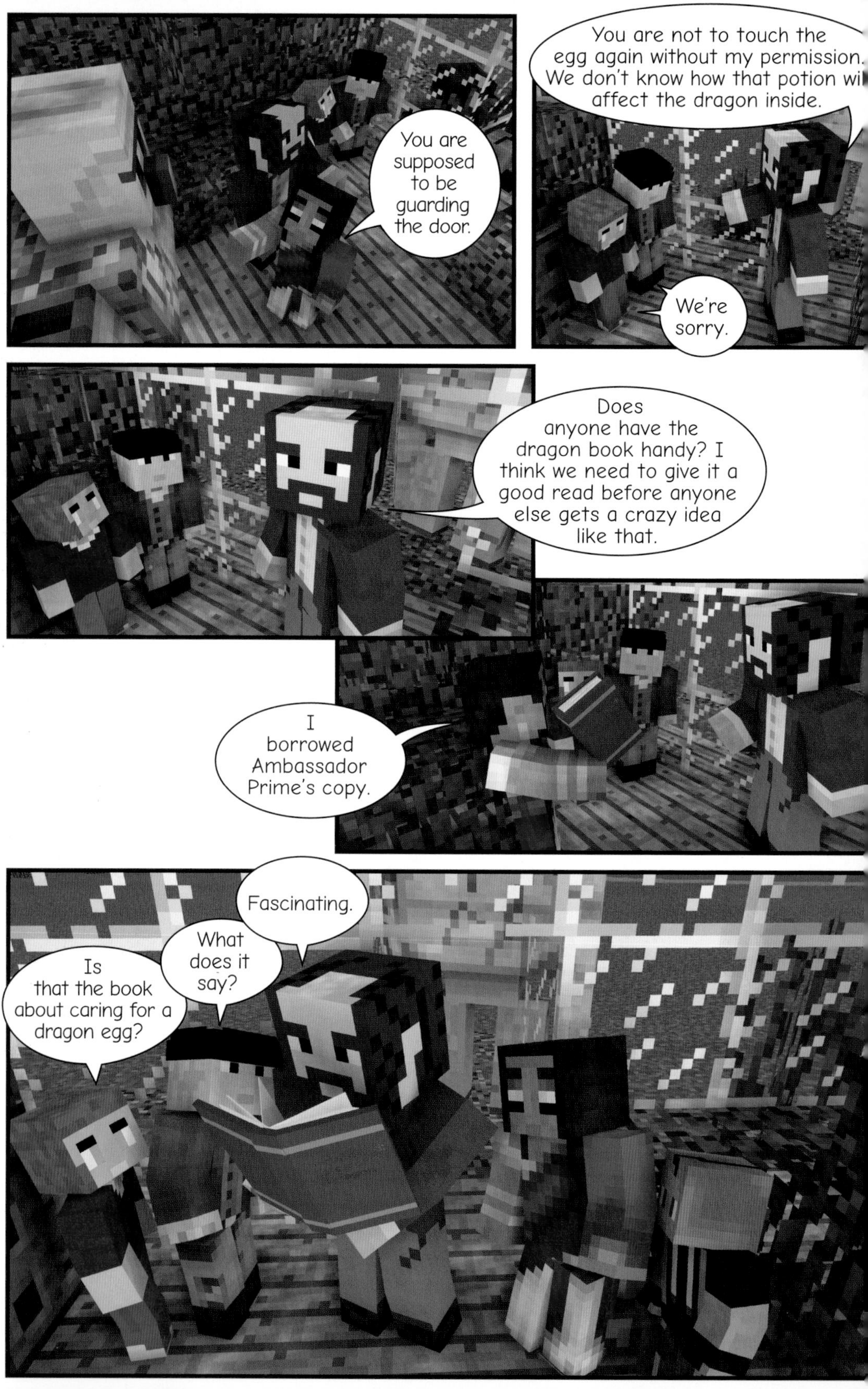
You are supposed to be guarding the door.
You are not to touch the egg again without my permission. We don't know how that potion wi
affect the dragon inside.
We're sorry.
Does anyone have the dragon book handy? I think we need to give it a good read before anyone else gets a crazy idea like that.
I borrowed Ambassador Prime's copy.
Is that the book about caring for a dragon egg?
What does it say?
Fascinating.

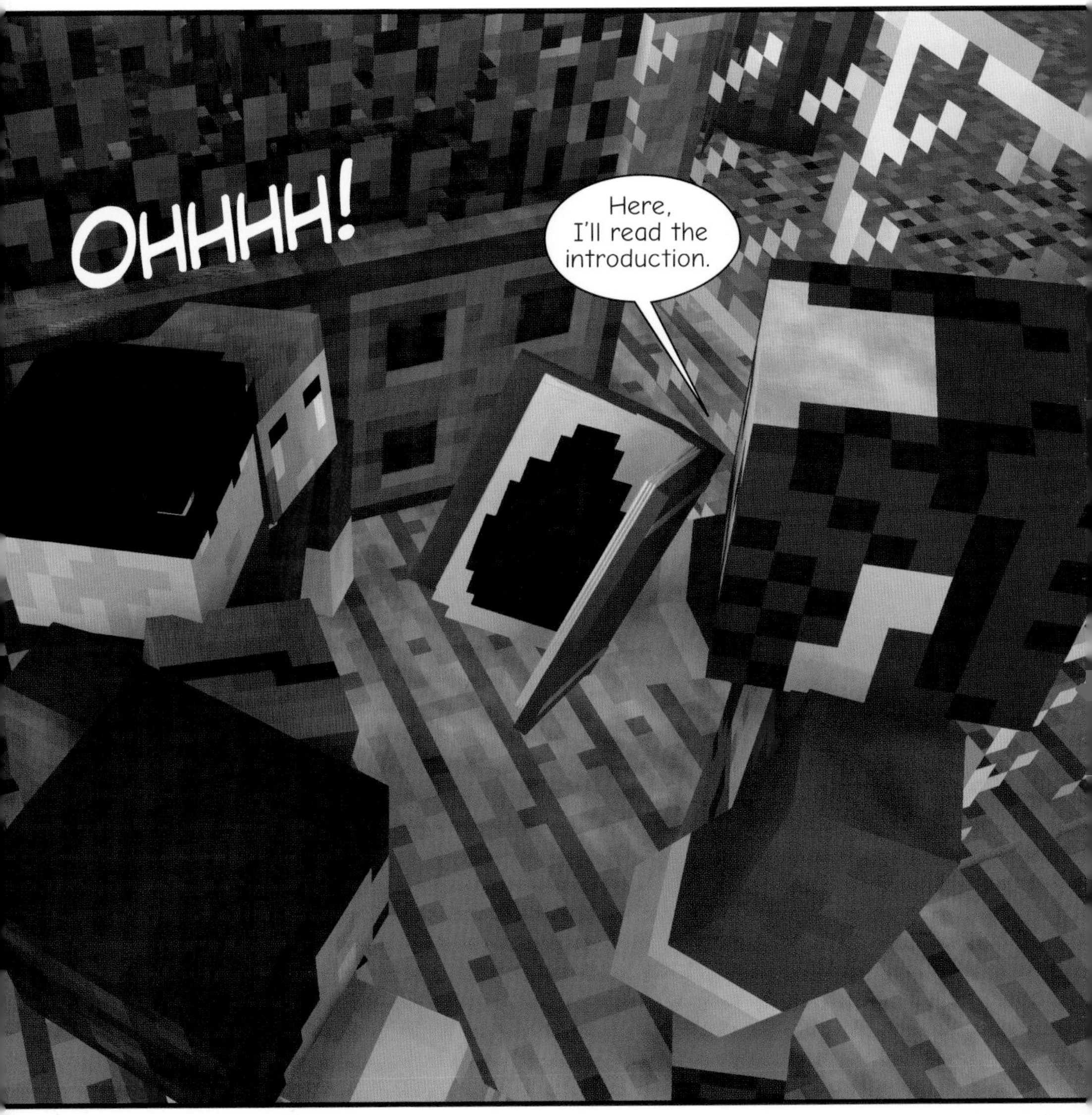
OHHHH!
Here, I'll read the introduction.

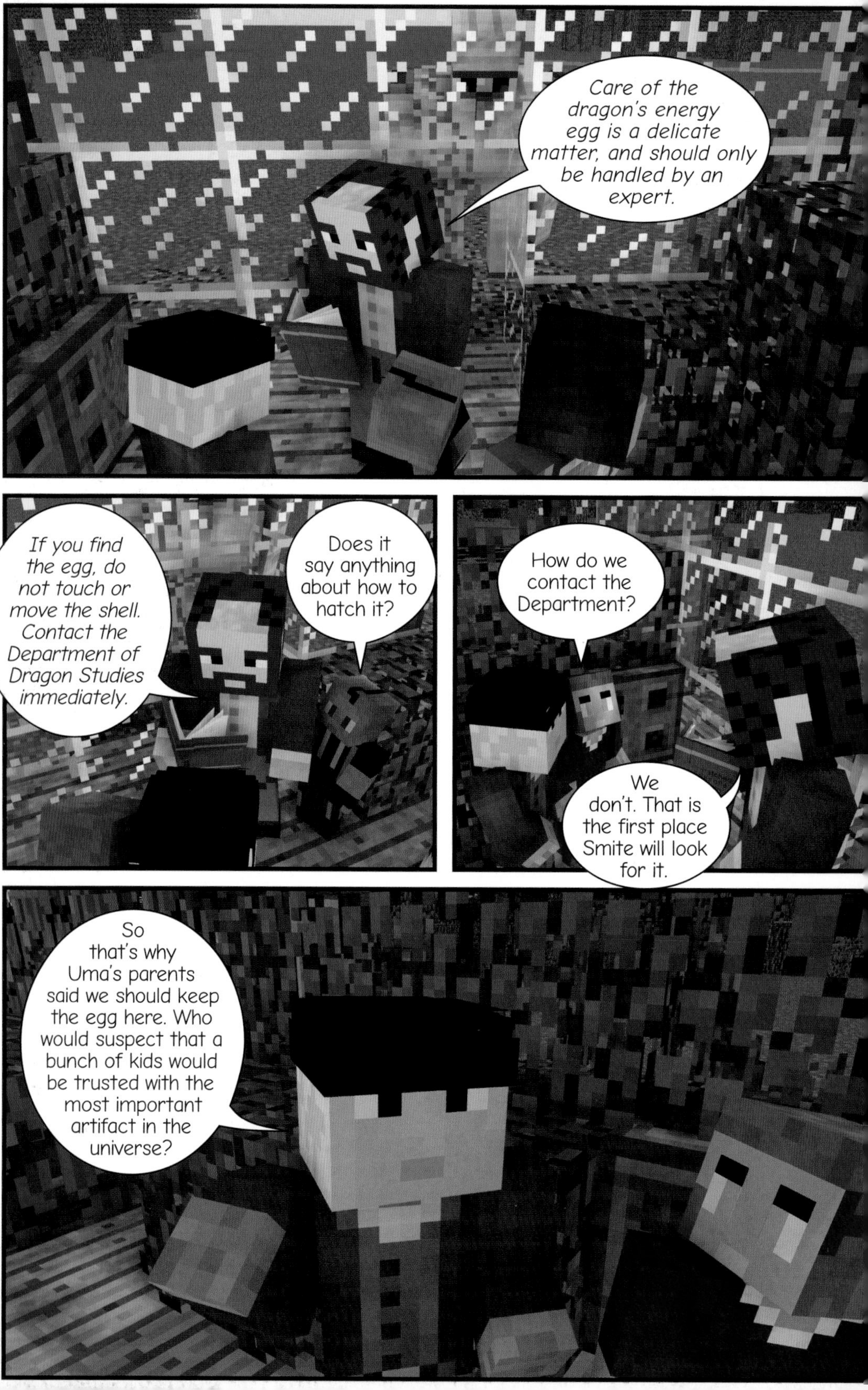
Care of the dragon's energy egg is a delicate matter, and should only be handled by an expert.
If you find the egg, do not touch or move the shell. Contact the Department of Dragon Studies immediately.
Does it say anything about how to hatch it?
How do we contact the Department?
We don't. That is the first place Smite will look for it.
So that's why Uma's parents said we should keep the egg here. Who would suspect that a bunch of kids would be trusted with the most important artifact in the universe?

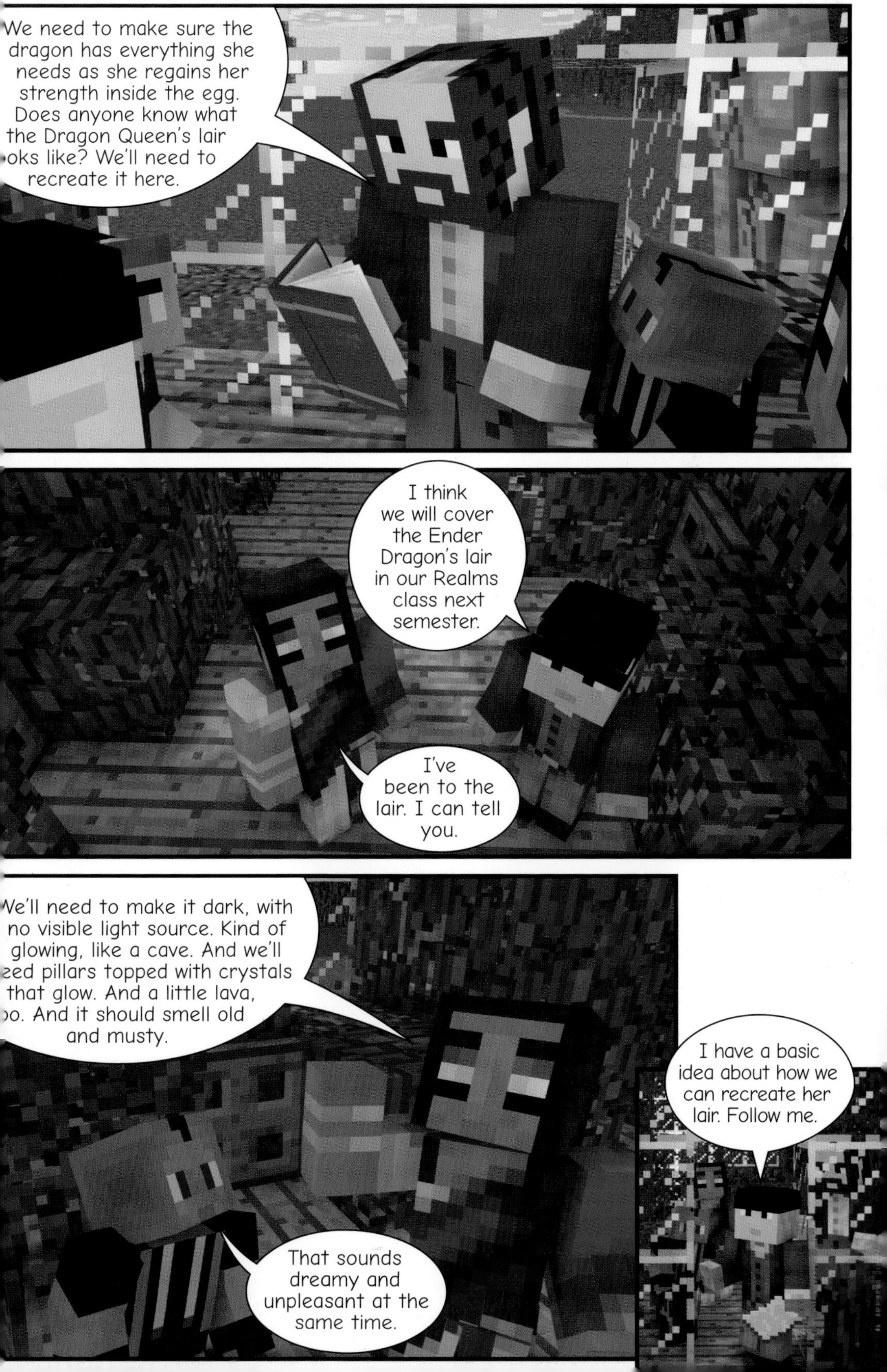
We need to make sure the dragon has everything she needs as she regains her strength inside the egg. Does anyone know what the Dragon Queen's lair oks like? We'll need to recreate it here.
I think we will cover the Ender Dragon's lair in our Realms class next semester.
I've been to the lair. I can tell you.
e'll need to make it dark, with no visible light source. Kind of glowing, like a cave. And we'll eed pillars topped with crystals that glow. And a little lava, o. And it should smell old and musty.
That sounds dreamy and unpleasant at the same time.
I have a basic idea about how we can recreate her lair. Follow me.

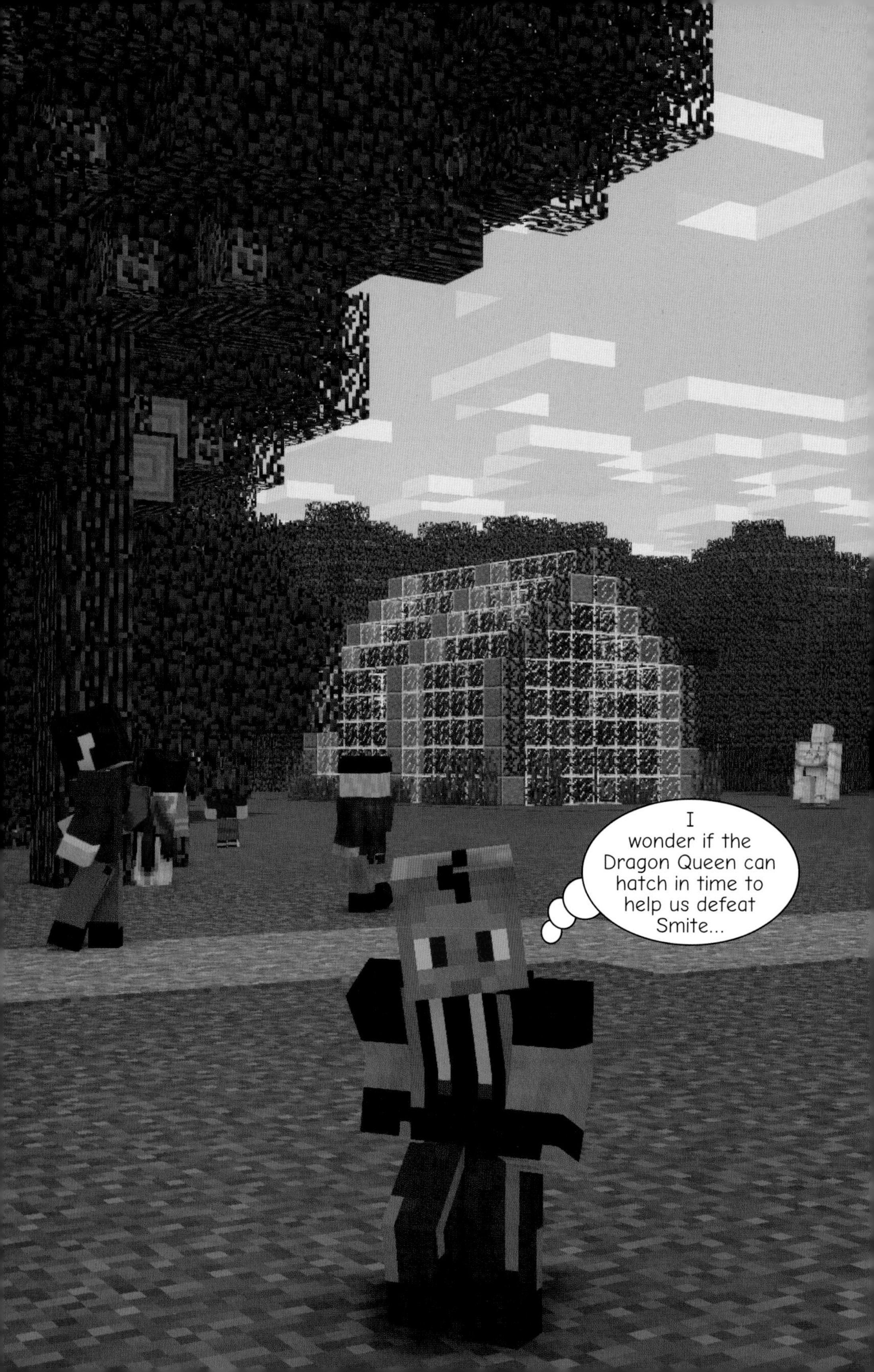
I wonder if the Dragon Queen can hatch in time to help us defeat Smite...

CHAPTER 10

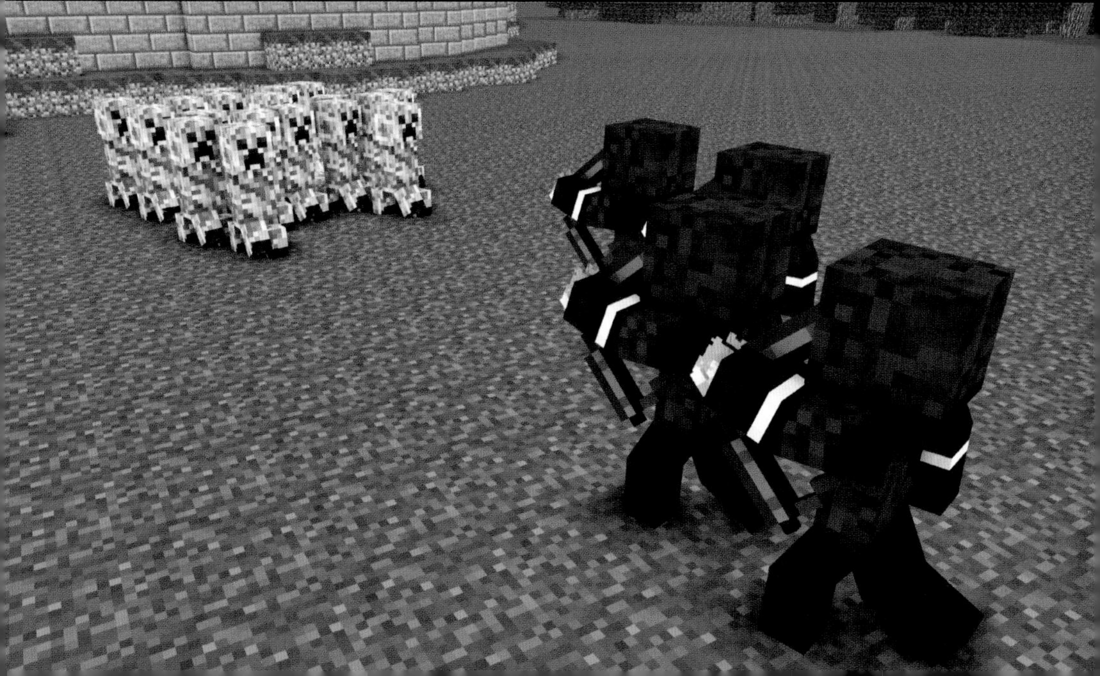

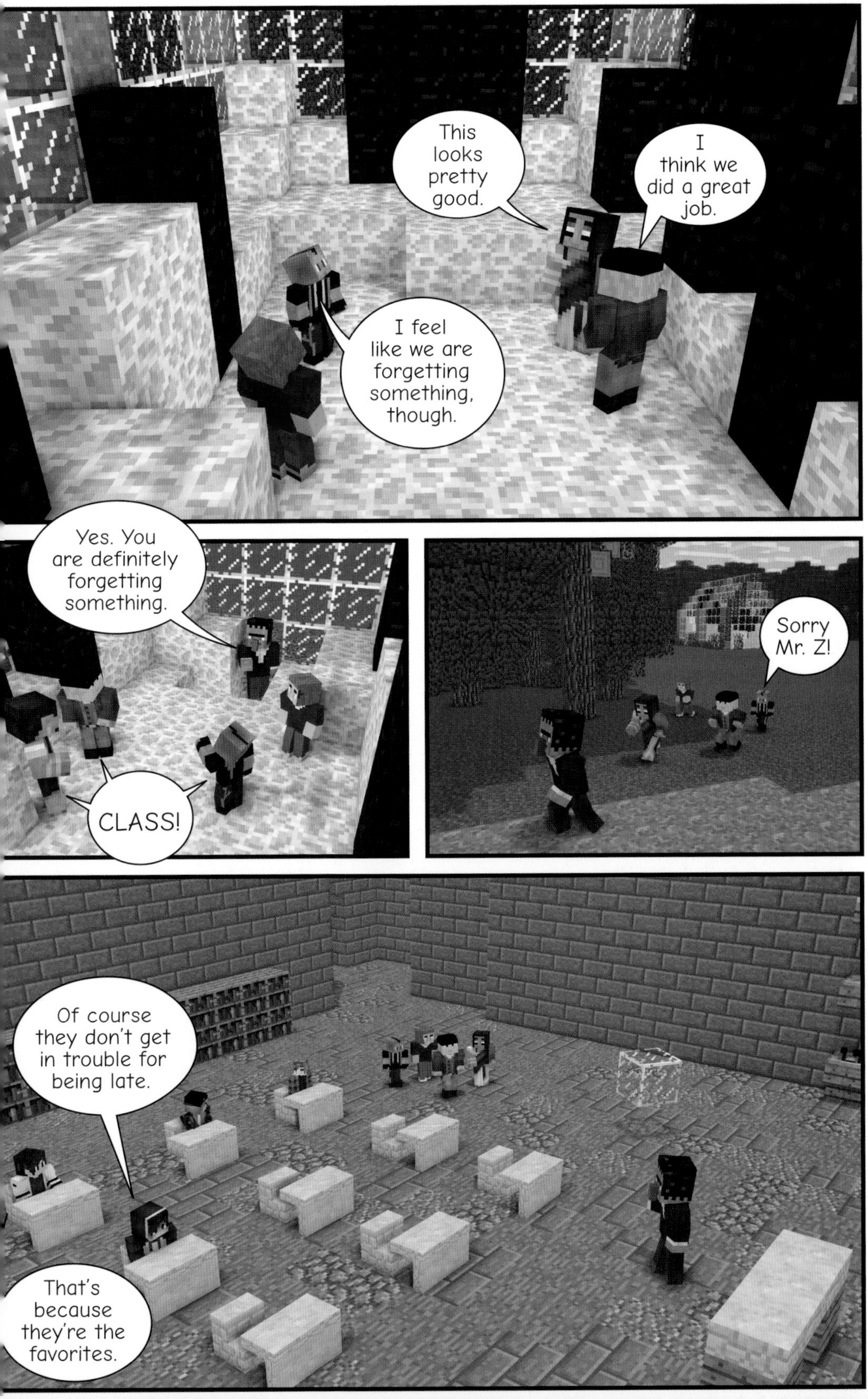
This looks pretty good.
I think we did a great job.
I feel like we are forgetting something, though.
Yes. You are definitely forgetting something.
CLASS!
Sorry Mr. Z!
Of course they don't get in trouble for being late.
That's because they're the favorites.

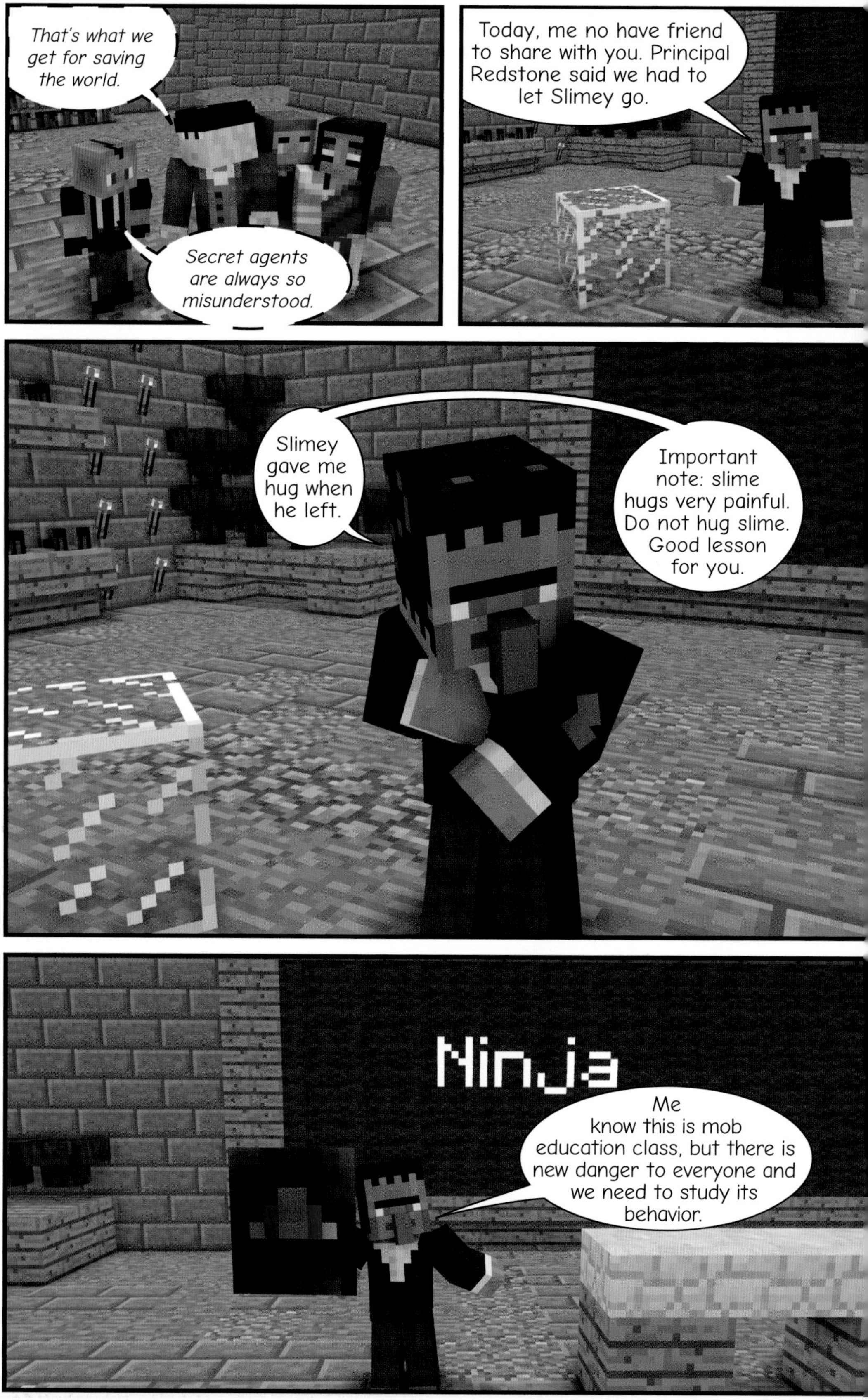
That's what we get for saving the world.
Secret agents are always so misunderstood.
Today, me no have friend to share with you. Principal Redstone said we had to let Slimey go.
Slimey gave me hug when he left.
Important note: slime hugs very painful. Do not hug slime. Good lesson for you.
Ninja
Me know this is mob education class, but there is new danger to everyone and we need to study its behavior.

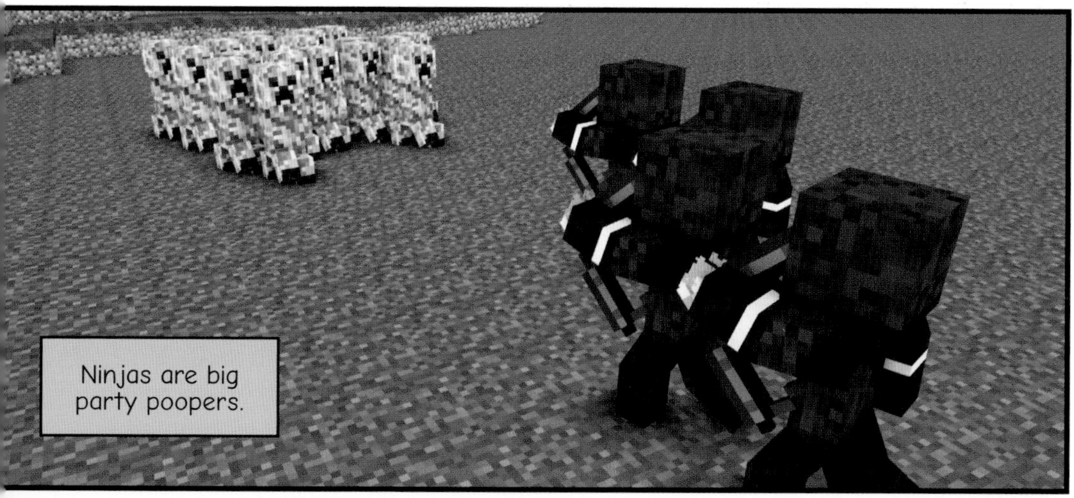
Ninjas are big party poopers.

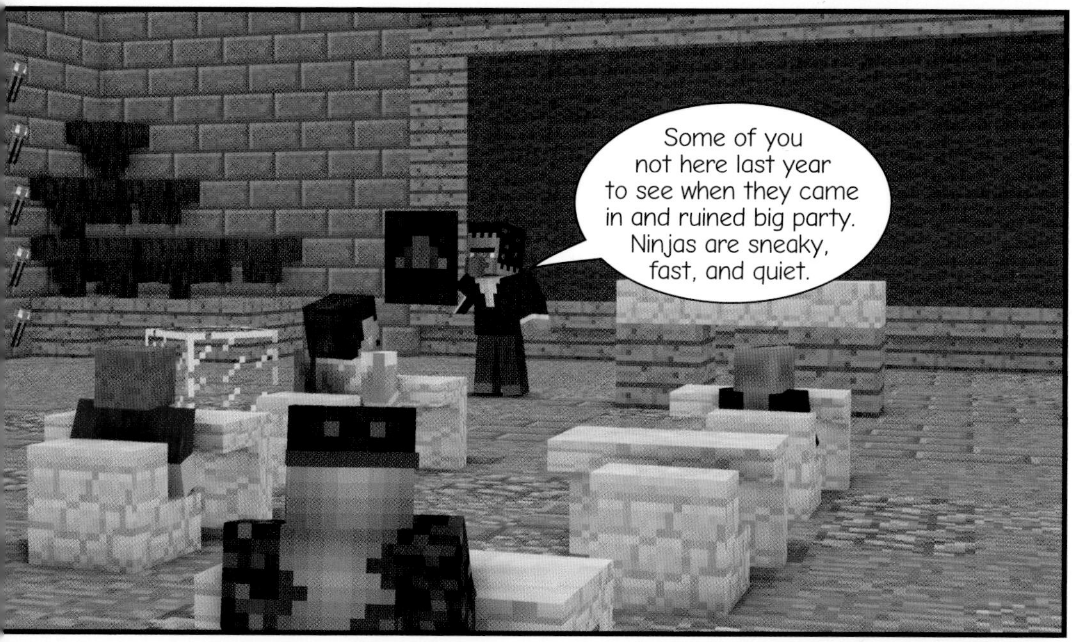
Some of you not here last year to see when they came in and ruined big party. Ninjas are sneaky, fast, and quiet.

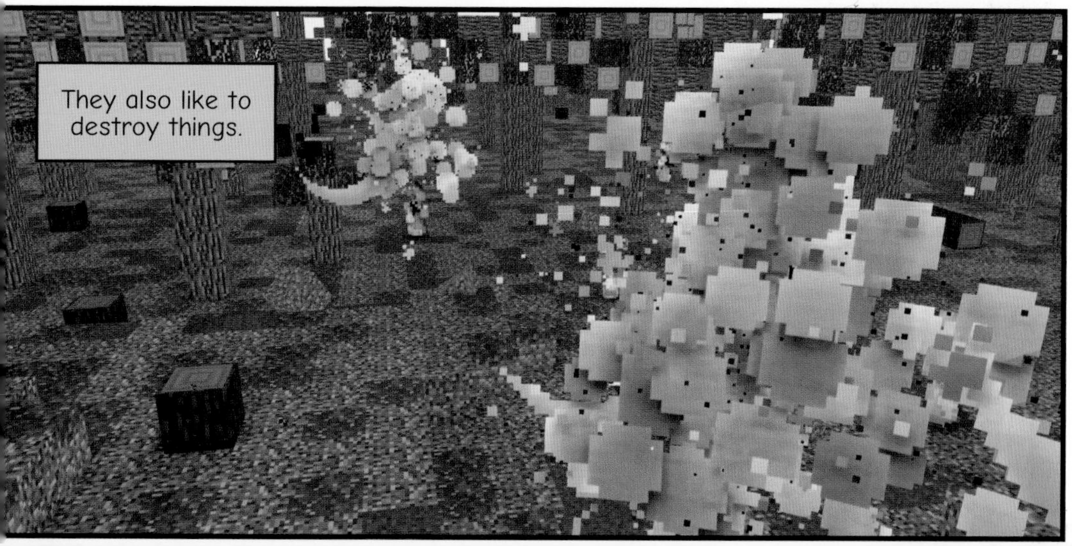
They also like to destroy things.

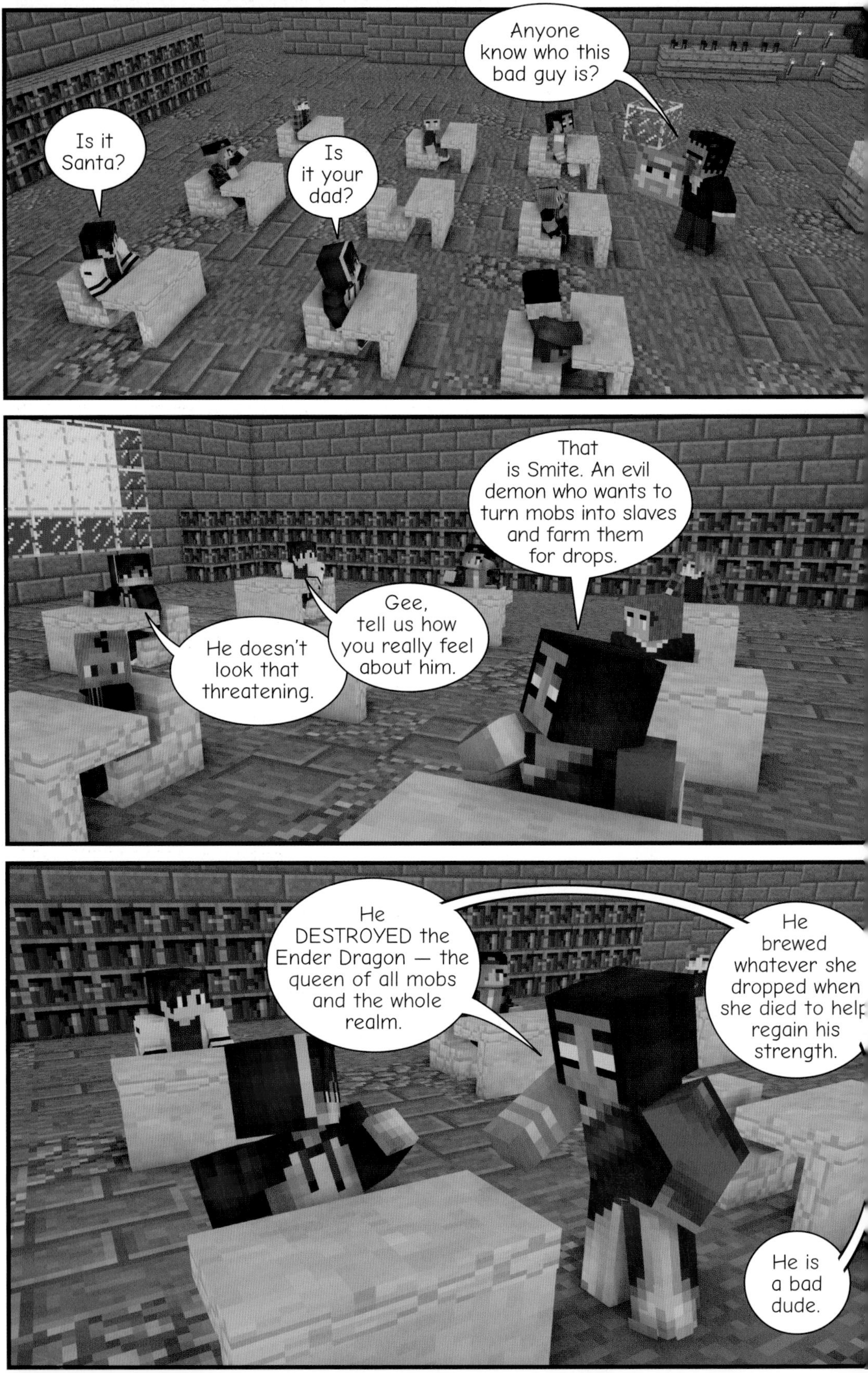
Anyone know who this bad guy is?
Is it Santa?
Is it your dad?
That is Smite. An evil demon who wants to turn mobs into slaves and farm them for drops.
He doesn't look that threatening.
Gee, tell us how you really feel about him.
He DESTROYED the Ender Dragon — the queen of all mobs and the whole realm.
He brewed whatever she dropped when she died to help regain his strength.
He is a bad dude.

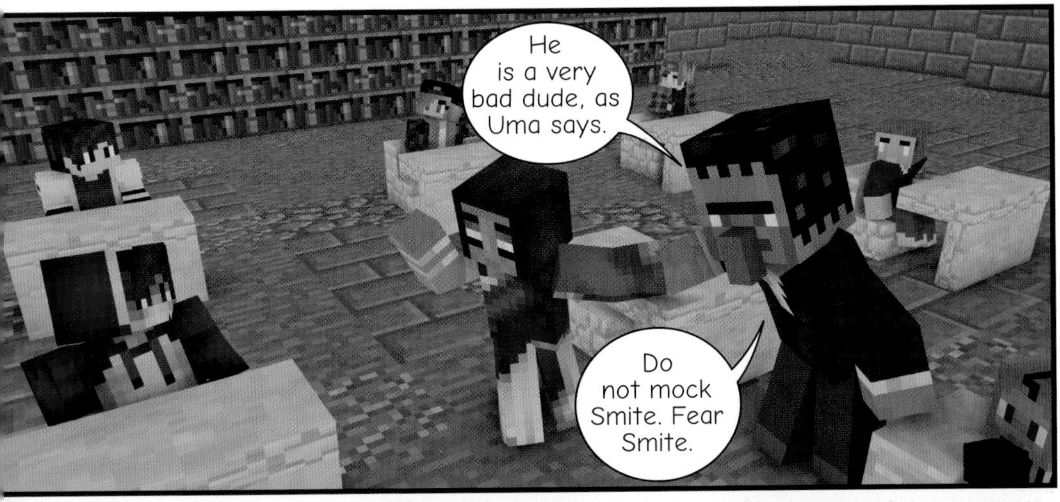
He is a very bad dude, as Uma says.
Do not mock Smite. Fear Smite.

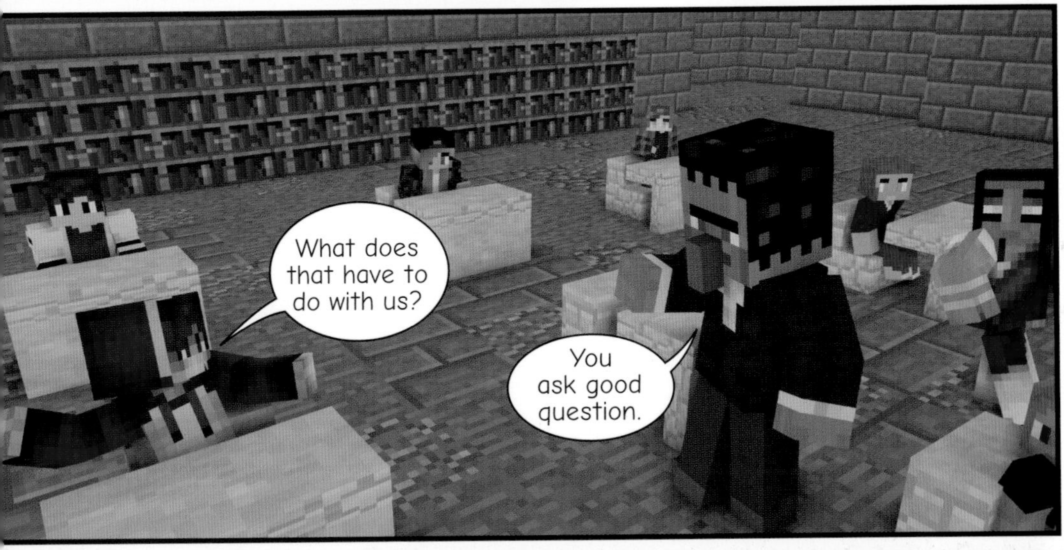
What does that have to do with us?
You ask good question.

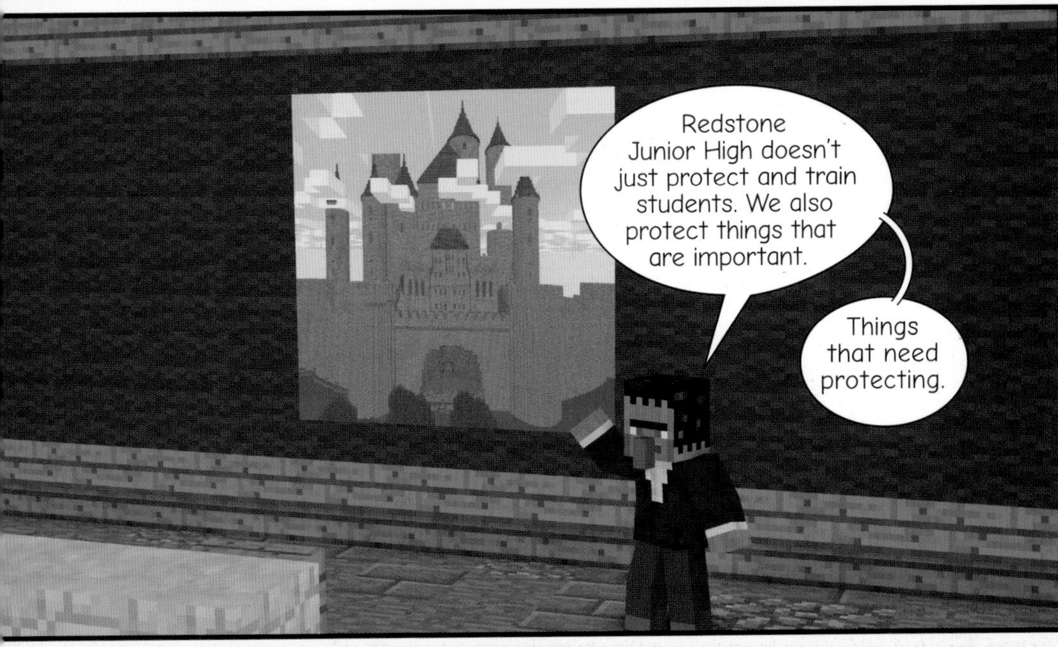
Redstone Junior High doesn't just protect and train students. We also protect things that are important.
Things that need protecting.

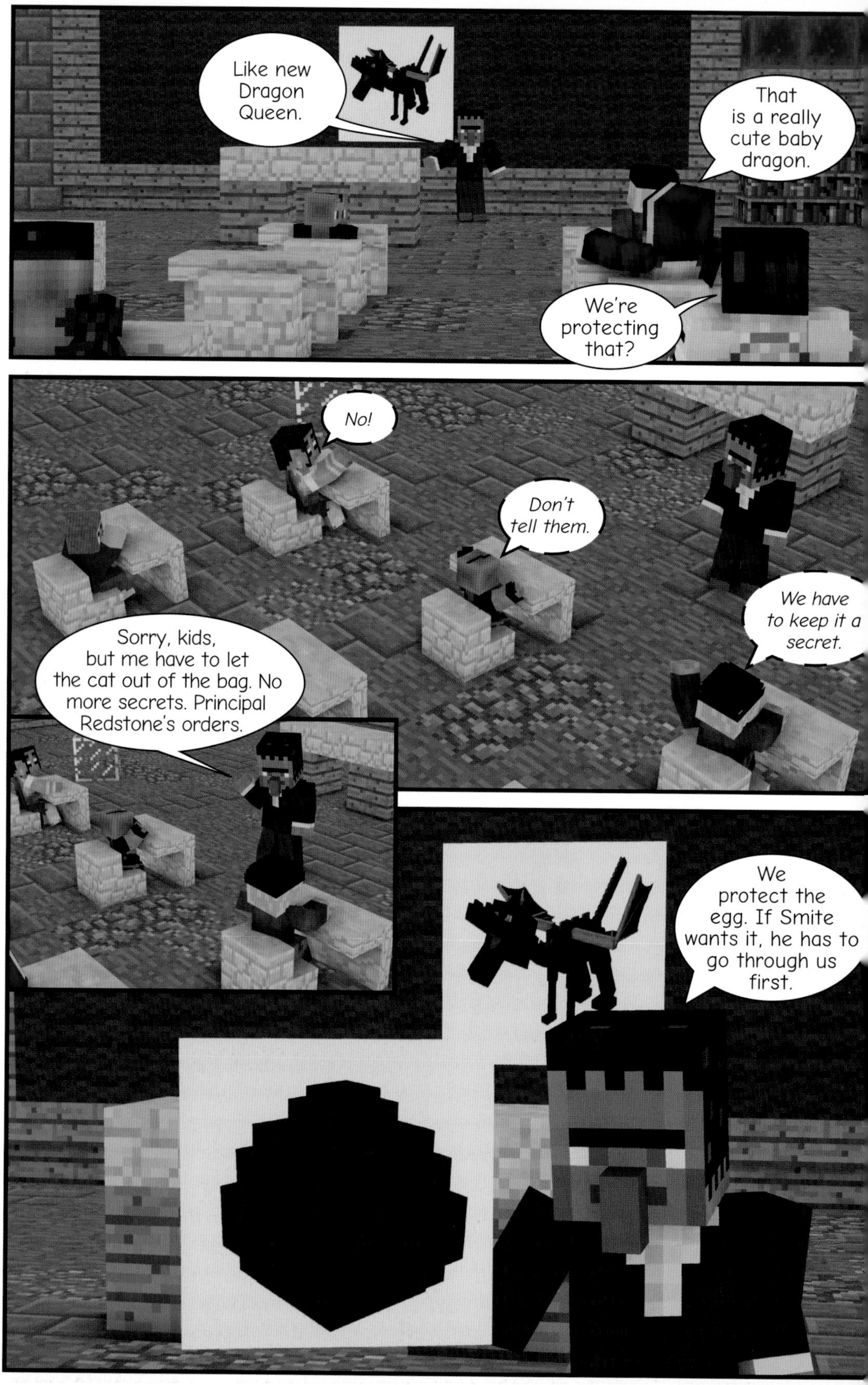
Like new Dragon Queen.
That is a really cute baby dragon.
We're protecting that?
No!
Don't tell them.
We have to keep it a secret.
Sorry, kids, but me have to let the cat out of the bag. No more secrets. Principal Redstone's orders.
We protect the egg. If Smite wants it, he has to go through us first.

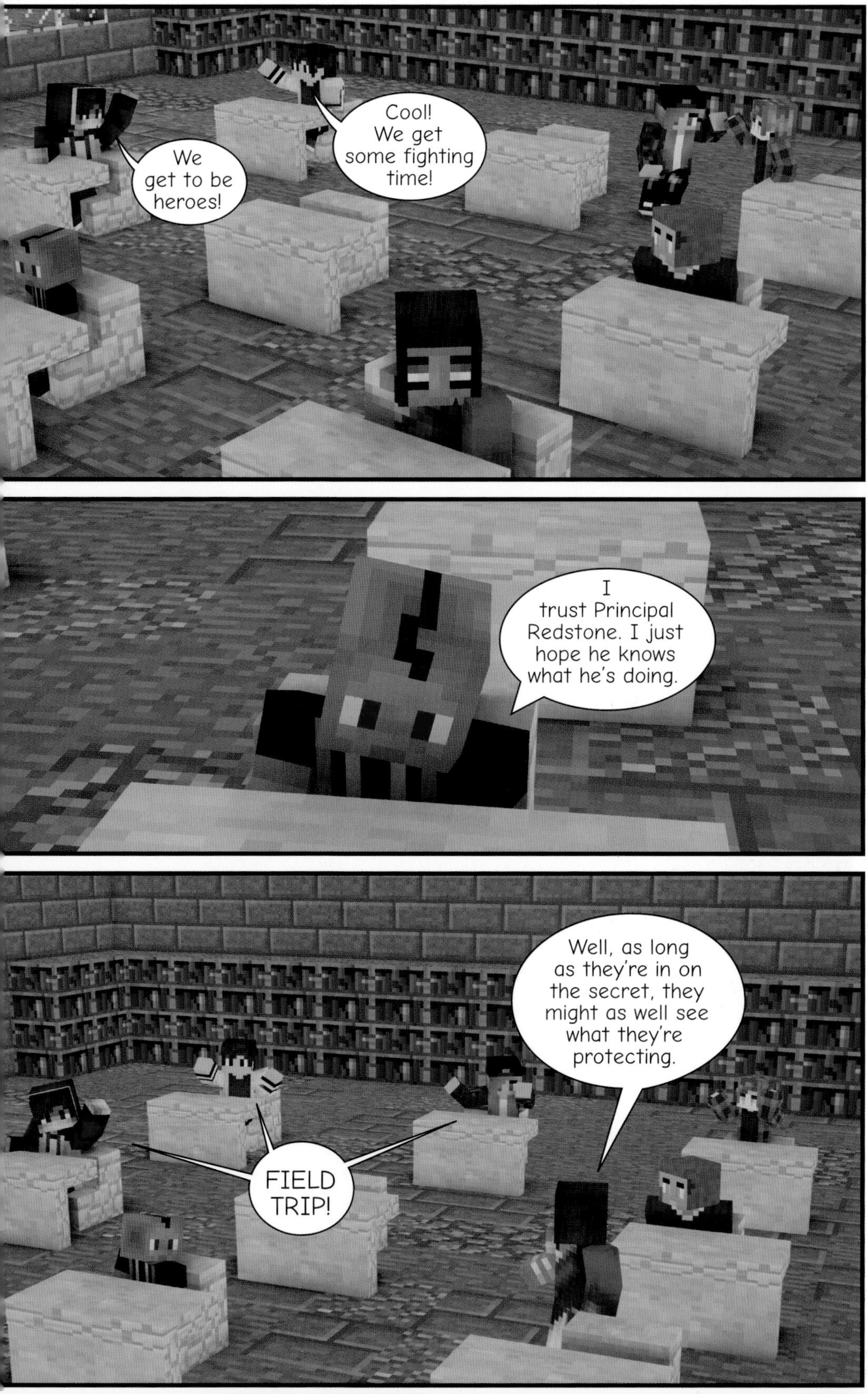

We get to be heroes!
Cool! We get some fighting time!
I trust Principal Redstone. I just hope he knows what he's doing.
Well, as long as they're in on the secret, they might as well see what they're protecting.
FIELD TRIP!

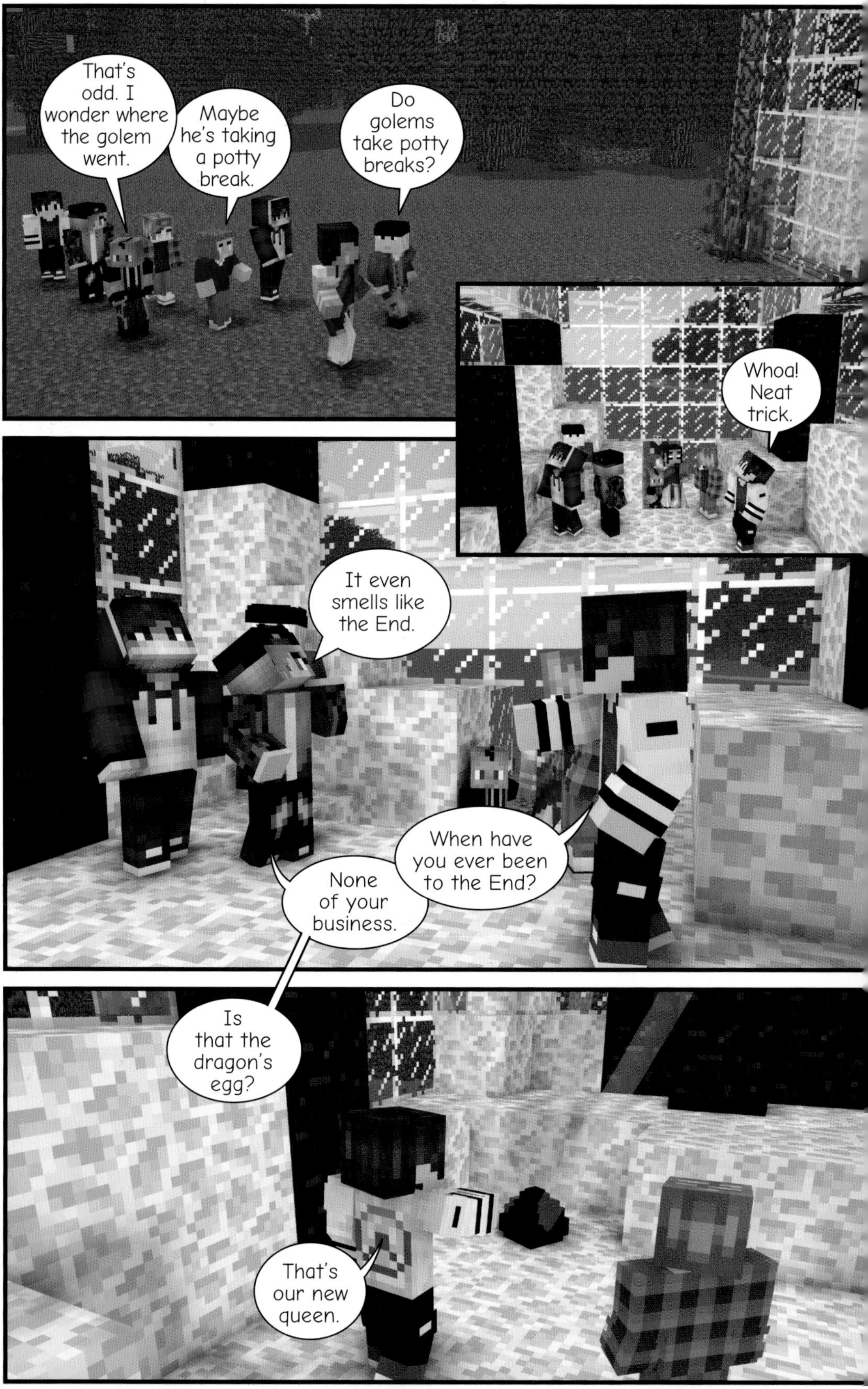
That's odd. I wonder where the golem went.
Maybe he's taking a potty break.
Do golems take potty breaks?
Whoa! Neat trick.
It even smells like the End.
When have you ever been to the End?
None of your business.
Is that the dragon's egg?
That's our new queen.

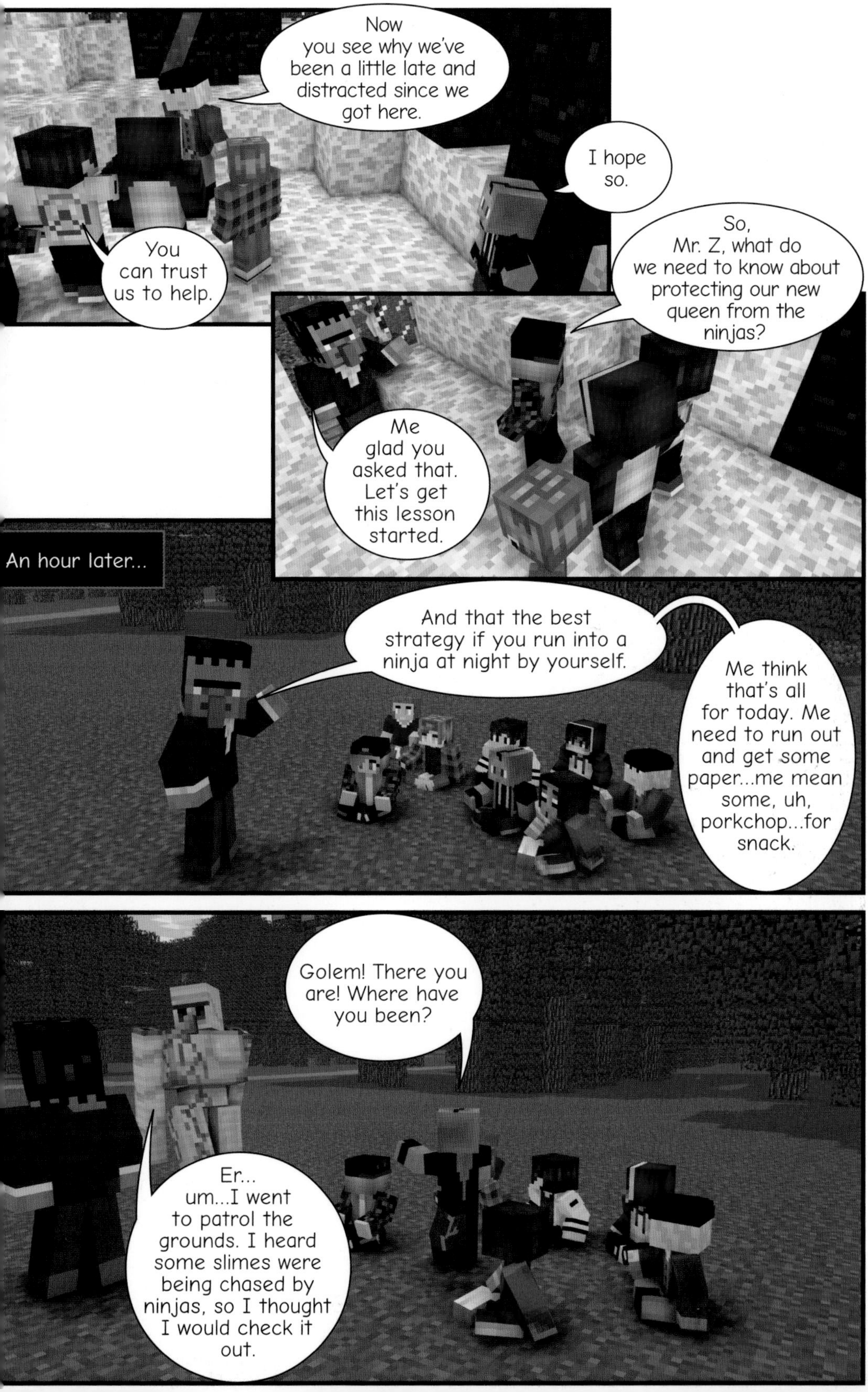

Now you see why we've been a little late and distracted since we got here.
I hope so.
You can trust us to help.
So, Mr. Z, what do we need to know about protecting our new queen from the ninjas?
Me glad you asked that. Let's get this lesson started.
An hour later...
And that the best strategy if you run into a ninja at night by yourself.
Me think that's all for today. Me need to run out and get some paper...me mean some, uh, porkchop...for snack.
Golem! There you are! Where have you been?
Er... um...I went to patrol the grounds. I heard some slimes were being chased by ninjas, so I thought I would check it out.

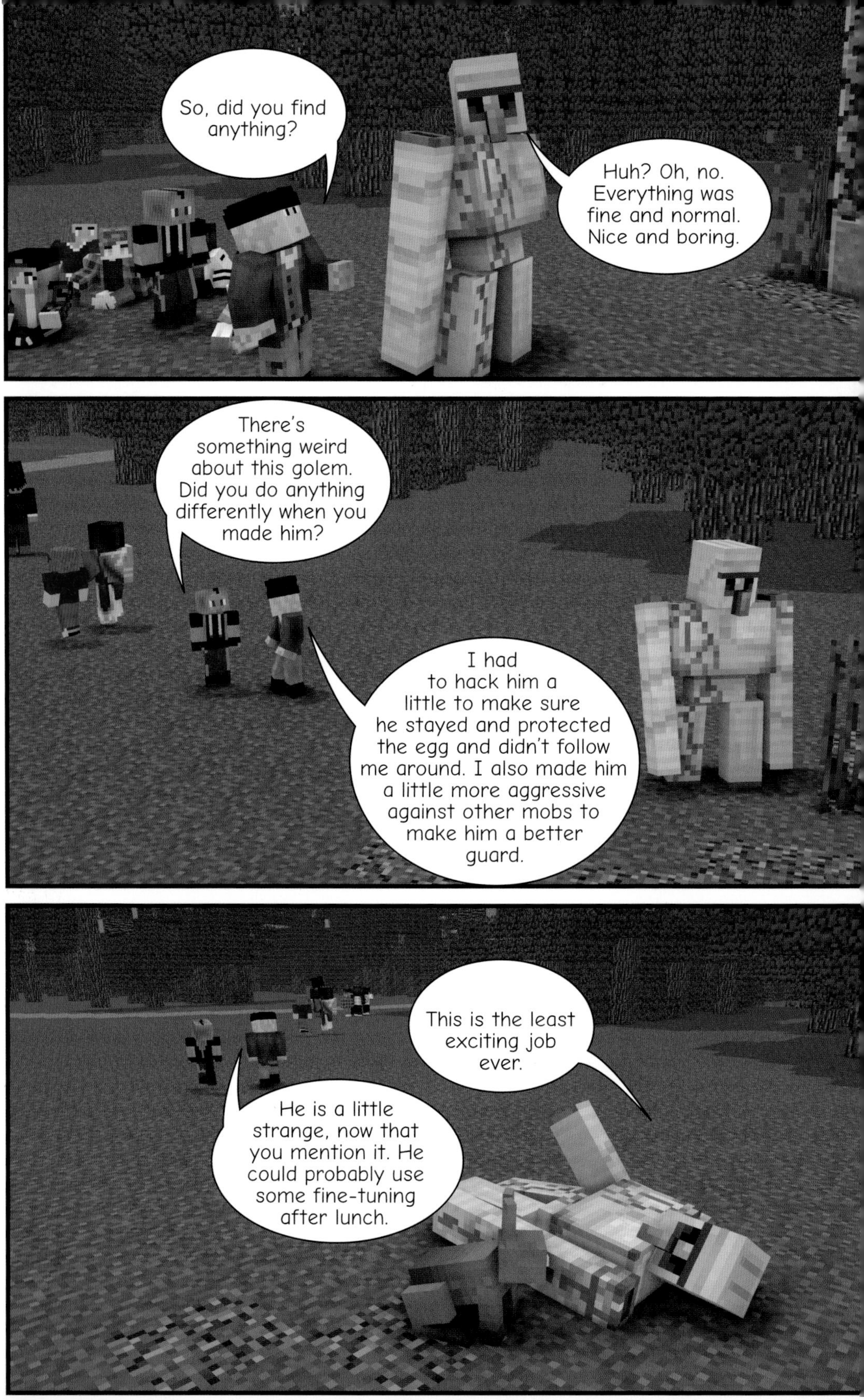
So, did you find anything?
Huh? Oh, no. Everything was fine and normal. Nice and boring.
There's something weird about this golem. Did you do anything differently when you made him?
I had to hack him a little to make sure he stayed and protected the egg and didn't follow me around. I also made him a little more aggressive against other mobs to make him a better guard.
This is the least exciting job ever.
He is a little strange, now that you mention it. He could probably use some fine-tuning after lunch.

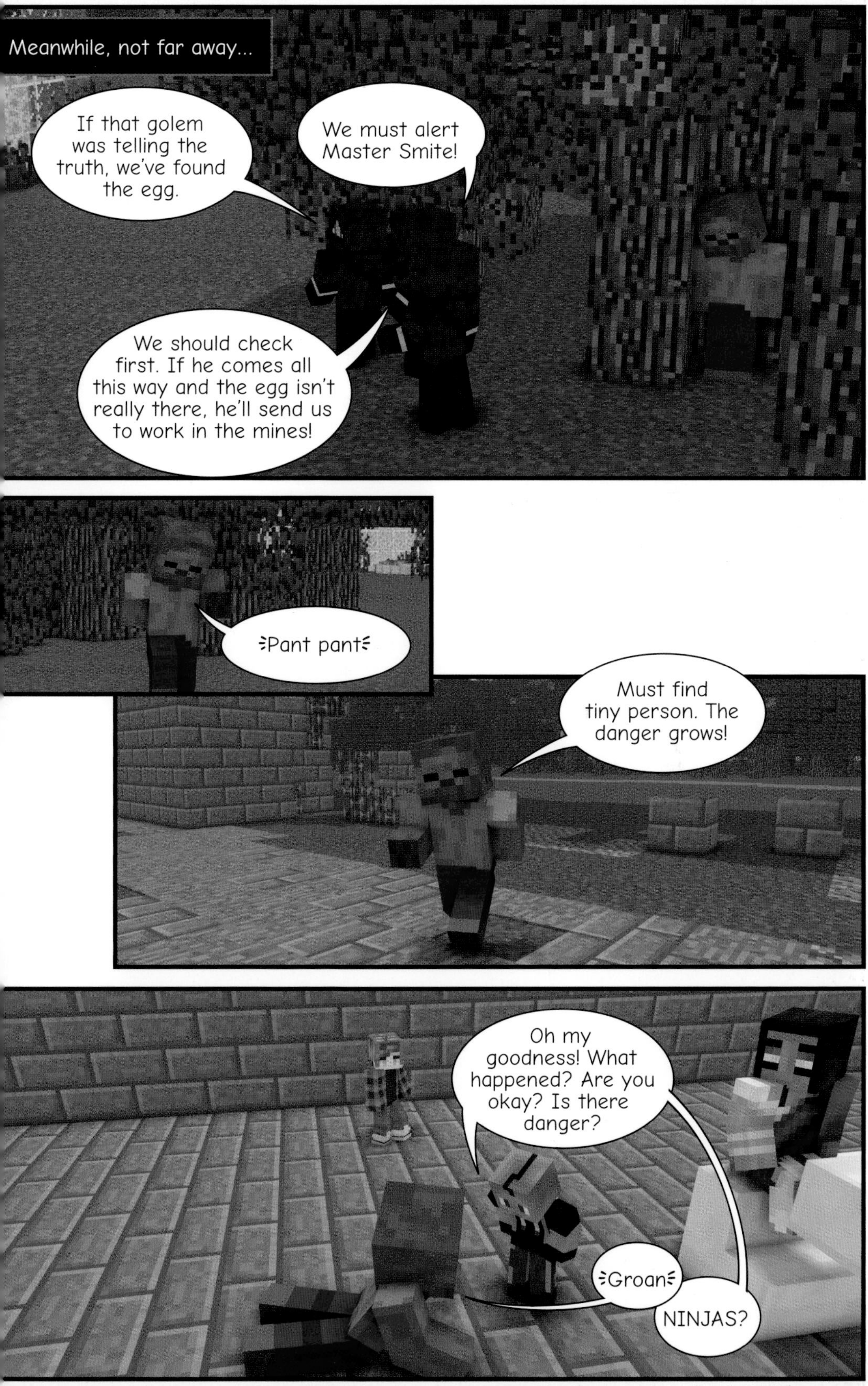

Meanwhile, not far away...
If that golem was telling the truth, we've found the egg.
We must alert Master Smite!
We should check first. If he comes all this way and the egg isn't really there, he'll send us to work in the mines!
Pant pant
Must find tiny person. The danger grows!
Oh my goodness! What happened? Are you okay? Is there danger?
Groan
NINJAS?

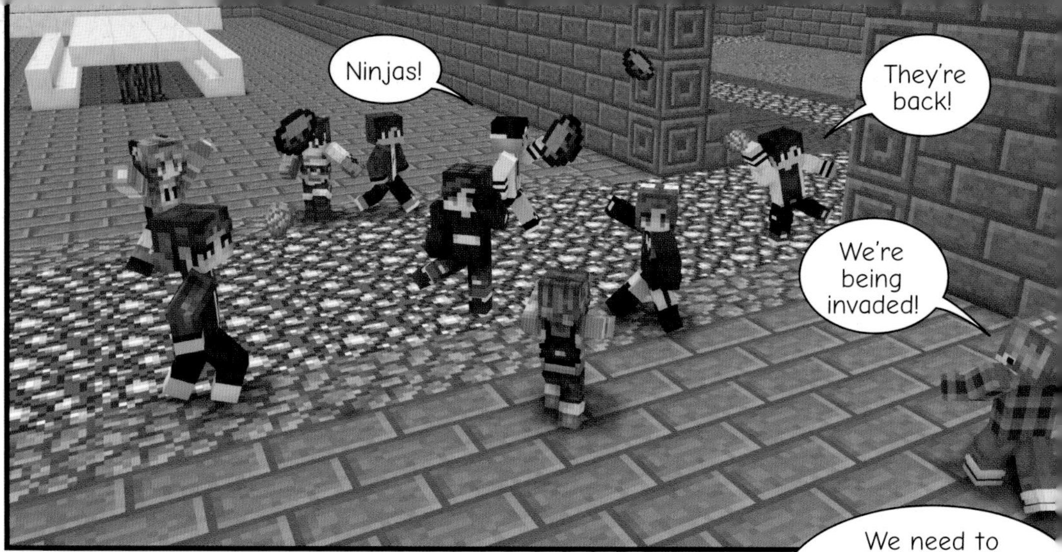
Ninjas!
They're back!
We're being invaded!

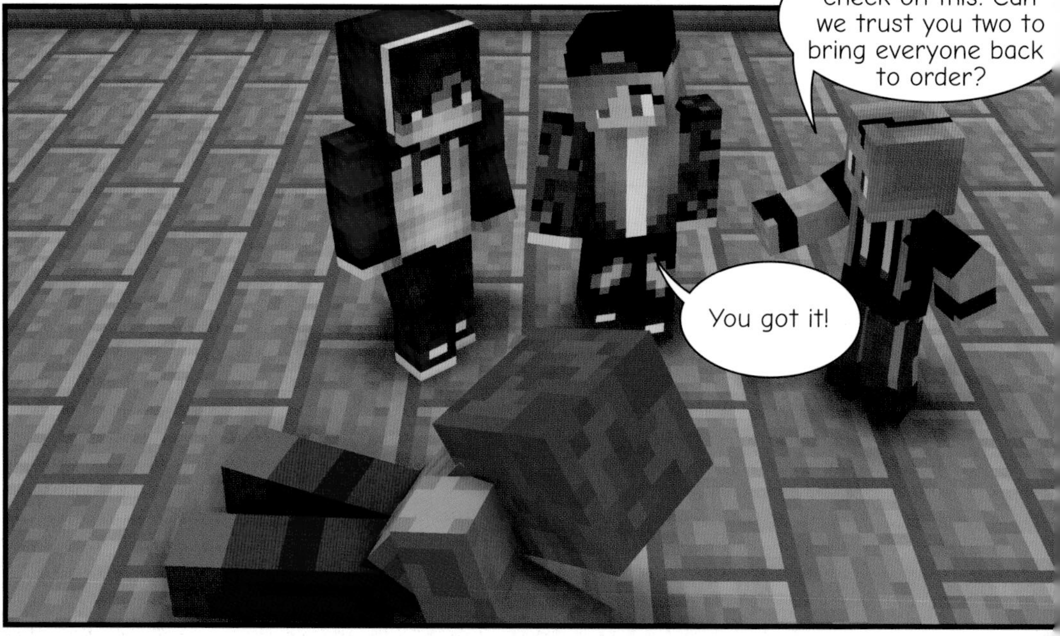
We need to check on this. Can we trust you two to bring everyone back to order?
You got it!

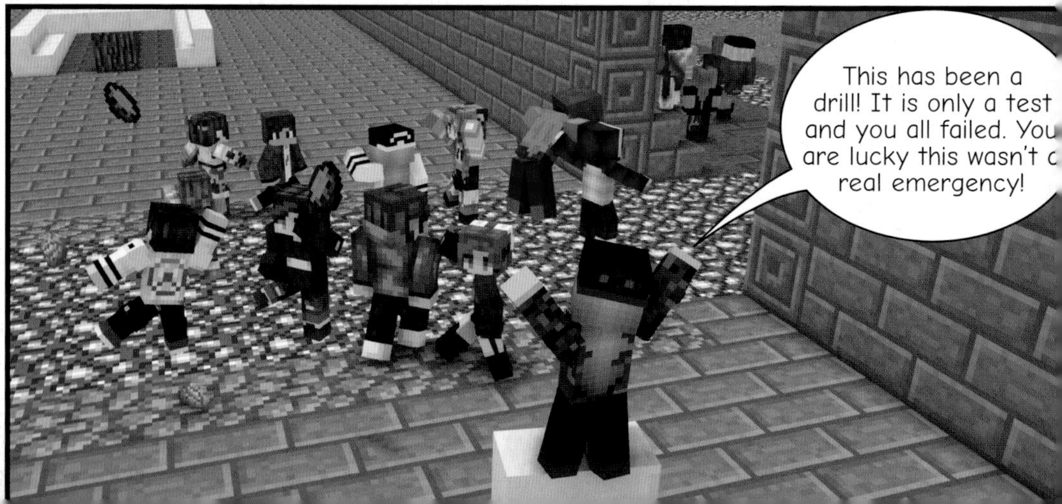
This has been a drill! It is only a test and you all failed. You are lucky this wasn't a real emergency!

CHAPTER 11

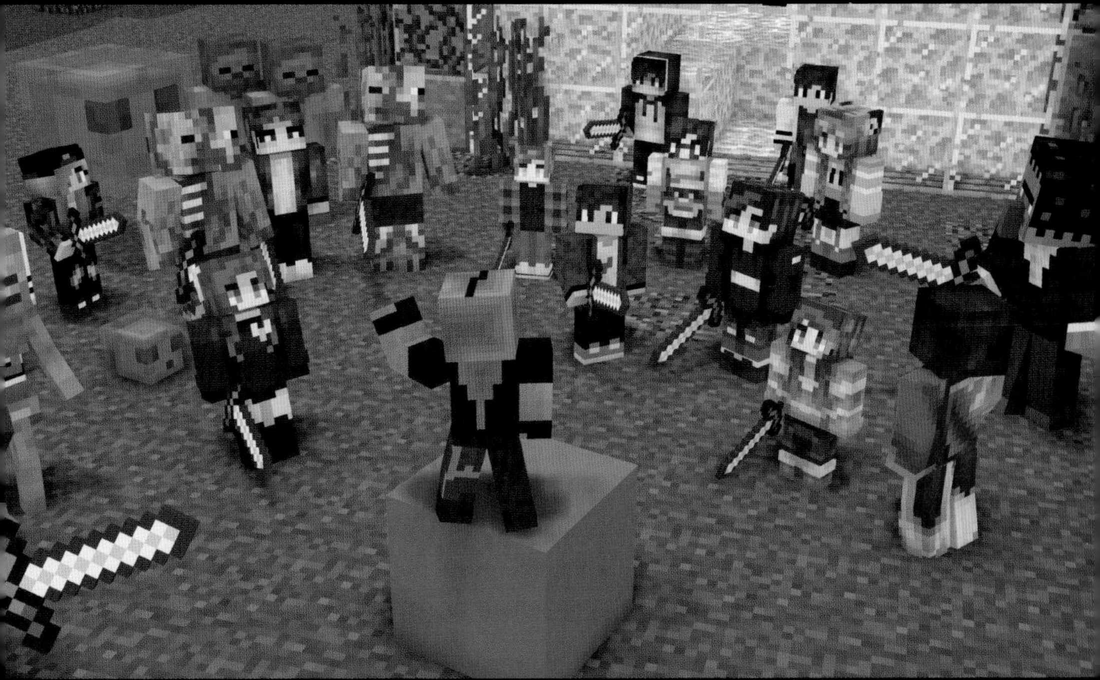

THE BATTLE

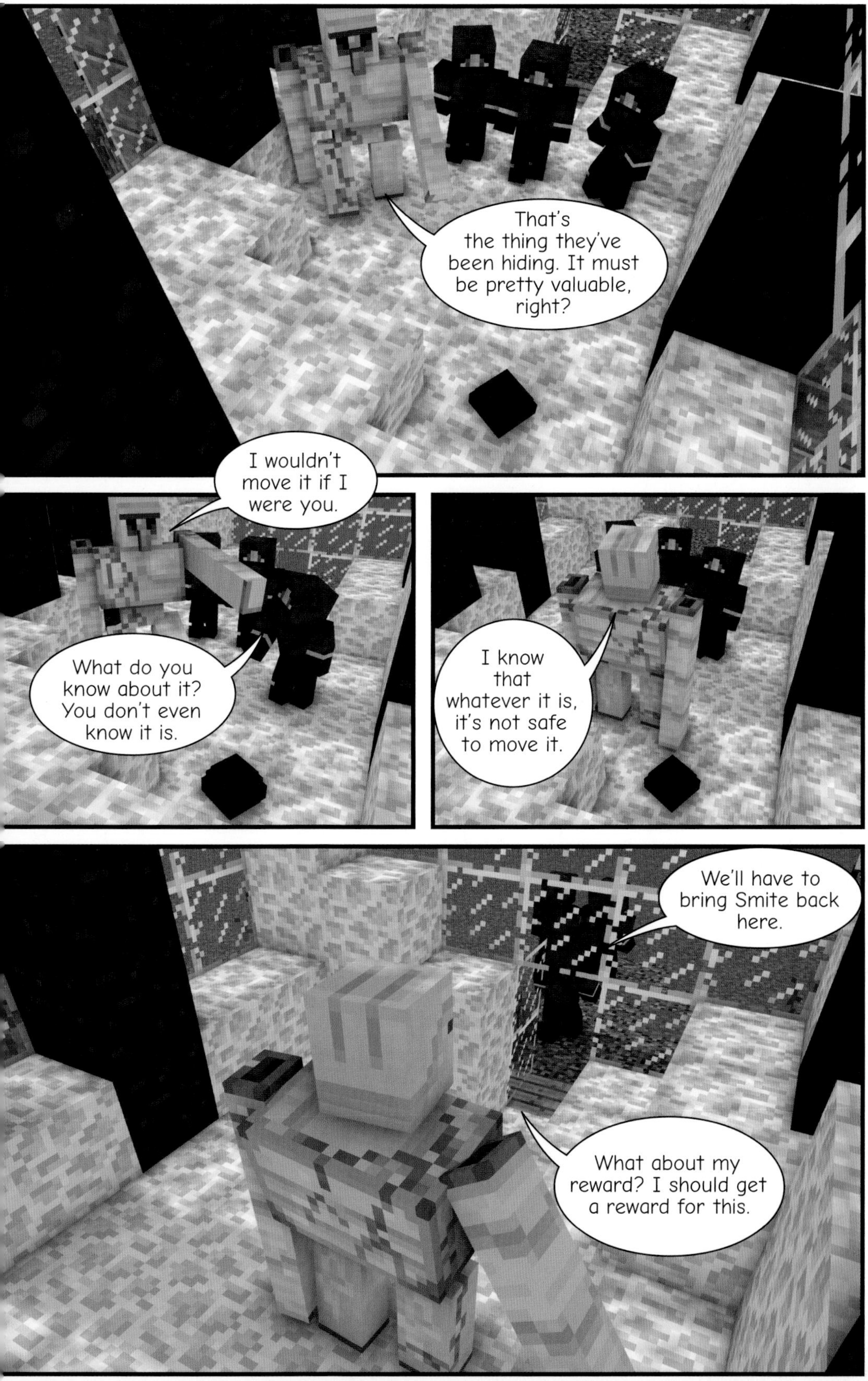
That's the thing they've been hiding. It must be pretty valuable, right?
I wouldn't move it if I were you.
What do you know about it? You don't even know it is.
I know that whatever it is, it's not safe to move it.
We'll have to bring Smite back here.
What about my reward? I should get a reward for this.

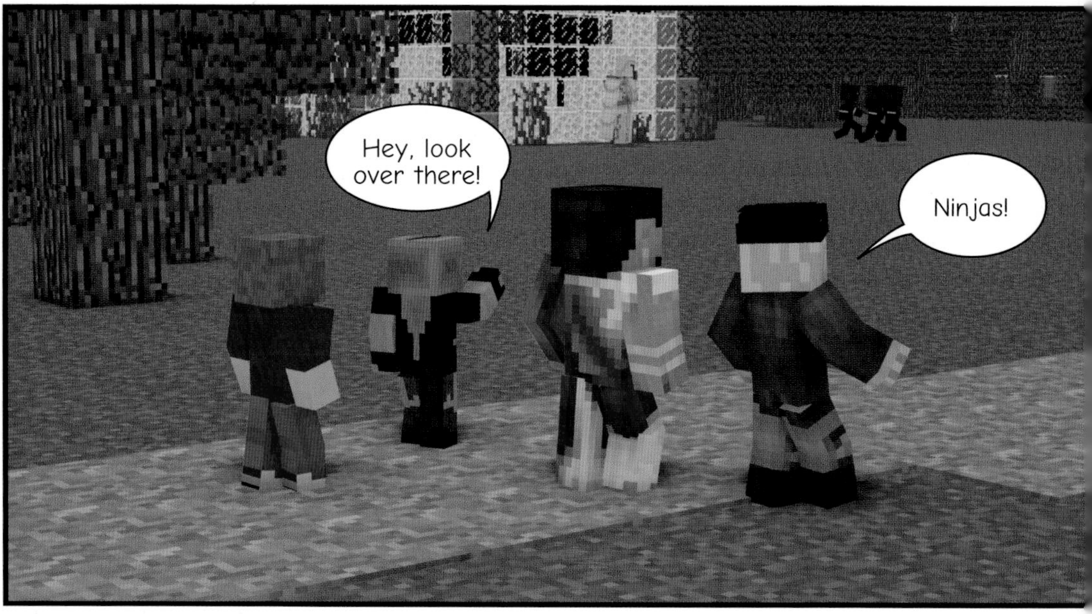
Hey, look over there!
Ninjas!

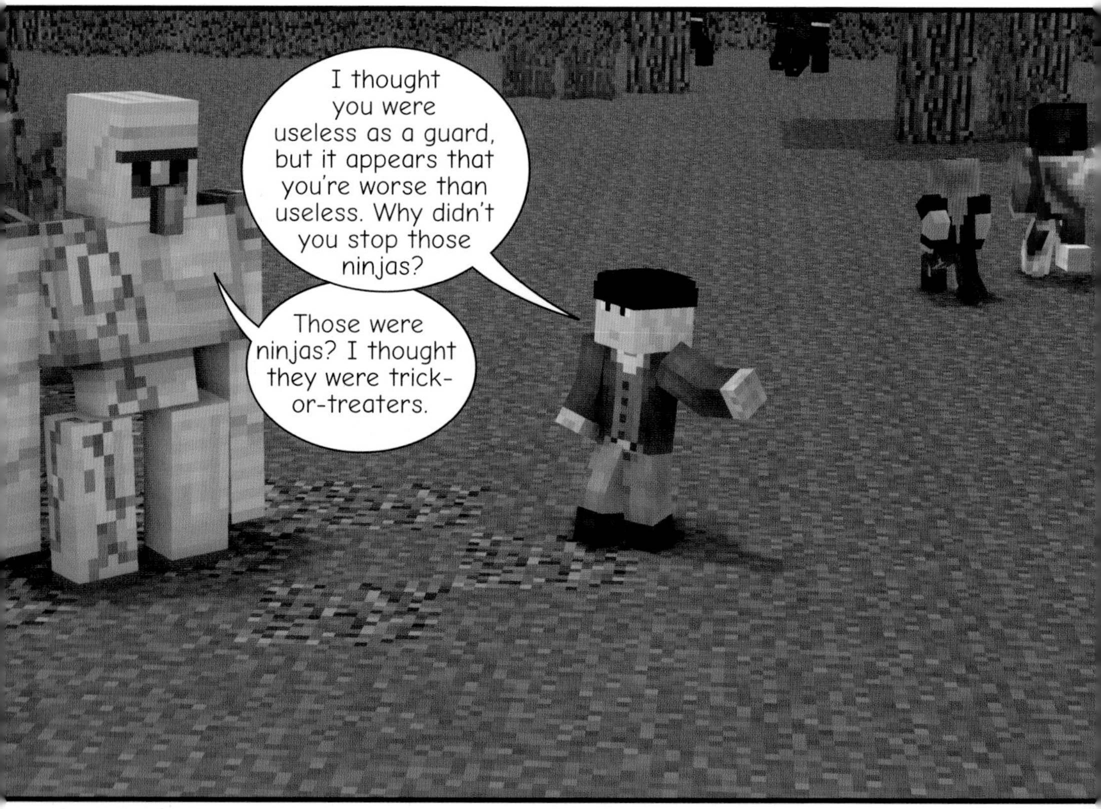
I thought you were useless as a guard, but it appears that you're worse than useless. Why didn't you stop those ninjas?
Those were ninjas? I thought they were trick-or-treaters.

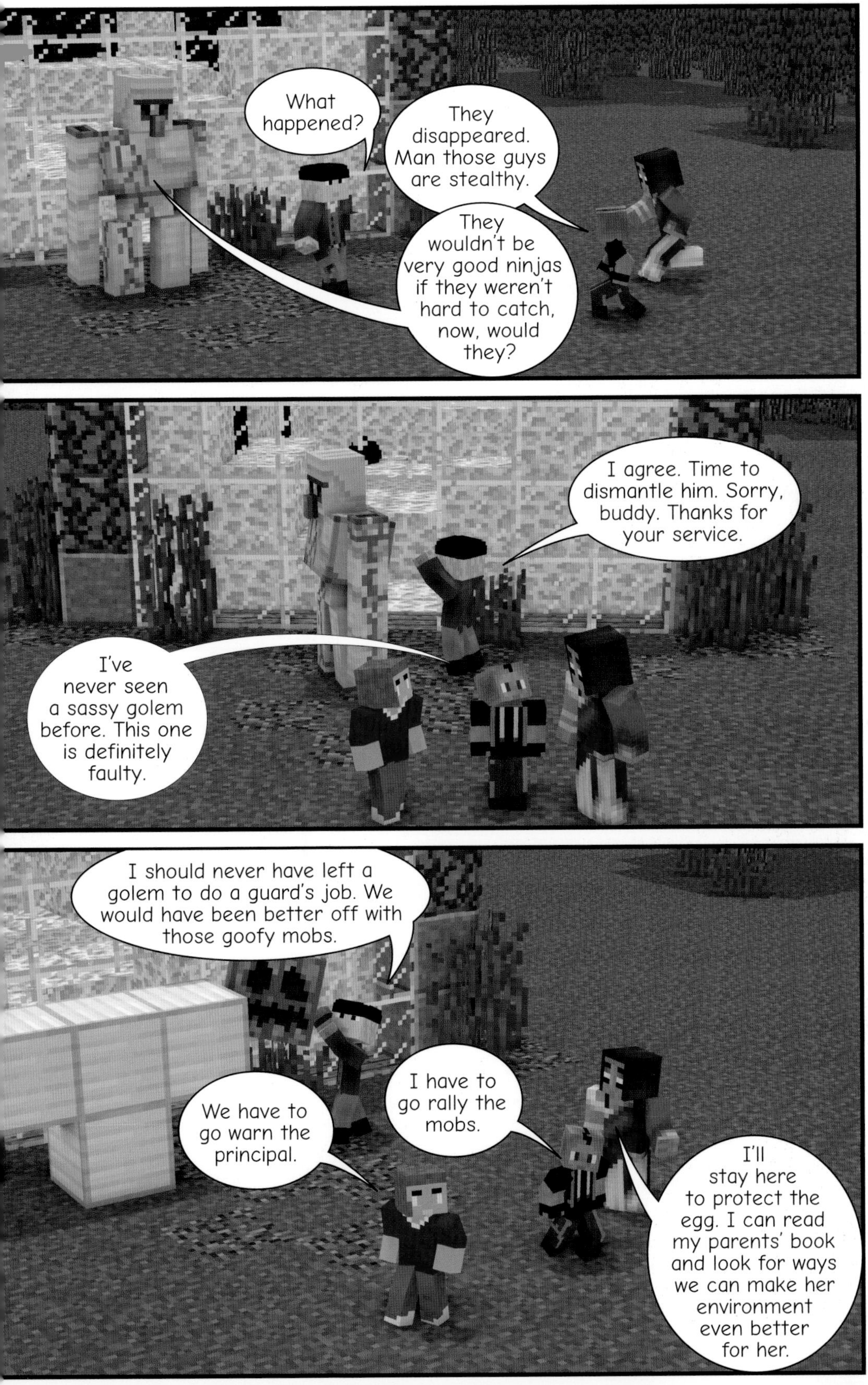

What happened?
They disappeared. Man those guys are stealthy.
They wouldn't be very good ninjas if they weren't hard to catch, now, would they?
I agree. Time to dismantle him. Sorry, buddy. Thanks for your service.
I've never seen a sassy golem before. This one is definitely faulty.
I should never have left a golem to do a guard's job. We would have been better off with those goofy mobs.
We have to go warn the principal.
I have to go rally the mobs.
I'll stay here to protect the egg. I can read my parents' book and look for ways we can make her environment even better for her.

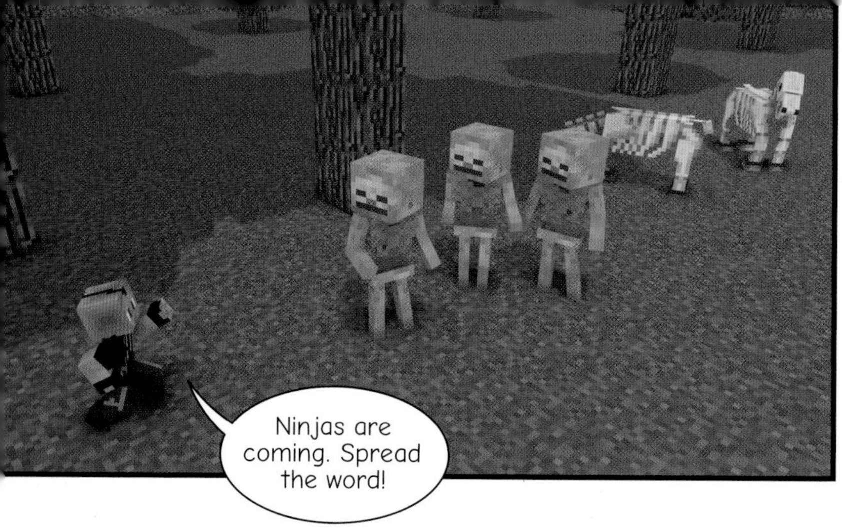
Ninjas are coming. Spread the word!

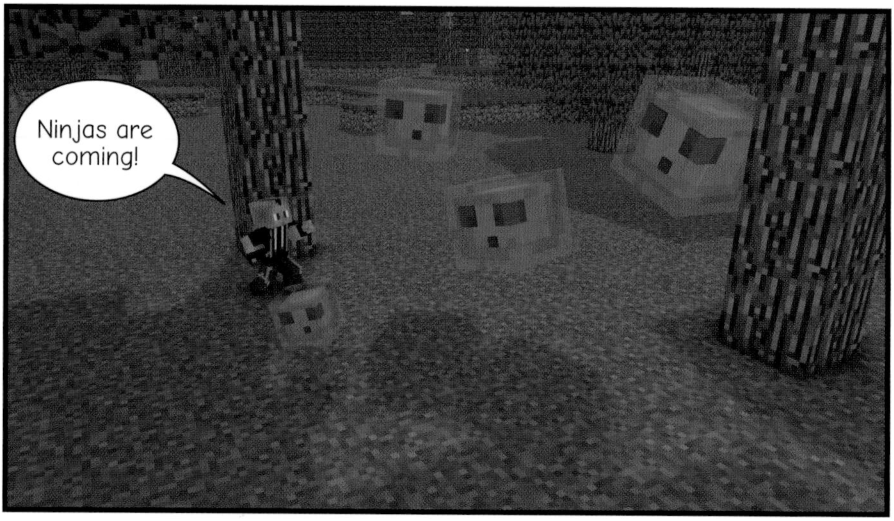
Ninjas are coming!

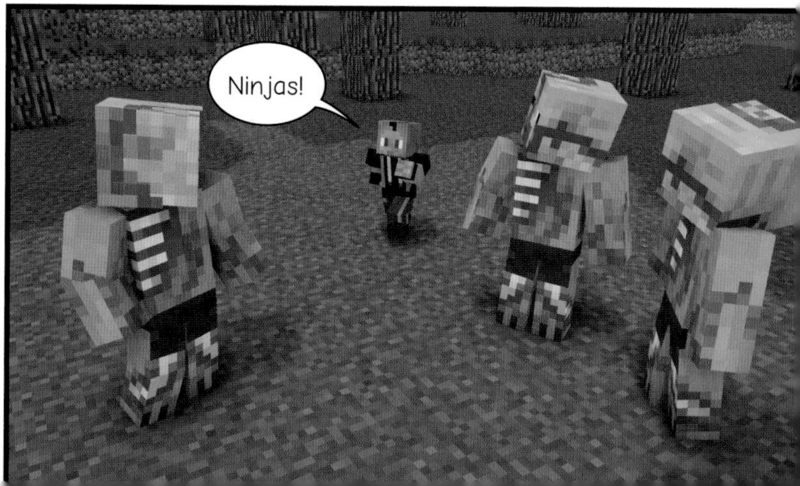
Ninjas!

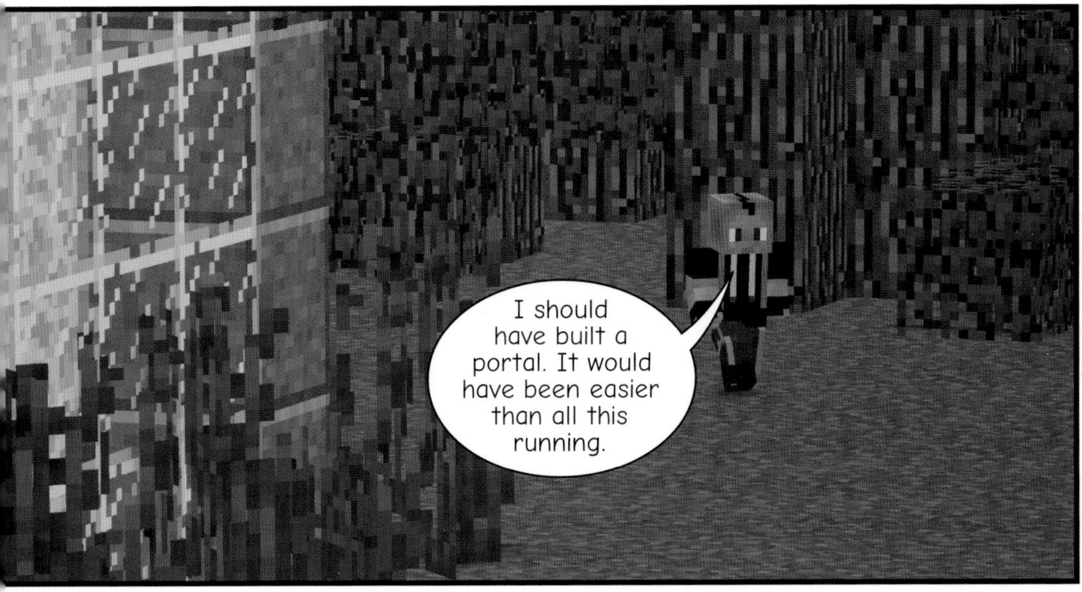
I should have built a portal. It would have been easier than all this running.

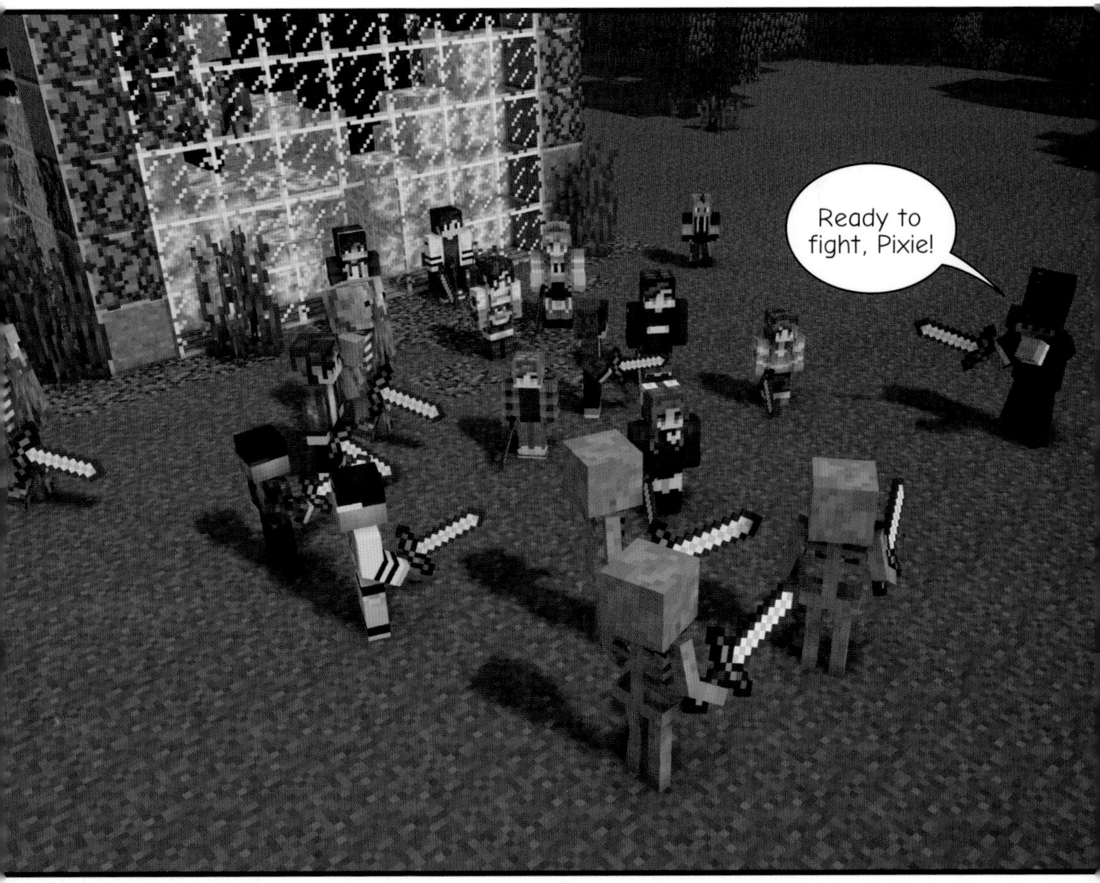
Ready to fight, Pixie!

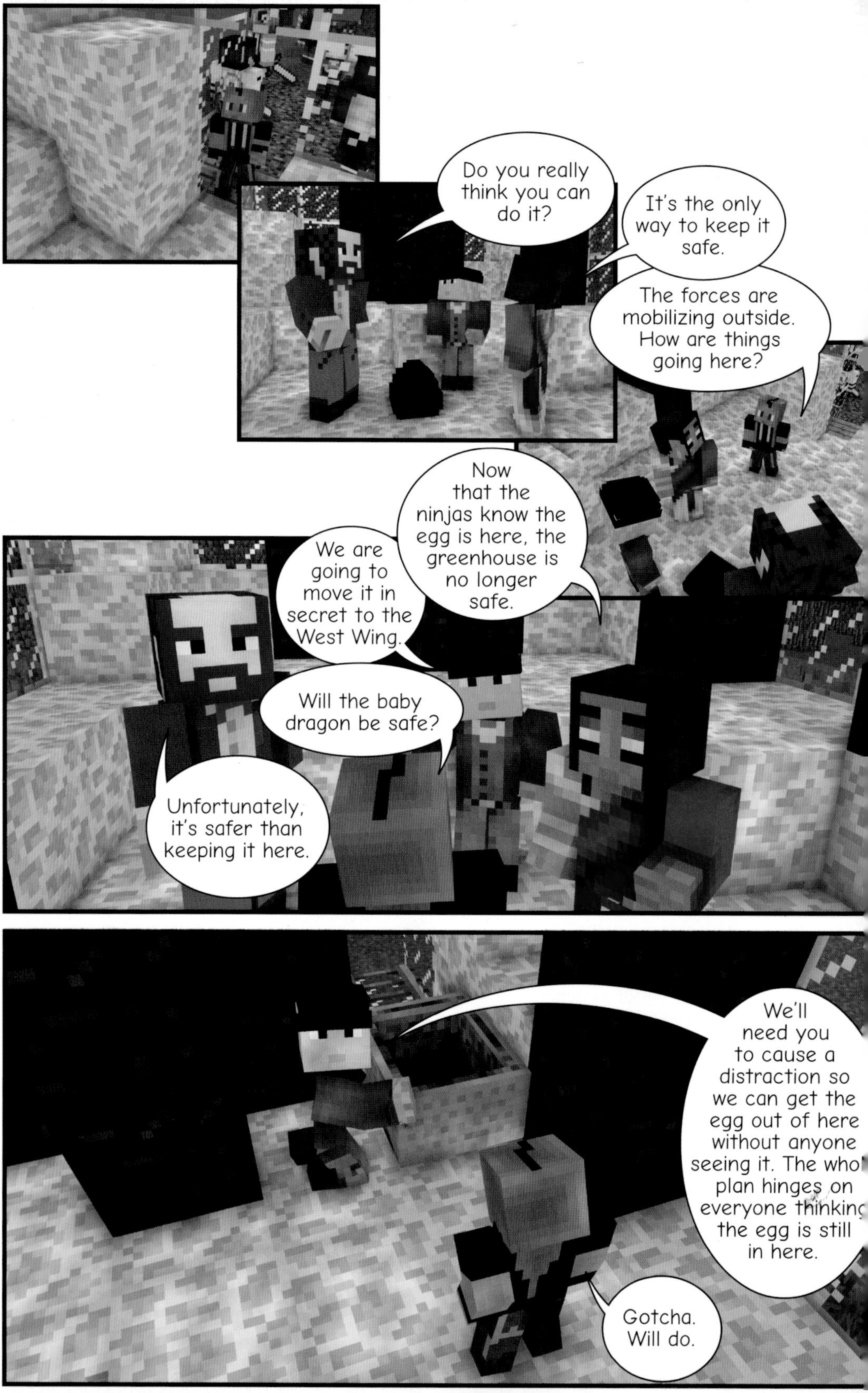
Do you really think you can do it?
It's the only way to keep it safe.
The forces are mobilizing outside. How are things going here?
Now that the ninjas know the egg is here, the greenhouse is no longer safe.
We are going to move it in secret to the West Wing.
Will the baby dragon be safe?
Unfortunately, it's safer than keeping it here.
We'll need you to cause a distraction so we can get the egg out of here without anyone seeing it. The who plan hinges on everyone thinkin the egg is still in here.
Gotcha. Will do.

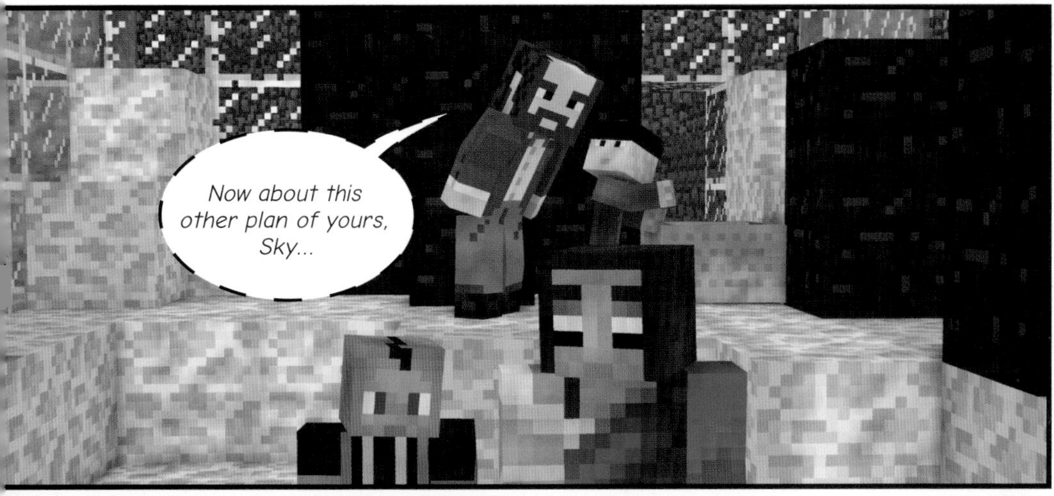
Now about this other plan of yours, Sky...

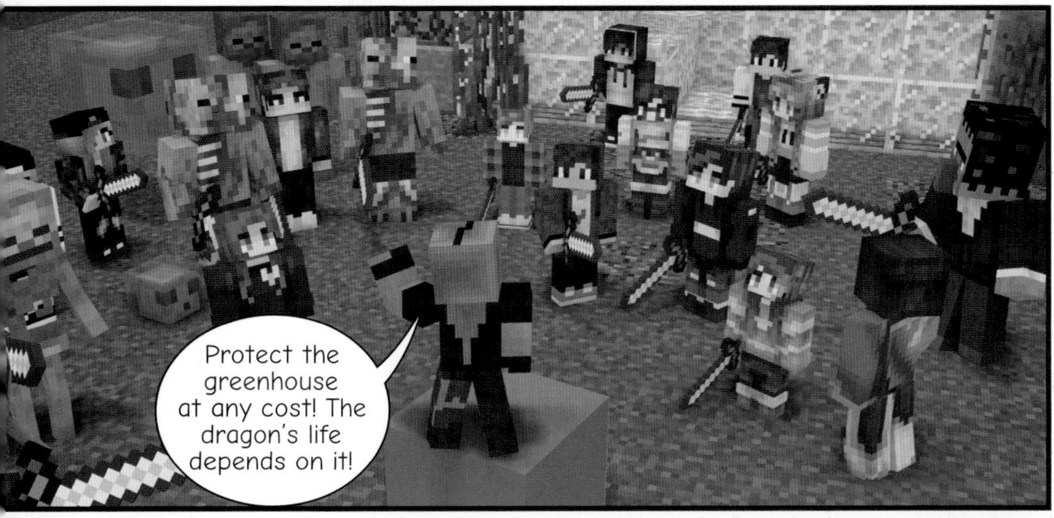
Protect the greenhouse at any cost! The dragon's life depends on it!

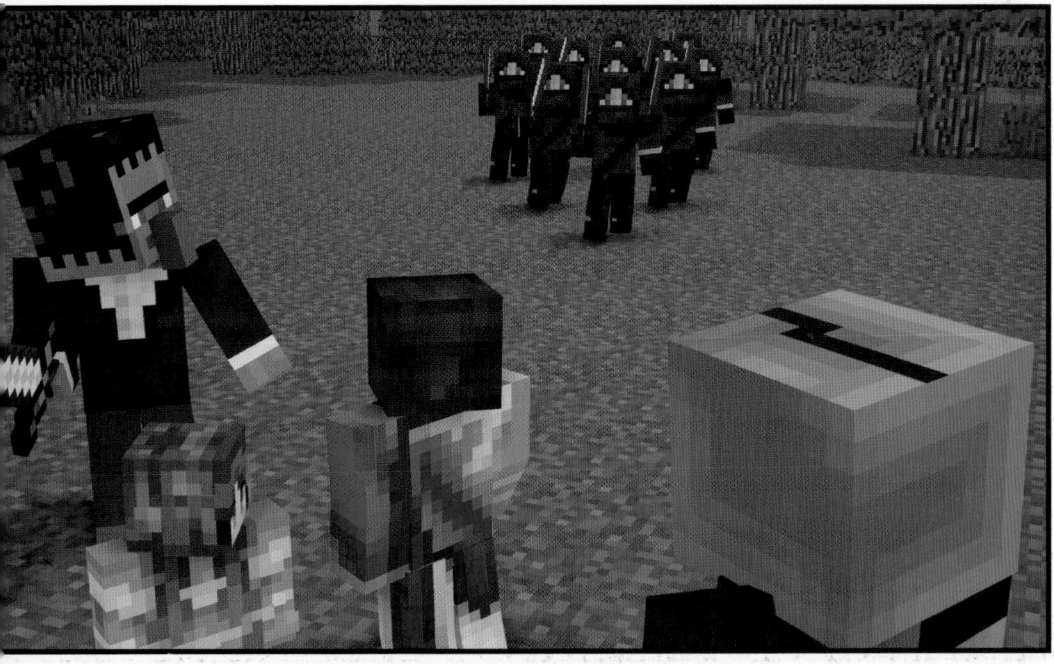

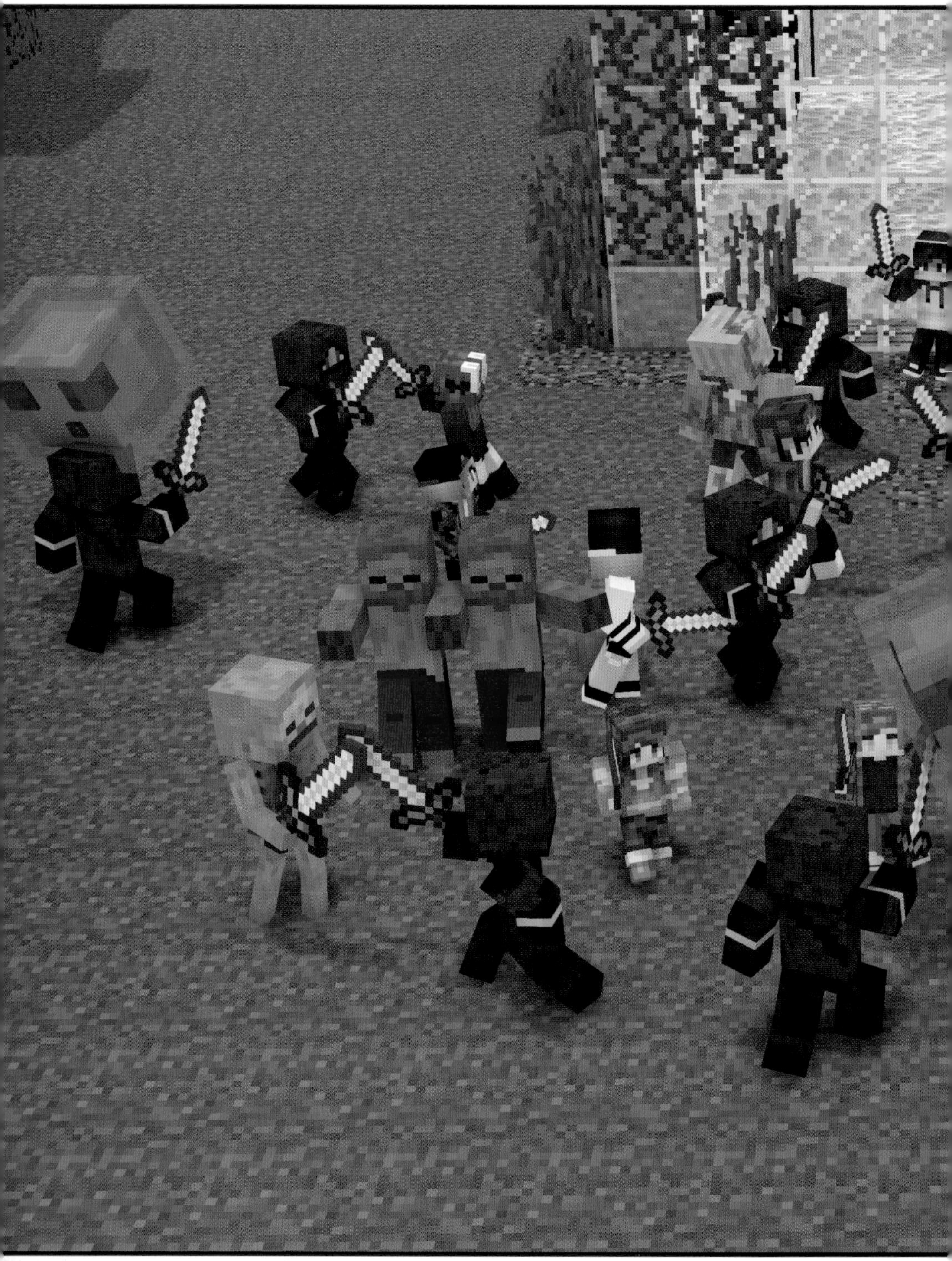

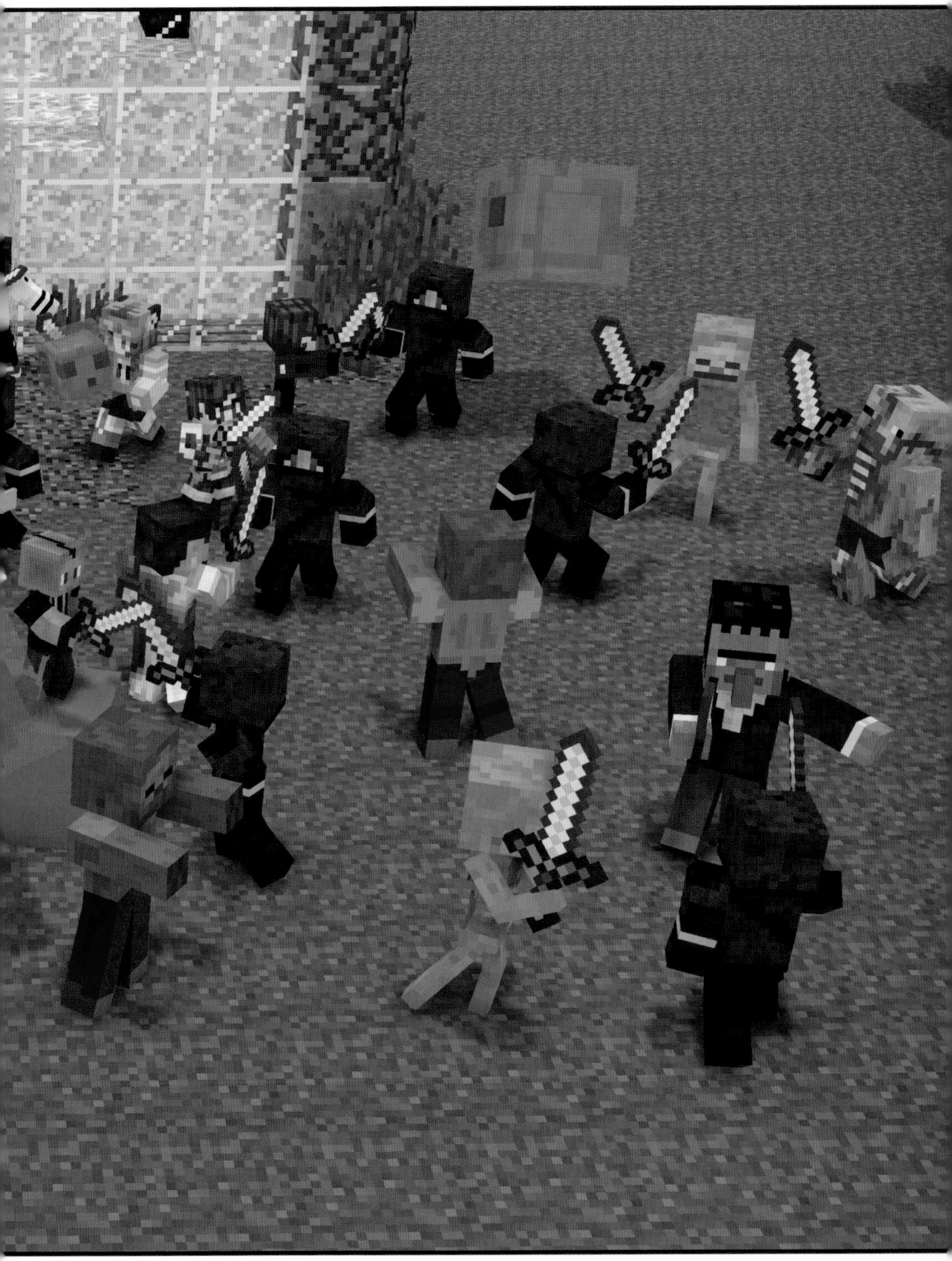

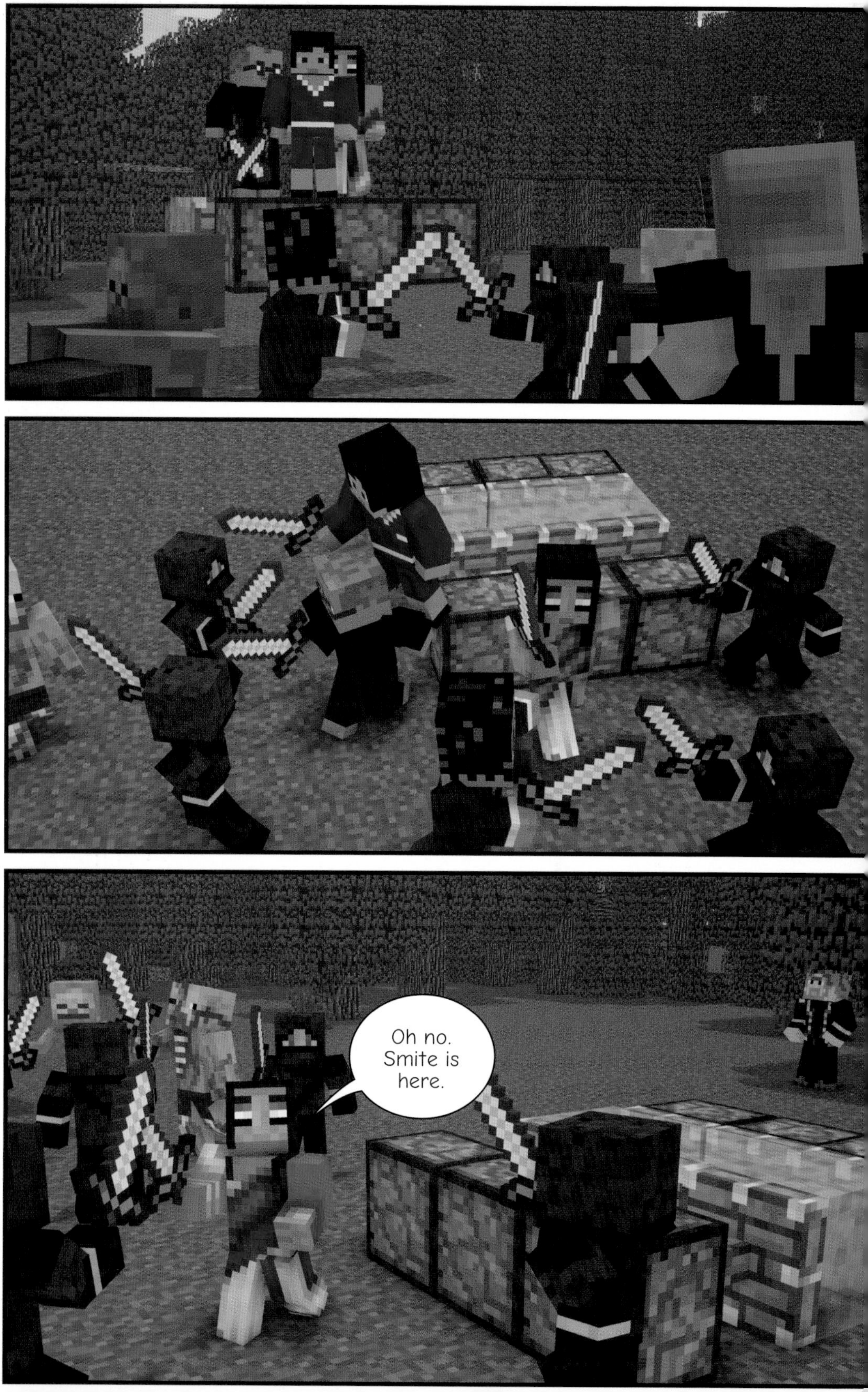
Oh no. Smite is here.

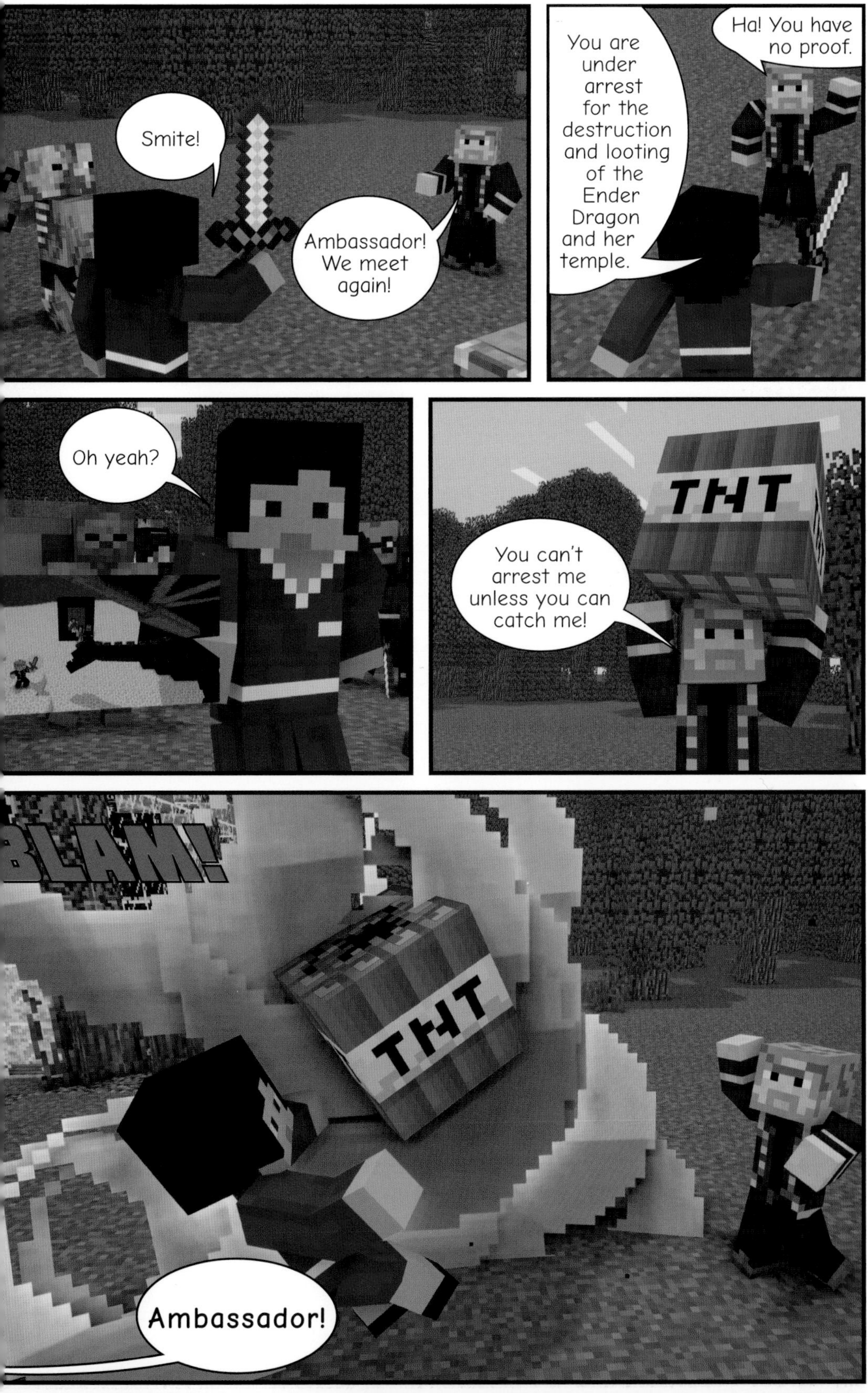
Smite!
Ambassador! We meet again!
You are under arrest for the destruction and looting of the Ender Dragon and her temple.
Ha! You have no proof.
Oh yeah?
TNT
You can't arrest me unless you can catch me!
BLAM!
TNT
Ambassador!

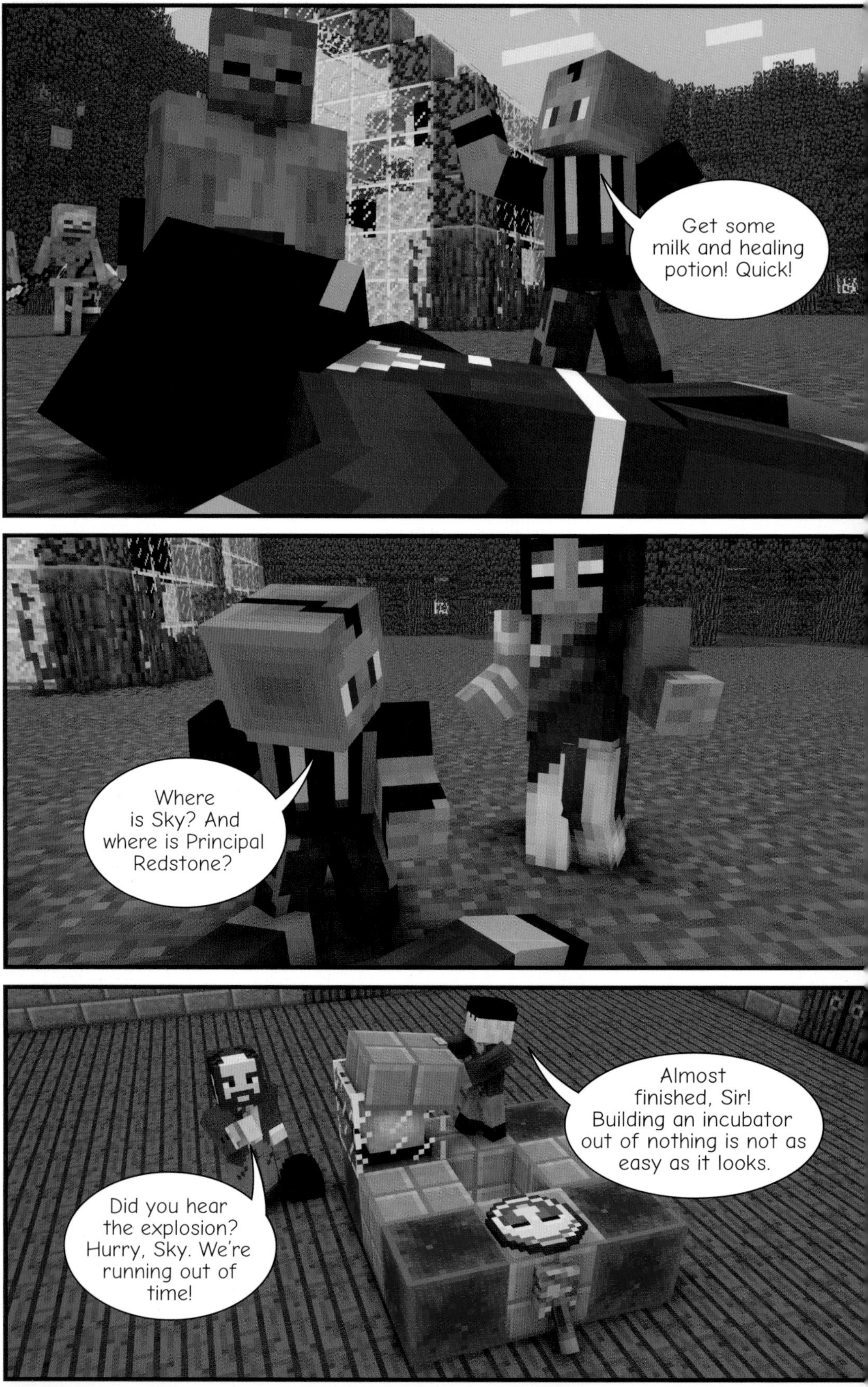
Get some milk and healing potion! Quick!
Where is Sky? And where is Principal Redstone?
Almost finished, Sir! Building an incubator out of nothing is not as easy as it looks.
Did you hear the explosion? Hurry, Sky. We're running out of time!

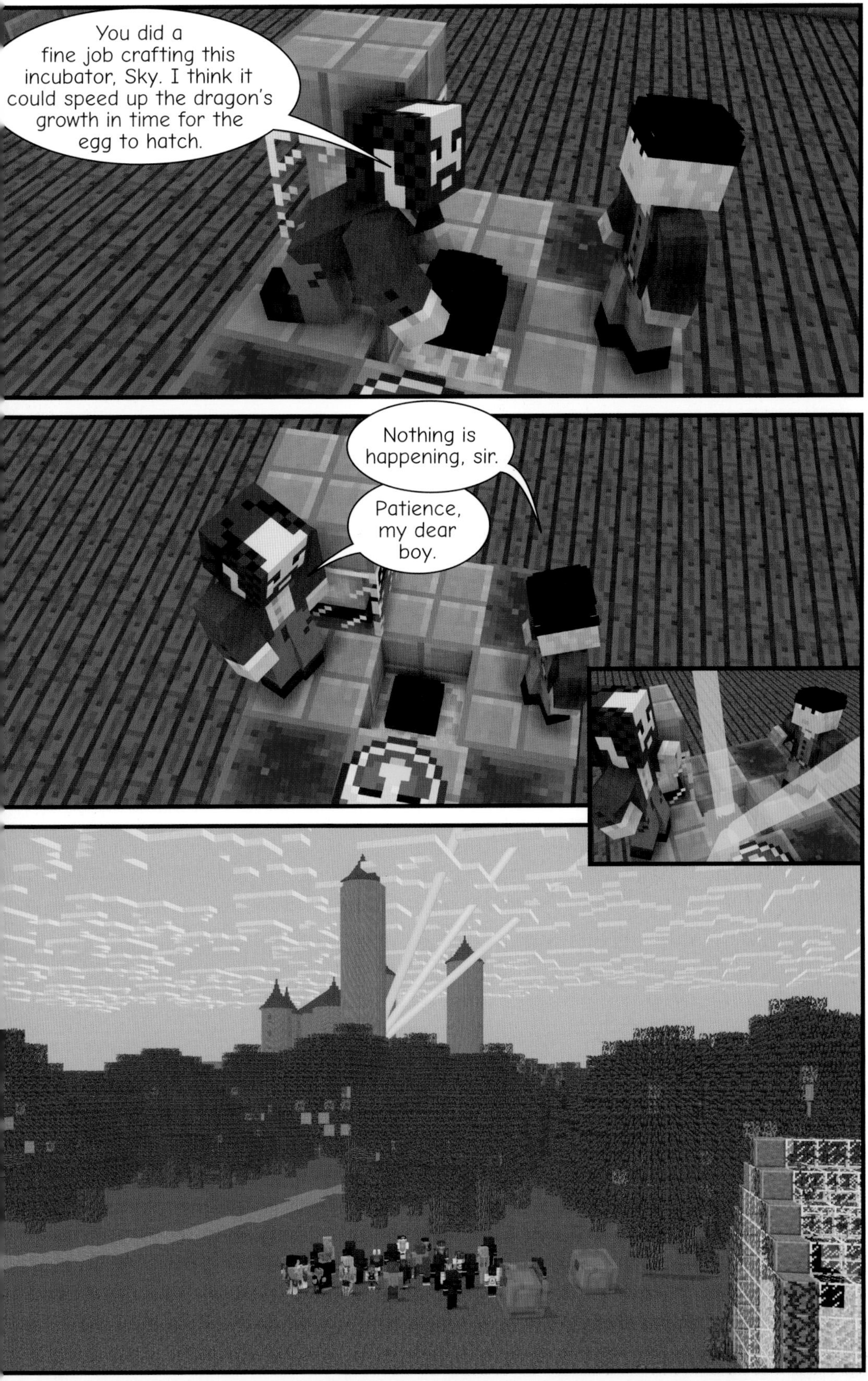
You did a fine job crafting this incubator, Sky. I think it could speed up the dragon's growth in time for the egg to hatch.
Nothing is happening, sir.
Patience, my dear boy.

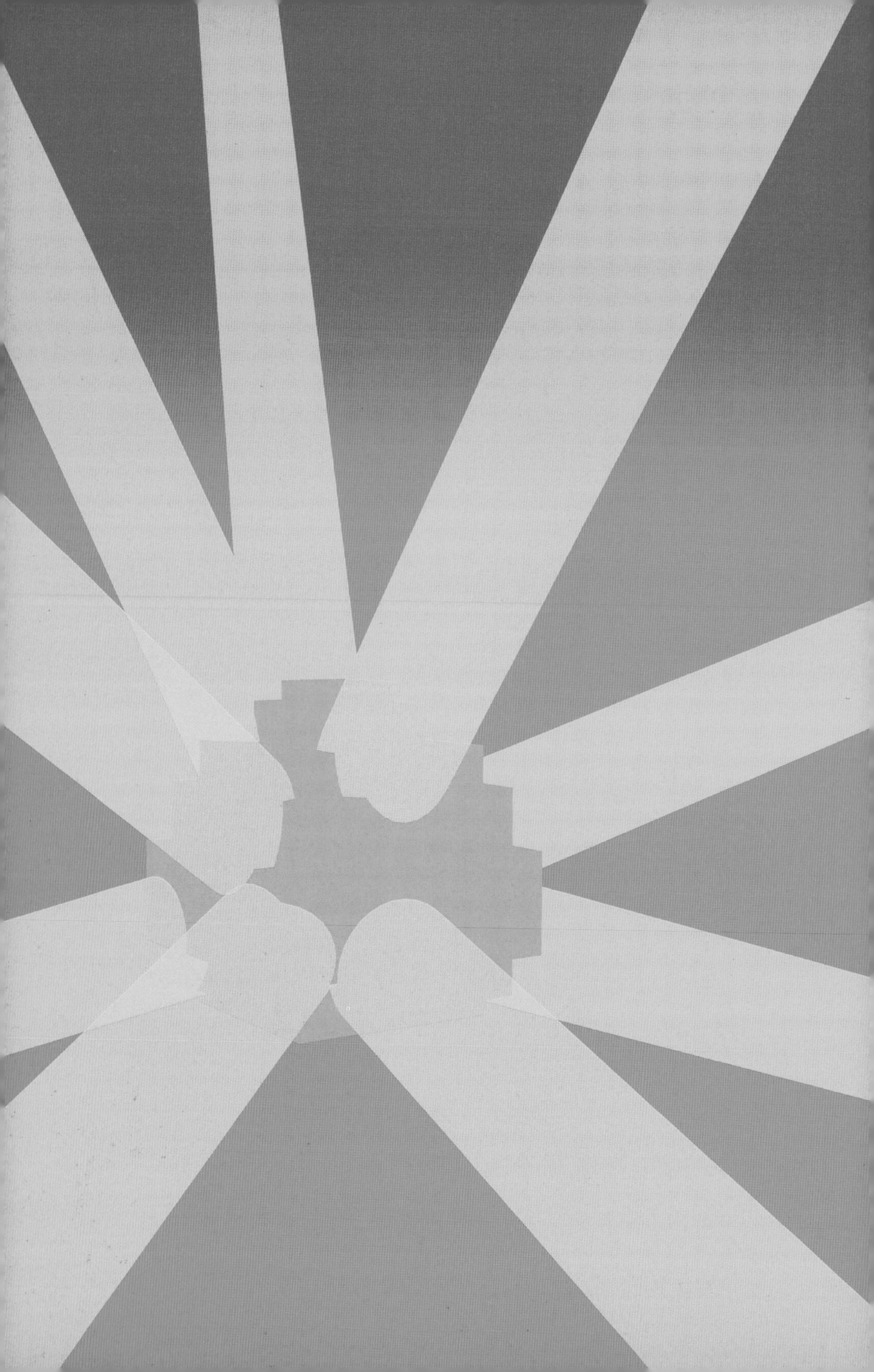

CHAPTER 12

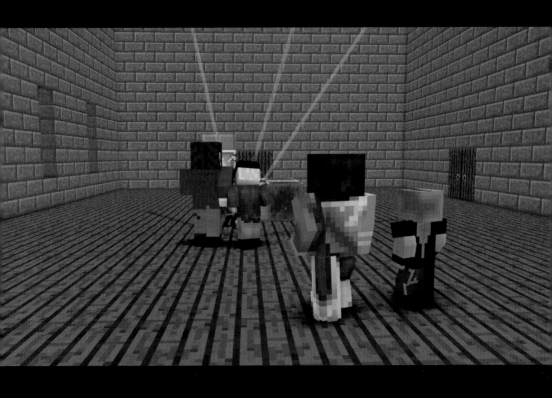

A QUEEN
IS BORN

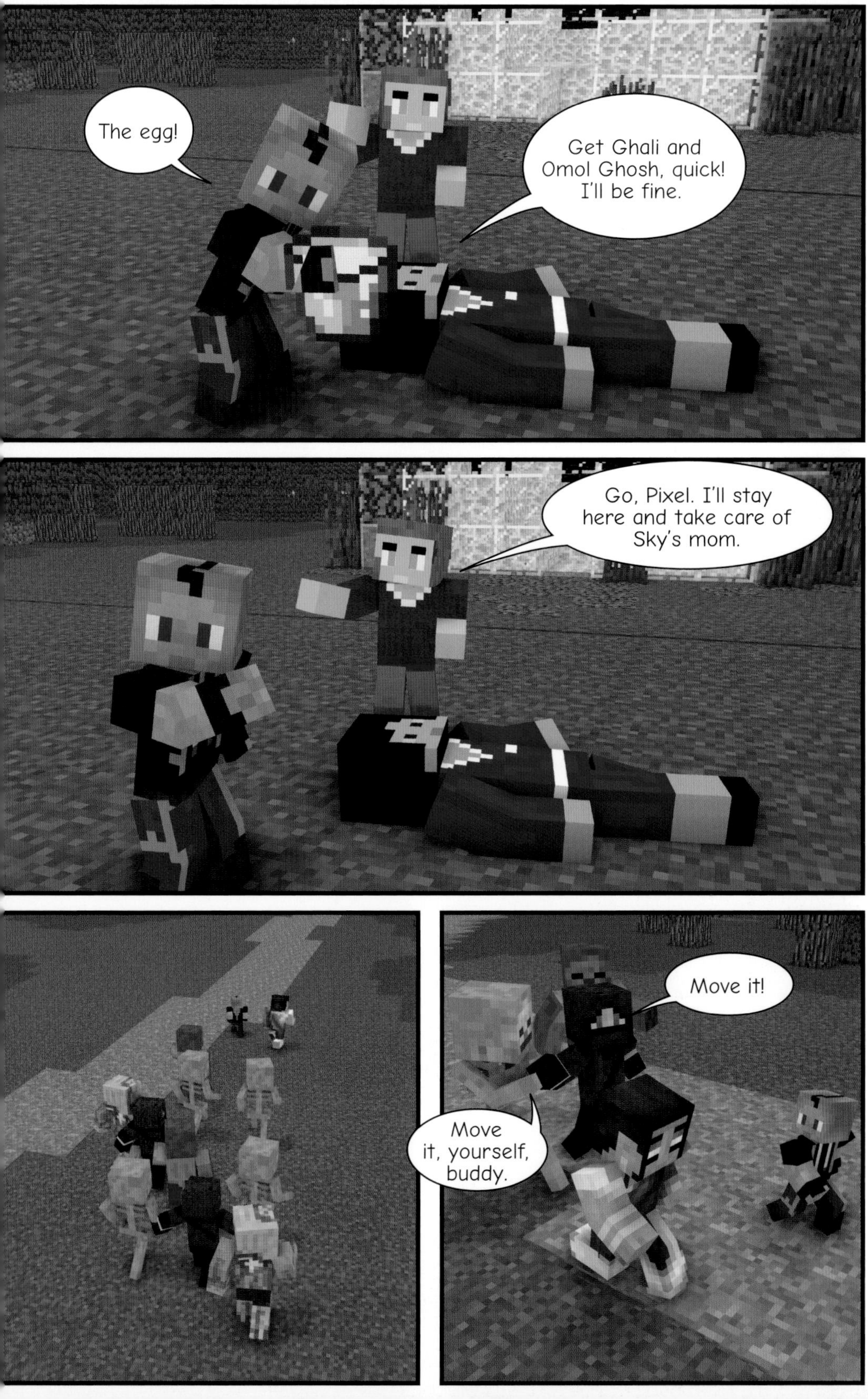
The egg!
Get Ghali and Omol Ghosh, quick! I'll be fine.
Go, Pixel. I'll stay here and take care of Sky's mom.
Move it!
Move it, yourself, buddy.

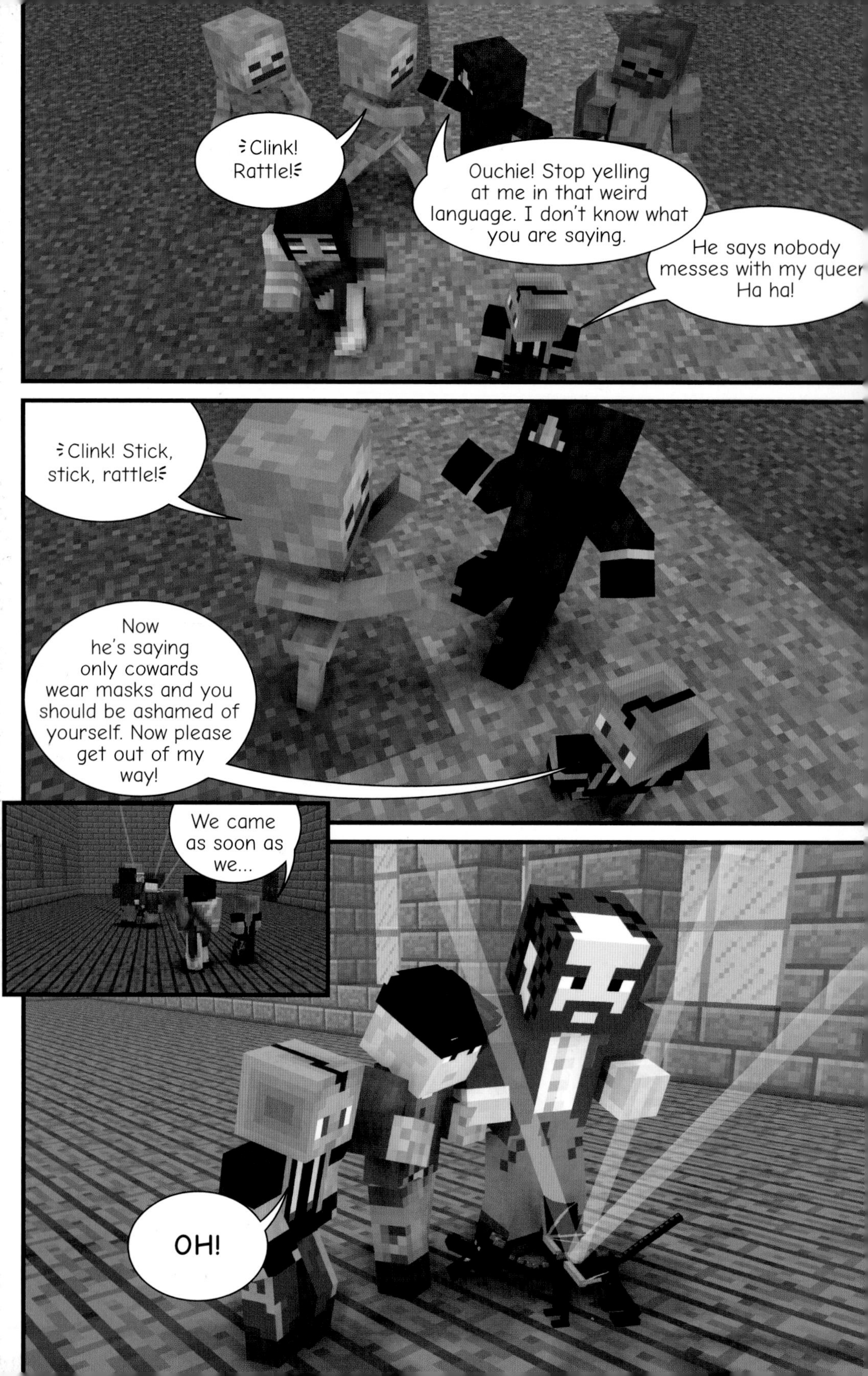
Clink! Rattle!
Ouchie! Stop yelling at me in that weird language. I don't know what you are saying.
He says nobody messes with my queer Ha ha!
Clink! Stick, stick, rattle!
Now he's saying only cowards wear masks and you should be ashamed of yourself. Now please get out of my way!
We came as soon as we...
OH!

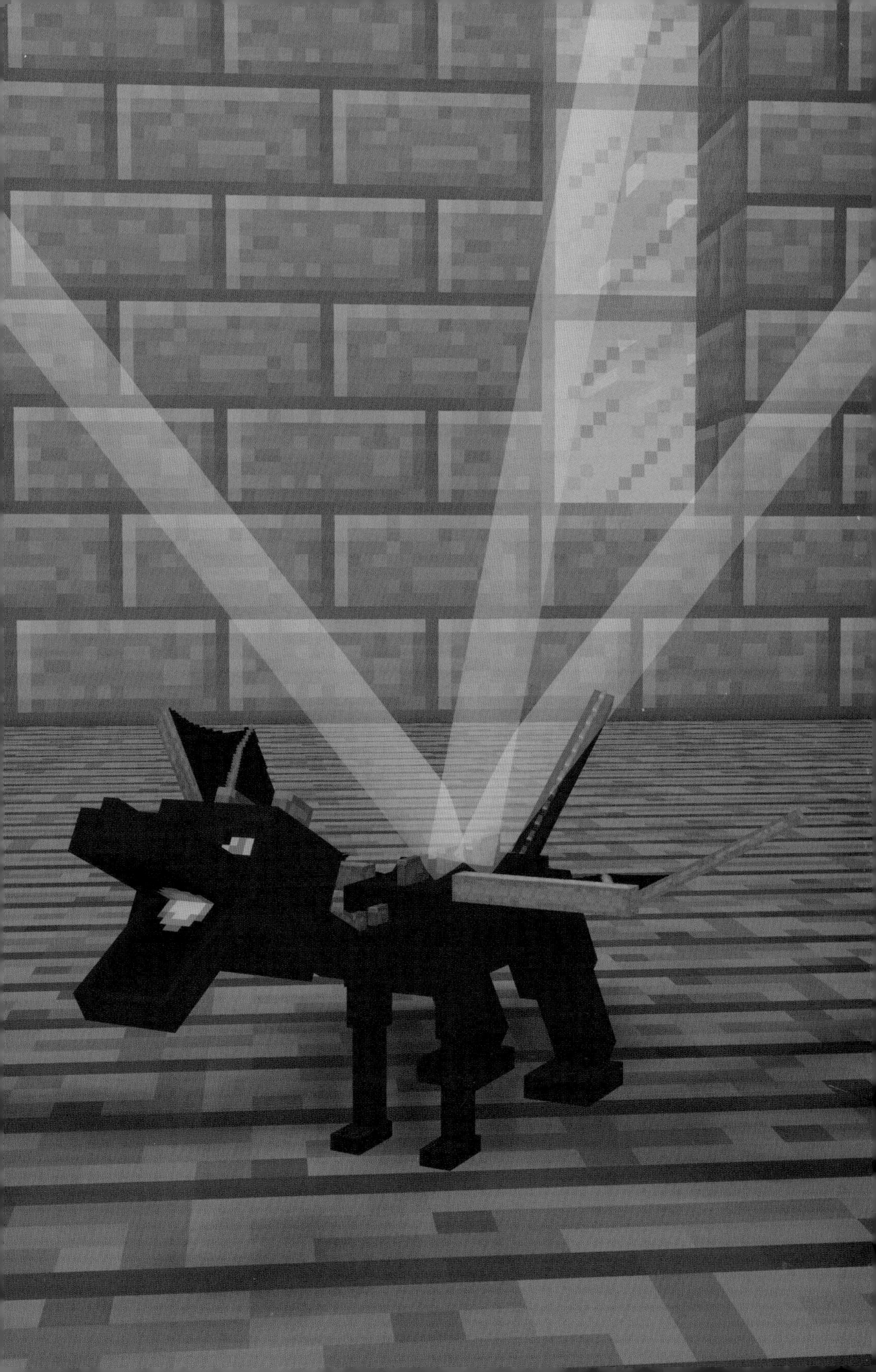

Is it okay to pet her?

Dragons are not friendl by nature, but since she hasn't burnt your hand wit her dragon breath by now, I'm guessin you're safe.

Whoa!

Oh my!

Careful!

≥Skrixxxxx!≤

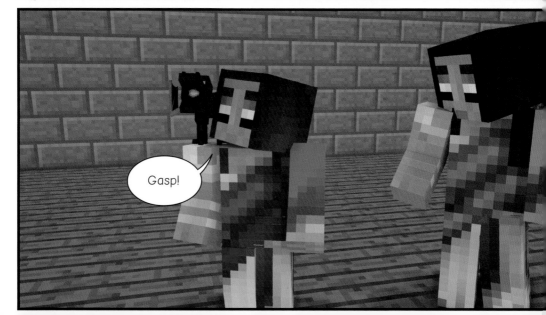

Gasp!

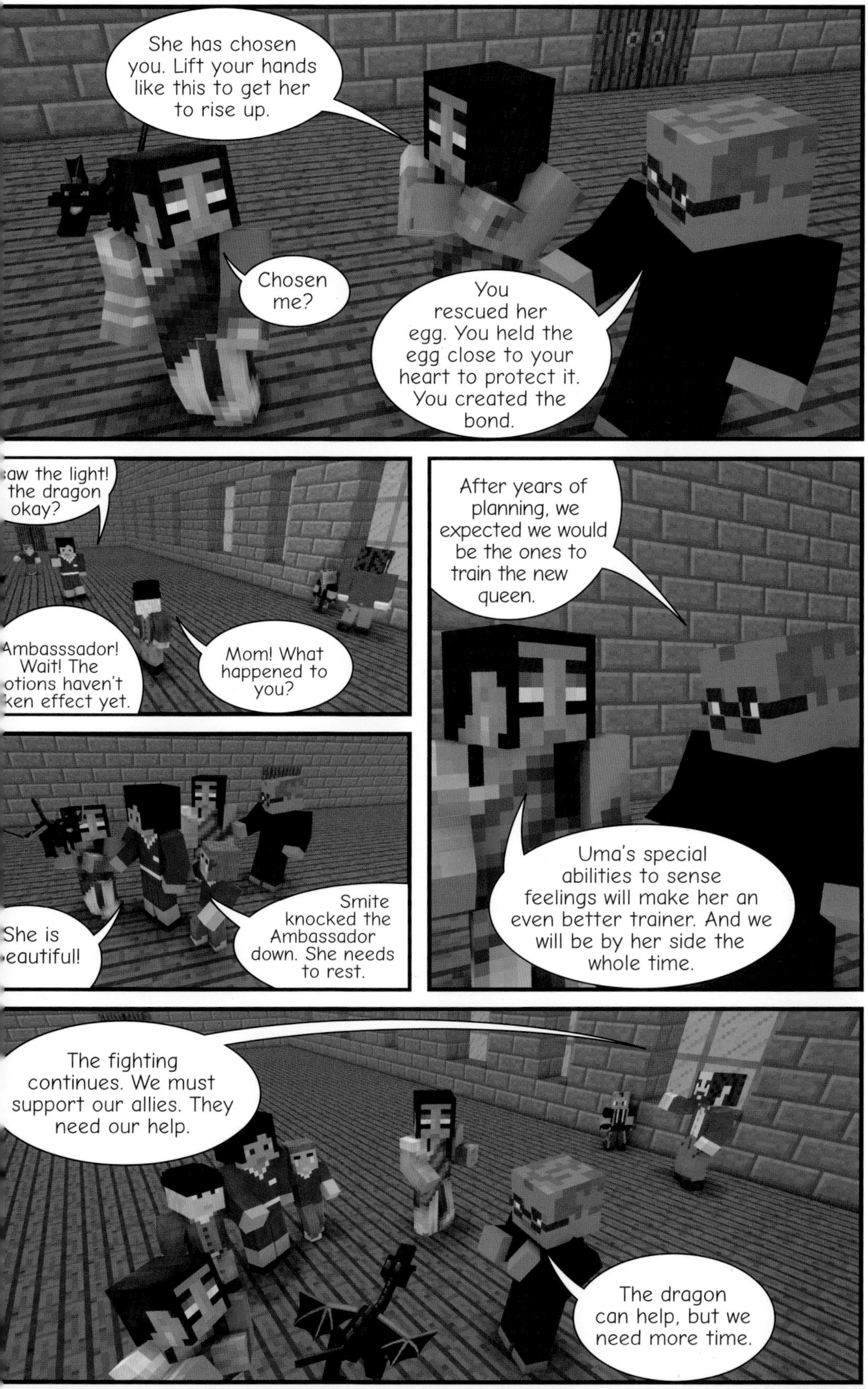
She has chosen you. Lift your hands like this to get her to rise up.
Chosen me?
You rescued her egg. You held the egg close to your heart to protect it. You created the bond.
aw the light! the dragon okay?
Ambasssador! Wait! The otions haven't ken effect yet.
Mom! What happened to you?
She is eautiful!
Smite knocked the Ambassador down. She needs to rest.
After years of planning, we expected we would be the ones to train the new queen.
Uma's special abilities to sense feelings will make her an even better trainer. And we will be by her side the whole time.
The fighting continues. We must support our allies. They need our help.
The dragon can help, but we need more time.

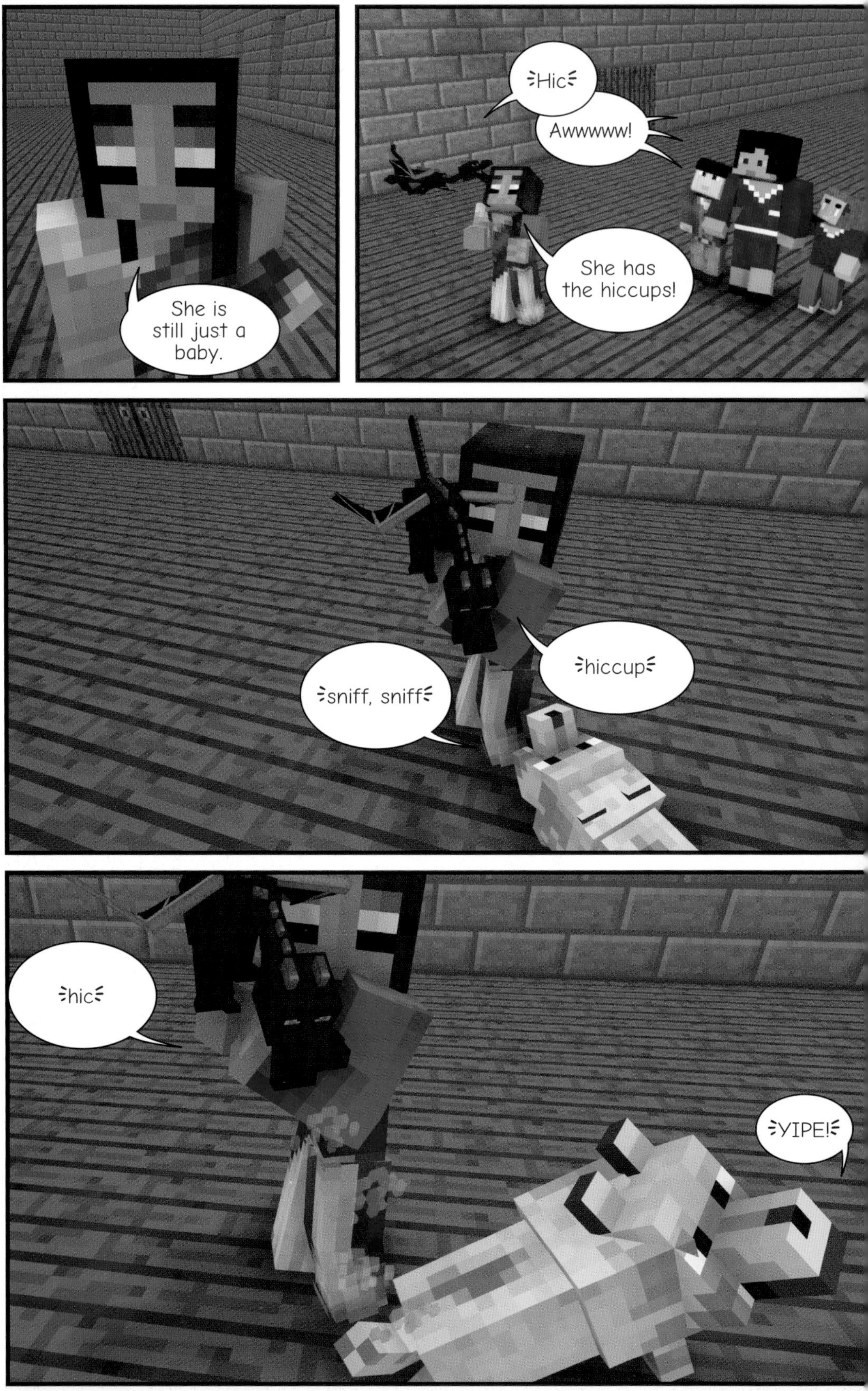
She is still just a baby.
Hic
Awwwww!
She has the hiccups!
hiccup
sniff, sniff
hic
YIPE!

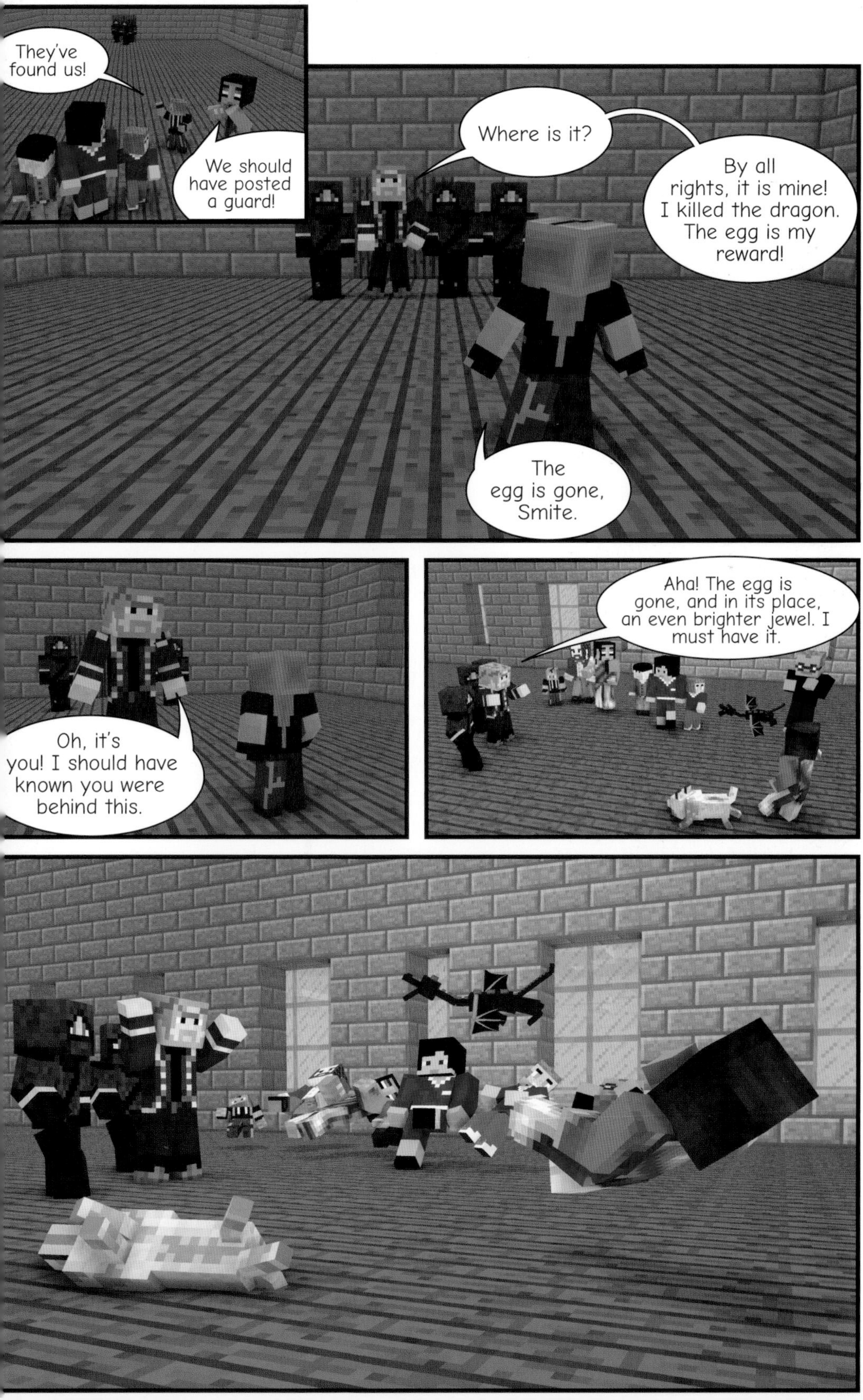
They've found us!
We should have posted a guard!
Where is it?
By all rights, it is mine! I killed the dragon. The egg is my reward!
The egg is gone, Smite.
Oh, it's you! I should have known you were behind this.
Aha! The egg is gone, and in its place, an even brighter jewel. I must have it.

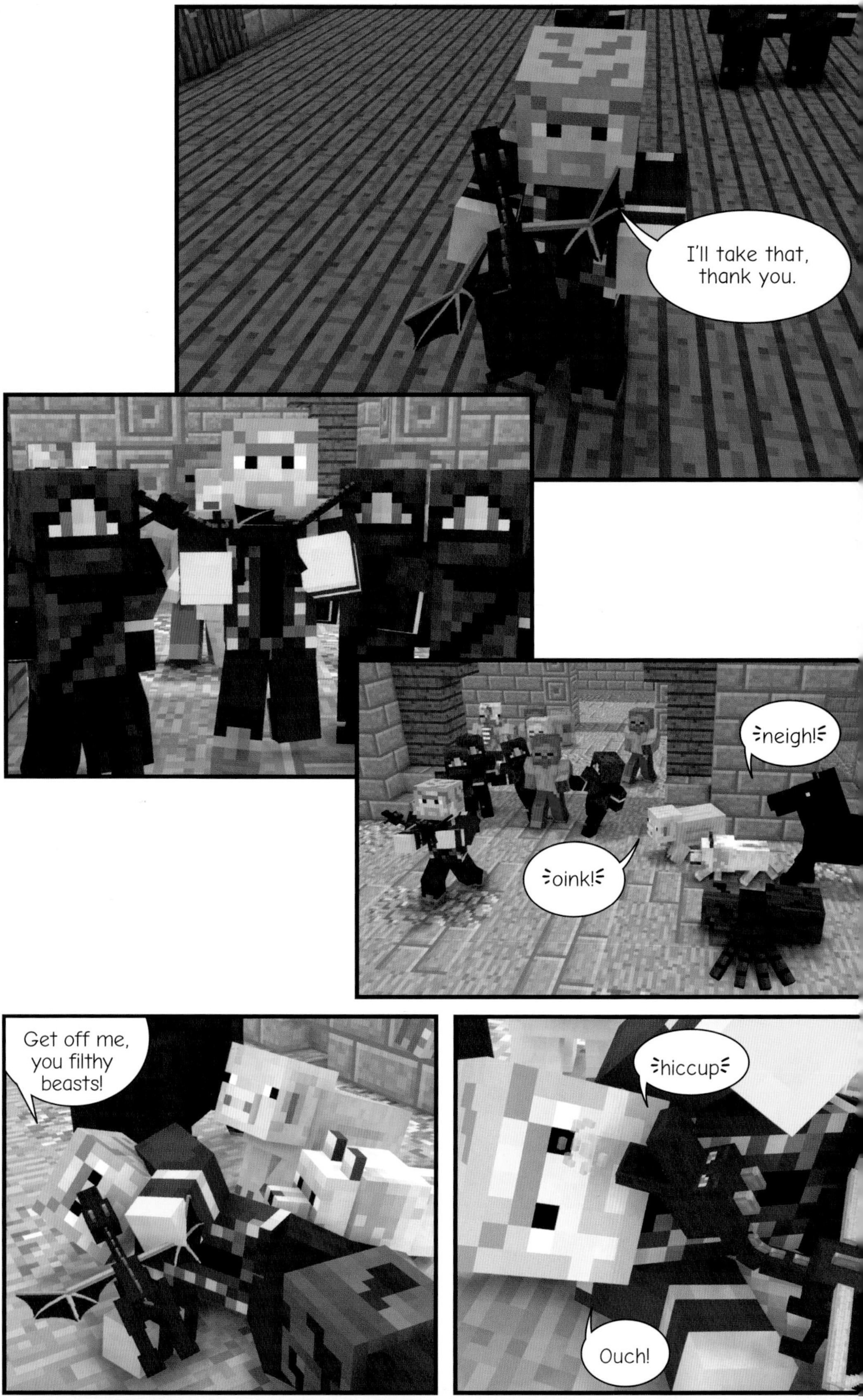
I'll take that, thank you.
neigh!
oink!
Get off me, you filthy beasts!
hiccup
Ouch!

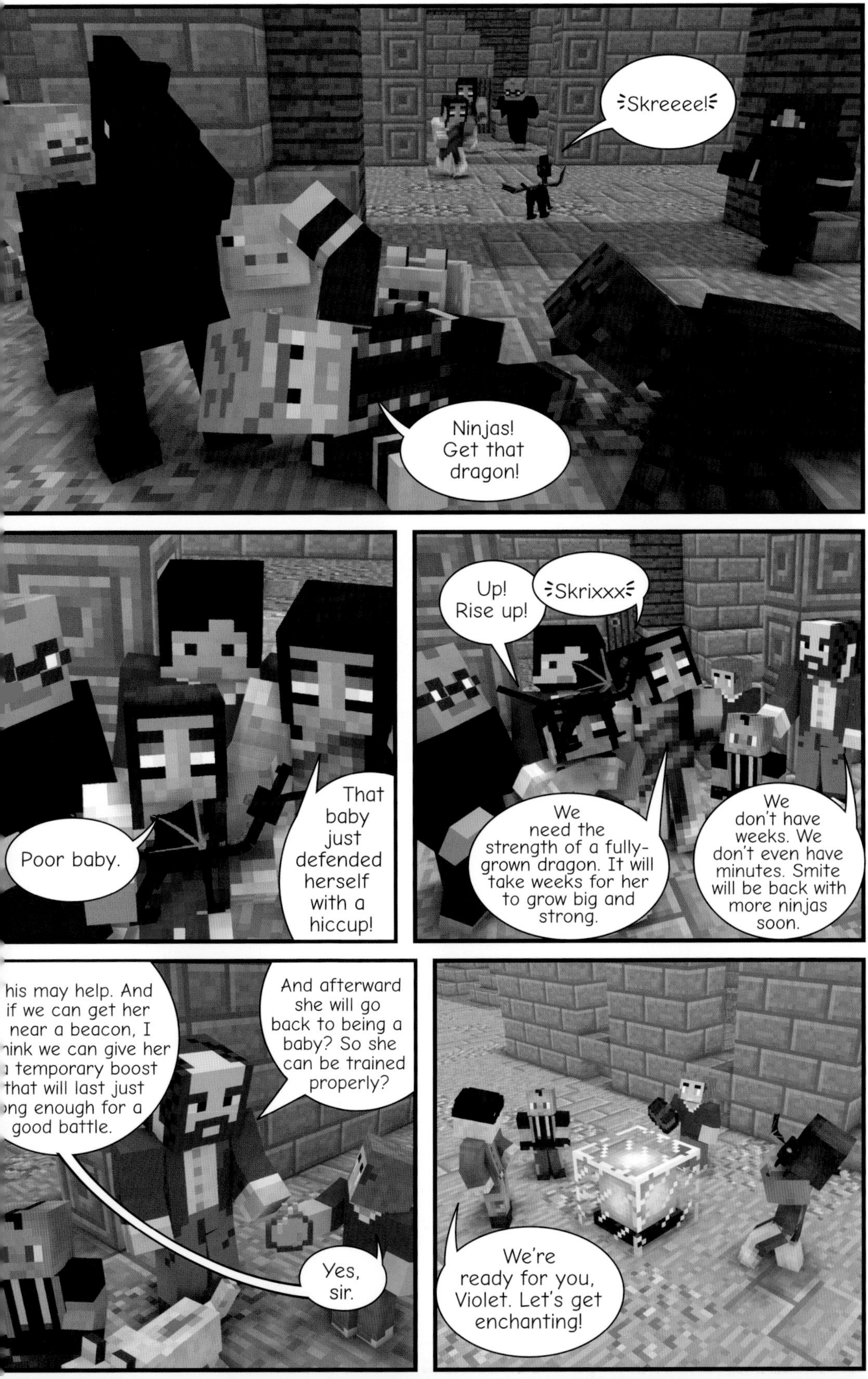

Skreeee!
Ninjas! Get that dragon!
That baby just defended herself with a hiccup!
Poor baby.
Up! Rise up!
Skrixxx
We need the strength of a fully-grown dragon. It will take weeks for her to grow big and strong.
We don't have weeks. We don't even have minutes. Smite will be back with more ninjas soon.
his may help. And if we can get her near a beacon, I ink we can give her a temporary boost that will last just ng enough for a good battle.
And afterward she will go back to being a baby? So she can be trained properly?
Yes, sir.
We're ready for you, Violet. Let's get enchanting!

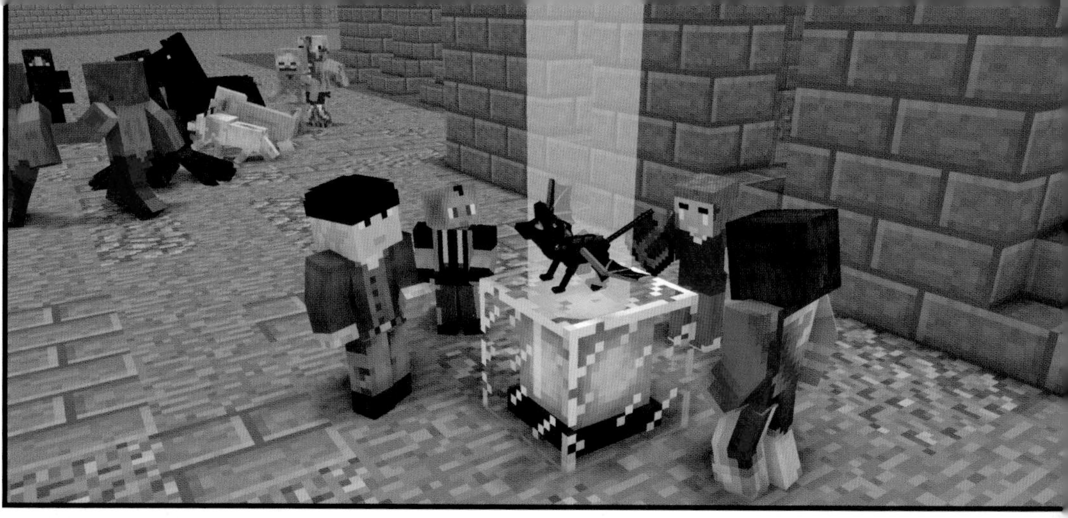

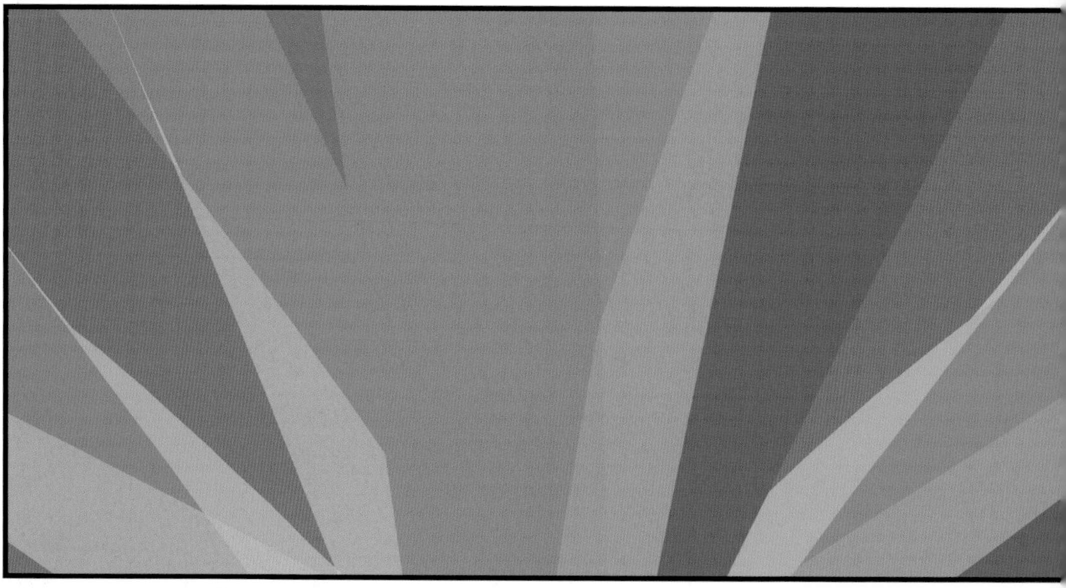

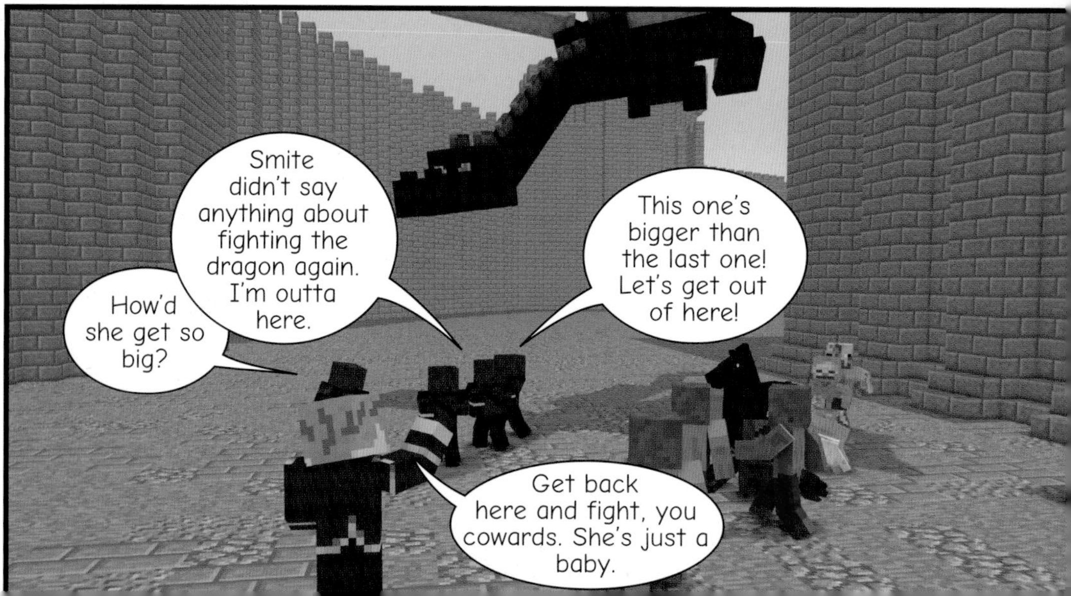
How'd she get so big?
Smite didn't say anything about fighting the dragon again. I'm outta here.
This one's bigger than the last one! Let's get out of here!
Get back here and fight, you cowards. She's just a baby.

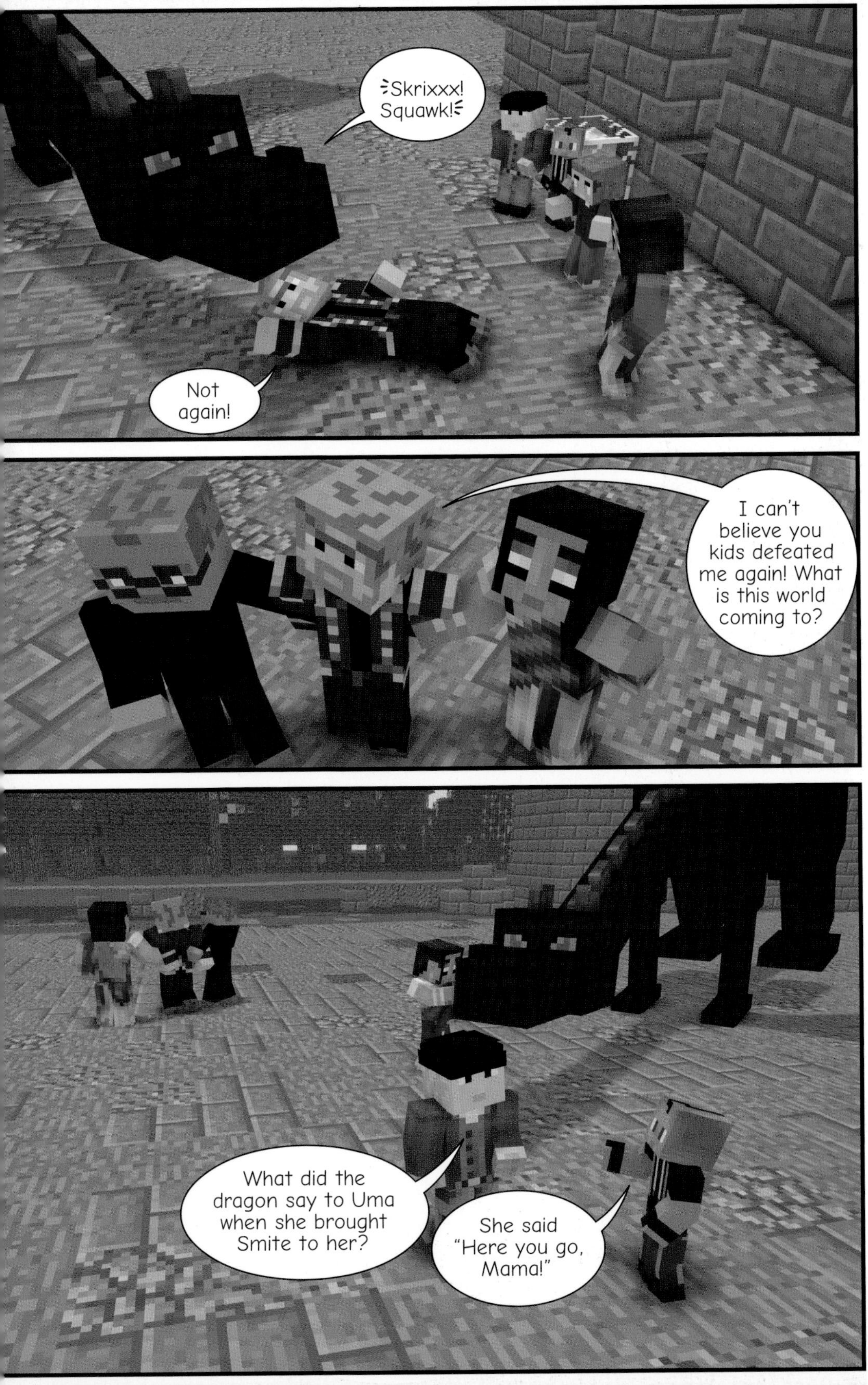
Skrixxx! Squawk!
Not again!
I can't believe you kids defeated me again! What is this world coming to?
What did the dragon say to Uma when she brought Smite to her?
She said "Here you go, Mama!"

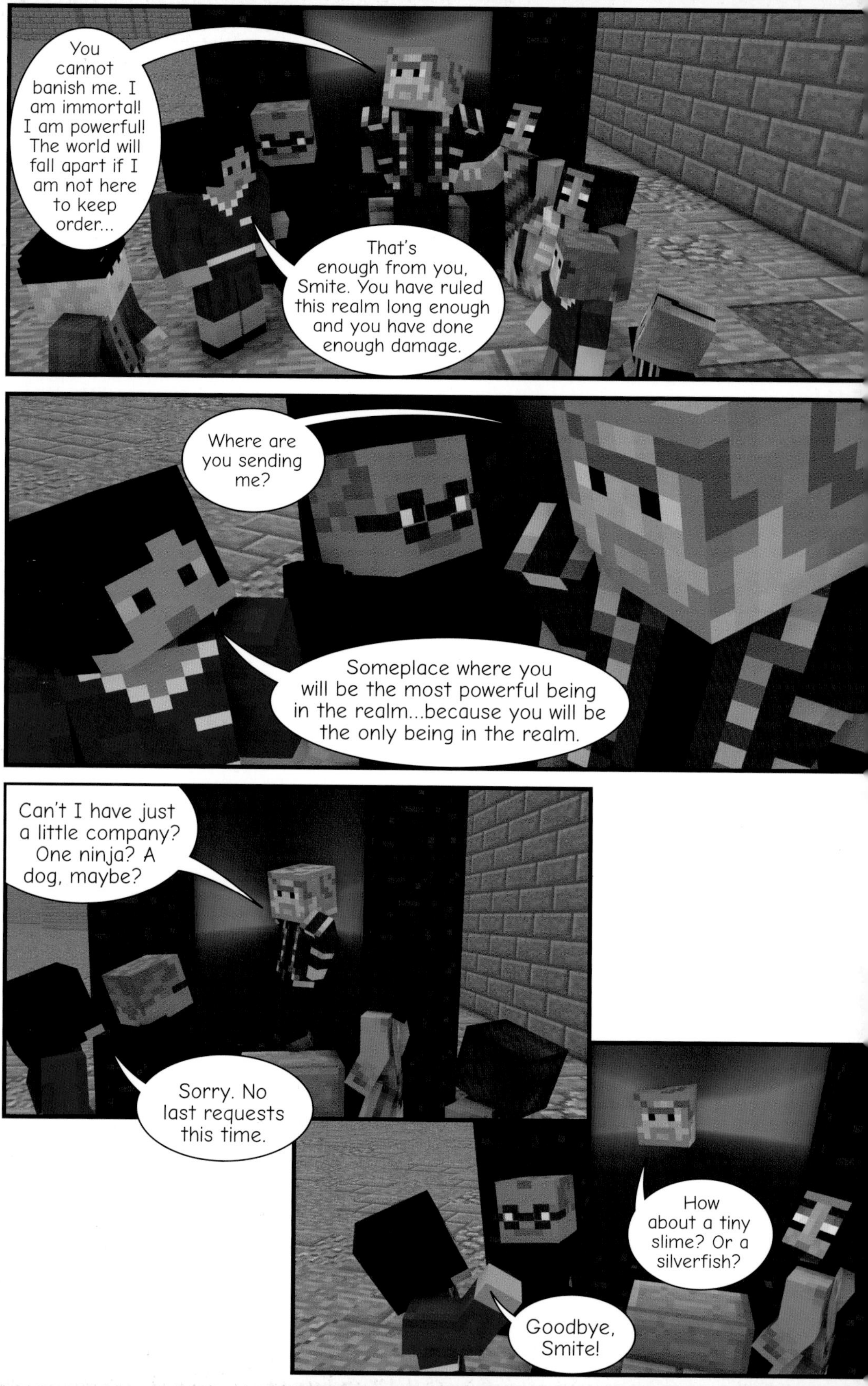
You cannot banish me. I am immortal! I am powerful! The world will fall apart if I am not here to keep order...
That's enough from you, Smite. You have ruled this realm long enough and you have done enough damage.
Where are you sending me?
Someplace where you will be the most powerful being in the realm...because you will be the only being in the realm.
Can't I have just a little company? One ninja? A dog, maybe?
Sorry. No last requests this time.
How about a tiny slime? Or a silverfish?
Goodbye, Smite!

CHAPTER 13

THE QUEEN'S
GUARD

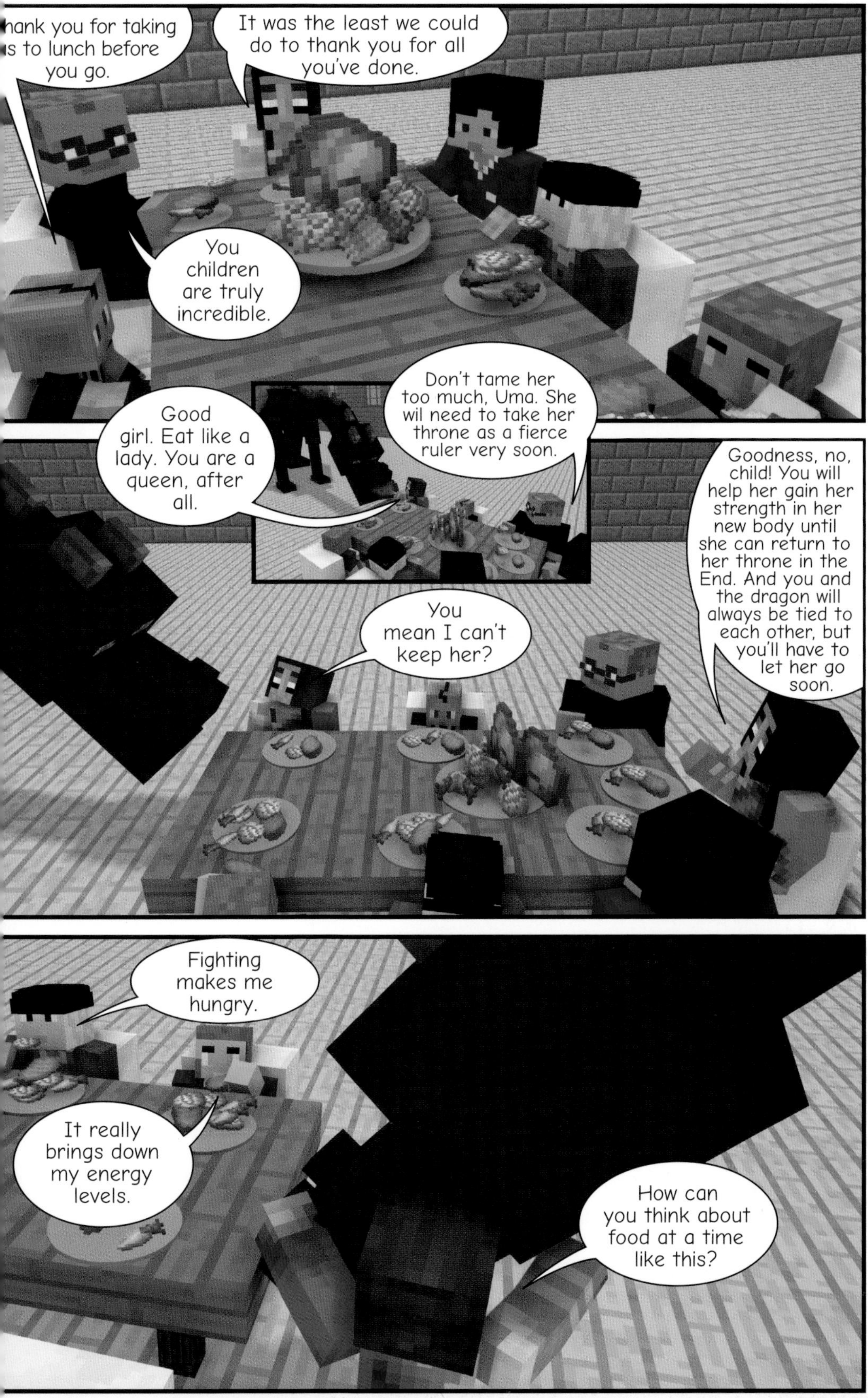
hank you for taking
s to lunch before
you go.
It was the least we could do to thank you for all you've done.
You children are truly incredible.
Good girl. Eat like a lady. You are a queen, after all.
Don't tame her too much, Uma. She wil need to take her throne as a fierce ruler very soon.
Goodness, no, child! You will help her gain her strength in her new body until she can return to her throne in the End. And you and the dragon will always be tied to each other, but you'll have to let her go soon.
You mean I can't keep her?
Fighting makes me hungry.
It really brings down my energy levels.
How can you think about food at a time like this?

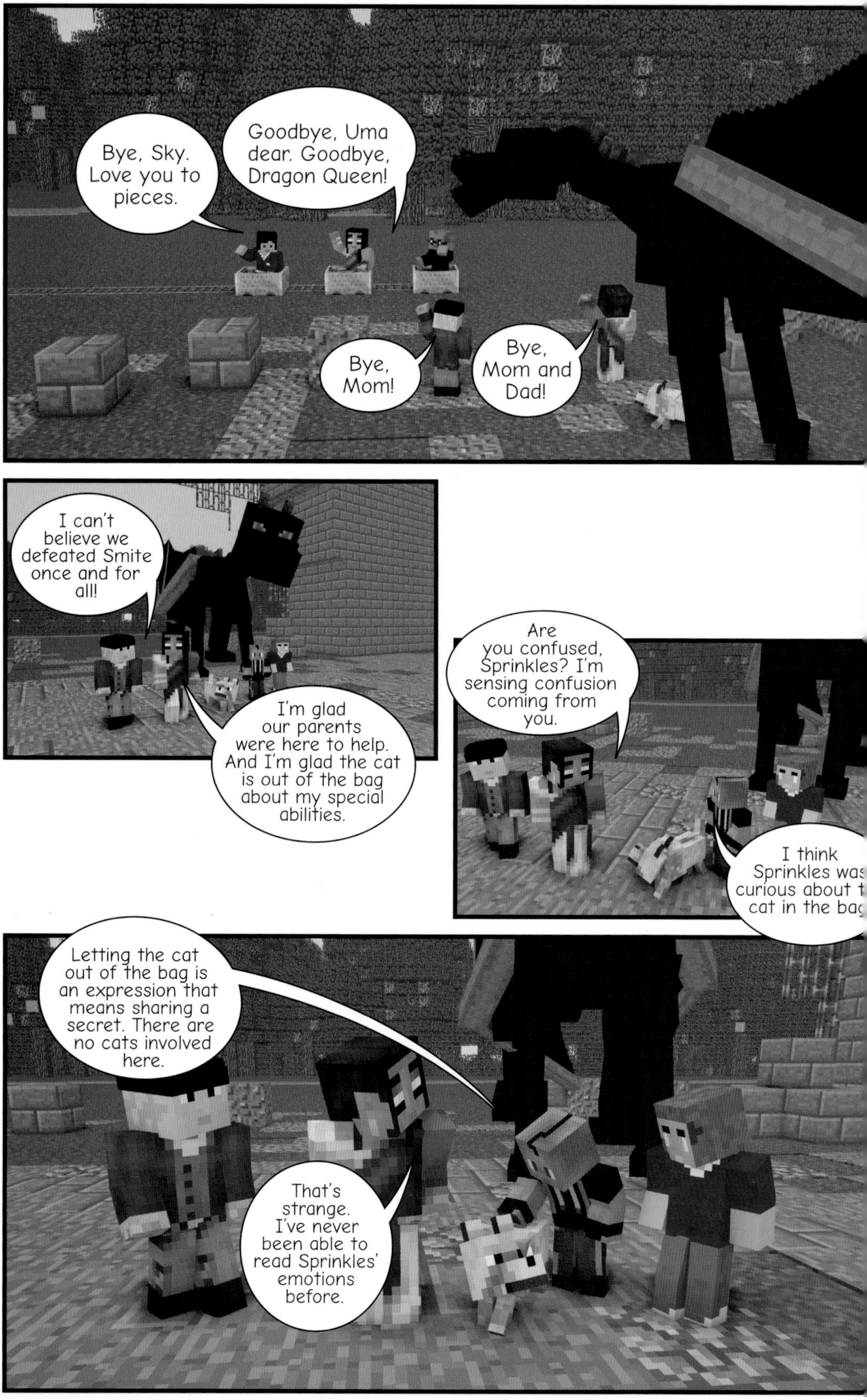
Bye, Sky. Love you to pieces.
Goodbye, Uma dear. Goodbye, Dragon Queen!
Bye, Mom!
Bye, Mom and Dad!
I can't believe we defeated Smite once and for all!
I'm glad our parents were here to help. And I'm glad the cat is out of the bag about my special abilities.
Are you confused, Sprinkles? I'm sensing confusion coming from you.
Letting the cat out of the bag is an expression that means sharing a secret. There are no cats involved here.
That's strange. I've never been able to read Sprinkles' emotions before.

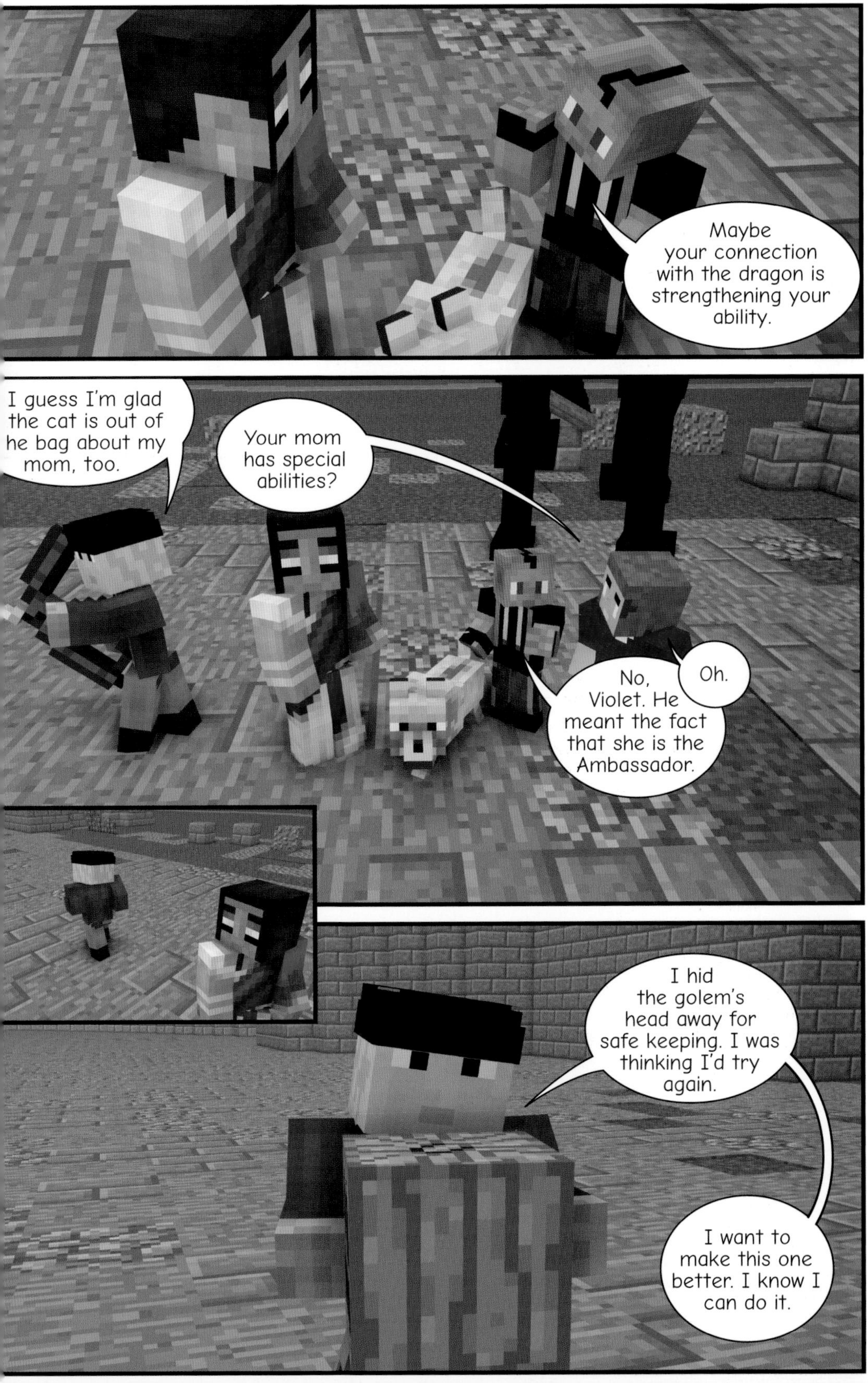
Maybe your connection with the dragon is strengthening your ability.
I guess I'm glad the cat is out of he bag about my mom, too.
Your mom has special abilities?
No, Violet. He meant the fact that she is the Ambassador.
Oh.
I hid the golem's head away for safe keeping. I was thinking I'd try again.
I want to make this one better. I know I can do it.

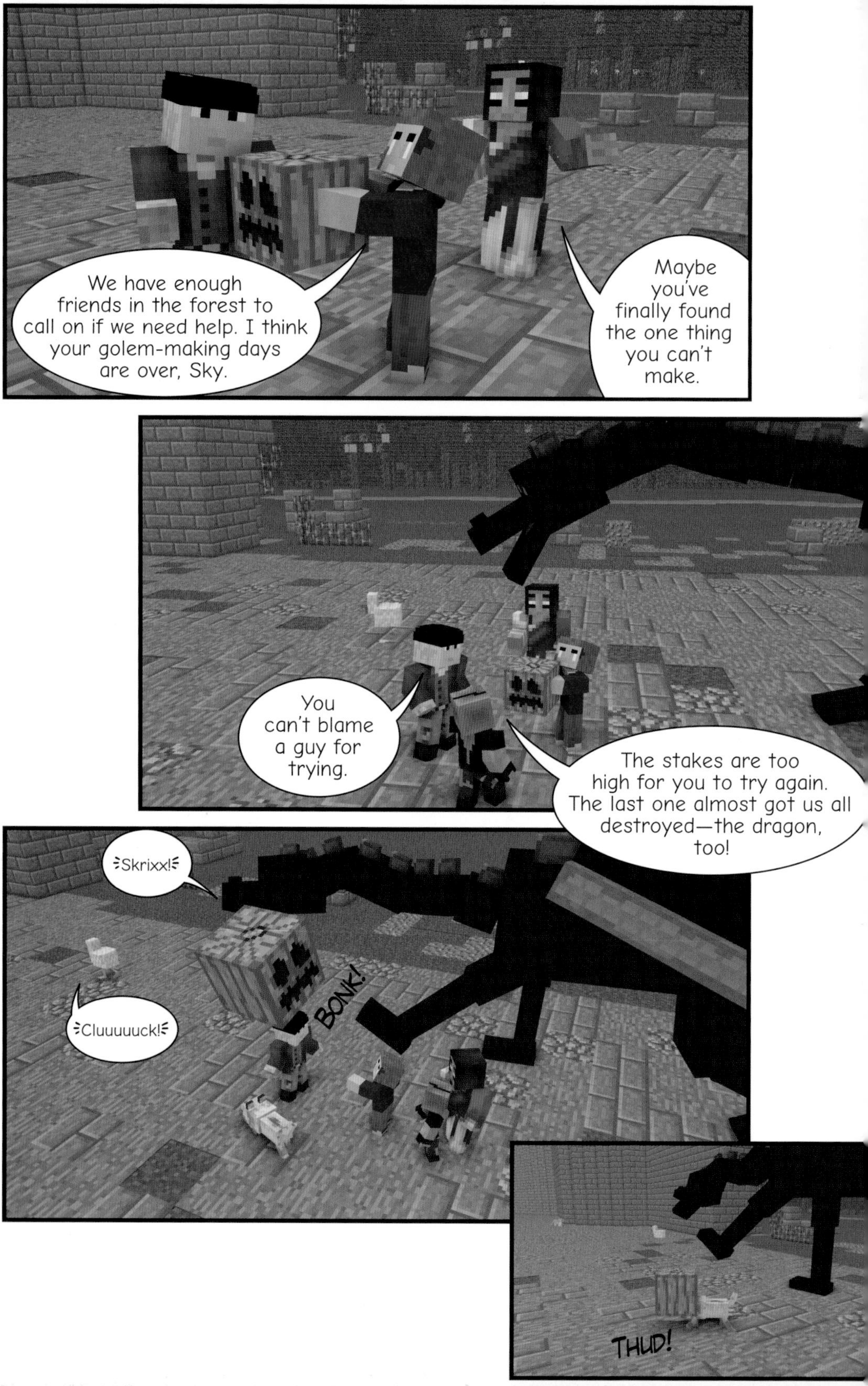
We have enough friends in the forest to call on if we need help. I think your golem-making days are over, Sky.
Maybe you've finally found the one thing you can't make.
You can't blame a guy for trying.
The stakes are too high for you to try again. The last one almost got us all destroyed—the dragon, too!
Skrixx!
Cluuuuuck!
BONK!
THUD!

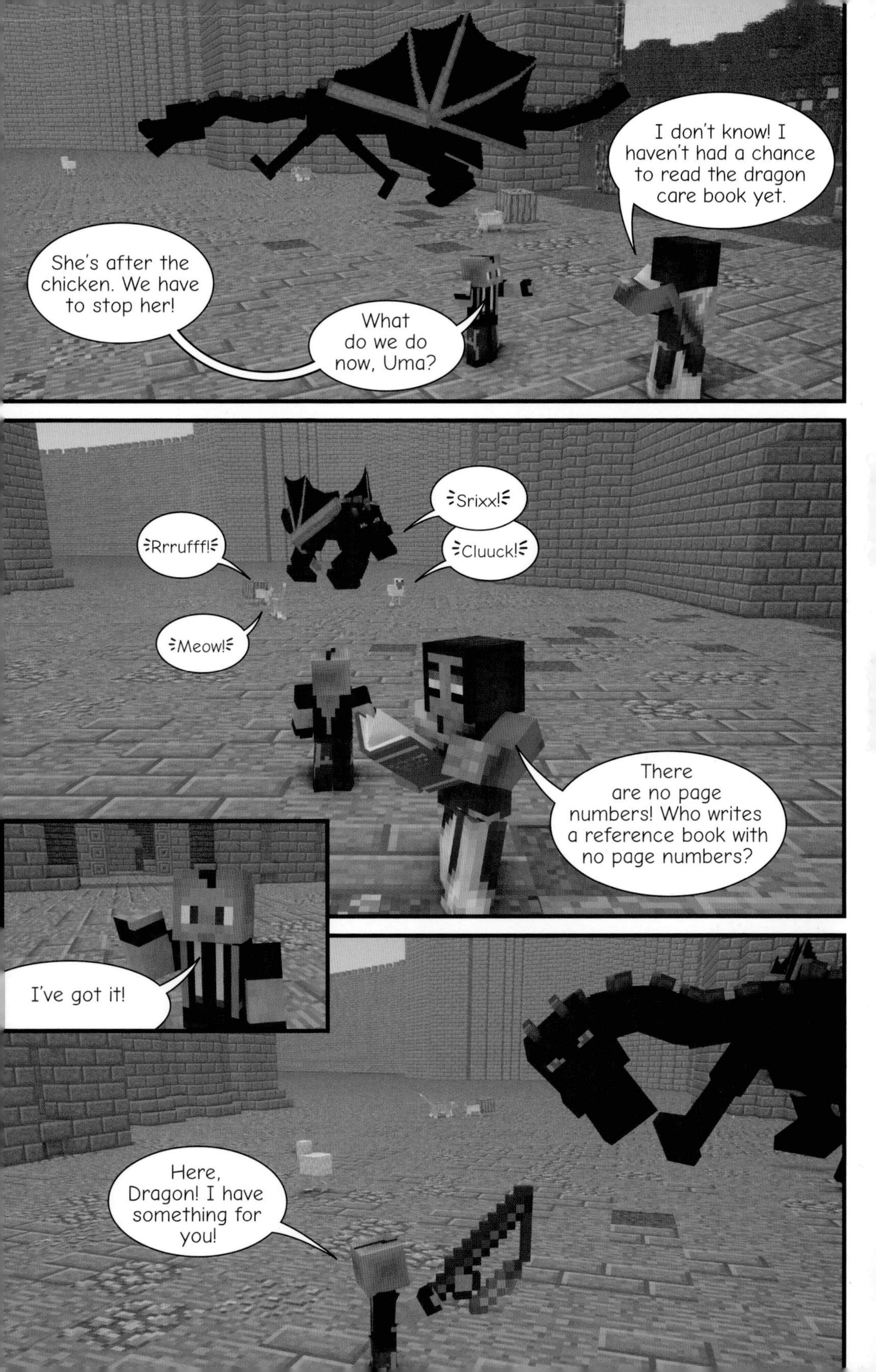
She's after the chicken. We have to stop her!
What do we do now, Uma?
I don't know! I haven't had a chance to read the dragon care book yet.
Rrruffff!
Srixx!
Cluuck!
Meow!
There are no page numbers! Who writes a reference book with no page numbers?
I've got it!
Here, Dragon! I have something for you!

I guess she likes carrots. Nice job, Pixel.

Hey Sky, we are going to need a way to keep our little dragon friend safe and out of trouble.

I'm way ahead of you, friend!

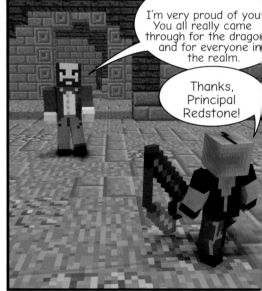

I'm very proud of you. You all really came through for the dragon and for everyone in the realm.

Thanks, Principal Redstone!

I'm sorry we made such a mess of the school again.

That's all right, Uma. It all turned out for the best.

I have a big favor to ask of you. It's about the dragon.

I have a few ideas for how to make her stay here more comfortable for everyone, if you'd like to see them.

If you're going to ask if we can keep the dragon at the school while you train her, the answer is yes. Mr. Z and I are making arrangements for her to stay in the West Wing.

I would. As long as it doesn't involve creating another golem with artificial intelligence.

One week later...

This is a lot more exciting than learning about slimes!

Today, we have new special guest in Mob Education: Dragon Queen.

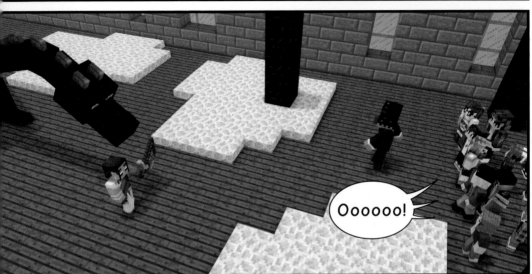

Ooooooo!

Huh?

Gasp!

Noooo!

Bad dragon!

That's better. Good girl!

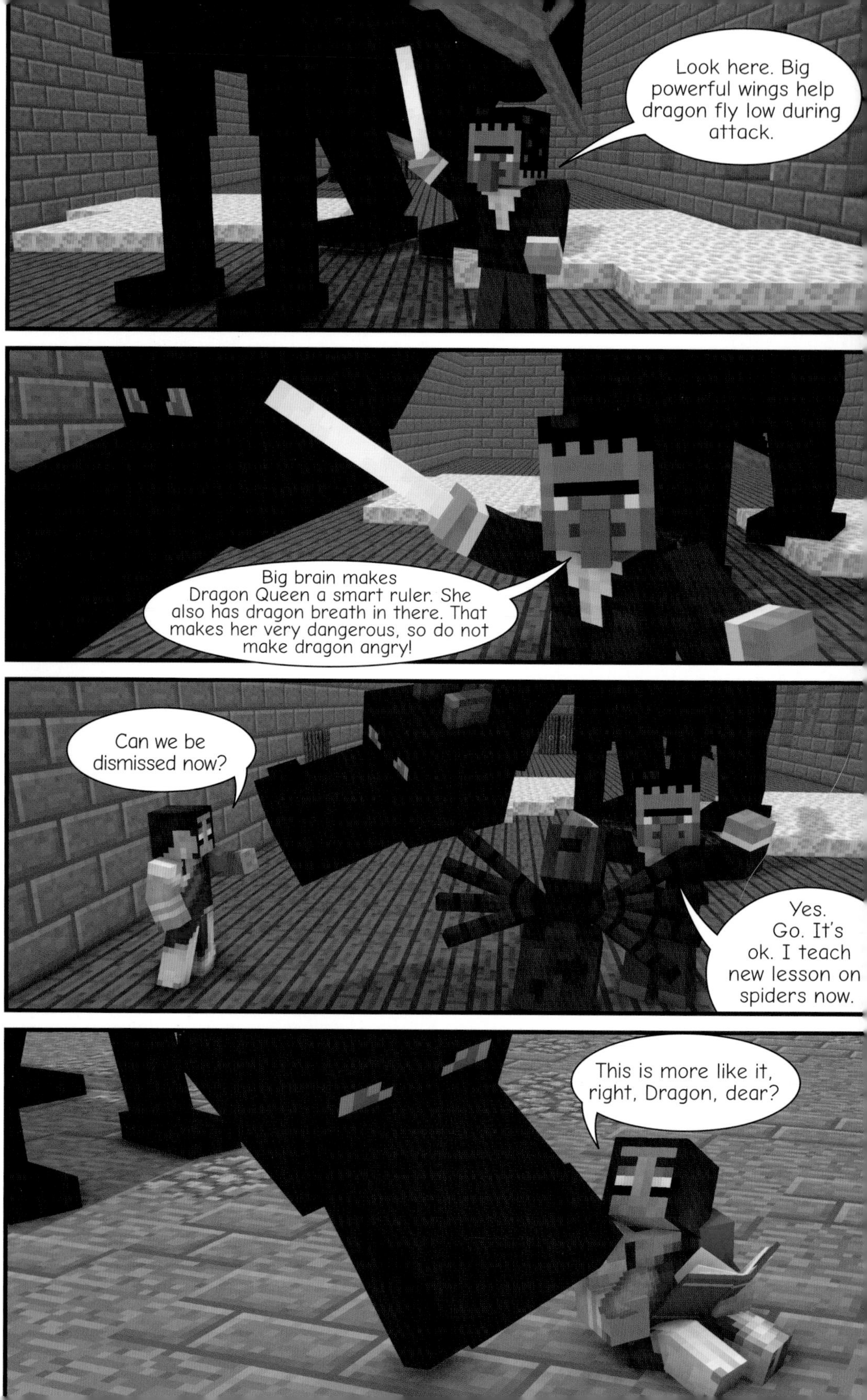
Look here. Big powerful wings help dragon fly low during attack.
Big brain makes Dragon Queen a smart ruler. She also has dragon breath in there. That makes her very dangerous, so do not make dragon angry!
Can we be dismissed now?
Yes. Go. It's ok. I teach new lesson on spiders now.
This is more like it, right, Dragon, dear?

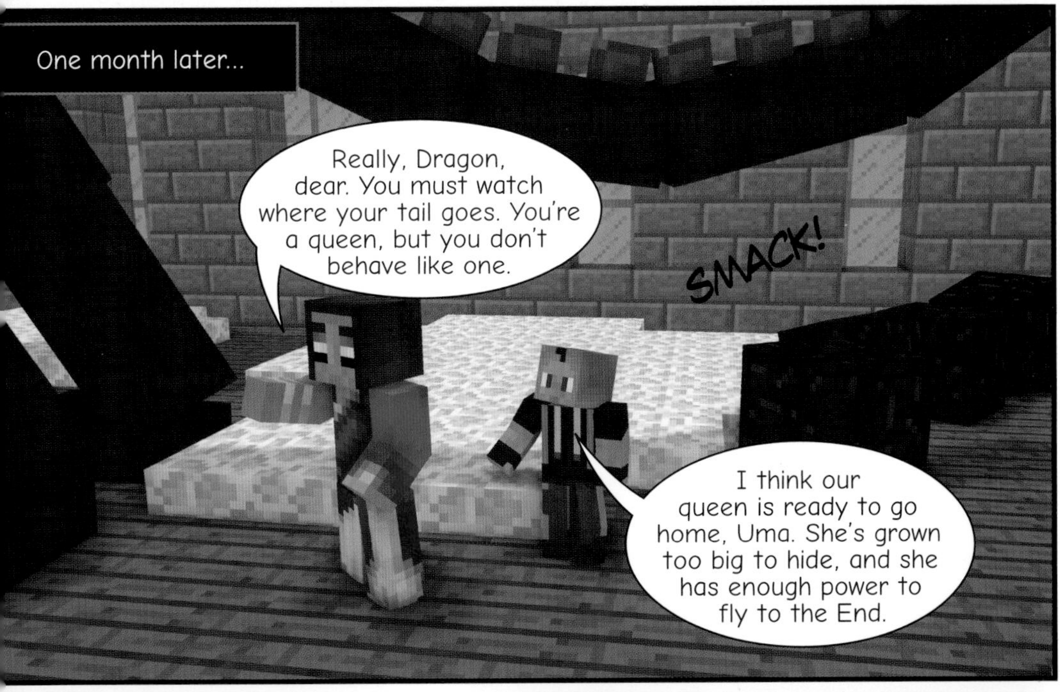
One month later...
Really, Dragon, dear. You must watch where your tail goes. You're a queen, but you don't behave like one.
SMACK!
I think our queen is ready to go home, Uma. She's grown too big to hide, and she has enough power to fly to the End.

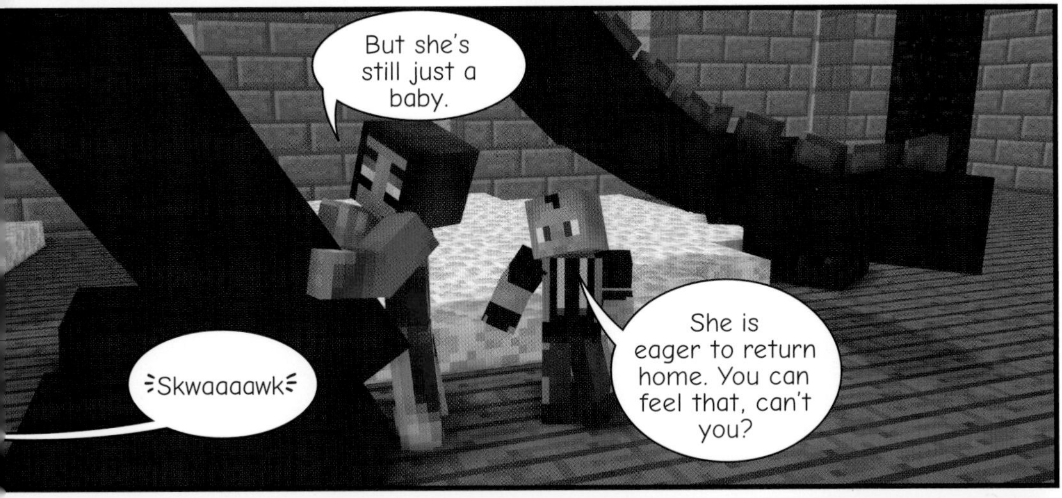
But she's still just a baby.
She is eager to return home. You can feel that, can't you?
Skwaaaawk

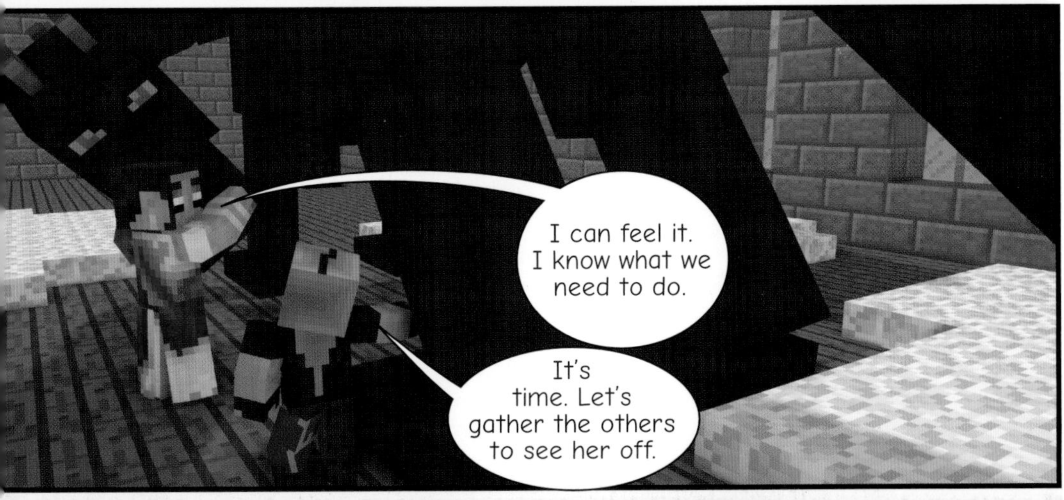
I can feel it. I know what we need to do.
It's time. Let's gather the others to see her off.

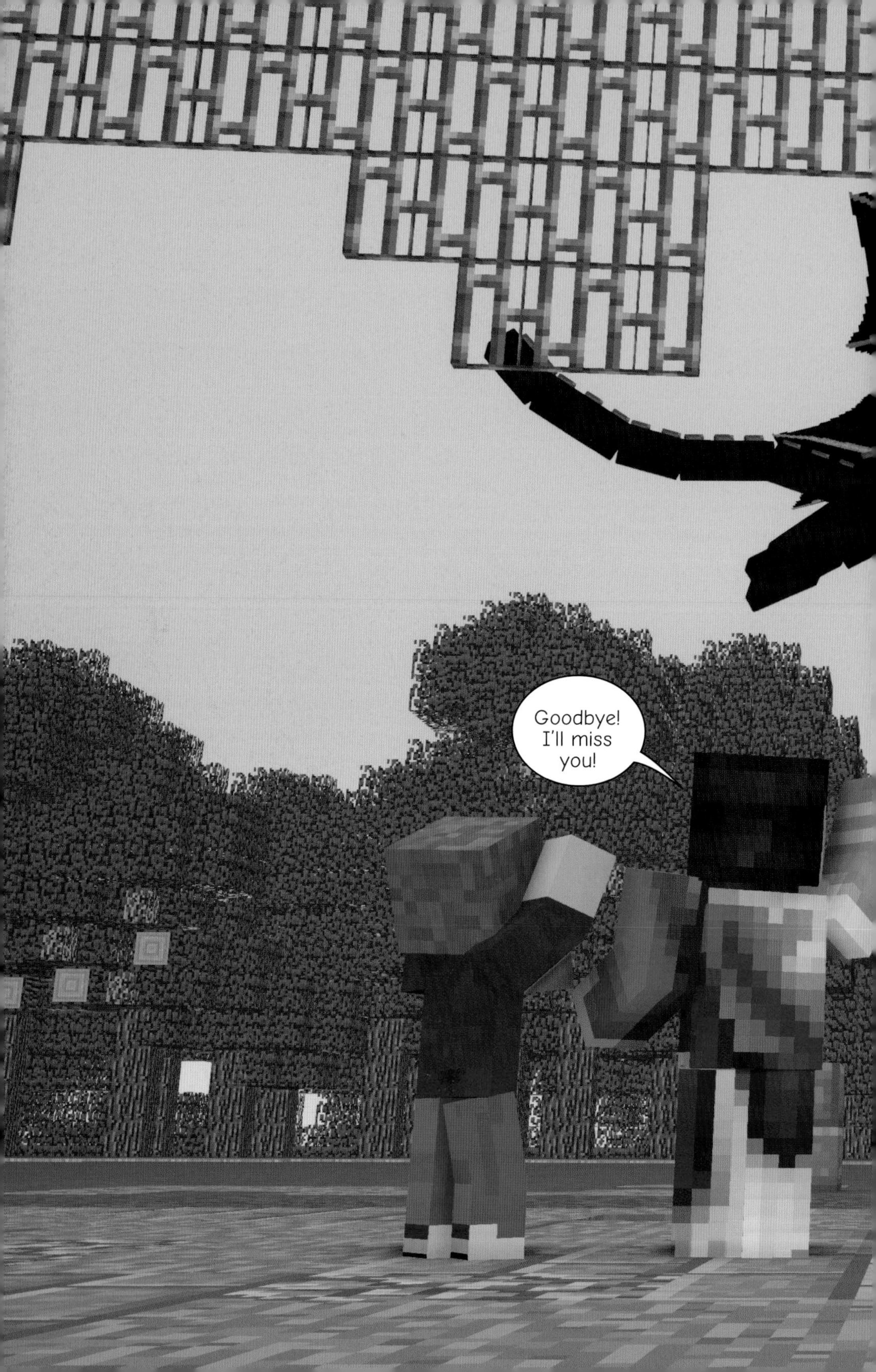
Goodbye! I'll miss you!

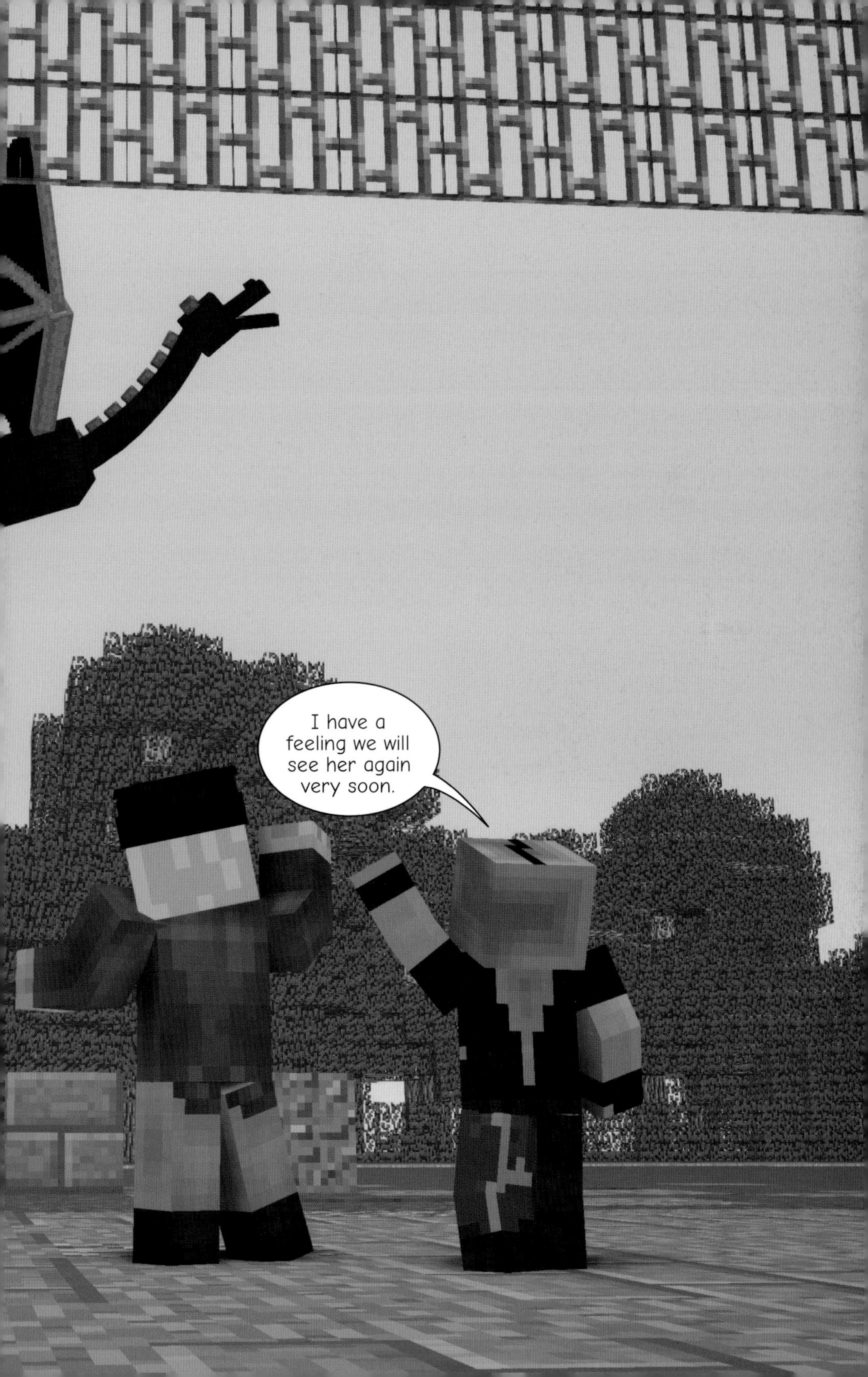
I have a feeling we will see her again very soon.